Following My Nose

FOLLOWING MY NOSE

ALEXEI PANSHIN

ARC MANOR
ROCKVILLE, MARYLAND

＊

SHAHID MAHMUD
PUBLISHER

www.caeziksf.com

Following my Nose © 2025 by The Estate of Alexei Panshin. All rights reserved. This book may not be copied or reproduced, in whole or in part, by any means, electronic, mechanical, or otherwise without written permission except short excerpts in a review, critical analysis, or academic work. Originally published by Tom Doherty Associates

Cover art by Dany V.

ISBN: 978-1-64710-134-3

March 2025.
1 2 3 4 5 6 7 8 9 10

An imprint of Arc Manor Inc.

www.CaezikSF.com

To the memory of my teachers

ROBERT HEINLEIN and IDRIES SHAH

CONTENTS

INTRODUCTION ... 1

FOLLOWING MY NOSE ... 5
1. THE LAND OF MAKE BELIEVE ... 7
2. LIFE IN AN IMAGINATIVE DESERT ... 9
3. DISCOVERING SCIENCE FICTION ... 11
4. WHAT IS SCIENCE FICTION? ... 15
5. IN SEARCH OF WONDER ... 18
6. THEFT AND DISCOVERY ... 21
7. "SO YOU WANT TO BE A WRITER" ... 23
8. LEARNING TO WRITE ... 28
9. WRITING SCIENCE FICTION CRITICISM ... 31
10. THE VILLIERS BOOKS ... 35
11. DOWN ON THE FARM ... 38
12. CREATIVE IMAGINATION AND TRANSCENDENCE ... 42
13. ENCOUNTERING THE SUFIS ... 46
14. THE WORK OF THE SUFIS ... 50

MIRACLES CAN HAPPEN ... 55
1. "BRIDGE ENOUGH FOR ME" ... 57
2. "THEREFORE, HE DIDN'T KEEP SHEEP" ... 62

3	"ALYOSHA, WHERE IS YOUR HORSE?"	67
4	"PUT YOUR TRUST IN GOD"	71
5	THE END OF THE TRACKS	74
6	"YOU CAN TELL BY THE WAY THE LEGS MOVE"	77
7	STORMS RAGING BELOW	81
8	AMBUSH AT BATALPASHINSK	84
9	"DO YOU BELIEVE IN MIRACLES?"	89
10	LIKE FAIRYTALE GIANTS	92
11	THE GOOD WILL OF OTHERS	97
12	SOME OTHER PLACE ENTIRELY	100
13	ANYTHING THAT INTERFERED WITH REASON	103

SYMPATHY FOR THE DEVIL — 109

PART ONE: MAKING K-O DUST — 111

1	THE RIDDLE OF "SOLUTION UNSATISFACTORY"	111
2	MANNING TAKES A JOB	116
3	THE INVENTION OF K-O DUST	121

PART TWO: USING THE DUST — 127

4	THE DEATH OF BERLIN	127
5	SECRETARY OF DUST	131
6	THE FOUR-DAYS WAR	136

PART THREE: MANNING AND DEFRIES — 141

7	MR. COMMISSIONER MANNING	141
8	WHO'S ON TOP?	145
9	THE CHEESE STANDS ALONE	149
10	MANNING'S NATURE	153

PART FOUR: INTERPRETATIONS — 157

11	POINTING IN FOUR DIFFERENT DIRECTIONS	157
12	FOREIGN POLICY—WHAT FOREIGN POLICY?	159
13	WATCHING THE WATCHERS	162

| 14 | DIRTY BOMBS DON'T WORK | 166 |
| 15 | DR. NO NO NO | 171 |

PART FIVE: SOLVING THE RIDDLE — 175
16	NOTHING CAN BE BELIEVED	175
17	THE TRUTH THAT COULD NOT BE SPOKEN	179
18	JOHN CAMPBELL'S RESPONSE	184

AFTERWARD — 191
| 19 | AFTER THE BOMB | 191 |

FALLING DOWN A RABBIT HOLE — 193
1	PICTURE YOURSELF IN A BOAT ON A RIVER	195
2	LIFE IS BUT A DREAM	206
3	FREE FALLING	215
4	A DREAM WITHIN A DREAM	225

MAN BEYOND MAN — 237
1	AN ORGANIC UNIVERSE	239
2	COSMIC HOSTILITY	250
3	THE MUTATION-AFTER-MAN	263
4	HOLISTIC PERCEPTION	277
5	MORAL RESPONSE	291
6	ONENESS	303

INTRODUCTION

My Mandate

All my life, I've been following my nose in pursuit of my inner mandate. It's told me to write, what to write, and how to write it.

I think everyone is given that same mandate, by the way, which is that we're all here with an assignment to take part in the ongoing transformation of our species from apes with ambition into fully realized human beings. Speaking generously, I think you could say that presently we're only part way through the process.

Each of us has our own individual version of this mandate. As Bob Dylan was once overheard saying: "There's a voice inside each of us that speaks only to us. We have to be able to hear that voice."

But not everyone hears the voice and recognizes it for what it is. Daily life and personal concerns can block us from picking it up. And even if we do hear the voice, we may not make a commitment to live by it. There are many of us who don't.

Qashani—you do remember "Abd al-Razzaq al-Qashani," don't you?—talks about this voice. Qashani was a Sufi scholar 700 years ago who said that our inner voice speaks to us in the form of ideas—"something which arrives without any conscious effort on the part of the individual."

Qashani lists four kinds of ideas, good and bad: Divine Ideas, Angelic Ideas, Selfish Ideas, and Satanic Ideas.

Divine Ideas are the means by which the mandate makes itself known to us. They manifest themselves as overwhelming experiences of illuminative certitude which arrive unbidden from out of the blue and are instantly recognized [or not] as orders from a higher authority—directive imperatives from the unknown we find compelling.

I had a small handful of these revelatory experiences in the course of my early life. They identified the nature of the human task for me and then set forth my specific job assignment, made its paradoxical nature evident, and pointed to the means by which I was to pursue it. Having accepted the mandate, I've been left to deal with practical details of procedure and to actualize and execute them with the guidance and support of subsequent Angelic Ideas—the small flashes, fortuities, intuitions, accessions, and happy chances that attend us daily and make pursuing our lives possible.

The first Divine Idea to come to me was the basic one of "growing up," an idea I haven't let go of yet. As long as I can remember, from earliest childhood, I yearned to grow up. At first, I took that to mean the attainment of physical adulthood and legal majority. But by the age of fourteen, I'd come to the conclusion that the grownups I was observing in the world around me weren't all that grown up themselves. Their sort of adulthood wasn't all it was cracked up to be, and it should be possible to continue developing past that level. The real challenge I'd been given wasn't merely gaining my own personal maturity but working on how all of us might become more like the most developed among us.

A second Divine Idea came to me when I was ten or twelve as I was walking down a dirt road in Indian Hills, then a still mostly empty residential area across the Red Cedar River from Okemos, Michigan. After World War II, my parents built a passive-solar-powered home there with no less than sixty feet of giant Thermopane windows along its southern exposure. A Frank Lloyd Wright house would be built next door and another one directly across the street. It would have been three if my father hadn't had a falling out with Wright before the war over the insufficient rationality of his design. But our little cul-de-sac of architectural aspiration would prove to be atypical of the subdivision as a whole as it gradually filled up during the course of the fifties with houses of a more conventional nature.

That day I was walking along Woodcraft toward Arrowhead Road where I lived, and as I got to the bend before the two roads met in a T, I was suddenly struck by an imperative revelation: What I was meant for and what I should be doing was knitting together incompatibilities.

You can understand this as a command from on high for me to be creative, original, and holistic.

The next step in my process of self-recognition came when I was sixteen and sitting in the library reading room of the boarding school in Massachusetts to which I'd been sent that year. On impulse one fall afternoon, I got up from my chair, crossed the room, and picked a Bible off the shelf—a thing it had never occurred to me to do before. The book fell open to The Book of Ecclesiastes, and my eyes landed on Ecclesiastes 9:10, "Whatsoever thy hand findeth to do, do it with thy might …"

The grave awaits us all—this book of wisdom told me—so while we're here we should be serious about everything we choose to do. I closed the Bible then and placed it back on the shelf where I'd found it having gotten the message I'd been guided to find.

This wouldn't be the only time the same thing would happen to me, by the way—having a book leap into my hand and fall open to the right place in order for a significant passage to force itself on my attention and for no other reason. But this would be by far the most significant of the three or four occasions I can recall this happening, delivering me a new imperative rather than just feeding me something I could use to know.

Much later I would discover Lewis Carroll offering advice to the young in his introduction to a simplified version of *Alice in Wonderland* intended for little children and quoting the very words from Ecclesiastes I'd taken to heart, declaring he'd found them in an old book he'd read.

The last of my formative Divine Ideas struck me one day shortly after I'd graduated from Mt. Hermon School while I was standing on the lawn behind the House of Tomorrow. As my graduation gift, my parents had given me a Smith-Corona portable typewriter, no doubt thinking I'd be needing one in college. The weekend after I received it, I had my last epiphany. A hand, as it were, fell on my shoulder there in our backyard, and a voice spoke in my ear: "Go indoors and write. Write stories. Write science fiction stories."

And so, I did. I went inside and began writing. Eventually, I would write my first five books on that typewriter.

There would be two Angelic Ideas afterwords to these instructions to grow up, be creative and original, be dedicated, and write. One was that I wasn't to do the same thing over and over. Everything I wrote had to be different from anything I'd written before in some significant way, which chipped away at the limits of what I hadn't yet done but still needed to do. I'd also be informed that everything I wrote had to be a part of the same thing. Both of these true at once—ever different and always the same. And storytelling, in general, and science fiction, in particular, were to be my worldly medium for this reconciliation of incompatibles.

There you have my personal mandate, the cluster of commands that I would live by thereafter: My task in life was to become a true adult and develop as a writer while working on the unfinished business of human self-transcendence, with storytelling in general and science fiction in particular as my specific means, and with an obligation to be both original and single-purposed as I went about it.

With this as my inner agenda, it's no wonder that I would never prosper as a commercial writer, being altogether too painstaking, too stubborn, and too wayward to serve anybody as a reliable wordsmith. Nor would I ever qualify as a serious writer, either, since I was working in unrecognized intellectual territory—the true nature of science fiction—while making everything up for the first time. I wasn't to be popular, and I wasn't to be widely known. Instead, I would have to be content to write in marginal spaces at the edges of public perception, and with any successes and recognitions I received coming rarely, randomly, and unexpectedly.

And yet I've continued to work on the Work that I was first assigned to do, of which this book can be considered both a display of examples and a summation. Take it as a multifaceted expression of the path I've followed—a holistic story about the creation and significance of stories.

The first part, "Following My Nose," tells how I learned to recognize the formative power of creative imagination through science fiction and Sufi teaching stories.

Next, "Miracles Can Happen" is a critical commentary upon my father's account of how he made the transition from life as a boy before the Russian Revolution as the youngest of thirteen children in a family of provincial aristocrats to a radically different adulthood in America as a professor of wood technology who built and lived in a house of the future, this metamorphosis being the consequence of a dozen miracles, only one of which my father ever acknowledged as such—significantly, the only one of them he rejected.

"Sympathy for the Devil" is an unveiling of the conscious unreliability and true nature of Robert Heinlein's 1941 story, "Solution Unsatisfactory," concerning the invention of the first nuclear weapon and the diabolical effect of its use.

"Falling Down a Rabbit Hole" tells of the afternoon boat ride when Charles Dodgson was goaded by three young sisters into improvising the beginning of *Alice's Adventures in Wonderland* and about the shamanistic mind state he was in, which allowed him to do it.

Finally, "Man Beyond Man" presents A. E. van Vogt's intuitive exploration in his earliest scientific fairytales of the idea of a higher order of human being to come.

FOLLOWING MY NOSE

1
THE LAND OF MAKE BELIEVE

WHEN I was small, my imagination was formed by *The Land of Make Believe*, a 1930 poster by Jaro Hess of the world of nursery rhymes, fairytales, and original quirkiness, with myriad wonders to look at, along with danger and mystery.

Here it was simultaneously night and day. The poster featured the house of the Three Bears, Jack and the Beanstalk, a Magic Carpet, the Cow That Jumped Over the Moon, the Talking Bird, and the remote House of Grandfather Know-All at the top of an impossible peak where my kids would say I lived. There were ships and mermaids, castles and mysterious places like the Enchanted Woods and the Bottomless Lake. At the end of a side road was a hole labeled Do Not Go In Here. Best of all, the whole was united by The Path That Leads to No Place. Eventually which wound through and around the entire picture.

Following an Angelic impulse, one day I went looking for it in a local map store, but when I asked if they had a map of Fairyland, they showed me something obvious and crude. I described the map I remembered, and they actually had it among their racks of maps on display, but they no longer had copies for sale. When I asked whether I could purchase the display copy since they were no longer selling it, they gave it to me outright. I had it framed in red, just like the one we had when I was young, and I have it hanging on the wall of my workroom today.

In recent times, *The Land of Make Believe* has become available once more in many forms, including a play rug for little children.

My favorite picture book in those days was *The Tenggren Tell-It-Again Book*, with pictures by Swedish-American artist Gustaf Tenggren and twenty-eight stories, among them "Hansel and Gretel," "Beauty and the Beast," and "Rapunzel"—including a number represented on *The Land of Make Believe* poster—retold by Katherine Gibson.

Whether we knew his name or not, and mostly we didn't, Gustaf Tenggren was every child's favorite artist. He did brilliant work in a variety of styles. He drew designs for Walt Disney movies, in particular for *Snow White* and *Pinocchio*. And he illustrated many Little Golden Books including the all-time best seller *The Poky Little Puppy*. But *The Tenggren Tell-It-Again Book*, published in 1942, was his masterpiece, with memorable otherworldly illustrations, a few of them like the ogre and his minions in "Puss in Boots" just scary enough to be challenging for a small child like me to peek at.

Another book that made a lifelong impression on me was *Old Peter's Russian Tales*, gathered by Arthur Ransome in 1915 and illustrated by Dmitri Mitrokhin. A copy of it was given by my father to my older brother Danny as a Christmas present in 1945 when he was seven and I was five. I was fascinated by these stories of firebirds, horses of power more clever than their masters, and malevolent witches with iron teeth.

I was particularly struck by the ur-witch Baba Yaga who "lives in a little hut which stands on hen's legs. Sometimes it faces the forest, sometimes it faces the path, and sometimes it walks solemnly about."

The little girl in the story is sent off to Baba Yaga by her cruel stepmother, who is another bad 'un armed with iron teeth. "How shall I find her?" asks the little girl, and the witch pinches her nose. "Follow your nose and you will find her," she says.

I loved that line for its multiple meanings and have always done my best to heed it.

Then the book mysteriously disappeared, and I never knew where it had gone.

However, years after its disappearance, in 1954, when I was in eighth grade, I followed my nose one day to a window box in my homeroom and there I spotted *Old Peter's Russian Tales* again, inscribed to my brother and stamped and dated by him. I proved ownership of the book to the teacher and regained possession of it.

Danny was sixteen then and didn't care about having it back, but I did, and do, and I have it yet.

LIFE IN AN IMAGINATIVE DESERT

AS a youngster during the 1940s, I was a voracious reader with a hunger for the imaginative. But the imaginative was all but impossible for a child to find. From a distance, the 20th century begins to appear flat, mundane and materialistic, short on spirit and the magical. But the forties, in particular, were not a heady time to be young and in search of otherness.

This was an era when public libraries like mine abhorred the fantastic except for the hints in the more outlandish Dr. Seuss books like *The 500 Hats of Bartholomew Cubbins*. The East Lansing public library wouldn't even admit fairytale books, let alone anything as strange as L. Frank Baum's Oz stories which were looked down upon and excluded. I was lucky enough to read two Oz books passed along from my mother's childhood, Baum's own favorite, *The Scarecrow of Oz*, and his final book, *The Magic of Oz*. The Dr. Dolittle books from the twenties, featuring a talking parrot as a figure of wisdom, intelligent animals, and a two-headed beast called a pushme-pullyou were about as imaginative as anything I could find to read in those days.

I had to be taken to the State Library in Lansing to discover books of any kind which were other than mundane, and they were rare. There was Tolkien's *The Hobbit or There and Back Again* from the late thirties. The one other truly different library book I can remember encountering was *The Angry Planet* by John Keir Cross, a story about a trip to Mars populated by weird alien creatures, and then back to Earth again.

During the forties there weren't many imaginative movies for children. The ones that existed were mostly from Disney, and they were either based on fairytales or 19th century sources like *Pinocchio* and the Uncle

Remus stories in *Song of the South*. Then when I was eight, there was a revival of the 1939 version of *The Wizard of Oz*, which enchanted and frightened me. But during the entire decade there were few films like that.

The one place that I might have found anything of what I was seeking was in pulp magazines in their years of decline, but the pulps were too racy, too adult, and too déclassé for my parents to accept.

It wasn't until I was ten when I read the serialized abridgment of Robert Heinlein's *Farmer in the Sky* about a colony on Jupiter's moon Ganymede in my older brother's *Boys' Life* that I encountered anything at all like what I was looking for. The story wasn't exactly magical, but it was as near to something of the right kind as I could find in those barren years.

In order to borrow more Heinlein juvenile SF in the early fifties I would have to drive with my mother to the State Library. They had just three titles—*Space Cadet*, *Farmer in the Sky*, and *Red Planet*. Whenever we went there, I was always hoping I'd find a new one waiting for me, and eventually I would.

I followed Heinlein from one book to the next through his Scribners period, missing only one of them, *Starman Jones*. Eventually I'd catch up with that one, too, in the Ingham County Library branch in Okemos.

Robert Heinlein was the standard by which I would come to measure science fiction. He may not have set my imagination alight, but he definitely broadened my imaginative horizons. I learned more from him than from anyone else, and I thought of myself as his greatest fan.

I wanted more stuff like that and looked for it everywhere in hopes of finding it somewhere. But Heinlein was the best there was. I read everything he wrote that I could find.

This was during the fifties when I caused my parents to be afraid I might be reading too much science fiction and be too heavily invested in a single writer. They never dreamed there would come a day when Heinlein Idolators would take me for the Anti-Heinlein, and Heinlein himself would be agitated by me like no one else. But those things would eventually come to pass.

3
DISCOVERING SCIENCE FICTION

WHEN I became a reader of science fiction at the age of ten, thanks to the *Boys' Life* serialization of Robert Heinlein's *Farmer in the Sky*, there was precious little of it to be found. In those days, science fiction was rare, marginal, and ill thought of. It was the product of low-class pulp magazines which were dying then under the paper shortage of World War II and the postwar advent of television. And as yet, there were almost no paperback books to take their place.

After the war, thanks to the dropping of the Atomic Bomb, two large anthologies of pulp magazine SF stories had been published by Random House and Crown. But these books stood alone. Consequently, in the absence of interest in imaginative fiction by professional book publishers, science fiction fans with enough knowledge and experience to do the job began founding their own specialty publishing houses to issue book versions of favorite authors—most notably Fantasy Press, Gnome Press, and Shasta. These books would include titles by Robert Heinlein, E.E. Smith, A.E. van Vogt, Jack Williamson, L. Sprague de Camp, and L. Ron Hubbard. But libraries would never buy anything so questionable and obscure. These were strictly limited editions, well-done fan productions for a specialized fan audience.

In order to feed my hunger for the fantastic, I had to settle for the first four Heinlein juveniles which I would read over and over. There was no other SF available to a child like me.

But that would change radically in a number of ways in the early fifties. And when it did, by following my nose, I was able to find science fiction in every place it was manifesting itself but one.

Three major science fiction magazines existed then, all of them digest sized, meaning the 5½ × 8¼ inch size of *Reader's Digest*. First amongst them was *Astounding*, founded in the early thirties, which had survived the war and the death of the pulps by making itself small, plus two new titles, *The Magazine of Fantasy and Science Fiction*, whose first issue was in the fall of 1949, followed by *Galaxy* one year later. At the time, however, since my parents denied me access to the few places they were available locally because of their sales of tobacco and alcohol, science fiction magazines like these were still off-limits to me. At most, I might catch glimpses of their covers from a distance, so I kind of knew that forbidden fruit existed but without any clear idea of what it might be.

Starting in 1952, however, because of the example set by Scribners with their yearly books by Heinlein, juvenile science fiction began being published. There was Andre Norton's *Star Man's Son*, which, to my disappointment, proved to be a post-nuclear war survival story and not the interstellar adventure suggested by the title. And there was a series of original novels from Winston.

My parents gave me a subscription to the Junior Literary Guild for my birthday that year, and the first book I received was a Winston juvenile—*Rocket Jockey*, a planet-to-planet race-through-space story by Philip St. John, a pseudonym of Lester del Rey. "This is great," I thought and hoped more such books would follow. But they didn't. This would prove to be the only science fiction book the Junior Literary Guild ever sent me during the year my subscription lasted.

However, other books from Winston's initial offering of ten titles, identifiable by their brightly-colored jackets with a rocket symbol on the spine, would make it into the children's stacks of the State Library before I left the children's room behind me. But none of them were a match for the Heinlein books which had called them into being.

During the forties, a handful of adult novels deriving from the SF pulp magazines—just six books that I can think of—had been issued by established publishing houses. The East Lansing Public Library owned one of them—Fredric Brown's *What Mad Universe* from Dutton, a mind-bending trashing of pulp story conventions that had first been published in the pulps. Knowing no better, I took the novel straight, and it scared the bejesus out of me. It would be several years before I could summon the nerve to read it.

Then, in 1950, Doubleday began a continuing line of hardcover science fiction books which included *Pebble in the Sky* by Isaac Asimov, and *Waldo and Magic, Inc.*, two long stories by Robert Heinlein. Through somebody's misapprehension, the Heinlein book showed up in the State Library shelved with his Scribners juveniles. That book was scary to me, too.

Grosset & Dunlap, known for their unconventionally marketed cheap hardcover editions, issued four reprint SF titles, two in 1950, one more in 1951, and finally, Heinlein's *Beyond This Horizon* in 1952. This was Heinlein's first adult novel, originally issued by fan publisher Fantasy Press. I spotted it on the mezzanine of Knapp's Department Store in Lansing and bought it for a dollar.

New paperback lines sprang up at this time, too, and these would also begin to issue science fiction books mostly derived from the SF magazines. When I was in seventh grade, two of them, both single-author story collections that had originated with the fan presses, would be offered to me at school through the Scholastic Book Service: Heinlein's *The Green Hills of Earth* and Fredric Brown's *Space on My Hands*. I snapped them up, of course, the only kid in my class who did. The principal publishers of these paperbacks would be Signet, Ballantine, and Ace, a company that offered two short books bound back-to-back.

Most importantly, however, I followed my nose downstairs at the State Library and checked the adult card catalog under the words "science fiction." The only titles listed under the heading had the number 808.3. And, feeling like a daring intruder as a kid barely turned twelve, I tracked them down back in the adult stacks.

The number "808.3" proved to be the Dewey Decimal number for American story anthologies. And there among them I would discover a motherlode of significant science fiction—seven books in particular, three of them brand new.

Historically important were the two classic postwar anthologies from 1946: *Adventures in Time and Space*, edited by Raymond J. Healy and J. Francis McComas, and *The Best of Science Fiction*, edited by Groff Conklin. And there were three further fat Crown anthologies edited by Conklin—*The Big Book of Science Fiction* from 1948, *The Treasury of Science Fiction* in 1950, and *The Omnibus of Science Fiction* in 1952. There was also the recently published *The Astounding Science Fiction Anthology*, edited by John W. Campbell, Jr. Finally, there was *The Galaxy Reader*, edited by H.L. Gold, which reprinted every story from the first year of this new magazine without omitting a single one. *That* was a head-bending collection.

When I found them, I checked these books out again and again, taking on the stories as I could, reading and rereading them because I only had a partial understanding of what I was reading, gradually working my way through the books. I had to learn a whole new conceptual language to cope with them at all, and I was challenged both intellectually and imaginatively by what I discovered.

These were stories which were an imaginal match for the Heinlein juveniles and more, discovered as they were reborn in book form.

4

WHAT IS SCIENCE FICTION?

AFTER being a kid of ten who liked the kind of thing he was discovering in the novels of Robert Heinlein but couldn't find more of it, suddenly, in the course of 1952, I found myself inundated by science fiction stories old and new, juvenile and adult, coming at me from every direction. I was swamped. I didn't know what to make of it all, and I didn't know anyone else who read SF and understood it better than I did who could guide my comprehension of what I was encountering. I was all alone in the midst of strangeness—a lot of it much harder to get my head around than the Heinlein juveniles—challenged to work out for myself and by myself where I was and what it was all about.

Hugo Gernsback, the pioneer magazine publisher who named the genre in 1930, may have wanted it to be a literature of future invention educating and entertaining young technologists-in-the-making. But by my day in the early fifties, science fiction had long since escaped his hands. And no one was ready to tell me what it *really* was.

Clearly, it wasn't merely stories about imaginary science. As an example, just a decade after Gernsback, Heinlein was able to publish a story like "Waldo" in *Astounding* in which the reality of our world isn't stable but is subject to change by the power of thought. And during the course of the forties, Fredric Brown could write one story in which someone falls in love with the thought projection of a cockroach on another planet and a second in which a writer is faced with an alien spaceship temporarily stranded in the sandwich he's eating, and these would be considered science fiction, too.

By the fifties, a number of publishing houses—albeit few of the most distinguished—might begin to issue SF because money was to be made from it, but academics and established cultural commentators still had no use whatever for this new popular imaginative literature. The only people who had any interest in the subject were writers and fans of science fiction, so if I wanted to understand what SF was really about, it was to them I'd have to turn.

The initial book on the subject was *Of Worlds Beyond: The Science of Science Fiction Writing*, edited by Lloyd Arthur Eshbach, the person behind the first serious fan publishing house. This 1947 symposium consisted of seven brief essays by writers like Heinlein, Jack Williamson, and A.E. van Vogt, who were authors of Fantasy Press' first titles. But the book was more a collection of individual accounts of personal writing choices and methods than a coherent discussion. Even if I had been able to find a copy of this little book—an impossibility for me at the time I was most in need of guidance—it wouldn't have been much help in the task of comprehending science fiction.

More useful would be two books published in 1953 for people in the same position I was—new to SF and in need of orientation—but who were some years older than me: *Modern Science Fiction: Its Meaning and Its Future*, edited by Reginald Bretnor, and *Science-Fiction Handbook* by L. Sprague de Camp.

(Those were the days when it was debated whether there should be a hyphen between the word "science" and the word "fiction.")

Modern Science Fiction was a book of essays intended to legitimize SF culturally which I tracked down in the Michigan State College library. It contained eleven essays divided into three parts. The first group was about SF publishing and the appearance of science fiction in media like the movies and radio. The second section considered science fiction's strengths and weaknesses and the ways in which it differed from conventional mundane fiction. And the final part of the book was about science fiction's relevance to the world around us—society and science, morals and religion—and what was to be expected of the genre in the future.

L. Sprague de Camp, the author of *Science-Fiction Handbook*, had a long essay in Bretnor's book entitled "Science Fiction and Creative Imagination" on the way in which science fiction stories were conceived. He said they were a product of the creative imagination but didn't believe science fiction was inspired literature. It merely recombined sensory data in new and provocative ways.

I didn't find this argument compelling. I'd learned a great deal from the factual knowledge I picked up from science fiction, probably than from any other source. That was one of the things I valued most about the Heinlein stories I'd read over and over which had provided me with a wider window into the world around me.

But what I personally liked best about the imaginative material I was finding was the head-bending stuff—the simultaneous night and day of the Jaro Hess poster, Gustaf Tenggren's fairytale pictures, the reality creation in Heinlein's "Waldo," even Fredric Brown's thought projections of an alien cockroach. And it was the absence of this mind-moving quality that I would come to feel was the major weakness in de Camp's own stories.

L. Sprague de Camp's *Science-Fiction Handbook* was a more instructive book than the Bretnor symposium. It told about science fiction's antecedents and history, what its present markets were, who its editors were, who read it and who'd been writing it, and how a good science fiction story was crafted.

This was a book I loved when I first read it. It filled me in on a great deal I needed to know and did the same for others. Many years later, at a science fiction convention room party, Roger Zelazny told me he wished he owned a copy. I answered that he was in luck because I had seen one just the day before in a glass-fronted bookcase near the checkout counter in the Strand Bookstore in lower Manhattan. It was, in fact, the only time I would ever see a copy for sale in a bookstore.

But *Science-Fiction Handbook* was an artifact of its time. Many years later, a second edition of the book would be published without all the elements in it that screamed "1953." However, without them the book now seemed limp and lifeless.

These two books—and a little book by Basil Davenport several years later, *Inquiry into Science Fiction*—would be the beginning and the end of serious public discussion of science fiction. There would be no others. Thereafter for many years, SF would be left to its fans and writers to scrutinize.

In 1956 eight Chicago fans—one of whom, Sidney Coleman, would later become a prominent theoretical physicist noted for his humor—banded together as Advent: Publishers to produce serious books on science-fictional subjects. The motive figures of the group would be Earl Kemp who had the ideas and George Price who executed them.

Advent's first book, *In Search of Wonder*, was a collection of reviews and essays by Damon Knight, an SF writer and anthologist who would become the founder of the Science Fiction Writers of America, the Milford Science Fiction Writers Conference, and the Clarion Science Fiction and Fantasy Writers' Workshops. Knight cared deeply about the craft and meaning of science fiction and probed the question unmercifully in his analyses.

Since the search for wonder was what I cared about most, this was a book I'd been waiting for. As soon as I learned of its existence, I sent off for a copy from the boarding school where I'd been imprisoned in Massachusetts, putting a little space monster doodle I'd worked up the year before under the return address on the envelope.

5
IN SEARCH OF WONDER

WHEN Damon Knight's *In Search of Wonder*—the first critical book I ever owned—arrived in my hands at Mt. Hermon School, it proved to be a joy to read, the only source I'd seen specifically concerned with the quality and meaning of individual science fiction stories. The book was informative, snarky, and acute in its perceptions. But it didn't resolve the fundamental question of what kind of thing SF really is.

The title of Knight's book was a reference to the phrase "sense of wonder" coined by fan historian Sam Moskowitz. SaM was the editor of *Science-Fiction Plus*, Hugo Gernsback's short-lived final attempt at publishing an SF magazine, as well as a hedge scholar devoted to documenting the history of science fiction fandom, uncovering SF's forgotten antecedents, and writing brief biographies of its major writers.

Moskowitz felt that in the course of the development of modern science fiction, something vital had been lost—the quality of wonder. Knight's book was a promise to seek wonder again.

However, what Knight actually cared about wasn't wonder but rather what he and his friend James Blish thought of as "technical criticism." Blish said that the technical critic "should be able to say with some precision not only that something went wrong—if it did—but just *how* it went wrong," while Knight declared that his concerns were originality, sincerity, style, construction, logic, coherence, sanity, and garden-variety grammar. Wonder wasn't on their list, or anyone else's, during the 1950s.

By that time, it was generally, if not universally, agreed that the true nature of science fiction was neither scientific nor prophetic—the original defining characteristics laid down by Gernsback. The vital question now for most commenters was whether SF was extrapolative or speculative in nature.

I first ran into the term extrapolation in a 1952 article by Robert Heinlein in *Galaxy* entitled "Where To?" and later called "Pandora's Box." Here Heinlein said, "'Extrapolation' means much the same in fiction writing as it does in mathematics: Exploring a trend. It means continuing a curve, a path, a trend into the future, by extending its present direction and continuing the *shape* it has displayed in its past performance …"

A story title expressing the essence of extrapolation is Heinlein's first short novel in *Astounding*, "If This Goes On—."

Speculation was another term owed to Heinlein. His 1947 essay in *Of Worlds Beyond* had been entitled "On the Writing of Speculative Fiction," a sly way of proposing an alternative to the name "science fiction," which he failed to develop further in his essay. Five years later, however, in the "Where To?" article in *Galaxy*, Heinlein said that speculation took the basic facts admitted by extrapolation and then threw in some additional wonky element like little green men from Mars. A title that could be considered speculative might be my story collection, *Farewell to Yesterday's Tomorrow*.

"Speculative fiction" would become an occasionally used alternative to the name "science fiction" which had the virtue of retaining the "SF" abbreviation familiarly understood to indicate both science fiction and fantasy. At the outset of *In Search of Wonder*, Damon Knight declared that "science fiction" was a misnomer we were unfortunately stuck with, but he personally thought "speculative fiction," which he credited to Heinlein, was a better name for the genre.

What the terms extrapolation and speculation have in common is that both of them are based on the assumed primacy of the so-called real world. As L. Sprague de Camp said in his essay "Imaginative Fiction and Creative Imagination" in *Modern Science Fiction: Its Meaning and Its Future*:

> Please let us assume that the world of the senses *is* the real world. If you believe that in addition to sensory data, the mind also draws upon divine inspiration, universal consciousness, racial memory, or some other suppositious non-sensory factor, we shall have to agree to disagree.

The one notable exception to this standard set of assumptions would come from A.E. van Vogt. He wrote in his essay in *Of Worlds Beyond* in 1947,

> Ever since I began writing for the science fiction field, it has been my habit to put every current thought into the story I happened to be working on. Frequently, an idea would seem to have no relevance, but by mulling it over a little, I would usually find an approach that would make it usable.

That is, van Vogt held that the thoughts that popped into his head, rather than de Camp's "real world" plus extensions and variations upon it, were paramount in his creation of science fiction.

In later self-accounts, van Vogt would amplify this by saying that while he was writing a story, he would program his dreams to feed him ideas as he needed them, waking himself every two hours during the night to harvest the results. He said, "Generally, either in a dream or about ten o'clock the next morning—*bang!*—an idea comes, and it will be something in a sense non-sequitur yet a growth from the story. I've gotten my most original stories that way ..."

He declared, "I have tried to plot stories consciously, from beginning to end, and I never sell them. I know better, now, than to even attempt to write them that way."

6

THEFT AND DISCOVERY

MY access to science fiction increased radically starting in the fall of 1954. Instead of me continuing at Okemos School, where I'd gone from second grade through eighth, my parents sent me to high school in East Lansing as they had done with my brother before me.

And every day, I got fifty cents lunch money. But instead of wasting it on a school lunch, as I was expected to do, I walked up to Grand River Avenue, the boulevard separating the main shopping in East Lansing on one side of the street from Michigan State College on the other. And there, with fifty cents in my pocket every day, I ran wild.

Science fiction paperbacks priced at twenty-five or thirty-five cents had begun to proliferate as never before, and I obtained a new one every day. One day I would buy a book and spend the rest of my money on a bag of half a dozen day-old Spudnuts or a quarter pound of Spanish peanuts and an A&W fountain root beer at Kresge's. The next day, I would steal a book and spend the full fifty cents on a more substantial lunch.

I was very good at swiping books, slipping them under my arm inside my jacket, and holding them in place with my elbow while I eased out the door. I didn't steal too much or too often in any one place. And I made sure to buy books in the stores where I stole so my honesty never came into question. I was never caught.

My days as a thief lasted for my freshman and sophomore years of high school until I was sent off to boarding school as a junior. I never stole again after that except for the occasional olive. But between misappropriation of lunch money and outright theft, I obtained a lot of science fiction books during those two years, some of them new titles, some of them reprints. And I read them in class, too.

I also expanded my sources of reading from paperbacks to magazines. The first SF magazine I ever bought was the December 1954 issue of *Astounding* with a giant picture of Mars on the cover by Chesley Bonestell. I sat at the lunch counter in the five and dime store and thumbed through it. The issue had an editorial by John W. Campbell, Jr., illustrated stories with a cryptic little Campbell comment before each one, a speculative science article, book reviews by P. Schuyler Miller, and a letter column called Brass Tacks. All of this was new to me and had to be assimilated.

But what struck me the hardest was the unique odor of the paper the magazine was printed on. That odor, that tan paper, was typical of *Astounding* in the middle fifties and I imprinted on it strongly. If I smelled it again today more than sixty years later, it would affect me deeply.

I bought *Astounding* regularly from that day on and would read it for the next dozen years. Even when I stopped reading the stories I would still read Campbell's editorials at the newsstand. They were intentionally provocative and taught me even when I disagreed with them.

About six months after I started reading *Astounding*, my mother informed me that the son of her friend, Mrs. Schultz, was going off to grad school and was getting rid of his science fiction magazine collection. I could have them if I wanted, and of course, I said yes. I wasn't anticipating much, but when my mother brought the box of magazines home, it was a very large box.

I laid the magazines out on the floor of my bedroom and sorted them by title and date. What I'd been given proved to be a run of *Astounding* from 1947 until a few months before I started buying the magazine, a complete run of *Galaxy* from the first issue, and a complete run of *The Magazine of Fantasy and Science Fiction*. Wow!

A year later, I took a further step. I wrote a fan letter to Robert Heinlein tapped out on my mother's portable typewriter. I told him that he was my favorite writer and that while other science fiction stories might be nourishing, his stories were steak to their hamburger. That would be the one and only time I ever tried to catch the sound of Heinlein's prose.

A month after that, when I had newly arrived at boarding school in Massachusetts, I received a blue postcard from Heinlein forwarded by my mother. Heinlein took note that I'd said in my letter that he didn't need to answer, but said my letter was a pleasure to answer. Wow again!

At the beginning of summer in 1958, when I was still seventeen, I wrote Heinlein a second time on my own brand-new typewriter. I said I was heading west for a summer job and wondered if I could pay him a visit on my way. This time, he didn't answer me.

7

"SO YOU WANT TO BE A WRITER"

AFTER receiving a typewriter as a high school graduation present in 1958 along with a backyard revelation that I should use it to write science fiction stories, I began teaching myself how to do it. By that time, I'd read all the science fiction and the science fiction criticism I could lay my hands on, so I figured I had a basis to work from. From that time on, I thought of myself as a writer and not just another science fiction reader.

I didn't think of myself as an SF fan since I had no contact with science fiction fandom and had no idea what fans did except for the ones who had published *In Search of Wonder*. The one exception to this is that somehow, I obtained an Australian fan parody of an issue of *Astounding*, which I was prepared to find funny. In those days, each issue of *Astounding* had a symbol in the upper lefthand corner of the cover with the revelation of what it represented on the contents page. The parody had a rubber band as the cover symbol. The explanation was "Propulsion."

In the fall of 1958, I began college at the University of Michigan. I didn't take an English writing course because I didn't want my writing messed with. I concluded I was right about this when a friend told me that in his English writing course science fiction was not acceptable.

My first contact with another SF writer came that fall when I met Dean McLaughlin in a college bookstore down the street from my dorm. Dean, nine years older than I, was the go-to guy in the store who knew where everything was and was called upon constantly to aid less savvy employees. Ten years after we met, Dean's *Analog* novella "Hawk Among the Sparrows" would be nominated for both a Hugo and a Nebula.

I was familiar with Dean's name from L. Sprague de Camp's *Science-Fiction Handbook*, where his second published story back in 1952 had been used as an example of the inner inconsistency that de Camp advised was to be avoided in constructing an SF story. I overlooked this minor flaw in Dean's perfection and instead picked his brains relentlessly for whatever he could tell me about the science fiction writing world. Dean was incredibly patient with my daily drop-by visits at the store to learn more from him.

My first writing assignment at the University of Michigan came in my introductory psychology class where we were told to take some bit of psychological research and compare the reality with a popular representation of it. I chose the work of Samuel Renshaw as portrayed in the stories of Robert Heinlein.

Heinlein had treated Renshaw as a super-scientist in the novella "Gulf," and then in the juvenile novel *Citizen of the Galaxy*, and would again for a third time a few years later in *Stranger in a Strange Land*. Like Alfred Korzybski before him, Renshaw was presented by Heinlein as someone who could take smart people, eliminate impediments and imperfections, and make them much smarter—swifter readers, infallible witnesses, trained geniuses.

To check Heinlein out, I interviewed a couple of University of Michigan psychologists and read a 1948 three-part profile of Renshaw and his work in the *Saturday Evening Post* entitled "You're Not as Smart as You Could Be," which would prove to be Heinlein's primary source of information on Renshaw and his research. My conclusion was that Heinlein had inflated Renshaw's work for fictional effect. What I would say now is that Heinlein portrayed Renshaw as a maker of more competent people—Homo novis—whereas a more accurate characterization would be that Renshaw was a student of thresholds of perception.

I got an A for the paper and sent a copy of it to Heinlein who responded with a three-page letter. The one thing I recall from it now is that Heinlein said that while he was writing a story, he knew it so well that he could correct punctuation in it mentally after he went to bed, but once it had been published, he remembered so little of it that he could read it for pleasure.

That fall, Dean took me and graduate student X. J. Kennedy to Detroit to a meeting of the convention committee of the following year's SF Worldcon. Kennedy, who would become well known as a poet, had had a former life in the forties as science fiction fan, Joe Kennedy. I think he and I represented the past and future of science fiction fandom to Dean. In the event, I kicked my heels in a basement family room during the confab of the con committee and was introduced to the con chairmen Roger Sims and Fred Prophet, and that was about all. I never laid eyes on Kennedy again after that day.

But I did attend Detention, the Seventeenth Worldcon in Detroit, the following Labor Day weekend. There were 381 people in attendance. As I was checking into the hotel, the older man in front of me in line turned around, stuck out his hand, and said, "Hello, I'm Doc Smith. Don't I know you?" I was completely bowled over by his generosity and tact, which were not at all what I expected to encounter from a science fiction icon like Smith.

The first con members I met were Earl Kemp and George Price of Advent. They remembered me from the space monster doodle on my order for *In Search of Wonder*. Very soon after that, I spotted Damon Knight and began reciting bits of his book to him. I attached myself to him and followed him around all weekend pestering him with questions as I had with Dean McLaughlin before him.

I even bought an hour of the time of the convention's Guest of Honor Poul Anderson at auction for $25 and talked to him of my writing ambition.

Some weeks after the convention, I drove with Dean to Chicago to attend a science fiction pro party. I hadn't sold a story at that point, but because of knowing Dean, I was treated with a degree of respect that I hadn't yet earned. I was told we would be staying overnight with Earl Kemp.

On our way to Chicago, Dean informed me that I had a good science fiction writer name, like van Vogt, Heinlein, Sturgeon, or Asimov. I appreciated that.

I met a few writers at the party—Harlan Ellison, Theodore Cogswell, whose first story had made the cover of *Astounding*, and Indiana lawyer (later judge) Joe L. Hensley, with whom I would collaborate on a couple of stories, including my first anthologization, "Dark Conception." When Harlan and I were introduced, he fingered my blazer on which I had spent no less than $20, and said, "So you want to be a writer. The first check you get, ditch this and buy yourself a continental cut suit." He didn't know me very well. I haven't owned a suit to this day, continental cut or otherwise.

During the course of the evening, mention was made of a broadsheet that Heinlein had circulated the previous year. I said I hadn't heard of it, and what was it? Earl Kemp poked his head up across the room and said he would show it to me when we got to his place.

In fact, Earl would show me three things. He showed me the manuscript for "Who Killed Science Fiction?" a question-and-answer super-fanzine that would win him a Hugo and provide the basis for him chairing a Chicago Worldcon. He showed me Boris Artzybasheff's artbook, *As I See*, which I would eventually be fortunate enough to own a copy of. And he showed me Heinlein's newspaper ad titled, "Who Are the Heirs of Patrick Henry?"

This newspaper ad was an answer to a series of ads by SANE—The Committee for a Sane Nuclear Policy—opposing atmospheric bomb testing. I wasn't any too keen on those tests myself because I didn't fancy nuclear fallout in the milk I drank.

Heinlein not only supported atmospheric testing as a matter of patriotism but beat the drum for a new organization, The Patrick Henry League, and asked for people to sign up. He would then reprint the ad as a broadsheet and circulate it in Navy circles and in the science fiction community. But to his bitter disappointment, he would get little positive response from either quarter. Heinlein didn't let go of the piece, either, but would reprint it again more than twenty years later in his 1980 collection *Expanded Universe*.

I finished reading the broadsheet Earl had taken from a drawer and said, "Wow. This is a little over the top, isn't it?"

I was bothered by the ad as well as by the passage in Heinlein's new novel, *Starship Troopers*, in which he said that radiation was necessary for evolution to take place, which I took as a covert reiteration of his support for the atmospheric tests. So I wrote to Heinlein expressing my concerns about fallout and pointing out that in stories like "Solution Unsatisfactory" and "Blowups Happen," he himself had stressed the dangers of atomic weapons.

He answered me by saying, "The Russians are coming. The Russians are coming." And recommended that I read three books.

I found all three in the University of Michigan library and read them. The books were from vehemently anti-Communist, right wing publishers. I remember the point of one of them was that we had supported the Russians during World War II with money and machines, and they hadn't paid us back, the dirty swines. So I wrote Heinlein again, saying as nicely as I could manage that I had read the books but didn't think they answered the question I was asking about Strontium-90 in the atmosphere.

As I would find out however—and William Patterson would later confirm in his official biography—Heinlein couldn't abide disagreement, and not at all on this particular subject. He didn't answer me this time. Instead, I got a note from Virginia Heinlein saying that her husband was now occupied in writing a new book, presumably *Stranger in a Strange Land*, and had no time for correspondence.

But Heinlein didn't forget or forgive my having disputed him and would bring it up when he was trying to prevent the writing of *Heinlein in Dimension*, the first book on his work. In fact, however, this exchange of letters would be the point at which I ceased to be Heinlein's unquestioning Number One Fan and began to apply all I had learned from the critical opinions he presented in his stories to the man himself and his own work. I think it's fair to say that this aborted correspondence marks our parting of the ways.

8 LEARNING TO WRITE

WHEN I began trying to write stories in the summer of 1958, I was completely ignorant and totally inept. I proved as much that fall by writing an unpublishable SF novel, but I learned a lot in doing it. Mainly what I learned was to get my think-think out of the way and listen to the words I was being given to set down on paper.

For a year and a half I did nothing but collect rejection slips. But about six months after Harlan Ellison fingered my inadequate jacket and told me to buy a continental cut suit with my first writing check, I sold a story to *Seventeen* magazine for $300 called "A Piece of Pie" based upon the annual intramural cross country race at Mt. Hermon School.

After another year and a half with more rejections, while stationed at the headquarters of a US Army preventive medicine company in a compound outside Seoul, Korea, I got an idea for a science fiction story. I was still bothered by the chauvinism and belligerence Heinlein had shown in *Starship Troopers* and I wanted to write a story with a devastating conclusion that I imagined Heinlein would endorse, but I would not.

My approach to constructing the story was to accumulate a number of key factors I wanted to work with and then allow them to reveal themselves as a single narrative.

I had just read Harper Lee's new novel, *To Kill a Mockingbird*, and as much as I liked it, I hadn't been completely convinced by her portrayal of the mentation of a six-year-old girl. Neither had I been convinced by Heinlein's little girl character Peewee in another book I'd loved, *Have Spacesuit—Will Travel*. As of that time, Heinlein had yet to include a young female protagonist in any of his juvenile novels.

I'd never attempted such a character in any story I'd written myself. And I was always trying to do something I hadn't done before in every story. So a young female lead became my second factor.

Next, I'd just read an article in *Astounding* by G. Harry Stine called "Science Fiction Is Too Conservative." In it, he proposed the idea—not actually new—of giant spaceships carrying colonies to the stars. That was my third factor.

The final piece of my story fell into place when I picked up a new novel called *Walkabout* in the camp library. The blurb spoke of a rite of passage in which Australian Indigenous boys were sent off to survive for a month in the wild by themselves.

So there was my story: A young girl from a starship would be dropped on a human colony planet to survive for a month in order to become an adult and earn citizenship on her ship. But the starship would be offended by the colony and vote to destroy it.

Almost as soon as I thought of the story, I found myself transferred to the company detachment at Camp Red Cloud in Uijongbu. There I was drafted by the second lieutenant in charge to do his typing. This was the only opportunity to write that I would have during my two years of army service, and I made the most of it. Over the next several months, I wrote my story. At 20,000 words, it was the second-longest story I had yet attempted.

I sent the manuscript off to John W. Campbell at *Astounding*, by that time renamed *Analog*. But while it was gone and then being returned to me, I came to the conclusion that to bring off the devastating ending I aimed for, the story needed to be longer. I submitted it again to Fred Pohl, editor of *Galaxy* and *If*, and then set to work on the longer version.

Pohl offered to buy my story, but only if I cut it in half. I did the job in one night while on charge of quarters duty back at company headquarters. I typed furiously through the night, rewriting the story and eliminating the overwhelming ending for which it existed while I listened on the radio as John Glenn orbited the planet three times.

And Pohl did buy the shortened story which he retitled "Down to the Worlds of Men" and published a year and a half later in the July 1963 issue of *If* following the serialization of Heinlein's *Podkayne of Mars*, which had a young female protagonist, though not one whose voice I believed in.

That was my second story sale, this time for $100. For a time there, my story checks kept getting smaller and smaller—$50 from *Datebook* for "A Tale of a Trunk," then half of $50 from *F&SF* for "Dark Conception," a collaboration with Joe Hensley, and then finally, before the bounce-back happened, $20 for a story called "The Death of Orville Murchison" from a magazine called *motive*. After that, the checks started getting larger again.

I wrote new stories and criticism, as well as a whole other nonfiction book while continuing to work on my novel for four more years. My aim was to write a story of the future more plausibly textured than SF was accustomed to being, which told about someone growing up in a society with a substantial power advantage over others, at first accepting its values as natural and then coming to reject them. Just like me and America.

While I was still at work on the book, I submitted another portion of it to Fred Pohl as a stand-alone story. But he turned it down—not unreasonably—telling my agent, "I used to think that Panshin wrote this way because he was stubborn. Now I think he just doesn't have a very interesting imagination."

When *Rite of Passage* was done in February 1966, I attempted to sell the novel, but it was rejected again and again, thirteen times in all. Once the reason given was that it was about a young girl, and girls didn't read science fiction, or so I was told. Another time, the reason was my funny name, which casual readers would take as the product of a foreign writer and pass by in a bookstore. When publishers don't want to accept a submission, any excuse will do.

This was a very frustrating time for me. In the summer of 1967, I even wrote a *cri de coeur* called "How to Get Kicked in the Head and Learn to Love It." I showed it to one friend, who gave me the sympathy I was seeking, and then I deposited it in a wastebasket.

By that time, I was living in a fifth-floor walkup in Brooklyn Heights and sharing a half-sized football with Terry Carr, who lived a few blocks away. We would toss around the football in the street after his work hours. Terry was an assistant editor at Ace Books and had proposed a new line of more ambitious science fiction books to A.A. Wyn, the owner of the company. Wyn was then in his final months of life and apparently desirous of making a mark to leave behind him because he said yes to Terry.

Terry was seeking books to be published as Ace Specials. And one afternoon while we were chucking the football back and forth, he asked to have a look at the manuscript of the novel I couldn't sell.

And he accepted *Rite of Passage*! It would be published in June of 1968 between novels by R.A. Lafferty and Joanna Russ, a perfect place to attract notice. The following spring, *Rite of Passage* received a Nebula Award from the Science Fiction Writers of America as Best Novel of the Year. It won 21 to 17 over Joanna's Ace Special *Picnic on Paradise*.

I knew it was going to win but was forced to pretend otherwise. Barry Malzberg informed me in advance. He said he was sure I'd want to know, although I really didn't. That's the writing life for you.

9 WRITING SCIENCE FICTION CRITICISM

SHORTLY after "Down to the Worlds of Men" was finally published in 1963, I began writing science fiction criticism. I'd returned from the army and then spent the next eight months working on turning the story into *Rite of Passage* before taking up college again at Michigan State. One evening, while I was sitting in the grill in the basement corridor connecting the men's dorm Snyder, where I lived, and the twin women's dorm Abbot, it struck me that there was a weakness in Robert Heinlein's 1961 novel *Stranger in a Strange Land*.

Heinlein had stated that his book took on the assumed truths of the modern Western world and cast doubt upon them. But it came to me that his handling of the subject of sex in *Stranger*, with water brotherhoods where everyone screwed everyone and no one was jealous or unhappy because of their clear new Martian-style thinking, wasn't actually as radical or enlightened as Heinlein presented it, but rather was something of an adolescent fantasy.

That was presumptuous of me. I was completely sexually inexperienced myself at the time and more than a bit of an idealist where sex was concerned. When my soldier friends went off to fuck in a Korean whorehouse, I remained downstairs with a girl on my knee until they were done. By contrast, Heinlein was someone who considered himself a sexual sophisticate.

However, my insight wasn't totally mistaken. In his Naval Academy days, Heinlein was known as a guy who was led around by his dick. Sex was the root cause of many of his troubles in life. And when he proposed to his third wife, he admitted to her that he could lose his head where sex was concerned at any time and might well do it again. Sex was definitely a weakness in his self-presentation to the world as a mature master of knowledge and behavior.

So I got up from the table I was sitting at, returned to my room and wrote my first critical piece. It might be fair to say that it was half naive, but also half intolerably perceptive.

When it was finished, I had nowhere to send it. The obvious place of publication for it was a science fiction fanzine, but I had no contact with anyone who was in the business of putting out a fanzine. But then, by happy chance, I spotted a classified ad in *F&SF* that said that someone named Bill Blackbeard was looking for fanzine material, so I mailed the piece off to him in California.

Almost immediately, I got an answer back, not from Blackbeard, but from a person who signed himself Al haLevy. He asked if I was a known fan writing under a pseudonym. I assured him that I was me and pointed to the story I had just had in the July issue of *If*.

I got no reply to the note I wrote him. However, about three weeks later (!), I opened my dorm mailbox to find a manila envelope. Inside was an issue of the Los Angeles Science Fiction Society's clubzine *Shangri L'Affaires*, familiarly known as *Shaggy*. And there in the Table of Contents on the front cover was my name given as the author of a piece called "Heinlein: By His Jockstrap."

That was dismaying. I thought the title was half-clever as a play on Heinlein's story title, "By His Bootstraps," but it was also rude and crude. And I was none too thrilled to be identified as Heinlein's jockstrap. That wasn't at all the way I wanted to introduce myself as a critical voice. Not surprisingly, the piece also offended Heinlein mightily because of the vast gap between how he saw himself and how the piece represented him.

Poul Anderson wrote a letter to *Shaggy* saying that he knew me, and I was a good kid—which was generous of him—and pointed out that not everything a writer wrote was what he believed personally, but rather what markets would accept. So I wrote another article for the zine saying that you could begin to believe a writer meant what he said if he said the same thing multiple times, and I cited one of Anderson's own tropes as my example.

At that point, however, I really didn't want to write anything further for *Shangri L'Affaires*, feeling I'd been taken advantage of by Blackbeard, haLevy, and *Shaggy* editor Redd Boggs, who apparently had their own fish to fry. When I told Dean McLaughlin about this, he suggested that I might write for Buck and Juanita Coulson's fanzine *Yandro* and gave me their address.

During the next year, I would produce a number of serious constructive articles for *Yandro* on the subject of science fiction. The true nature of SF was still my question and I tested it from one angle after another.

My primary models were Damon Knight and James Blish. I didn't consider myself a technical critic in the same way they did since I thought I was still in the process of learning how to write, but I definitely thought of myself as the youngest member of the group of SF writers who were concerned with the true nature of science fiction and how SF might be made better.

Yandro was a marvelous place to publish. It was around thirty yellow mimeographed pages in length with a new issue every month, never missing an issue for years on end, with an editorial, essays of various kinds, book reviews by Buck who was a prodigious reader, and letters of comment.

You may think of this amateur publication as fannish activity at its best with no pretensions and no agenda, a more personal and haimish version of the creative expression exemplified by the Chicago fans who had created Advent: Publishers in order to issue books by people like Knight and Blish. Roger Ebert would write testimonials about the formative power that involvement with *Yandro* had on him when he was a young fan. My contributions to the Coulson's magazine were so frequent during 1964 that when *Yandro* won a Hugo as Best Fanzine the following year, I was pleased to think that my sercon essays were part of the reason why.

I must have made an impression with what I was writing, too, because that summer at Midwestcon, my first regional science fiction convention, Earl Kemp called to me at a crowded room party, "Hey, Alex, want to write a book about Heinlein?" I hadn't seen Earl since he'd showed me the "Who Are the Heirs of Patrick Henry?" broadsheet back in 1959, and I thought he was kidding me about "Heinlein: By His Jockstrap." But he wasn't because he said it again at a party at the Coulson's in rural Indiana a month later. And I agreed to do it, returning to Michigan with a singing heart and a buzzing head.

That winter, before my final term as an undergraduate at Michigan State, I told my advisor that I was presently at work on two books, *Rite of Passage* and another on Robert Heinlein, and I wondered if I could get credit for either one. He answered, "Well, we can't give you credit for a novel, but we can call your book on Heinlein your senior thesis and give you credit for that."

Robert Heinlein was the first person I wrote to when I was researching the book, but he failed to answer my letter. However, in February, when I was two-thirds done with what proved to be the initial draft of the book, Heinlein wrote to Earl Kemp. He said that if Advent was serious about a book on his work, they would have engaged a more established critic. He accused me of having conned his best friend's widow out of a file of personal letters. He refused to read the book in progress and threatened to sue me and Advent if it were published.

Advent was intimidated by this, exactly as intended, and immediately withdrew from publication, sending me a check for $50 and no fewer than three letters—one official, one from Earl, and one from George Price—saying how sorry they were. I wasn't intimidated, however. The book was to be my senior thesis. It was the next step in my development as a critic. And no one, not from Heinlein's list of established critics nor anyone else, had yet written a book about the work of any science fiction writer, and I wanted to do it.

During the following month, I wrote the text of *Heinlein in Dimension* as the book now stands. I didn't think of it as anti-Heinlein in any way, but rather as a fair-minded first look at all his stories and a raising of issues like sex and solipsism that merited further consideration.

After it was done, I had the problem of finding alternate publication for it. So I wrote a piece for *Yandro* entitled "Lese Majesty, an offense against the King"—setting forth the situation. And it was effective. Over the next year, *Heinlein in Dimension* would appear in pieces in four different fanzines. So word of it got around.

Heinlein's attempt to kill the book outright before it was written turned out to be counter productive. Specifically because of the fanzine appearances of *Heinlein in Dimension*, the only fan writing I published in 1966, I would win the initial fan writing Hugo presented at the World Science Fiction Convention held in New York the following year.

Advent got its nerve back and decided they would publish the book and be damned. And *Heinlein in Dimension* appeared as a hardcover book in the spring of 1968 with an introduction by James Blish two months before the publication of *Rite of Passage*.

After it was published, Damon Knight took me aside at a Milford Writers Conference to tell me that he didn't like the book. But I couldn't tell you now what it was that he didn't like about it.

10 THE VILLIERS BOOKS

AFTER my period of getting kicked in the head and learning to love it finally came to an end in the fall of 1967 when I signed a contract with Advent for *Heinlein in Dimension* and another with Ace Books for *Rite of Passage*, Terry Carr of Ace suggested that I write a series of science fiction novels for him. I said yes, but working up a proposal for the first one didn't come easily to me since my approach was not to plot out a book in detail beforehand but rather to accumulate crucial factors I wanted to include until they reached what I thought of as "critical mass," and then just start writing.

In this case, marijuana was getting around in my circle of acquaintances just then. Our expectation of it at that early date was to get stoned and then scarf down a Sara Lee cake. But what I valued in the experience was that it triggered a series of strange insights, weird cross-connections, and funny perspectives in me. I jotted down any number of them on notecards, some of which I retain to this day. I wish I had more of them, particularly the half-dozen I posted on the wall in front of my typewriter as a reminding factor, and perhaps I still do somewhere if I dig hard enough. Here are a few examples:

> A sentient rock: I'm not stupid. I'm dull normal.

> A person does nothing all his life but sit and think. Ask him why. He has observed that actions can have untoward consequences. He's still thinking about things. At last, he leaps up, does something enigmatic or decisive or … and bops off down the road.

Rational people are always bumping into rocks. I used to be a rational person. I could show you scars.

"I don't understand you, sir."
"I don't propose that you should."
"But you don't understand me, either."
"And you don't propose that I should."
"Exactly."
"Understood."

The first factor was to write a book that was full of stuff like that. Editor Fred Pohl had said to my agent that he used to think I wrote the way I did because I was stubborn, but now he thought I just didn't have a very interesting imagination. I wanted to show him that he was right the first time and that my stubbornness was that I was working on *Rite of Passage* at the time and following the voice of that book—but I was also quite capable of writing in totally different ways. The voice of this book wouldn't be at all the same.

A second factor was that I thought science fiction was too committed to a sober meta-narrative constructed over the years by the writers of *Astounding* and *Analog*. I wanted to fight against the Empire of science fictional convention by presenting a quirkier and more amusing state of existence in which fanciful and unanticipated things might take place: Peels could grunt at midnight, large furry alien toads could ride red tricycles if the opportunity arose and they were of a mind to, and little pink clouds could claim to be God.

And yet a third factor was that while I was in graduate school at the University of Chicago, I'd found stacks of Canadian paperback copies of the books of Georgette Heyer in a local bookstore and read my way through them all. One book of hers which didn't knock me out in general was *The Grand Sophy*. But the last several chapters of it were a hoot with different characters wandering on and off stage, interweaving in an almost dance-like way. I wanted to do something like that myself—write prose performance pieces depending on timing and tempo—but at book length.

I once had someone suggest to me that P.G. Wodehouse was my model for doing this, but that's not so—even if it should prove to be so. I've never been a reader of P.G. Wodehouse. My inspiration was the last two chapters of *The Grand Sophy*, which I've never reread.

I didn't want to imitate anyone. I wanted to catch a dynamic and let it determine what things happened and how.

But how do you write a plausible book proposal which says that you aim to write a science fiction novel, or a series of them, which don't have ordinary plots but instead are pure improvised interactive quirkiness and fun? Somehow, I managed to cobble together something about a young lord who's a remittance man in a dinky future "Galactic Empire" encompassing a few hundred stars within a galaxy of stars by the hundreds of billions, together with his amiable but inscrutable traveling companion, an illegal alien being with the power to cloud men's minds. This was plausible enough to satisfy Terry, and he gave me a contract for it.

I quit my job at the Brooklyn Public Library, figuring that I could finally make a living by writing. I turned out to be wrong, but I did it anyway.

I dashed off the first book, *Star Well*, in two months. The second book in the series, *The Thurb Revolution*, took me three. But the third book, *Masque World*, came harder. It would take a full year to write. I've never written *The Universal Pantograph*, which was to be the fourth book, although I've carried materials for it around in my head for nearly fifty years.

The reasons for never writing it were manifold. First of all, I didn't want to repeat myself. I could get away with three Villiers books, but I wasn't sure about doing yet another one, only to find myself writing a template series like John D. MacDonald's Travis McGee books in which the elements were all familiar and cut to a pattern. Secondly, the sixties, which provided the cultural context and social climate in which books like mine could be written, were now over, and the seventies wouldn't offer as friendly an atmosphere for writing tightly phrased but intuitively imagined sixties-style whoop-de-do. Not least, however, was that A.A. Wyn, the not-completely-honest one-man owner of Ace Books, had finished dying near the beginning of the period of small publisher acquisition that was starting to happen then. The company was sold to Charter Communications, a many-headed monster oriented toward possession and profit rather than authenticity. In this new corporate climate, Ace's resourceful editor-in-chief, old-time fan Donald A. Wollheim, left the company after twenty years on the job to start his own line of books. My editor, Terry Carr, would depart for the West Coast, as well, and once again, I was stranded without a publisher.

However, the result of the whole cosmic arrangement of events in 1968 was that I, who a year or so earlier had been getting nowhere at all with my writing, had no fewer than four books published in the course of one volatile, heady year. So when I made my appearance in public awareness within the science fiction microcosm, I made a splash.

That gave me all the cultural capital I would live on for the next twenty years.

11
DOWN ON THE FARM

STAR *Well* was published in October 1968. A few weeks later, I received a fan letter—my first fan letter ever—from Cory Seidman telling me how much she liked the book and setting forth her take on what it was I'd done.

I first laid eyes on Cory at Tricon, the 24th World Science Fiction Convention in Cleveland, in 1966. She was the girl in the leafy brown dryad costume. Cory was a Radcliffe student in linguistics at the time and hung out with the MIT Science Fiction Society. She even took a course at MIT with Noam Chomsky. Over the next several years she and I would see each other from time to time at gatherings at Charlie and Marsha Brown's apartment in the Bronx.

If Cory related to *Star Well*, I won her heart with *The Thurb Revolution*. We were married the following June. It may tell you something about us that our initial wedding present to ourselves was the acquisition of the four-volume boxed set of Joseph Campbell's *The Masks of God*.

Three months later, in the spirit of many others who were leaving the city at the end of the sixties and moving to the country, we found ourselves living in a converted carriage house on a farm in upper Bucks County and acquiring a pushy tuxedo kitten named Fang who demanded to live with us and wouldn't be denied.

One consequence of our move to Open Gate Farm was losing direct contact with the science fiction professional and fan world within which we had previously functioned.

It may have been no accident that we would be confronted by a mass invasion of crickets that fall, something I'd never seen before and haven't witnessed since.

But being isolated on a farm which had no gate of any kind but a very long driveway while listening to a symphony of crickets bespeak, our situation had its advantage inasmuch as it threw us back on our own company. Cory and I spent the next several years working on reconciling our respective concepts and vocabularies. In the process, I discovered just how bright Cory is, something that took me time to properly appreciate.

Her particular skill was research and organization of data. In 1971, while I was teaching a course in science fiction at Cornell inherited from Joanna Russ, Cory spent the summer in the university library going through the Golden Age of the Campbell *Astounding* one issue at a time, making intensive notes on each one which she kept in a black binder I still have on my shelf of science fiction indexes today. In times to come, it would prove a unique and invaluable resource.

In the meantime, in spite of my newly established success as a writer of novels, I'd never let go of my basic inquiry into the true nature of science fiction and I pursued it in a bi-monthly column for *Fantastic* called "Science Fiction in Dimension."

In October 1966, during my period of intense frustration over *Heinlein in Dimension* and *Rite of Passage*, I received a commission from Twayne Publishers to contribute a general book on SF to their United States Authors series, and between May and July of the following year, I wrote one for them called *Science Fiction: A Critical Introduction*. But by the time I submitted the manuscript, the editor who'd asked for the book had departed from the company, and I got no response whatever from them for month after month until I'd finally had enough and took the manuscript back. I tried submitting it elsewhere a couple of times without success, but it was so tailored to the specifications of Twayne that I was never really happy with it and soon killed it altogether.

However, even as the sixties were on their way out the door, my friend Ted White inherited the editorship of *Amazing* and *Fantastic*, two SF magazines of minimal circulation, and asked me to write a column for him. With the turmoil then going on at Ace my fiction-writing career was in limbo, so I accepted.

At first, I thought of the column as an extension of the essays on the nature of science fiction I'd written for *Yandro* in 1964, only paid for this time. And I would manage to keep writing them for eighteen issues over the next three years—making a grand total of $630 for doing it—while I was simultaneously at work on a novel called *The Son of Black Morca*, a fantasy set against a science fictional background.

The final seven installments of "Science Fiction in Dimension" were devoted to an alternate history of science fiction that Cory and I were evolving based around the idea that science fiction wasn't really about future science and outer space as it was ordinarily considered to be, but rather was about inner space—the head states of the people who wrote the stories and of the audience that received them. These columns would be the first work to be signed by both of us.

Our contrary thinking in "Science Fiction in Dimension" had two direct results. The first of these was that I made myself persona non grata, apparently for life, with the academic community then beginning to teach science fiction at the university level.

First, I wrote a column entitled "Science Fiction and Academe," questioning whether academics were qualified to teach science fiction at all. If that weren't bad enough, a month after it was published, Cory and I attended a Secondary Universe Conference, an academic gathering held in Toronto that year, where I delivered a talk, later another column, entitled "Metaphor, Analogy, Symbol and Myth." My fatal sin then occurred when I told the whole gathered conference that science fiction couldn't be addressed effectively using the same analytical conventions they were accustomed to applying to mundane fiction but had to be addressed on its own terms. Science fiction criticism needed to be science fictional in nature.

Maverick professor Leslie Fiedler, who I think was positively disposed toward us, rose at that point to ask whether I really meant what I was saying. I said I did mean it. And ever since then, science fictional academia has treated me as a nonperson—and who could blame them? It has to be affronting to be told that the peripheral territory you think unoccupied and unexploited and ripe for possession is in fact, not a secondary universe at all and is not your property, and what's more, you haven't got the key to it.

The second result was that three years after we finished our column, we would be contacted by Ricardo Valla, editor for Italian publisher Editrice Nord. He proposed to publish those final seven columns as a book, and we agreed to it. It was duly issued in the spring of 1978 under the title *Mondi Interiori*, which is to say, *Worlds Within*.

In February 1973, having learned of the forthcoming publication of *Time Enough for Love*, a new novel featuring Lazarus Long, the central character of Heinlein's 1941 *Astounding* serial *Methuselah's Children*, I wrote a long essay of the same title in a single week discussing what the book would need to be in order to satisfactorily attend to the unfinished business of the earlier story. When I was done, I sent a copy of the manuscript to Heinlein. He read it and made copious notes in the margins addressed to me. But then he didn't share them with me.

I've only managed to catch up with Heinlein's marked copy in recent times in the Heinlein Archives. He protested that it was a book review of a book I hadn't read. He didn't understand that the essay was speculative criticism—along the lines of his "speculative fiction"—a science fictional reading of a forthcoming science fiction book, exactly the kind of reading I didn't think the academicians were capable of doing.

Ah, but then I did it again. On the heels of the last seven columns for *Fantastic*, I tested out our new alternate interpretation of science fiction on Robert Heinlein in an essay called "Reading Heinlein Subjectively."

Heinlein didn't appreciate it. When asked by young fan Gary Farber, he wouldn't admit to having read it, but he didn't like it. He thought I was reading his mind when I was only reading his stories and what they really said about him.

12
CREATIVE IMAGINATION AND TRANSCENDENCE

IF the sixties were a period of difficulty and frustration for me during the years in the wilderness before my *annus mirabilis* of 1968, the seventies would prove to be an even more trying time for me and my writing.

Throughout the decade it seemed that nothing could go right. New material failed to sell. Anthology proposals went nowhere. I couldn't crack non-SF markets. There were stories I tried to write but couldn't finish. I had work commissioned that was never used. I even had a signed contract for a hardcover version of *Rite of Passage* torn up because "Ace stole our accounting department. We don't do business with Ace."

I tried selling *The Son of Black Morca*, now called *Earth Magic*, without success. *Rite of Passage* was turned down a mere thirteen times. *Earth Magic* was turned down twenty-eight times before it was finally mis-published.

Larry Niven may have come the closest to telling me why. He said the story was about surrender. And I told him that he was right about that.

Larry said, "I could never surrender."

I said, "That's because you've already surrendered. Muslims say there are a hundred names of God. I don't know what they are, but one of them might be 'science,' and 'science' is the name to which you've made your surrender."

But the biggest hangup during that difficult time was writing a definitive book on the nature of science fiction with which I could live. Starting with *Science Fiction: A Critical Introduction* for Twayne in the sixties, we made six different attempts at it.

Perhaps the most interesting of these failures was *The F&SF History of Modern Science Fiction*, a compilation of book reviews from the magazine together with extensive commentaries.

The book that went the farthest was called *Masters of Space and Time*. David Hartwell at Pocket Books liked it enough to give us a contract for it but thought we should start it at an earlier point than we had. However, before we had completed the necessary research and writing, David lost his job and once again we were left without an editor, writing on pure speculation.

Money was always a problem for us. We lived month to month and hand to mouth, getting by on occasional sales and erratic payment, temporary jobs, credit card advances, help from both sets of parents, and finally, welfare and food stamps.

I might have regularized my income by taking a day job like a normal person, but I never did that. Instead, I adopted Bob Dylan's attitude that I was doin' God's work and just kept grinding away at it.

I lost a year altogether in 1975–1976. In what was a bad time for the industry, it had become clear to me that the royalty statements I was receiving from Ace were completely unreliable. There was one printing of *Rite of Passage* I wasn't even notified of let alone paid for.

Ace had long had a reputation for shorting their authors including one notorious case when a writer had both sides of an Ace Double and then received wildly different sales figures for each of them. When I had had enough of being jobbed, I circulated a questionnaire to the members of the Science Fiction Writers of America asking about their experiences with Ace.

Writers are vulnerable and are used to being cheated, but the results of my survey were so unmistakable that the SFWA was compelled to act. The organization audited Ace's financial books and as a result the company had to pay its authors no less than half a million dollars they had wrongfully withheld.

I personally was told I was owed $4000. But I had all my statements and that was clearly much less than I was due. So I rejected the settlement, and took Ace to arbitration as called for in my contract. Ace was overwhelmed by my stack of paper and offered me $10,000, and even though I knew the true figure was higher than that, at that point I was thoroughly exhausted and took what I was offered.

But the result of instigating the audit and then following it up with successful arbitration was that I made myself anathema in the SF publishing world. This meant that I'd now managed to alienate three different powerful parties—Heinlein and his Idolaters, science fiction academics, and science fiction publishers. And once again, I wouldn't be forgiven for my transgressions.

The weird thing was that Cory and I continued to survive. When the money had to be there, somehow it always was. That wasn't an easy way to live, and I wouldn't recommend it to anyone who doesn't have a mandate and know it, and a nose to follow.

Even so, in the midst of all this failure and frustration, the work we were doing went on. The most important result of this was that Cory and I had the time and solitude to develop two new key concepts.

The first of these was that the essential quality that made science fiction and fantasy different from ordinary "realistic" fiction was what we termed transcendence.

In any SF story—in order for it to be SFnal—there is always some nonexistent element. And that quality was what all the future science and unknown realms of being of science fiction have been about.

The other idea we developed was that the interior element expressed by SF writers wasn't merely a matter of personal psychology as we'd suggested at first but rather was creative imagination.

This phrase had first been used by L. Sprague de Camp in his essay for Reginald Bretnor's "Modern Science Fiction: Its Meaning and Its Future" back in 1953. But de Camp hadn't made the most of its implications because he immediately denied that creative imagination derived from "divine inspiration, universal consciousness, racial memory, or some other suppositious non-sensory factor." Instead, de Camp insisted that it meant moving around known pieces of knowledge and information and arranging them in novel ways.

The two of us picked up on the phrase in Henry Corbin's 1969 book *Creative Imagination in the Sufism of Ibn 'Arabi*, which these days passes by the alternate title *Alone with the Alone*.

Muhyiddin ibn al-'Arabi (1165–1235) was a Sufi master, a prolific writer and poet who was born in Spain and died in Damascus, known to this day by those who follow him as the Highest Teacher. There's even a current American group founded in 1977 called The Ibn 'Arabi Society.

In Corbin's book a distinction is made between the imaginary—which was what L. Sprague de Camp was actually invoking when he spoke of recombining elements received through the senses in new and meaningful or useful ways—and the imaginal, which is the expression of things not previously existent.

Cory and I came to a recognition that the creative imagination is the means by which transcendence is perceived and then expressed. And The

World Beyond the Hill—the realm of that which lies beyond ordinary knowledge—is the place where transcendence dwells.

What's more, that country of nonexistent things is the very same place that's represented in the Jaro Hess poster *The Land of Make Believe* which first captured my imagination when I was a small child and that I was seeking thereafter by reading fairytales and then science fiction.

With these concepts in place, it was finally possible for us to write the book on science fiction we'd been struggling with for so long, but it would take us a further ten years to do it.

13 ENCOUNTERING THE SUFIS

IT was no accident that we found the concept of the creative imagination in a book about the Sufis' greatest teacher.

I first encountered the Sufis as a freshman at the University of Michigan in the fall of 1958. In my first semester, I had four required courses—or perhaps it was three—and one free elective. So I went through the catalog of courses available, most of which weren't open to freshmen, and for whatever reason picked out one titled Great Books of the Near East, at that point having no idea of what college courses were like or what the great books of the Near East might be.

The teacher was George Makdisi. There were only four students in the class, three upperclassmen and me, and we all sat around a rectangular table in a small room with me on the right side and Mr. Makdisi at the far end.

The one book we were to read that I can recall nearly sixty years later was *The Confessions of Al Ghazali*. But the books in the course weren't available at the college bookstore. We had to order them from Blackwell's in England. And the books didn't arrive and didn't arrive. At least half the term went by before they came.

So there we were, the four of us, in a reading course with nothing to read. It became a matter of Mr. Makdisi talking and us asking questions. But the three upperclassmen—one at the end nearest the door and two across the table from me—didn't have much to say, so it largely became Mr. Makdisi talking and me, the new kid in school, asking questions of him.

It was a strange and intriguing experience because I soon came to the conclusion that while we were using the same words, they didn't mean the same thing to the two of us, and I had to figure out what he was getting at by guess and by gosh. It was far and away the most stimulating course I ever had in college, and I was spoiled by it because I thought all college would be that way, but it never was again until an open discussion course with Margaret Useem in my last two terms at Michigan State six years later.

I'm not sure that we ever talked about the Sufis as such—even though the books, when they did come, all proved to be Sufi classics. It was only years later that I came to the conclusion that Mr. Makdisi himself was a Sufi, and this was what Sufis were like. However, the course had a great impact on my way of thinking, which remained with me after that.

Finally, let me say that once late in the year and a half that I spent at the University of Michigan, I passed Mr. Makdisi in a busy hallway between classes. But I didn't speak to him, and he didn't speak to me.

In the years following my University of Michigan experience with Mr. Makdisi, I checked out what various reference books of the time could tell me about the Sufis. But I found what they had to say superficial, contradictory, and unhelpful. Here's a typical entry from *The Reader's Encyclopedia*: "Sufi. Member of a Mohammedan sect of mystics, mentioned, for instance, in Omar Khayyam. The literal meaning of the word is 'clad in wool.'"

In 1967, while I was working as a librarian for the Brooklyn Public Library, I found Idries Shah's *The Sufis*, a very strange book which began with a fable, followed by a series of jokes about a wise fool named Nasrudin, and eventually pointed to connections between the Sufis and a variety of Western manifestations like alchemy, the Knights Templar, and Francis of Assisi.

However, I got hung up in the passages on the abjad system of numerical word equivalence, which seemed dubious to me at best. Then I left the book on the subway by accident from where, fortunately, it was returned to the library. But I didn't go back to it and pick up where I'd left off.

What finally caught my attention was an essay by Doris Lessing entitled "What Looks Like an Egg and Is an Egg" in the May 7, 1972 *New York Times Book Review*, which cited no fewer than nine of Shah's books.

I found one of these books, a collection of Nasrudin stories—*The Exploits of the Incomparable Mulla Nasrudin*—in the Bucks County Free Library. It was illustrated by Richard Williams, the man who would do the animation for *Who Framed Roger Rabbit*.

Here's a Nasrudin story for you:

The Mulla bought a donkey. Someone told him that he would have to give it a certain amount of food every day. This he considered to be too much. He would experiment, he decided, to get it used to less food. Each day, therefore, he reduced its rations. Eventually, when the donkey was reduced to almost no food at all, it fell over and died. "Pity," said the Mulla. "If I had a little more time before it died, I could have gotten it accustomed to eating nothing at all."

I ordered more of the books named in Lessing's essay in paperback form from Kenny's bookstore in Doylestown. And the book order lady Mrs. White put me in touch with Gus Linton, somebody who was ordering the same books that I was.

Over the more than forty years of our friendship, Gus has proven to be the only person I've ever come in contact with who was also reading Shah's Sufi books. What is particularly interesting is that Gus and I have rarely if ever discussed the substance of those books.

All of Shah's books are subtly different in arrangement and outward appearance from each other, and each of them is the same in terms of having an unpredictable, enigmatic, and provocative nature. In addition to jokes, the materials they present include dervish teaching stories, anecdotes, original stories, translations from classical Persian poets like Rumi, lectures, and conversations.

Three of my particular favorites are *Thinkers of the East*, *The Way of the Sufi*, and *Learning How to Learn*. The first of these offers lessons in conduct and conception from various Sufi teachers. The second is translations and statements from different Sufi manifestations over a thousand-year period. And the third consists of lengthy responses to various questions received by Shah.

Someone else, like Gus, could as legitimately choose three other books.

I was amused and entertained by what I was reading, and I also learned from it. I certainly didn't understand everything that I read. Just as when I first encountered science fiction, I had to hold opinion in abeyance, accumulate and integrate information, and work out for myself what was really going on.

What was really going on was not indoctrination in a belief system. Rather it was learning the nuances of an operating system.

In recent times, I've encountered a Sufistic (because anyone can claim to be a Sufi) guru figure saying that people have read Shah's books for ten, twenty, thirty, or forty years and gotten nowhere with them. Which is quite true, I'm sure. What you get out of these books is what you are prepared to get out of these books, and the very fact of his own stuckness is evidence that he never did the necessary work.

It turns out that none of the material made available by Shah is actually Sufic in nature. Rather, it's the byproduct of past Sufic activity.

My takeaway is that even the name Sufi and the presence of Sufis in the shelter of Islam for a matter of centuries is only partial and temporary. What Sufis do and how they do it antedates Islam and can and does go on outside its parameters.

What Shah was teaching in his forty books was not Sufism, but rather learning what is necessary in order to be capable of operating in a Sufic manner.

Me, I haven't gotten to the bottom of those books yet. There's much in them that I still don't fathom after all these years, but I'm working on it.

14

THE WORK OF THE SUFIS

ONE night in the privacy of a hotel bedroom turned coatroom at a convention party for science fiction professionals, I said to Roger Zelazny that he was the last SF writer to have had an influence on me like writers such as A.E. van Vogt, Theodore Sturgeon, and Fredric Brown.

It was Robert Heinlein who'd been my first and primary science fictional mentor. I found him immensely broad and learned from that breadth. There's no question in my mind that after he entered the field, Heinlein widened the parameters of science fiction again and again.

Eventually, however, I found I had a talent for identifying Heinlein's limits. The primary one was that while he was very good at unifying information outside himself and presenting it in unusual and cleverly phrased ways, when he and his identifications were questioned, he would short out.

Roger—like Sturgeon—had demonstrated to me how well science fiction could be written. But I told him that influence had ceased after his novel *Lord of Light*, and I asked him what had changed. He indicated his baby asleep on the adjacent bed and said, "I had a living to make."

From the point I discovered science fiction by way of Heinlein until then, SF had given me information, broadened my horizons and fed my imagination, but after this it no longer taught me in the same way. I was still curious to know its essential nature, but it was no longer my primary teaching source.

This was when my attention shifted to learning from the Sufis.

What I particularly liked about the Sufi material Idries Shah provided was that it could be understood in multiple ways, each with its own validity. It could be both ha-ha and a-ha at the same time. Heinlein might have breadth, but the Sufis had depth.

I learned that one statement or joke might have as many as seven different levels of meaning. And the Sufis were also masters of "scatter"—providing bits of knowledge that readers had to accumulate and integrate for themselves. Shah provided the material, but you had to permit it to make its significance known to you and in the process raise your level of perception.

The difficulty was that Sufis were nowhere to be found. The Sufis weren't a public presence. You might show every sign of interest in them, but never be recruited or enlisted by them. Shah always said that in order to make Sufic progress, a teacher was necessary, but where were those teachers?

I only had a few glancing encounters with Shah. Gus Linton, Cory, and I traveled to New York City to view a screening of "One Pair of Eyes," a BBC program by Shah shown by Tony Hiss, the son of Alger Hiss, which is now available on YouTube.

The three of us traveled again to New York to the Roosevelt Hotel to listen to a well-attended lecture by Shah arranged by psychologist Robert Ornstein. Ornstein was the author of *The Psychology of Consciousness*, a book which introduced many people to the concept of the functional specialization of the two halves of the brain, and he would later write *The Mind Field* which discusses the Sufis in contemporary Western psychological terms.

A few years later, the lecture we heard that day would form the first half of a book called *Neglected Aspects of Sufi Study*. I remember two things in particular from the event itself. One was that Shah held up his right hand in front of the microphone and demonstrated—quite plausibly—the sound of one hand clapping. The other is that during a break in the session, I heard one person complaining loudly that Shah was only saying things that were already to be found in his books.

Lastly, I sent Shah a newspaper clipping about a campus goose which had been killed by a student who said the goose had startled him while he was meditating. I received a note back signed by O. M. Burke, whom I knew as the author of a book called *Among the Dervishes*, saying that Idries Shah hoped to meet me some day.

It's only been recently that I read *A Noose of Light*, the memoirs of Alan Tunbridge, who designed book jackets for Shah for twenty years. He said that Burke was a pseudonym of Shah's.

Shah never used the clipping as far as I know, and we never did meet—unless, of course, the statement meant that Shah hoped that I might learn something from his books.

During our period of failure and frustration in the seventies when Cory and I were attempting without success to write one book after another on the true nature of SF, I wrote to Leonard Lewin, a professor of electrical engineering at the University of Colorado and holder of many patents, who had edited a book called *The Diffusion of Sufi Ideas in the West*, saying that we had run into an impasse on the subject of science fiction and wondering how we might connect ourselves to the Sufi work. He answered by giving a page reference in *The Exploits of the Incomparable Mulla Nasrudin*. When I looked it up, the story was this:

> Someone saw Nasrudin searching for something on the ground. "What have you lost, Mulla?" he asked.
> "My key," said the Mulla. So they both went down on their knees to look for it.
> After a time, the other man asked: "Where exactly did you drop it?"
> "In my own house."
> "Then why are you looking here?"
> "There's more light here than in my own house."

I took that as a clue that I should look for my key in the dark where I'd dropped it. So we persevered at the work we had been doing and eventually produced *The World Beyond the Hill*.

What made *The World Beyond the Hill* different from what we had written previously and from other books on the subject of science fiction was that our central concern was not who had written science fiction or where it had been published but rather the cumulative development of its images of transcendence—its imaginal vehicles, the nonexistent places they went to, and the beings that were encountered there—and how these affected the familiar world of ordinary assumption and experience, the so-called "real world."

The World Beyond the Hill received praise from people outside science fiction, like Northrop Frye and Charles Tart, as well as from SF giants like Isaac Asimov. It also won a Hugo Award in 1990 for Best Related Non-Fiction Book.

I drew two conclusions from writing the book. The first was that it wasn't an accident that I'd been told by Leonard Lewin to keep working on the subject of science fiction.

What I would say now is that connections exist between the Sufis and science fiction. I don't know exactly what active hand the Sufis may have taken in seeding and feeding the development of SF, but I can tell you that at the beginning of the eighteenth century, when the Western world, mesmerized by its newfound rationalism, had largely lost touch with the creative imagination, the two means of its preservation and reintroduction in Europe were collections of fairytales like those by Charles Perrault and Madame d'Aulnoy and the publication of *The Arabian Nights*. Among the stories contained in that book were Sufi teaching stories.

The other conclusion that I came to is that the work of the Sufis has always been to help humanity grow up and complete its unfinished business of becoming fully human. The essence of Idries Shah's work was to break the grip of conventional Western habit and assumption in order to admit a more comprehensive form of knowledge access to our minds.

Before he died, Shah told his son Tahir two vital things. One was that his books constituted a complete Sufic teaching program. The other was that if Sufism came to the West, it wouldn't be called Sufism.

The purpose of what Shah had to offer would seem to have been to produce a new order of Sufically-developed people who aren't known as Sufis.

After Cory and I finally completed *The World Beyond the Hill*, as a writer who's not-a-Sufi, I was faced with the question of what I should write next. I've gathered some of the results in this book.

MIRACLES CAN HAPPEN

1
"BRIDGE ENOUGH FOR ME"

IN a fantasy novel called *Earth Magic* that Cory and I wrote, one of the characters is convinced that a bridge must exist just over the hill because the map in his hand shows a bridge there. He says, "By my map, there is a bridge, and I believe my map."

All that he may actually discover is the ruins of a former bridge, but it's sufficient to satisfy him. He declares, "That is bridge enough for me. My map was right."

My brother once told me that he thought this was really a description of our father.

Dad was a university department chairman and professor of wood technology. He was a relentlessly literal-minded and rational man who believed in always following maps, and who trusted the maps he followed far more than the world they represented.

If a song was called folk music, then he held the reasonable expectation that it was first sung spontaneously by a bunch of anonymous people in some day long past. The likes of Woody Guthrie and Bob Dylan had to be imposters. And it was his given opinion that nobody should write a story and permit it to be labeled science fiction who didn't possess at least a Ph.D. in advanced science, so you could be sure that he really knew what he was talking about.

If neither the world nor I always managed to live up to standards like these—and it was apparent that, at times we didn't—nonetheless, how things properly ought to be was clear to him. The word or the map or the book came first. The sometimes untidy way that things can actually be was the departure from truth.

Even so, there was a point in his life when my father turned his back on everything he'd loved and relied upon most and proceeded into the unknown with no map to guide him. And unaccountable things found a way of happening to him then which contrived to carry him away from one world and toward another.

The pivotal event may have been meeting Ahmed again. In his memoirs, my father—who didn't usually acknowledge the existence of the marvelous—would call it "the most incredible incident of my life."

Dad was born in the first year of the twentieth century in the city of Voronezh in Russia, one-third of the way from Moscow to the eastern tip of the Black Sea. He was the thirteenth and final child of a family of provincial aristocrats.

As it was told to him, there were two brothers named Panьshin at the court of Peter the Great who had refused to cut their beards and abandon the special clothing which identified them as boyars. In consequence, they were banished.

They traveled beyond the fringes of the northern forest to Voronezh in the black soil region, which was as far north as the rivers that flowed to the Black Sea were navigable. The elder brother became a property owner in the growing city, and the younger brother a shipbuilder. The story as it was handed down within the family was that one day he set off for America on one of the ships he built and was never heard of again.

As a boy, my father's favorite time of year was summer. When school had let out for the season, the children of the family would leave Voronezh in troika-drawn carriages for Mihailovka, the principal Panьshin country estate.

Mihailovka was a working farm. There were cows and pigs and chickens, fields of ripening grain and sunflowers, and great fruit orchards split by a broad avenue of linden trees and bounded by alleys of white birch, with cross-alleys lined with rowan, maple, and oak. Every week a wagon, or in winter a sleigh, would bring produce from the estate to the family in the city—eggs and poultry, butter and cottage cheese, fresh vegetables and fruit in season, mushrooms and root vegetables, jams and preserves.

But the real business of the place was the raising and training of racing horses and the provision of horses under contract to the army of the Tsar. There were thirty stables at Mihailovka. My grandfather's prized Orloff trotters were kept there, and for a period of several years until it managed to wear out its welcome, a camel, too. A round indoor horse arena was located where two wings of stables met at a right angle. And there was also an adjacent track.

The manor house had been built as the country home of my grandfather's grandfather, who first acquired the estate near the end of the eighteenth century together with two villages of serfs. It was a large comfortable split-level place with five bedrooms, a room for formal occasions, a family room, and a library full of books.

Dad's parents and their guests stayed there whenever they came out from the city. At those times, life would become more restricted and closely regulated.

There was a second house, as well, more sparely furnished and painted red. This contained another eight bedrooms built to accommodate the overflow of children. But my father looked on it as just a place to eat and sleep.

For him, Mihailovka was a boy's paradise with a million things to do.

There was a playground for the children. Or else you might play croquet or a game of gorodki. You could poke your nose into the office or the farm kitchen, the smithy or the machine shop. And it was always possible to hang around the stable foreman, illiterate yet horse-wise, who had once been my grandfather's childhood playmate. Or you might listen as the coachman told his stories, always familiar but always a little different, about Tsar Ivan and his foolish son or the Tsarevna Natalya and how she was turned into a frog.

It was also the kind of place where someone with parents who were proper and demanding and who had a dozen older brothers and sisters to evade could lose himself and never be missed. Between the houses and the orchard, there was a park full of ancient trees with a myriad snaking paths and hidden benches. One trail found its way to a hilltop where a circular shelter of glass had been built. My father thought of that as his special private place. It was possible for him to sit there for hours just dreaming, watching the herds of horses in the meadow below.

But what my father enjoyed most at Mihailovka were the nights he spent riding guard around the boundary of the estate with Ahmed.

Ahmed was a Muslim—a Cherkess from a village in the northern part of the Caucasus. He was a tall, wiry, catlike man who'd spent a life in the saddle. He wore a karakul cap on his head and a silver-ornamented dagger in his belt. Across the breast of his tunic, there were loops for rifle shells, and he carried a short-handled whip called a nagaika.

Local people looked on him with suspicion as an infidel, a dangerous and unpredictable man. Some thought that he had supernatural powers and could cast evil spells. There was even talk that he'd been seen in the act of changing into the form of some strange wild beast.

Old peasant women would cross themselves when they laid eyes on Ahmed and hurry away. But there were also said to be girls in the adjacent villages with babies that didn't look Russian.

If my father was shy of him at the outset, he overcame his wariness. Ahmed didn't act all that weirdly around the estate. For a wild man of the mountains, he seemed more gentle and patient than not. And he was even willing to allow a curious boy to accompany him when he rode on his rounds.

They would set off as night was falling, never following the same route or schedule so they couldn't be anticipated. If there was no moonlight, then Dad would have to rely on the horse to find its way.

The estate became another world after dark. My father would recall the sensuous feel of the summer air as they rode, and the sound the grain made as it rustled in the breeze. Most of all, he would remember the song of the nightingales.

During the night they would pause at the fire of the herdsmen watching the horses in the meadow and share their kettle of porridge or eat potatoes that had been baking in the coals. Then they'd resume riding the perimeter until daybreak.

My father only witnessed Ahmed act violently once. One night they stumbled across the hidden campfire of a horse thief. The man spotted Dad first and launched an attack upon him, and Ahmed came to the boy's aid.

He struck the intruder a blow with his nagaika and knocked him down. And then, when he continued to show his intent to fight, hit him again. That was all it took.

More unsettling were those occasions when he would sing sad, savage songs that sent shivers down my father's spine. Ahmed didn't like interruption while he was singing. At other times, he would tell stories about his past life.

Dad said, "Once he told me about his family, his chieftain father, and his beautiful younger sister who was stolen by a young man from another village, and how he and his father had avenged the family honor by killing not only the young brave but his entire family."

He wondered if that was why Ahmed was there so far from where he belonged.

"THEREFORE, HE DIDN'T KEEP SHEEP"

THE fortunes of the Panьshin family in Voronezh may have been at their zenith at the time my father was born. While he was in the process of growing up, however, they went rapidly downhill.

The easy life to which the Russian landed aristocracy had grown accustomed was fated to come to an end after the serfdom on which it was founded was officially abolished in 1861. My grandfather was a boy, not yet nine then. And although he couldn't foresee that the day would come when one of his own sons would inform him that he was "an oppressor of the masses," nevertheless he would understand and accept that it was going to be necessary for people of his class to change their ways.

My grandfather prided himself on his progressive views. He might still send his favorite black stallion off to Paris to win a prestigious harness race, but he only had contempt for his two sisters who continued to live their lives as creatures of society and fashion. He believed that every man had a duty to perform responsible work and to make provision for his family through his own efforts.

His chief occupation was the breeding, training and trading of horses. But even though he was successful at it, and his Orloff horses were respected, that wasn't enough to satisfy him. He didn't care to be just another horseman, heir to an outworn mode of life. The horse was not the way of the future.

A new century was coming, and he was determined to keep up with the times. So, as a man in his forties, he staked his wealth on becoming modern.

He took his greatest bit of unearned good fortune—Petropavlovka, his largest estate, bequeathed to him by the eccentric maiden aunt who lived there because he was the only person in her extended family who never bothered her—and worked to see this long-neglected place transformed into a model sheep ranch. Development of the project he placed in the hands of a professional agronomist, a young graduate in the study of scientific farm management.

Then, at the turn of the century, my grandfather erected a new grain mill in Voronezh, a four-story brick building filled with up-to-date equipment. His brother-in-law, who was a mechanical engineer, was in charge of its design and operation.

But the changes that he was making at Petropavlovka were not happily received, and in one of the popular uprisings that followed Russia's defeat in the Russo-Japanese War, a mob of peasants ransacked and burned the buildings and made off with the sheep. The young agronomist was lucky to escape with his life wearing the dress of a peasant woman smuggled to him by his village sweetheart.

He would be blamed by my grandfather for having antagonized the local people with displays of pride and arrogance. But the truth was that Mihailovka escaped suffering a similar fate only because the invading peasants became preoccupied with destroying two mechanical harvesters, the likes of which they'd never seen before, and my grandfather was given time to arrive from Voronezh with half a dozen troikas laden with extra bells to sound like an even greater force, and managed to scare them away.

However, he would not be able to go on with his experiment in sheep farming. He had already mortgaged Petropavlovka in order to pay for building the mill, and he was overextended. If he wanted to hold onto the grain mill, then he had to let go of the estate and the sheep.

So he sold whatever remained—with the sole exception of a boulder of red granite, six feet high, six feet wide, and twelve feet long, which had been discovered there, an anomaly in the black earth. My grandfather had that dragged through the snow on a sleigh drawn by oxen to Mihailovka, where he set it in place as the centerpiece of his main flowerbed.

And thereafter, he didn't keep sheep.

The grain mill operated successfully for more than a decade. But then a fire broke out in the building one Sunday, the day before my father's tenth birthday. The blaze could not be contained, and the mill was lost, too. The brick shell of the gutted building continued to stand as an eyesore for more than thirty years.

Eventually, Dad had to be told that all he could expect as his portion was an education. What that actually turned out to mean was that he would be able to spend a difficult year living at home while he worked in a medical supply warehouse for one hot meal a day, a pound of black bread, and money that had no value, and did his best to study botany at a university displaced from Estonia to Voronezh by World War I.

The First World War, even more than the Russo-Japanese War, put a strain on the ability of an autocratic and repressive Russian government to continue to keep the restiveness of its population under control. Riots, strikes and military insurrection escalated into a revolution in March 1917 that ended with the abdication of the Tsar.

This radical break with the past was widely welcomed within the country as something long overdue. But two attempts in the following months to create an effective successor government that would be more liberal and inclusive were failures.

Peasants and workers wanted an end to Russia's involvement in the grinding and inconclusive war in Europe and were hungry to see a redistribution of land and wealth. And these would become the avowed purposes of the Bolshevik revolutionaries who seized the government and major cities in a coup that fall.

Three more years would pass before the issue of who ruled Russia was finally settled. The story of this struggle is that the White Army, composed of everyone from monarchists to socialists, lost the Civil War they thought they were fighting because they had too many conflicting goals in mind, whereas the ideologues who directed the Red Army were able to carry the Revolution they'd launched through to a successful conclusion because they were more unified in purpose.

During most of this period, Voronezh was under the control of the Reds. But in October 1919, the Red Army withdrew from the city to defend Moscow against the threat of a daring White Army cavalry offensive, and the White Army then swung around to occupy a lightly-defended Voronezh.

By that time, few of the Panьshins' former possessions still belonged to them.

Losing Mihailovka had been a foregone conclusion, but they had hoped to be able to make the transition a smooth one. Instead, the estate had been seized by a committee of peasants. Both houses were burned down, and the tree-lined alleys, orchards and park were leveled. The cattle were parceled out, and the Orloff trotters were turned into plow horses.

In Voronezh, my grandfather's stables and half the Panьshin home were taken over by a Red Army cavalry unit—who then served as protectors of the family against the worst excesses of anarchy and terror in the city. But their orchard would be chopped down for firewood. And to keep themselves fed, they would have to barter away their clothing, their rugs and furniture, their silverware, even the frames from their ancestors' portraits.

The disastrous way that my grandfather's ventures into sheep ranching and grain milling had turned out—which the family would call his "reverses," as though they'd been losses at the gaming table—may in great part have been due to his own mistakes. He wasn't prudent. Anyone who fathers thirteen children and then mortgages his assets is presuming rather heavily on continued fair weather and smooth sailing. Instead, he was impatient and inclined to push his luck. At the same time, as someone who'd been educated at home by tutors, he was too ready to respect the authority of those more systematically knowledgeable than he. Impatient and imprudent gamblers who chase after the systems of others suffer reverses.

But the calamity sweeping over him now like a tidal wave was completely beyond his power to affect. It applied to all members of his class and every owner of property. And the only way that he could ever have avoided this disaster would have been by leaving Russia as a young man and ceasing to be a Russian aristocrat of his own accord.

In actual fact, however, my grandfather was sixty-five years old and completely incapable of being anything other than the man that he already was. He had no alternative but to stand by and watch while everything that his forefathers had gathered together was stripped away from him.

His former progressive sympathies deserted him. All that he could do was try to comprehend the full measure of what he'd lost, savor his own bitterness, and find vindication in the reiteration of old truths.

He blamed the current social chaos on a wayward younger generation that had lost its proper respect for the authority of parents, church, and state. In his impotence and anger, he would point to his own children as the nearest examples of this falling away. And they would then prove the truth of his words by attempting to evade his tirades.

Nobody paid any attention to him now—not even those people who in previous times would have been ready to think of him as a class enemy. When the Communist victory was finally secure, my grandparents would be allotted a single room in what had formerly been one of my grandfather's properties. And that is where he would spend the remaining years of his life.

A picture of my grandfather was taken when he was in his eighties. He looks like some cross between Father Time and King Lear—a grave old man with a high forehead, deep lines in his face, white hair, and a long white beard. He wears a heavy coat, and his hand rests on the head of a cane. But there is a distant look in his eyes as though his mind is really on other things.

3
"ALYOSHA, WHERE IS YOUR HORSE?"

MY father met Ahmed again at the moment that he most needed to. This was in the Caucasus Mountains during the Civil War, years after they'd last seen each other. Their encounter would be wholly unexpected, and a great relief to Dad.

He had just turned nineteen then. As a straggling soldier in the White Army, he'd agreed to join a prospective battle on no more than the hopeful promise that he would be able to find some weapon for himself after he got there. Instead, he'd jumped from the moving wagon that was taking him to the fight at the sight of mounted men bearing down on them with raised sabres and sought refuge in an unharvested field of corn.

Now he was running from the Red Army once more with no idea of what to do next beyond somehow finding his way back to the monastery where he'd been in hiding. He and Kyril, his companion, had spent a cold night in the woods, not daring to light a fire, with nothing more to eat than a few sour wild cherries they'd found.

They were walking along a mountain road when a voice called out for them to halt. Two men approached them from the brush with drawn guns. Dad was afraid they'd fallen into the hands of the Communists.

But these men were wearing traditional mountain garb. What's more, the taller of the two looked strangely familiar.

It was Ahmed! And even though my father was no longer the same boy that he'd once permitted to ride along with him, Ahmed knew him, as well.

"Alyosha!" he said. "We meet again. Where is your horse, and what are you doing here, so far from home?"

Exactly what Dad was doing there at that moment can't have been completely clear to him—which is what made meeting this way so utterly incredible.

When the White Army took Voronezh, there had been nothing to keep Dad at home any longer.

All that his father had to give him was further blame for the collapse of his world.

He'd said goodbye to Nadya Kotlerova, the daughter of a state prosecutor under the Tsar, as her family left town on the train. She and her brother had been the best friends that he had, his haven from the emotional thunderstorms raging at home. She gave him his first kiss as they parted, and she would send him her photograph by a hand-to-hand route through his sister Shura, but he would never set eyes on her again.

And he'd stood in the town square near Leon Trotsky as the organizer of the Red Army delivered an impassioned speech from the back of a splendid black horse urging resistance to the counter-revolutionary forces that were advancing from the south. He'd been impressive to watch and to listen to. But if the Communists were to come back to Voronezh, the only certainty they had to offer someone like Dad was that the older he grew, the more suspect and offensive they would be prepared to find him.

Soon after the White Army got to the city, their recruiting posters appeared on the streets. Many students were ready to enlist now that the chance was here. My father, nearly eighteen and a political liberal of largely untested conviction, joined a bunch of his fellows and they all went down to the recruiting office and signed up together.

He returned home to collect his underwear and say goodbye. His mother was at morning church service and had to be sent for. She and his sisters cried at having the youngest of the family leave so suddenly. Dad believed that his father was secretly proud of him but couldn't bring himself to say so.

When my father departed to join his group of forty new recruits, it would be the last time that he would see his home and parents.

Dad enlisted in the White Army with the expectation of becoming a cavalryman and riding on in triumph to Moscow.

But that wouldn't happen.

The offensive that took Voronezh and then stuck there was not the stuff of which triumphs are made. Rather, it was a last desperate act that had run out of breath and come up short of its goal.

Now the army was overextended. After less than a month the Reds counter-attacked to cut its lines of supply and isolate the occupiers of the city.

My father's platoon and the other that made up his company were thrown into the initial resistance. They were pulled from the training ground, placed in horse-drawn carts, and taken to the battlefield where they assumed positions on one side of a river. They managed to hold in place for three days. Then artillery was brought to bear on them, and they were forced to fall back.

Instead of moving on to Moscow, Dad went in exactly the opposite direction. And he wasn't riding a horse. He walked.

My father's fighting career was short, futile, and ugly. It only lasted for a period of two months. It consisted in its entirety of defeat and retreat.

And it would come to an end with him lying on a cot in a hospital with a case of typhus and with gangrene spreading through his left foot.

The stand they'd made by the river had helped to buy time for the army in Voronezh to begin its evacuation. His unit would then become part of the general pullback.

But they came under continual harassment as they moved. Again and again his company was drawn into skirmishes and small engagements. They kept suffering losses and continuing their retreat.

One month after they first began fighting, only two dozen of the forty youngsters who'd enlisted in Voronezh were still on their feet. The rest were sick, wounded, or dead. The other platoon had been even harder hit.

Dad took a superficial bullet wound in his left hand. That earned him a hot bath, the boiling of his clothes to rid them of lice, and a week of rest—each of which he valued. After that, however, he would be returned to his unit in order to retreat some more.

At the end of the second month of this, the army attempted to make a stand with a forest at its back. It was late December. The nights were frigid, and the toes of my father's left foot became frostbitten.

Once again, his company was in the thick of things for three days and held their ground. But at the end of that time, they had taken so many casualties that they were no longer an effective fighting force. Those who remained were pulled from the line, placed on a troop train, and sent south to become part of an attempt to regroup.

Before they left, however, they were forced to watch as a man was killed in reprisal for an incident in which three soldiers had been shot from ambush. Witnessing this was difficult for my father. Nobody seemed to care very much whether the person being executed was actually guilty, and that troubled Dad.

He had rejected the Russian Orthodox religious beliefs of his upbringing—that was one of the quarrels his father had with him. Nonetheless, this killing felt like an atrocity to him. When there was an outbreak of typhus on the train, and Dad was among the first to fall sick, it would pass through his mind as he was drifting into delirium that somebody who did believe would call this retribution.

But while he was lost to the world, they had the good fortune to overtake a hospital train at a railroad station along the way. His sergeant, Ivan Kashirin, took advantage of the opportunity and had the sick and wounded transferred from one train to the other.

When my father regained awareness several weeks later, he found himself in a military hospital in Ekaterinodar.

4
"PUT YOUR TRUST IN GOD"

ALTHOUGH he wasn't yet aware of it, Dad's active service as a rifle-toting warm body was already over. He wasn't able to point a gun just now, and the White Army would only continue to fall apart at the seams.

There really hadn't been much genuine substance to his military career. It could almost seem that the whole desperate cavalry gambit of the White Army had happened for the sole purpose of reaching out to him in Voronezh, snatching him up, and carrying him away, and then setting him down here in Ekaterinodar, just a little worse for wear.

He would gradually begin to regain strength from his bout with typhus. However, when he attempted to walk, he discovered that his left foot had now turned blue, and two of his toes were green. It was all that he could do to hobble a little on the outside edge of his foot.

A nurse told him that his foot should be amputated before the gangrene had a chance to spread to his leg. But the doctors were too busy just then to attend to the job, which would prove lucky since it left him some ability to move when he had to.

After the passage of another week, he looked up one day from his book to find a visitor at the foot of his bed. It was Ivan Kashirin, his sergeant. He had come here in search of his men. Ivan was the most experienced soldier in my father's unit, a twice-wounded veteran of the Great War in Europe. Dad admired his competence and the uncanny ability of the sergeant to keep a cool head even in the most heated moments.

In terms of the authority that he'd been forced to assume, if not his actual rank, Ivan was their company commander. It was he who'd given the youngsters what training they'd had. In the brief time available to him, he'd done what he could to teach them not to be either stupid or foolish when bullets were flying at them. He'd kept them together through the disastrous retreat as much by his bearing and example as by the orders he gave. And he was still doing what he could to look out for them now.

Ivan's path of spiritual advance was through combat. If he'd happened to live in a society which recognized people like him and made provision for them, he might have been an excellent samurai, Knight Templar, or Lakota warrior. As things were, his life served as a battleground for the contending sides of his nature.

In his youth in northern Russia, he'd been a leader of hooligans, thrown into jail on more than one occasion for disturbing the peace. He had also earned the highest Russian medal for valor, the Cross of Saint George.

When he first entered the army, Ivan's physique won a place for him in an elite guard regiment, where he rose to be a sergeant. But women had a way of hurling themselves at him and expecting him to catch them. He'd committed the error of making love to the wrong noble young lady and, as a consequence, found himself assigned to an infantry regiment in Siberia. Even so, it wouldn't be the last time in his life that he would toy with a mistake of that kind.

On the eve of the First World War, he was a novice in a monastery near Moscow. But with the permission of the Archimandrite, he'd left the monastery to rejoin his old guard regiment, and later to fight in the White Army. The last time that my father heard from him, he would be in another monastery in Serbia.

But he would never make a very good monk. Such were the conflicts in his soul that, in circumstances of routine, peace, and ease, he became a drunk.

It took the immediate challenge of wartime to call forth the best in Ivan. Combat gave him an active opportunity to exercise his higher nature at a time when it really counted. Under fire, responding creatively to the needs of the moment, he found it possible to be responsible, resourceful, unselfish, and persevering. And he did even better in circumstances of chaos and disaster.

My father would owe his life more than once to Ivan's ability to rise to the occasion and his refusal to ever give up. Dad would never really understand why the sergeant kept rescuing him, not realizing that Ivan was following the demands of an inner calling which would not let him do otherwise, or that his own degree of responsiveness might have anything to do with what happened to him.

The sergeant was here to tell him that the Red Army was now just fifty miles away and would soon be reaching the city. But if any of his men in the hospital were able to move, they were welcome to come with him. They would travel as far as they could by rail, and then go south.

That could only mean into the mountains—or over the mountains to Georgia, which had used the uncertainty of the moment to declare its independence from Russia. Ivan was telling him that they weren't merely retreating any longer. They were fleeing now.

Dad showed the sergeant his foot and said that he couldn't walk far.

Ivan said, "Put your trust in God. What have you to lose? Stay here and they shoot you. Go with us and maybe you will make it, God willing. I will help you if you decide to go."

My father placed no credence in religion, so it meant nothing to him to have the sergeant speak of reliance on the will of God. But he did understand that the Red Army was on its way, and he had no illusions about the mercy it would have for him when it got there.

During the period they'd run Voronezh, the Reds had revealed themselves as even more impressed by a technical solution to a problem than my grandfather. Not only had they taken Mihailovka away from the committee of peasants who'd seized it, they had confiscated the peasants' own holdings, as well. Then they'd merged all of the land into one gigantic state farm in the image of a factory.

The peasants longed to own more that was theirs alone and not to share everything while owning nothing, and so they'd risen once more. For this reactionary behavior and willful refusal to be properly grateful, they'd been put down harshly.

As somebody whom the Bolsheviks defined as a counter-revolutionary, Dad could hardly expect any greater sympathy from the Reds. Bad foot or not, his chances had to be better with Ivan. If the sergeant was willing to give him a hand when he needed it, he'd do all he could to keep up.

At the appointed hour, then, he rose from his cot. Ivan took his duffle bag and helped him down the stairs. My father was afraid that somebody would try to stop them, but so much had normal military and medical discipline broken down that nobody questioned their leaving.

However, he would be the only one who followed the sergeant from the hospital.

5

THE END OF THE TRACKS

MY father only began to appreciate the turmoil that he was being rescued from as he limped after Ivan through the streets of Ekaterinodar. Ordinary life had been suspended and there were military and civilian refugees everywhere trying to find some way out of the city.

It was late winter, and the passes in the Caucasus Mountains to the east and south were snowbound. The Black Sea laid to the west. And now the Red Army was coming from the north. People no longer had anywhere to go, and still, they looked for some miracle that would save them just as Dad was now being saved.

Looting was already starting to take place. They heard several shots being fired, and they passed a man lying dead in front of a broken store window.

Two trains were at the station. They made their way through a growing crowd of refugees held at bay by armed soldiers, and Ivan led the way to a boxcar at the end of one of the trains.

Inside it were three horses, three carts, and a dozen men. My father only recognized one of them—a young Ukrainian named Kyril from the other platoon. He was hobbling, too. Since Dad had last seen him, he'd been wounded, and he had a crude cast on his leg.

None of the other students who had enlisted with my father in Voronezh had managed to make it this far.

Soon the train began to move. The chaos of Ekaterinodar was left behind them, and they headed east.

Kyril filled Dad in on what had been happening to them while he'd been sick. The few members of the company who still remained had joined some Kuban Cossacks and the group of Kuban Assemblymen that they'd been ordered to escort.

Together, they'd hijacked this train. And Kyril had later gotten his wound in defending it.

Their intention had been to become a part of the ongoing evacuation of the White Army to the Crimean Peninsula in the Black Sea. But the boats had already left. Now the Kuban horsemen and foot soldiers were going back to their home in the mountains.

The train crawled along at a slow pace, stopping frequently. There was almost nothing to eat. All that Dad was given was one piece of black bread and a little salted fatback. But he'd developed dysentery again, and the lack of food helped to dry up his runs.

After they'd traveled for two days, they came to the end of the tracks.

At that point, the Kubans led their horses from the boxcars. They said farewell and set off for home, the Cossacks on their horses, the Assemblymen on foot.

Twenty soldiers were left by the train, along with the three carts and one horse.

It wasn't immediately apparent what they ought to do next, so they formed a circle to reach a decision. Although three young officers were present, Ivan Kashirin was chosen to preside.

Some of the men had become so hungry, tired, and dispirited by this time that if they had been left to themselves, they would have stayed right where they were until the Reds arrived. They didn't have much to contribute, though.

And there were those who'd just watched the last trace of security they knew disappearing into the distance and didn't want to lose contact with the Kubans. They thought the group should try to trail after them.

However, Ivan was in favor of going south to the mountain town of Batalpashinsk, not too far away. The prospect of a nearby town was appealing to all of them. And that is where it was decided they would go.

The horse was hitched to the best of the carts, and Kyril and my father rode in the cart along with the bags. Everyone else walked.

Batalpashinsk was assumed to be only two days away, but it took them four days to get there. My father would never be as hungry again in his life as he became on this trek into the mountains. During that time, all he had to eat was one egg that Ivan found for him, which he ate raw, and the corner of a piece of cornbread that a passing mountaineer broke off and gave him out of pity.

The six days of difficult travel and near-starvation that followed Dad's departure from his hospital bed took their toll on him. By the time they got to Batalpashinsk, he wasn't completely unconscious, but he was no longer aware of where he was or what was going on around him.

Ivan would tell Dad later of the cold reception they were given by the town. As soldiers with guns, they couldn't be ignored altogether. But they belonged to the White Army, and the local people were aware that the Reds were now winning the war. The townsfolk didn't want to make any moves that would get themselves shot. Neither did they want to make the mistake of doing anything they might be asked to answer for when the Communists came. So they kept as much distance from the men as they could.

Most of the soldiers were completely spent. They had been surviving on starvation rations for a longer period than my father, and they had just had four days of hard walking while he'd been riding in a horse-drawn cart. They could go no farther now. They were ready to remain in Batalpashinsk to await their fate.

But not Ivan. Never Ivan.

The sergeant was determined to keep on going as long as he was still capable of taking another step. Giving up was contrary to his faith, which demanded that he place his trust in God but never do less than his utmost.

Right now, this meant that through some marvel of transformation he contrived to alter the horse and cart into two donkeys and some food. Or perhaps he was able to find the one person in Batalpashinsk who was prepared to look upon a swap of that kind as too attractive an opportunity to pass up, even at this uncertain hour.

Ivan placed Kyril and my father astride the donkeys and pushed further on into the mountains. They were accompanied by the three officers, who were lent additional strength by their conviction that they were in greater danger from the Reds than the enlisted men who had chosen to stay behind.

Dad had nothing whatever to say about what was happening to him. He had just sufficient awareness and enough of his old horseman's seat to stay on the donkey as long as he was given support by the sergeant or one of the officers.

In his memoirs, he would describe his situation. He wrote, "Ivan's determination to go on in spite of all odds was typical of his conviction that our destinies were in God's hands. 'God willing' was for him no mere slogan but an article of faith. I was going with him because at this point, I had no will of my own."

6
"YOU CAN TELL BY THE WAY THE LEGS MOVE"

MY father would be grateful to Ivan for having chosen to rescue him once again when he was helpless. But why the sergeant had done it would always be a puzzle to him.

The only answer he was ever able to give was pretty feeble. It seemed to him that for some reason, Ivan had taken a liking to him.

A more apt answer would be staring him in the face, but it was at such odds with Dad's image of himself as somebody who always acted from reasoned judgment that he would never be able to recognize it.

You might say that he had a weak spot where the unreasonable was concerned.

I recall one time when Cory and I were visiting my parents in Michigan, and all of us were in the living room watching a magic special on TV. At a properly climactic moment in the program, the magician stood in a square open space formed by four panels lying flat on the stage. Then, the panels were raised to make an open-topped box enclosing him. When the walls were lowered again, we could see that the magician not only had managed to conjure up an elephant but he was now perched on it like a mahout.

The effect was so completely unanticipated and so well-timed that the audience broke into wild applause. The music swelled, and the magician rode the elephant around the stage in triumph.

Then my father said, "You can tell it's really not an elephant by the way the legs move."

Cory and I glanced at each other, but neither of us dared to utter a word. It would only have spoiled the moment.

There wasn't any doubt in our minds, at least, that what was before our eyes was a perfectly normal Indian elephant. It had an elephant's trunk. It had the oversized ears, the domed head, and the sad bags under its eyes. And its legs were moving just like the legs of an elephant as it lumbered along.

To say that it wasn't really an elephant seemed a strange act of denial.

However, even if we'd been ready to grant that Dad was right and it wasn't an elephant that we were watching, but a clever illusion projected from the basement, or the mechanical simulation of an elephant, or ten men balancing on each other's shoulders and hopping around the stage inside an elephant suit, that would only have made this trick that much more tricky. It wouldn't have changed the fact that something large and gray was there now that hadn't been there before and that it had a magician seated on its neck as it moved about.

But my father was satisfied that he had penetrated the deception. And that was enough to cancel the uneasiness he was feeling at having allowed himself to be fooled in the first place along with everybody else. Now that he knew better, it hadn't happened any longer.

Similarly, when Dad suggested that Ivan might have been prepared to go out of his way time and again to save his life just because the sergeant liked him, that would be another attempt by this man of reason to bring the disquietingly strange under control by trivializing it into submission.

What Ivan did would be reduced from an attempt by a warrior monk to emulate the example of Christ to mere comradely assistance from an older friend. And not only would the actual reciprocal nature of their bond not be acknowledged, but my father would do his best to disown all responsibility for the compact that he'd made with Ivan. It was too irrational for him to want to remember.

How irrational was it?

Do you recall the bridge in Cory's and my fantasy novel, *Earth Magic*, which appears on a map but is no longer standing? Well, later in the story—which, by the way, is dedicated to our fathers—another bridge of significance, but without worldly existence, manifests itself. The main character, a boy who is the son of a king who has just been overthrown, is sitting naked on a promontory of rock. He has been stripped of one thing after another which he took to make him who he is: Material possessions, relationships, expectations, ethnic identity, even his name. Now he is being hunted by his own kind and his own kin.

He's trapped there. He has no place to go, and his enemies are climbing to reach him.

Then, a bridge to nowhere appears before him over the void, suspended in nothing. And the boy walks out onto that impossible bridge.

That's just how nonrational the pact my father made with Ivan was.

Oh, Ivan's obligation was clear enough. In the hospital, the sergeant had told Dad that if he were to come with him, he would help him. So it wasn't a total mystery why Ivan should have taken my father along when he left Batalpashinsk, even though Dad was only semiconscious and a burden, rather than leaving him behind. That was what he'd promised he would do.

My father might act as though the sergeant had just happened to have a spare donkey on his hands and chose Dad to put on it because he had a liking for him. But, in fact, Ivan had deliberately set out to trade the horse and cart for two donkeys because neither Kyril nor my father was able to walk, and he needed transportation to carry them further into the mountains than a horse and cart could go at this time of year. The two boys were the last surviving chicks of this mother hen of the battlefield, and he wasn't about to abandon either one of them as long as he still drew breath.

However, what Dad had agreed to was a bit more problematic—for him, at least.

The sergeant had asked my father to trust in God. But it wasn't possible for him to do that.

Yet Ivan did rely on God, and clearly was going to continue to do it. So by agreeing to leave the hospital without permission and follow where the sergeant led him, Dad was tacitly authorizing Ivan to trust in God for both of them.

My father would rely upon the sergeant. And Ivan would strive for the impossible. If a miracle should take place, like the sudden appearance of the donkeys, Dad would accept the magic without questioning how the trick had been done, or whether they were actually donkeys at all.

That would be his part of the bargain. For the duration. For as long as he had need of miracles.

Afterwards, however, my father would do his best to put out of his mind that he could ever have made any agreement like that.

When they made camp that night, they had roast lamb to eat. It was the best meal they'd had in a long time and better than any they'd have for months to come.

Dad began feeling stronger for having eaten. The next day, he would be more alert.

However, Ivan began running a serious fever on that second day. It wasn't altogether surprising that he should become sick. He'd managed to remain on his feet while people all around him were falling ill. He'd also been pushing himself for far too long. Even though he was older than everyone else, he'd asked more of himself than of them, while taking less.

Sick or not, however, Ivan was still able to place one foot in front of the other, so he wasn't through yet. On he led them into the mountains by a path so precipitous that one of the officers was assigned to walk beside my father just to be sure that he didn't slip off his donkey and fall into the gorge of the River Tiberda below.

On the third day, they came upon a stone church on a level place on the far side of the river. It was surrounded by smaller whitewashed stone buildings, with another church from earlier times set on a height above. Beyond it rose snow-covered peaks.

This was the convent of Spasso-Preobrajenski. Twenty nuns lived here with as many novices, a dozen aging monks, and a retired general and his wife who were here on retreat.

The six men who crossed the rickety bridge that led to this monastery for women were a sorry-looking lot, ragged, unshaven, and dirty. The wild-eyed sergeant who led them was wobbling as he walked. Both boys riding donkeys had one leg swathed in filthy bandages. And three emaciated young officers came trailing after.

They were met by an elderly nun on the far side of the bridge. Ivan asked to speak to the Mother Superior, and he was taken away to see her.

Kyril and Dad were led to the infirmary where a brusque nun cut away their bandages. After she'd rewrapped Kyril's leg, she cleaned the stinking rotting flesh from Dad's blue foot and then put something on it which stung fiercely. She informed him that the foot would heal better if it weren't bandaged again.

Before she was finished, Ivan came lurching through the door, looking like some mad mountain hermit. But he was the bearer of good news. Another marvelous thing had taken place.

At the request of the Mother Superior, Sister Nina, the sergeant had told her about the two years he'd spent in a monastery near Moscow. And not only did it turn out that she was familiar with the place, having served in a nearby convent, but she was acquainted with his superior. In fact, the Archimandrite had been the one who'd proposed her for her position here.

Sister Nina decided that the three officers were to be taken by a reliable guide to a village of safety. The three sick men were to be given refuge.

Ivan had striven.

God's will had been done.

7
STORMS RAGING BELOW

TEN days later, five Red Army Cossacks came riding into the monastery from Batalpashinsk. The old general and his wife were quickly spirited out the back to higher ground.

When the Cossacks arrived, the three men—Dad, Kyril and Ivan—were still recovering in the infirmary. And there would be one tense moment when the leader of the detachment spied my father's boots—the felt boots of a White Army officer.

But Dad told the man the truth. A nurse in the hospital at Ekaterinodar had given him the boots because his had gotten worn out walking south from Voronezh. So far, he'd only been able to get a foot into one of them because of the gangrene, and he'd carried the other along with him.

Perhaps because my father looked too young to be an officer, his story was accepted, and he wasn't shot on the spot.

Before the Cossack left, he told them that as soon as the road was clear of snow and ice, a wagon would be sent along to pick them up. But the wagon never came.

Dad wasn't sure whether this was because the mountains around held too many White Army stragglers or because they'd somehow been forgotten.

After three weeks, my father had recovered sufficiently to leave the infirmary. He moved into a shed in the orchard.

Several dozen beehives were kept among the trees in the orchard. And boys from a nearby mountain village thought it was great sport to steal them.

Dad was given the assignment of guarding the beehives. To do this job, he was handed an 18th century blunderbuss, a weapon which couldn't be aimed, but only fired in a general direction.

Then, one spring night, he thought he heard a sound. He loosed a shot into the sky, just as he'd been instructed to do.

The noise woke the nuns. However, it was less successful than the gesture of intimidation it was intended to be. In the morning, a hole was discovered in the woven fence that surrounded the orchard, and several beehives were missing.

Each year toward the end of May, when the snows had melted in the high meadows, a few of the old monks would set forth from the monastery with a couple of herd dogs and drive a dozen cows and a flock of goats up the mountain to summer pasture. The monks would live in rude huts in the alpine meadow until snow came again, milking the animals twice a day and making cheese.

This year, it was thought prudent for Ivan, Kyril, and Dad to go with them.

So up the mountain they went after the monks, the dogs, the cows, and the goats, not to come down again until the first snow fell in the middle of September. All around them, Russia might be in flames and turmoil, but the three soldiers would pass this summer as though they were on a long vacation in a world apart.

They went swimming in a cold mountain stream. They fished for trout and then cooked their catch over an open fire. They drank fresh milk and ate new-made cheese, and they poked fun at the monks, telling them what an easy life they had and how lazy they were.

Once or twice a week, with the aid of the donkeys that Dad and Kyril had ridden from Batalpashinsk, novices would bring food up the mountain. They would cook a meal for the men and then go back down with a load of cheese to be ripened in the monastery's cave.

The only work the soldiers did that summer was to cut hay during two intense weeks of effort at the end of June, and then several more in the middle of August. Ivan and Kyril, who were experienced at this, wielded the scythes. My father had the job of raking the long grass they cut and stacking it.

The most vivid memory Dad would retain from this summer would be the experience of standing high on a mountainside, with blue skies above them, looking down at thunderstorms raging below. They could see black clouds lit here and there by lightning, and they could hear the sound of distant thunder. But they were above it all, unaffected.

Storms like these were even more striking at night—the stars overhead calm and remote, the storm flaring below. At a moment like that, Dad felt tiny and insignificant.

In September, with the cheese and hay all moved to the monastery, they followed the cows and goats down the mountain through newly fallen snow.

Sister Nina had invited the three soldiers to spend the winter at Spasso-Preobrajenski. "God willing," she had said, "everything will be all right."

My father returned to his shed in the orchard. Ivan and Kyril found space for themselves in the monks' dormitory. During the following month, Dad helped to move the beehives from the orchard to winter shelter and assisted the gardener in trimming the fruit trees. Ivan and Kyril fed the livestock and did the fall plowing of the monastery's extensive vegetable garden.

After a time, they would be joined by a White Army major, a stocky little Siberian who had grown tired of hiding out in the mountains and fending for himself and wanted a warm place for the winter.

The major made himself right at home at the monastery. He might be a married man with three children at home, but his greatest need at the moment was for a woman. So he singled out a middle-aged nun and moved in on her like a lion with an eye for the vulnerable zebra in a herd, and began an affair.

8
AMBUSH AT BATALPASHINSK

THEN, one morning in late October, a group of horsemen came to the monastery.

The men were Kuban Cossacks. My father recognized some of them from the train the previous March.

They said the Red Army only held the Caucausus lightly, and resistance was still alive in the mountains. In a few days, an attack would be launched upon Batalpashinsk. Every able-bodied man was needed. Who would come?

The major was the first to volunteer. His behavior was about to be made an issue at the convent and he'd worn out his welcome here. This gave him a good reason to leave.

And the call of patriotic duty was more than either Kyril or Dad could resist. They agreed to join the fight, too, even though they had no weapons to fight with, not even a blunderbuss.

When fifty mounted men appeared at the monastery on the appointed day, my father climbed willingly into one of the two empty carts they'd brought with them, along with Kyril and the major.

However, Ivan didn't go.

Dad would write that he couldn't remember why Ivan stayed behind. And he would suggest that he may have thought that the attack had little chance of success.

No doubt that was true. Even had the raid on Batalpashinsk gone exactly as it was supposed to, there was no chance that a little beehive-stealing escapade like this off in the Caucausus Mountains was going to turn into the rallying point for a defeat of the Red Army throughout Russia.

However, that kind of thinking doesn't sound like Ivan, who was never a man to duck a fight for a good cause simply because the odds were against him. It's much too sober, rational and after the fact. Even if he'd been given to calculation, I doubt that Ivan had either enough information or sufficient perspective on the overall state of the war to make any strategic assessments just then.

It seems more likely to me that the sergeant reacted to the moment as he encountered it. And if he didn't volunteer when they were first approached or climb into the cart when all the others did, it was because something about the situation didn't feel right to him.

A cavalry strike in hopes of finding a store of weapons and ammunition in a Batalpashinsk held by only a few defenders may have seemed both under planned and over hopeful to him. Or maybe he smelled a rat.

In the event the would-be attackers never reached their goal.

As soon as they got to more open country, the Cossacks went trotting on ahead of the slowly-moving carts, which were now filled with men, all of them officers but Kyril and my father. In their hurry to push on, the Kubans were soon out of sight.

And then they came pell-melling back, pursued by men on horseback. The Reds had known in advance they were coming and had been waiting for them in ambush.

It was as though the opposition to the Bolsheviks, which had been scattered through these mountains like so many separate blades of grass, had conveniently gathered itself all together in a bunch, and now the scythe was being swung to harvest the crop.

When Kyril and Dad took in what was happening, they went over the side of the moving wagon during the one moment in which it could be done. They dove into a field of corn that by some happy chance was still standing unharvested this late in the season, and then did their best to make themselves invisible.

In the final glimpse my father caught of what was going on, one cart had already been brought to a halt. The Siberian major had taken over the reins of the other. He was standing up, desperately whipping the horse on, but he was being rapidly overtaken by mounted men, bared sabers in hand.

And that was the last my father would ever see of him.

If, throughout the summer, Dad had been above the storm, he'd put himself right back in the middle of it now.

He and Kyril spent a miserable night lying low in the woods, afraid they might get lost and also afraid of being found. It rained. They got wet and then cold, but they didn't dare to light a fire lest they give themselves away.

What they ought to do next wasn't clear. In the morning, all they could think of was to set off back up the road to Spasso-Preobrajenski, as though if they were to ask Ivan, he might have some answer for them.

Then, in this moment when my father was most in need of guidance and direction, out of the brush stepped one more miracle, gun in hand. It was the most romantic figure of his former life—Ahmed, the Muslim guard with whom he'd ridden the boundaries of Mihailovka when he was a boy.

What an unanticipated thing to happen! No wonder Dad could think of this as the most incredible incident of his life.

Ahmed was taken by surprise, too, but he recognized my father as the boy he'd once known now grown up, and he called him "Alyosha." He asked Dad in a joking way where his horse was and what he was doing here so far from home.

My father explained what had happened to him and Kyril and said they were on the run now.

Ahmed said: "Why don't you go to my village with me? They will not get you there. I will find you a pretty girl. You will marry her and settle among us."

What a golden prospect to hold in front of Dad at a moment like that! Just to be asked cheered him.

Ahmed and his companion led them to a clearing not far away. And there my father saw mounted horsemen forming two separate circles.

The riders in the larger ring were Cherkessi, like Ahmed, more than a hundred strong. They'd arrived on the scene the previous day just in time to turn back the Bolshevik pursuit of the Kuban Cossacks. They were now gathered around their chieftains, imposing-looking men at the center of the circle.

The smaller ring of horsemen was what remained of the Kubans. At their heart was a respected general named Savin, whom my father didn't know.

Nearby stood a handful of White Army officers in their tattered uniforms. None were men who'd been in the carts with Kyril and Dad. But the two of them were recognized by one of the young officers who had walked behind their donkeys from Batalpashinsk to the monastery, and he brought them into the group.

The men in the clearing had been trying to decide what to do next, just like my father and Kyril. There appeared to be three choices open to them—to continue to fight, to go back home, or to flee Russia altogether.

The Cherkessi had come to a decision. To fight further would be to invite the destruction of their villages and families. They were going to return home and lay down their arms.

Hearing this settled matters for the Kubans. Without the assistance of the Cherkessi, there weren't enough of them to fight on. Nor was it possible for them to go home. Unlike the tribesmen, they were men in uniform, and, at the least, the officers among them would all be shot.

The only course remaining open now, General Savin told them, was to cross the Caucausus Mountains into Georgia.

The Cherkessi declared that it couldn't be done. It had been snowing in the mountains for nearly two months and the passes were closed. But General Savin and the men who followed him saw no other choice, and they were determined to try.

So a deal was struck. The Cherkessi would attempt to guide them over the mountains, and in return, they would take possession of all the Kuban horses.

There was one person who did have an option as to which way he would go—my father. However, when the Cherkessi turned off onto a separate trail for home, Dad said goodbye to Ahmed. He'd thanked him for his offer but told him he couldn't accept.

The reason my father would give was that the cultural gap was just too wide for him to bridge. It was too late for him to become Cherkess now, let alone a Muslim.

Once again, no doubt that was true. Dad would have made a very bad Cherkessi and no Muslim at all. At the same time, it also sounds like another rational gloss to me.

I think it was more like this:

Ahmed and the picture of possibility he painted were a romantic dream sprung to life from out of Dad's past. When my father was a boy, a storybook adventure like that would have held the greatest appeal for him if Ahmed had ever proposed such a thing some moonlit night when they were riding fence together or eating porridge by the herdsman's fire in the meadow.

However, while he was growing up, every easy dream that Dad had ever had was stripped away from him. First, there'd been his father's successive losses of property, then the hardships and narrowing of horizons of the First World War, followed by further reductions in the family's fortunes and his future prospects under the Red occupation of Voronezh. During the past year, he had enlisted in an army about to begin its retreat, been under fire and been wounded, been forced to participate in an arbitrary execution, suffered the threat of death from typhus and of amputation for gangrene, and spent months in isolation on a mountain top.

I think my father's participation without a weapon in the abortive attack on Batalpashinsk was his last futile gesture at holding onto a life for himself in Russia. And now he'd become so hopeless and disillusioned that an outright impossibility like crossing mountains deep in new snow to an unknowable future could appear a more plausible course for him to pursue than the fulfillment of some fantasy he might once have entertained about going home with Ahmed, settling down among wild and free tribal horsemen, and marrying a pretty mountain girl.

When the Cherkessi went their own way, my father was among those who continued after General Savin and the Kuban Cossacks back up the road to Spasso-Preobrajenski.

9

"DO YOU BELIEVE IN MIRACLES?"

IT was not until the 26th of November, New Style, that they were finally able to leave the monastery to begin the attempt on the pass through the mountains. It was snowing when they left.

They hadn't been able to go as promptly as they would have liked. They'd held the defile that led to Spasso-Preobrajenski while they gathered necessary provisions and informed everyone who might want to join them.

Altogether, there would be more than eighty people in the party. Among them were the retired general and his wife, who'd been on retreat at the convent.

They felt they couldn't remain there. They had to go, too. So Ivan, Kyril and Dad were appointed by General Savin to assist them in making the crossing.

At the outset, the old couple wanted to take everything they owned with them. But Ivan pointed out that nothing could go that couldn't be carried, and the soldiers were already burdened. Their considerable possessions would all have to be left behind.

And they would be, for the most part. But one object couldn't be abandoned.

The three men would be asked to lug the physical sign of the general's rank over the mountains—his splendid-looking but cumbersome ceremonial greatcoat, silver-gray and lined in red. The coat was excellent for standing in a single place and looking imposing, but it wasn't made for fleeing over mountains. It would be a trial for them to carry, and they would take turns doing it.

However, before they left the monastery, the old general was able to exercise the powers of his rank that he still retained to do a useful turn for

Ivan, Kyril, and my father. They lacked documents. Taking considerable pleasure in being able to use his official seal again, he made out certificates for each of them, identifying them as members of his old command—the 2nd Ordnance Commission of the Southern Russian forces—and then signed and sealed them.

When Red Army troops moved in to occupy Spasso-Preobrajenski two days after they departed from the monastery, the snow had turned into a blizzard. There would be no pursuit of their party, which was large and well-armed. Instead, the mountains and the bad weather were counted upon to do their work.

General Savin planned to make the crossing in three stages.

First, he moved the party to an abandoned military camp halfway between Spasso-Preobrajenski and the foot of the pass. In former times, it had been used for the training of mountain troops.

The Cossacks rode their horses through the falling snow. The old general and his wife traveled in one of three horse-drawn sleighs. The other two were filled with provisions. Dad was among those who walked.

This place was to serve as their base camp. There was an assembly hall here, and a dozen cabins with fireplaces and bunk beds. They would make the bunks more comfortable with hay from old haystacks that still remained. The Cossacks established two great fires in the clearing and began to roast sheep.

But it was snowing harder now, and there in the camp they would stay while the snow continued. They would find it discouraging to be stuck in this place for one uncertain day after another, listening to the wind howl and watching the snow get deeper.

The snow was still falling late on the fifth day when Ivan Kashirin—who always knew what was going on—informed my father that they were about to break camp and move closer to the pass to wait for the blizzard to end.

Then Ivan asked Dad, "Do you believe in miracles, Alyosha?"

My father answered with a denial and a recitation of the direness of their plight: "Miracles? I don't. All this looks like a bad dream to me. The Reds may be 15 versts behind us, the mountains are all around us, and we are trapped like hunted animals, with only that pass ahead."

Do you find it at all strange that my father could be so adamant about denying any belief in the miraculous at this moment when it looked like nothing short of a miracle could be enough to get them over the mountains to Georgia?

It seems strange to me. By my reckoning, at least, in order for my father to get to this moment of denial, an astonishing series of unlikely happenings and fortuitous events—call them miracles—had been necessary, from the cavalry paying an unexpected visit to Voronezh to snatch Dad from the hands of the Communists to the convenient existence of a cornfield still standing in November for him and Kyril to hide in.

And yet, the only one of my father's experiences that he would ever suggest had appeared extraordinary to him, and not just his good fortune or the way things happened to go, was having Ahmed pop out of the bushes to offer him a fairytale future as a prince of the mountains.

In short, the only miracle that Dad would ever be capable of acknowledging as such would be the one miracle that he'd turned his back on. And so great would be his determination to be rational at the moment Ivan asked his question that my father wouldn't even remember that his encounter with Ahmed—which he'd later call the most incredible incident of his life—had taken place just a few weeks before.

Dad did not believe in miracles. And he wasn't going to believe in miracles.

Even so, here they were in a predicament my father could see no rational way out of, but which still had to be coped with.

Ivan said, "Well, I do believe in miracles, Alyosha. And I believe in God's will. Remember, I was a monk once. Well, almost a monk. But now we'd better get ready."

And he picked up his pack and started for the door.

Whatever was Dad to do now?

He remembered what Ivan had said to him when he'd been lying in a hospital bed in Ekaterinodar with a blue foot and the Red Army approaching, and he'd just doubted his ability to keep up with the sergeant. It seemed that once again, he had the choice of following Ivan and his reliance on God's will or giving up and waiting to be shot.

My father took one last look around the cabin. And then the man who refused to believe in miracles followed the man who did believe out the door.

It was still snowing when the party set out from the base camp, the Cossacks astride their horses, and the old general and his wife in the only sleigh.

But the timing of their move was just right. As they moved higher something happened that helped to lighten their spirits. The clouds fell away beneath them, and they emerged above the storm into a starry night, with the trail ahead of them brightly lit by the moon.

10

LIKE FAIRYTALE GIANTS

DURING the next week, Dad set down the events of the crossing in a journal. (He would call it a diary, but it was clearly begun just afterwards.) Fifty years later, he would incorporate what he'd originally written in December 1920 into his memoirs.

The second entry—which is quite remarkable—is titled "At the Mountain Camp." It tells of a dream that my father had very shortly after they arrived there and then reports a speech made to them by General Savin.

Dad wrote:

> We reached a snow-covered clearing, surrounded by tall fir trees, by nightfall the next day. There were several small log cabins on one side of the clearing, and the Cossacks had already lighted several huge campfires. They had their horses tethered and were clustered around the fire. It was an eerie picture or perhaps a wild dream.
>
> I joined a group of Cossacks who were singing one of their beautiful haunting songs, and then I dozed off. The tall fir trees and the campfire gave way to the familiar surroundings of our living room in Voronezh. I was sitting on the sofa with Shura, and then someone else entered the room and I recognized Nadya. She was smiling as she paused on the threshold.
>
> I wanted to rise to greet her, but suddenly I realized that my legs were gone and in their place were hideous-looking stumps. I stretched out my arms to Nadya, but I could not move. The smile left her face, and with a mournful cry she was gone.

> I woke up with a start to the cry of a hyena. My legs, extended away from the fire, were numb with cold.
>
> The return to reality was so startling that, for a moment, I thought I was losing my mind. I got up, stamped my cold feet, and then sat down again by the fire, shivering, not so much from the actual cold as from the emotional upset caused by the dream.

In his memoirs, my father adds that for years afterward, he had recurrent terrifying dreams in which he needed to escape from something but was unable to do it because his legs refused to move.

This vision of Nadya Kotlerova, Dad's friend and almost-sweetheart, and of the old life she represented which was now beyond his ability to reach was so disturbing to my father that he went looking for Ivan and Kyril to tell them about his dream.

He found them in one of the log cabins. Kyril was sleeping, and Ivan was repairing one of his boots.

Ivan asked Dad if he'd fallen asleep outside. And my father described the shock he'd just had.

When he was finished, Ivan told him that General Savin was going to address them shortly.

In the journal he kept, Dad wrote:

> Half an hour later, everybody gathered around one large fire. The general sat on a log, looking as if he was still trying to come to a decision. Then he spoke:
>
> Friends, last night I got a message that General Wrangel evacuated all his forces from the Crimea on November 15th. This means that all organized resistance to the Communists now is at an end, and we are entirely on our own. We still have two choices: One is to go back to the monastery and wait there for the Bolsheviks to come. The other is to try the pass. If we go over and make it—and I must tell you that a party of some 20 tried it a week ago and did not make it—there is no assurance of how we will be received on the other side.
>
> I am no longer your commander. I am just one of you. I have made my decision, and you must decide for yourselves. There is no disgrace if you decide to stay behind. But those who want to go with me must be ready at daybreak.
>
> It will be a long, hard day ahead of us. And, of course, we must leave our horses here. I have made arrangements with the

Cherkessi to pick them up. This is our payment for the provisions and the guides that will lead us.

The third entry in Dad's journal is entitled "Over the Hump."

As soon as there was light enough to see, we started walking. It was snowing again, but not hard, and once again we soon broke through the clouds, and this time into the rising sun. We were told to go in single file, and above all, to be quiet. Loud shouts or a shot could start an avalanche, an ever-present danger at these altitudes. We, with the old General and his wife, were placed toward the end of the line.

The sun was now shining brilliantly, and it made my unprotected eyes ache from the reflection on the unbroken stretches of the whitest snow I ever saw, all around us. The panorama was breathtaking. We were ascending in a zig-zag formation up a steep incline. The men ahead of us trampled the snow down so that we, at the end of the line, were walking in a snow tunnel, with only our heads above the snow banks.

We were told later that the guides, of whom there were five, took turns breaking the trail. It was hard and dangerous work, because one false step could plunge a man into the deep, snow-covered crevasses. But somehow through years of experience these men knew all the landmarks and kept unerringly climbing up the mountain.

I was told that all of them are smugglers who make a number of trips a year over the pass, but never after the trail is covered with deep snow. Each of them carried a long staff with which he probed carefully before taking the next step.

Our line of people looked now like a gray snake wriggling its way up the white, snow-covered mountain. To the left of us, we could see a glacier, and all around us were snow-covered peaks looking like white fairytale giants. Below us, the view was cut off by the gray clouds through which we had emerged not long ago.

And all around us was silence such as one encounters only in the mountains when the air is still. One realized how complete the silence was when several times during the ascent it was broken by the rumble of avalanches, a frightening roar that I cannot compare to anything I ever heard before.

The summit of the pass looked like a saddle among the peaks, but it seemed incredibly far away above us. I did not have a watch, so I cannot say when we reached the summit, but it must have been at least two o'clock in the afternoon.

The ascent did not involve such a long distance, but it was a slow and fatiguing climb, even for those of us at the end of the line. We moved without stopping, and I wondered at the stamina and the astonishing determination displayed by our elderly couple. Even though we carried most of their possessions, it was a feat for them to keep moving through all those hours of uphill climbing.

Before we reached the summit, we passed a small lake, now mostly snow-covered. It must look like a gem in the summer. Though there was no visible vegetation anywhere around, the lake must be surrounded by an alpine meadow. A frozen cascade descended at our end of the lake, and the ice shone brilliantly in the sunshine. It would be a roaring stream in the summer.

When we reached the top of the pass, we found those ahead of us gathered in a group. There would be a half hour's rest we were told before we started down. We must reach some cover before dark. It was not safe to remain for long on the unprotected mountainside. The wind could start up, and the blowing snow meant disaster.

We found going down easier and faster. Perhaps the mountain sloped more gently, or maybe it was the knowledge that we had made it that spurred us on. Our spirits soared, and if not for the repeated warning to keep quiet, we would have shouted, yelled, sung, or even danced with joy. But whatever the reason, we forgot how tired we were and made our descent in what seemed like record time.

Before it got completely dark, we reached the first scrubby mountain growth, and camped there for the night. There was even dead wood around to build small fires. Some had cooking utensils with them, and were seen cooking something, but most of us were happy to have boiling water from the melting snow to drink, with bread and whatever other food we had with us.

We shared the food with our old couple. They were so very grateful for our assistance in crossing the mountain and wanted to give us something as a remembrance. Since we would not accept any of their jewelry, they presented each of us with a silver ruble as a souvenir.

It would not take very long before Dad's silver ruble had been spent on necessities. The certificate the general had signed would serve him a little longer—until he was given another certifying him a genuine (honorary) Kuban Cossack. The last that my father would see of the old general was about a week later in Sukhum, Georgia. He was walking down the street with his greatcoat over his arm. He was taking it to the bazaar to sell, having decided that even as sentiment it was only a burden to him.

11
THE GOOD WILL OF OTHERS

WAS this large party's successful crossing of the Caucausus Mountains in December a miracle? Or was it just the way things happened to go?

At the least, you would have to say that Dad was uniquely fortunate in having guides who knew the way, testing the footing for him at every step and taking turns breaking trail, not to mention having eighty people walking ahead of him trampling down the snow. Add the contrast between the week-long blizzard in which they began and the bright, clear, and calm weather they found at the pass. You can begin to appreciate their extraordinary luck when you realize that theirs was the only party that was successful in making it across the mountains after new snow began to fall. They may have been the last organized party out of Russia.

But how in the world had my father ever gotten to this point?

Of all the eager young students who'd flocked to enlist at the same time as Dad when the White Army came to Voronezh, he was the only one still on his feet and moving—the sole one among them who'd managed to survive and to escape from Russia. Yet, on the face of things, my father had done nothing for himself. One way or another, everything had been done for him.

He'd been on his own only for the briefest of moments. The rest of the time, he had just done what he was told to do—mainly by Ivan Kashirin, but also by the White Army, by the nurses and doctors at Ekaterinodar, by Sister Nina, by the Kuban Cossacks, by General Savin, and by the Cherkessi guides who'd led them on tiptoe over Kluhorskii Pass.

All too often, the result of putting himself in other people's hands had proven to be disaster, futility, and retreat. Except that somehow, in the midst of all that was going wrong, miraculous things had just happened to happen, which had made it possible for him to continue and to make it over the mountains.

After this, the miracles would never again come along in clusters and bunches the way they had during the thirteen-and-a-half months it took Dad to travel the six hundred miles from Voronezh to Georgia, walking most of the distance. Nevertheless, until my father's life finally stabilized again with him studying at a university in Syracuse, New York, and he no longer had the same need for miracles, his unbelievable good fortune would continue to operate whenever it was necessary.

The most blatant example of this would be Dad finding money in the streets of Constantinople when he had to have it. This was something that never happened to him before, and neither would it ever happen again.

In the spring of 1923, my father had just been getting by in Turkey for a period of more than two years. First, Ivan had turned into a moody and belligerent drunk in idleness and exile, then his application to join a monastery in the Balkans had been accepted, and he'd departed for Serbia. Now, Dad was sharing one large room with five other men, collecting, washing, and delivering laundry, and doing odd jobs when he could find them, but otherwise just marking time.

That spring, the U.S. Congress passed a special immigration bill making places for former Russian university students and graduates. My father knew nothing more about America than that it was the place for which his ancestor's brother had set sail from the heart of Russia and the impressions he'd picked up reading books like *The Last of the Mohicans* and *Huckleberry Finn*. But no other countries were offering special opportunities to refugees from the Russian Revolution.

Dad would be successful in passing an oral screening given by a board of three Russian and two American professors designed to identify real students and to weed out opportunists. He was accepted to go to America.

But for him to reach the United States, he had to be able to pay half the passage money in advance, and riding in steerage from Constantinople to New York cost $90.

Forty-five dollars may not seem like very much, especially if you have forty-five dollars. However, at a time when my father was barely earning enough money to pay for the food to keep him alive and his part of the room rent, it was an overwhelming amount.

Then, one morning that spring, Dad was making a little extra money by helping to carry another Russian's luggage two miles to the train station. As they were crossing a busy intersection in the heart of the city, my father spied a small roll of paper held together with a rubber band lying against the curb. Without pausing to look at it, he picked it up and put it in his pocket.

After delivering his burden to the station and receiving his payment—"the equivalent of ten American cents," Dad says—he checked to see exactly what he'd found. And inside the rubber band were several hundred Turkish piasters.

This money wasn't enough in itself to pay for my father's passage, but it was almost half of what he needed. And a few of the piasters bought him a rare decent meal.

For the rest of the money, Dad appealed to his sister Katya, who was now living in Poland.

She'd had adventures, too. Katya was a nurse who'd fled Voronezh after being denounced as a counter-revolutionary and an enemy of the proletariat by the wife of a Red official to whom she'd refused admission to the hospital with a trivial complaint. She'd then attached herself to the field hospital of a Polish army unit stranded in southern Russia by Russia's withdrawal from World War I. She had come down with typhoid fever, and later married her doctor, Josef Szulc.

Polish money wasn't worth very much in 1923. But Dr. Szulc cashed in his life insurance policy for its current value and sent the proceeds to his young brother-in-law, whom he would never meet. And thousands of zlotys turned into the $25 my father still lacked.

So there you have it—one more time, the good will of others and a happy accident were able to do for Dad what he would have been completely incapable of doing for himself. And in June he sailed for America on the Greek steamer *King Alexander*.

12
SOME OTHER PLACE ENTIRELY

HOWEVER, there is more to my father's story than just being blessed by benefactors and kissed by dumb luck. He didn't make it to America only by being wafted there on fortunate breezes.

If you look beyond the superficial fortuities, you can see that Dad made a number of decisions at critical moments that were all his own. And these had a determining effect on what happened to him.

The first vital decision that he made—along with some but not all of his fellow students—was to enlist in the White Army. That was a statement that he wasn't going to stay in Voronezh any longer but was going to do something about his situation.

The second major decision he made was to defy army and medical authority, rise from his bed, ignore his pain, and limp after Ivan through the streets of Ekaterinodar when no one else in the hospital was ready or able to do it.

The third decision he'd made was to attempt to cross the Caucausus Mountains in winter with General Savin when he might have chosen instead to remain behind in Russia with Ahmed.

And his last crucial decision was to follow Ivan out the door into the ongoing snowstorm when it seemed that only a miracle would be enough to get them over the pass to an unknowable future.

Even when it all looked like nothing but a bad dream to him, my father's feet had still kept moving.

In fact, what I really think happened was this:

I don't think that the bad dream had just begun for Dad when he spoke of it to Ivan before they left the base camp. I think that the nightmare had started long before that, back in Voronezh.

Life in Voronezh must have seemed incomprehensibly weird to my father.

He'd done his best to pretend that he was living a normal life as a botany student in spite of the capriciousness and hostility of the Communist rulers of the city. But day by day, his family's possessions had continued to slip away from them, and the possibilities of his future grew more uncertain, and the only hope they had of any protection from sudden, arbitrary destruction was the Red cavalry unit that had taken over their stables, occupied half the house, and chopped their orchard down. And all the while, his father was there to tell him that everything that had gone wrong in the world was the fault of people like him who'd lost proper respect for traditional authority, as though if Dad had just been willing to go back to church, all would have been well.

There was madness all around him. And I think that my father wanted nothing more than to be in some saner place than this where it was possible to live a rational life. I think that he wanted it so much that he made it come true.

He didn't accomplish this by rational means, however, because that wasn't possible.

Instead, the method that he adopted—although, of course, Dad would never be capable of admitting it either then or later, not even to himself—was to act like the innocent, good-hearted, foolish youngest son in one of Tihon the coachman's folk tales. He had just followed his nose and put one foot in front of the other until almost magically he'd found himself over the mountains and across the sea.

Or, to put it another way:

My father wanted desperately for the bad dream of his current life in Russia to be over. But since there wasn't any reasonable thing to be done about it, every decision that he'd made he'd necessarily had to make by intuition—his nose had told him what to do. And all those unreasoned decisions put together amounted to a fundamental resolve to keep on moving until he'd walked through the bad dream and out the other side.

I think the fundamental difference between Dad and the rest of his platoon which made every difference was that he really, *really* wanted to be some other place entirely and he never stopped until at last he found himself there.

And if it took the goodwill of other people and more than one miracle for it to happen, well, that's the way things work in this world: Goodwill—like the goodwill that was shown to my father by Ivan—is attracted by a determination to persevere. And miracles are able to happen—or are perceived as happening—only when they are absolutely necessary.

But this assistance was just the means for my father to get to the sort of place that he was secretly longing to be. And the evidence of what he actually had in his heart of hearts all along is the moves he made when he wasn't under any outside authority or following anybody else's direction and when the opportunities that were available to him didn't have the appearance of miracles.

It was his choice to go to the United States. And I don't believe that it was just an accident, but rather highly significant, that in order to qualify to go there, my father had to pass an academic examination. I think this was a confirming sign for him and that nothing less would have been acceptable.

13

ANYTHING THAT INTERFERED WITH REASON

IN America, it would be possible for Dad to be the kind of man that he wanted to be.

If he hadn't accepted the offer made by Ahmed, it was because he didn't think that at his age, he could make a Cherkess out of himself. And, in his memoirs, my father would regret the time that he'd wasted while he was in Turkey, and his complete failure to make any connection with a cosmopolitan city like Constantinople. He'd also turn down a suggestion from Ivan that Dad join him at his monastery in Serbia and become a monk.

However, he was prepared to work hard to make an American out of himself, and he would be successful at it. He would even find himself criticized by fellow Russians for being "too American."

My father knew no English when he landed at Ellis Island. Later, however, he wouldn't sound like a movie Russian, unlike the two friends he stayed in contact with through the years. Dad learned to speak American English with an accent so slight and so rare that it would be possible to overlook the fact that English wasn't his first language.

During my childhood, our family would travel from Michigan to visit my mother's sisters in upstate New York. To shorten the route, we would cut across Ontario, and when we passed through Canadian customs, we'd all be asked where we were born. On the first trip we made, my father said, "Voronezh, Russia." But these were the Commie-fearing fifties, and that answer cost Dad a lot of unnecessary explanation while the rest of the family sat in the car and waited for him. So, on later trips, he would say, "Syracuse, New York," just like my mother, and the answer was delivered so flawlessly that he was never doubted.

During the year after he arrived in the United States, my father took jobs that paid him much better than he had been getting in Turkey but which he didn't like very much. For the better part of the year, he put Lorna Doone cookies into the oven and took them out again at the National Biscuit Company—a job that would leave him with a lifelong aversion to Scottish shortbread. And then, during the summer, he cut grass with a sickle at a cemetery in Brooklyn. Far more important, however, he discovered something called the Russian Student Fund. He passed their examination for financial aid, and with their help, he was accepted as a student at the New York State College of Forestry at Syracuse University.

The other Russians he knew in the immigrant community in New York told Dad not to go. But he was afraid that if he didn't go then, he would never be able to, and it was with a distinct sense of relief that he left New York City for Syracuse in September 1924.

At first, he found it very difficult. He could barely understand anything his teachers said, and he had to write his assignments in Russian and then translate them word by word into English. But a little at a time, he began to get the hang of the culture. He says that what helped him most at the outset was the casualness and lack of inhibition that he found at college football games. That helped to break the ice for him.

His father wrote to ask whether he had a horse and to remind him that it was a mark of a gentleman to have one. But the reassertion of class privilege wasn't the direction Dad was headed. Instead of that, he did whatever he had to do, from washing windows to mowing lawns, to turn himself into the kind of technical man—the person able to bridge the scientific and the practical—that his father had been impressed by but been unable to be himself.

He earned a bachelor's degree in only three years—and owed the Russian Student Fund $1,758.31 for the help they had given him—then continued on for a master's degree, and finally, in 1931, a Ph.D. It was the only doctorate granted that year by the New York State College of Forestry.

So prominent would my father become in his field of specialization—the cell anatomy and uses of different kinds of wood—that people would come to study with him from Germany, Finland, Iran, and India. Even today, you'll find his books cited as authoritative on the Web.

Along with the other changes he went through in this country, Dad modified his name. In Russia, he'd been Alexei Ivanovitch Panьshin—with a distinctive soft sign after the first n—known to his family as Lyolya and to his friends as Alyosha. But in the United States, he would regularize his name, cutting it down to Alexis John Panshin, known professionally as A.J., and familiarly as Alex.

In America, my father was free to trim away anything and everything that interfered with reason. He became a man so regular and four-square that he could set out to build a modern house, pick Frank Lloyd Wright to design it for him, and then fall out with him and fire him for being insufficiently rational.

I only knew Dad to revert once to the risk-taking behavior which marked the year which carried him from Voronezh to Georgia. And significantly, it happened in Russia.

In 1959, my father was asked to be a member of an exchange mission, a U.S. Forestry Delegation traveling in the Soviet Union. On the last day they were in Moscow, Dad changed into old clothes so he wouldn't be conspicuous, gave the slip to their Intourist watchdog, and went looking for an address that he'd been given by his sister Katya.

He found a bleak, three-story cement building, one of a number forming a quadrangle. He says that it reminded him more of a prison than a place for free people to live.

He rang a bell on the second floor, and when an elderly woman answered the door, he recognized her after the passage of forty years.

He said, "Shura! I am Lyolya."

His sister Shura gasped and pulled him inside. She lived in this apartment together with another sister, Lyena, and Lyena's husband who was at the racetrack for the day and wouldn't be home soon. The three of them hugged. And my father had three full hours to talk to his sisters and find out about his family.

His eldest brother, Nikolai, had been sent to Siberia for eight years. When he returned from exile, he was a broken man who had essentially been allowed to starve to death. His second brother, Vanya, had been a factory manager. He was shot in 1923. His third brother, Volodya, the would-be revolutionary who'd told their father that he was an oppressor of the masses, had left home during the turmoil and had never been heard of again. He was presumed dead. And my father—the youngest of thirteen children—was now the eldest male in his family.

His sisters had done their best through the hard years to hang onto something of what the family had once owned. And they gave what they had managed to save to Dad as his inheritance. He brought it home with him from Russia.

His patrimony consisted of a silver soup ladle, six ornately engraved gold teaspoons, and a little silver cup in the shape of a horse's head, struck to celebrate the trotting race that my grandfather once won in Paris.

For myself, I still have a few questions:

What happened to Ahmed? And what would have become of my father if he'd gone off with the Cherkessi?

Ivan Nikiforovitch Panьshin 1852–1938

Alexis John Panshin 1901–1993

Once they established control of Russia, the Communists had been ruthless in their remaking of reality. They changed the name of the country. Ekaterinodar had been renamed Krasnodar. Batalpashinsk had become Cherkessk. Mihailovka was now a part of Krylovsky State Farm. Spasso-Preobrajenski was turned from a convent into a tuberculosis sanitarium.

Ahmed wouldn't have escaped that. Did he die from a bullet, too, or did he end his days selling newspapers at a kiosk in Kyiv?

What happened to that anomalous red granite boulder found in the black earth of Petropavlovka and dragged by my grandfather to Mihailovka after the destruction of his experimental sheep ranch? Is it where he placed it, or has it moved on once more in its inexorable progress from its unknown place of origin to its unguessable destination?

Most of all, I wonder what happened to the Panьshin who sailed from Voronezh for the New World. Was his determination to get there aided by well-wishers and benefactors along the way? And did miracles also happen to him when he needed them?

If he did reach America—and I think that if he really, really wanted to, he did—how long did he retain his boyar's beard and distinctive clothing after he arrived? Did he change his name, or only have daughters?

Is it possible that, unbeknownst to either of us, his descendants are living across the street from me today?

◆ ◆ ◆

This essay is primarily based on my father's memoirs, *I Remember*, printed for his family in 1972 in an edition of about twenty copies.

As an adult, my brother Dan learned Russian and made a number of trips to Russia. He visited both Voronezh and Krylovsky State Farm. And he worked on a public edition of *I Remember*.

I've tried to follow Dad's perceptions and memories exactly. But, as might be expected of any of us, despite his allegiance to exactitude and factual accuracy, his memory wasn't always perfect. For instance, he remembered that anomalous rock as six feet high, six feet wide, and twelve feet long. A mighty big boulder.

But Dan, who looked for it, found it, and took pictures, reported that it's actually more like two feet high, two feet wide, and six feet long. Still large, but not as large as it seemed to Dad as a child. However, a rock that big is still out of place in that country, and since my father's time it's moved on some more.

SYMPATHY FOR THE DEVL

"We did the devil's work."
—J. Robert Oppenheimer

"A lie is no good if it's not believed—unless it is told to be disbelieved."
—Mellrooney

PART ONE: MAKING K-O DUST

1
THE RIDDLE OF "SOLUTION UNSATISFACTORY"

AFTER World War II was brought to a sudden conclusion in August 1945 by the detonation of a new American superweapon over the Japanese cities of Hiroshima and Nagasaki, there was a change in the status of science fiction.

Science fiction was the last pulp magazine genre, named as recently as 1929. It was rarely published in hardcover book form. It wasn't reviewed by reputable newspapers and magazines. And it wasn't to be found on the shelves of most libraries, and only by people prepared to hunt to find it.

Now, with the appearance of atomic weapons in the world, it stood vindicated. Its direst imaginings had come true.

In the new postwar climate of elation and dread, it was suddenly possible to present science fiction as a form of literature almost as serious and farseeing as its most ardent fans and boosters had always wanted to believe it was.

In February 1946, just six months after the United States dropped the Bomb, the first hardcover science fiction anthology, *The Best of Science Fiction*, edited by Groff Conklin, was published by Crown. This was a fat book of forty stories intended to demonstrate the breadth and depth of the genre, from the near and infinitesimal to the most remote times and places—the far future, the stars and other dimensions.

As an acknowledgment of the major new concern of the day (as well as to stake science fiction's claim to special regard), the initial seven stories were grouped under the heading "The Atom."

The lead story, a novelette entitled "Solution Unsatisfactory," told of the end of war between England and Germany in 1945 after the dropping of an atomic superweapon made in America.

That was close enough to what had just happened to get people's attention.

The author of "Solution Unsatisfactory" was given as Anson MacDonald. This was the byline the story had appeared under when it was originally published in the May 1941 issue of *Astounding Science-Fiction*. But it had actually been written by Robert Heinlein the previous December.

A year before Pearl Harbor and four years prior to the termination of the war then being fought in Europe, Heinlein had dared to imagine the conflict brought to a conclusion by an atomic weapon of unprecedented deadliness made at a US Army facility in Maryland. In the story, the lab's director, Col. Clyde Manning, then maneuvers to make himself dictator of the world in order to keep the overwhelming weapon he's brought into existence in safe hands, namely his own.

The title Heinlein placed on the story was "Foreign Policy." This suggests that he saw its central subject not so much as the development of atomic weapons as the impact their existence would have on the international balance of power.

It was John W. Campbell, Jr., the editor of *Astounding*, who altered the title to "Solution Unsatisfactory" in order to make it clear to the readers of his magazine that in his view the story was a thought experiment which didn't offer an adequate answer to the problem it posed of controlling this demonic weapon once it had been made and used.

Four years later, as the architect and chief promoter of modern science fiction, as well as the original editor of one-third of the stories included in *The Best of Science Fiction*, John Campbell would be asked to contribute a preface to this pioneering anthology to justify and explain science fiction to an audience presumed to be unfamiliar with it.

Campbell viewed himself as a practical engineer concerned with what works. So in his preface, he took advantage of the moment to use "Solution Unsatisfactory" as an example of science fiction in action. In the context of this book for a general readership he wouldn't dwell on any inadequacy the story might have. Instead, he began by describing it as an "uncannily accurate prophecy."

This would be true, of course. But it would also not be true, as he had reason to know.

For one thing, Heinlein hadn't been a very good predictor of the future course of the war. Almost as soon as his novelette was published, it had been contradicted by events. In this story, neither the Soviet Union (here called the "Eurasian Union") nor Japan nor the United States ever directly participates in World War II.

On the timeline in which "Solution Unsatisfactory" was written and read however, just two months after the story appeared on the newsstand, in June 1941, Germany would invade the Soviet Union. And before the end of the year, Germany's ally Japan would launch a surprise attack on the US Pacific Fleet stationed in Hawaii and America would be brought into the war, as well.

Having not foreseen this radical expansion of World War II, Heinlein hadn't envisioned that the cities attacked to bring the war to an end would be Japanese. Instead, the metropolis atomically sterilized in his story was Berlin, the capital city of Germany.

There'd be another major difference between what had been written by Heinlein and what actually did take place. The weapon he imagined was radioactive dust—what today would be called a radiological weapon or "dirty bomb." It wouldn't be the brilliant humungous explosion capped by a roiling mushroom cloud that we've all become familiar with.

Writing in the immediate postwar moment, however, Campbell felt no inclination to linger on minor details like these. Instead, he wanted to establish the premise that the projections of science fiction deserved to be taken seriously, and for this it was sufficient that in "Solution Unsatisfactory" Heinlein had foreseen the United States developing an atomic weapon which had then been used to end the war. What's more, he'd even gotten the year right. That was close enough to pass for uncannily accurate prophecy.

By contrast, even though Groff Conklin, too, saw the story as possibly predictive, the editor of *The Best of Science Fiction* would regard this more negatively than Campbell did. What concerned him about "Solution Unsatisfactory" wasn't the part that had come true more or less, but the part that hadn't happened yet but still might.

In Conklin's introduction to the anthology, printed after Campbell's preface, he said: "The story which leads off in this book, 'Solution Unsatisfactory,' is included here with the greatest reluctance. It is one instance where science fiction has dangerously sinister overtones of possibility."

What disturbed the editor was not the invention of atomic weapons or the prospect of atomic war. What made him resist the story was its second half—the coming to power of a dictator who means to keep the Bomb under control by keeping the world in line.

The narrator of "Solution Unsatisfactory" says:

> ... Manning was no ordinary man. In him, ordinary hard sense had been raised to the level of genius. Oh, yes, I know that it is popular to blame everything on him and call him everything from traitor to mad dog, but I still think he was both wise and benevolent. I don't care how many second-guessing historians disagree with me.

Conklin didn't want to endorse anything like that. He had no use for dictators. If there'd ever been any doubt about the matter, World War II had just shown what dictators were like. Yet the storyteller would end his account by inviting the reader to empathize with poor Clyde Manning, reluctant dictator of the world who is only doing what circumstances determine must be done.

The editor saw this as giving Manning far too much credence. In his introduction, he wrote, "I do not agree ... with the author's political bias as it is exemplified in this tale. It seems quite dangerous to me."

The person who would ultimately be responsible for the inclusion and privileged placement of "Solution Unsatisfactory" in *The Best of Science Fiction* was Conklin's editor at Crown, Edmund Fuller. While working on this book, he'd developed so much of a taste for science fiction that Conklin sometimes suspected him of wanting to hijack the project and make it his own.

Fuller was particularly impressed by the stories of Robert Heinlein and Anson MacDonald. Struck by the timeliness of "Solution Unsatisfactory," he wanted to use it to lead off the book.

But Conklin didn't want the story in his collection at all. He only gave in at last—"against my better judgment"—after seeing a headline in the *Washington Post* for November 2, 1945, which read: "ATOMIC WAR THREAT MAY FORCE U.S. TO SELECT DICTATOR."

The story below the headline said that Harold Urey—a Nobel Prize-winning chemist who had helped develop the atomic bomb—had offered the opinion that the United States might have to establish a dictatorship in order to react to the threat of atomic war.

"I do not see any way to keep our democratic form of government if everybody has atomic bombs," Urey said. "If everyone has them, it will be necessary for our government to move quickly in a manner now not possible under our diffused form of government."

If an actual Bomb-maker of prominence was ready to suggest that with the Bomb on the loose, America might need to have a dictator in control, then, perhaps, distasteful though it might be, "Solution Unsatisfactory," the story of a master Bomb-maker who carries out a coup d'état and makes himself just such a dictator, *should* be in the book, if only as a cautionary tale.

Nevertheless, Conklin continued to harbor great reservations about this story, so that even though he may finally have given his assent to its inclusion, he still found it necessary to make it clear to everyone who read his book that he hadn't wanted to do it.

So just what was "Solution Unsatisfactory"—this story that was both celebrated and condemned in *The Best of Science Fiction* even before it led the way in the first showcase anthology of science fiction?

Was "Solution Unsatisfactory" an uncannily prescient anticipation of American invention of the Bomb, as John Campbell's preface and Edmund Fuller's premier placement of the story encouraged readers to perceive? Or was it an ultimately unsatisfactory first attempt to solve the problem of how a horrendous superweapon might be brought under control, as its Campbell-chosen title declared?

Was the story really about American foreign policy and how the existence of atomic weapons would force this policy to change, as indicated by Heinlein's original title? Or was it a dangerously sinister story about power politics and how a man makes himself world dictator, as Groff Conklin thought?

A case may be made for each of these interpretations. But objections can be raised to all of them, too. And none of them explains everything in "Solution Unsatisfactory." Unless, of course, the story is really an elephant in the dark, giving the appearance of being any number of different things while actually being something of another kind.

2 MANNING TAKES A JOB

IF for no other reason than because the narrator is not a reliable voice, it isn't easy to be sure what Heinlein's actual intention was when he wrote this story in December 1940.

If we believe the character who tells us the tale, Col. Manning never entertained any ambitions to make himself dictator. It was all a kind of accidental inevitability, something that circumstances happened to make necessary.

Before the war, Manning was a military officer—"one of the army's No. 1 experts in chemical warfare"—until a heart condition forced him into early retirement. Then he became a first-term congressman, a liberal.

Manning may be a liberal, but he's also said to be "tough-minded." Once he's come to recognize the logical necessity of a dictator controlling atomic weapons, he's not one to turn away from the job, even though he may find what he's called upon to do personally distasteful.

We could even think of what happens to Manning as a tragic act of self-sacrifice and empathize with the pain he must be feeling as he does what is necessary, even though it goes against his nature.

The full name of the all-but-invisible man behind the narrative voice of "Solution Unsatisfactory" is never given in one place, but we can add it up as John DeFries. As a high school teacher of sociology and economics, he was a member of the political search committee that chose Manning as an insurgent candidate for Congress. He becomes Manning's campaign manager, and after that Congressman Manning's executive secretary. And then, when Manning is asked to rejoin the army and head its atomic weapons program, at Manning's insistence, DeFries is instantly commissioned and brought along as his adjutant.

DeFries is no disinterested bystander. He's Manning's main man. And when it is Manning's man who assures us that Manning is really wise and benevolent and a genius of hard sense, can his words be believed?

At times in the story, DeFries seems to be only half-aware. Manning even calls him "downright stupid" to his face, and he accepts this as a compliment. It's possible that he is a bit dim and is kept around as a convenient tool when one is needed. Or perhaps he really knows more than he's telling and is acting as a loyal mouthpiece, like a Presidential news secretary covering his boss' ass and passing on to us what the boys upstairs think we should be told. It's even possible that DeFries is a secret spin doctor himself, actively seeking to manipulate our perceptions and sentiments from the outset.

Whatever the case may be, however, it's apparent that DeFries is never frank with us. There's a great deal that he doesn't bother to explain, there are crucial points of transition that he slides right past, and much of what he does tell us doesn't stand up under examination.

If we persist in pursuing the questions that he fails to address, a very different picture of Manning begins to emerge.

At the outset, the narrator tells us that Manning is a strong liberal. He ought to know since he helped select Manning as a candidate and then worked for him while he was in Congress. But liberals, even of the tough-minded sort, are by definition dedicated to achieving gradual progress by working for changes in the system. They don't turn themselves into dictators. You have to be an extremist of one kind or another to take over the system altogether and make all decisions yourself.

It seems highly doubtful, then, that Manning, whatever he may actually have been, could really have ever been a liberal—which ought to make us question both DeFries' truthfulness and Manning's sincerity from the start.

Then we learn that despite his bad heart, Manning was personally singled out to be called back to active duty by the army to head its atomic research and development program. And that seems unlikely, too.

In fact, this may have been the expression of a Robert Heinlein wish fulfillment. He'd been a Lieutenant (jg) when he was involuntarily retired from the Navy in 1934 after he developed tuberculosis. And he kept clinging to the hope that he would be recalled to duty when the US finally became an active participant in World War II.

However, this would never happen, even though Heinlein went knocking on a lot of doors after Pearl Harbor trying to make it happen. The best that he'd been able to do was to have an old service friend take him on as a civilian engineer at the Naval Air Experimental Station in Philadelphia.

Life moves on. And officers like Manning (or Heinlein) who've been retired from the service for a serious uncured ailment are seldom, if ever, unretired and called back to active duty, let alone singled out to be given crucial command assignments.

Moreover, Manning already has a job, and one of some significance, too. He's a Congressional Representative with a district and a party and his own strong liberal principles to stand up for.

So when the congressman is first called to come to the War Department for a chat about returning to duty, he tells his secretary, "It's impossible, of course." He thereupon sets off for the meeting at so eager a pace that DeFries worries about his heart.

And, of course, it is every bit as impossible as Manning says it is. Congressmen with bad hearts don't jump ship in mid-stream to go off and be army colonels, even important ones.

Sorry—I'm going to have to take that back, because DeFries goes on to say, "But it *was* possible, and Manning agreed to it, after the Chief of Staff presented his case."

A pretty impressive case it must have been, too, since the narrator tells us that no one has the power to make a congressman leave his post, and Manning had to be convinced.

But DeFries doesn't share any details with us of how this was done—nor even what the exact nature of the task offered to Manning was. These are points he goes gliding past, leaving us to try to figure out for ourselves what must have been said from what we see Manning do.

All we know for certain is that the general talked for a time and Manning, who's declared that leaving Congress is impossible and who must have reason to change his mind, found what he was told so compelling and persuasive that he agreed to the proposal. But, hey, if it was the Chief of Staff himself asking—I mean the top man in the whole damned army—how could he say no?

We might not be permitted to hear the siren song that was sung for him, but we can hazard a guess as to what it may have been since not much later, the narrator says of Manning, "… There was certainly no one else in the United States who could have done the job. It required a man who could direct and suggest research in a highly esoteric field but who saw the problem from the standpoint of urgent military necessity."

DeFries can't possibly be talking from his own knowledge here. He's just been sworn into the service himself and he isn't any better qualified than the next former high school teacher to offer opinions about the army or military necessity or who else other than Manning might be capable of carrying out this job. What's more, he admits that he knows no more about atomic physics than he's read in the Sunday newspaper supplement. He has to be repeating what he's heard from someone else.

However, if the source he had it from was the Army Chief of Staff as he was making his case to Manning, then we can understand how Manning's mind might have been changed. It has to be pretty heady stuff for someone who was a career military officer retired before his time to have the person in command of the whole army tell you that he has a critical job and you're the only person who is capable of doing it.

But if indeed this was what convinced Manning, then he screwed up badly in allowing himself to be sweet-talked into making such a disastrously wrong move. If Manning ever had it in him to be wise, this was the moment for him to speak.

If he were farseeing, he might have said something like this:

> Sir, the offer you are making is very flattering, but I'm afraid I must refuse for a number of reasons, any one of which would be sufficient.
>
> First, I have a previous obligation to my constituents that I must honor. Having asked them to elect me to office, I can hardly turn my back on them now and walk away after serving for only a few months.
>
> Second, as you know, my heart isn't in great shape. I'm not sure it would withstand the stress of the work you're asking me to undertake. If I were to die along the way or be forced to withdraw for reasons of health, and I'm as crucial to the task as you say, the program could be unnecessarily compromised.
>
> Third, as a human being and a liberal, I couldn't possibly direct a project like this one. I can see where it's headed, and its end is a weapon that will kill every living thing it affects and that can only be used on helpless civilians massed in cities. In my opinion, to make and use that kind of weapon would be a crime.
>
> Lastly, speaking as a member of Congress, I have to tell you I think it would be a bad precedent and bad policy for us to introduce a weapon of indiscriminate terror. We would likely frighten our allies as much as our enemies, set off an arms race, and destabilize the world. If you make an omelet, you have to eat it—you can't turn it back into an egg. With a weapon like this, we may find that we've won the war, but at the cost of the freedom for which we're fighting.

If indeed Manning is the only person in the country capable of directing this particular project—and if he really were as wise and benevolent as DeFries says he is—then perhaps speaking out this way at this pivotal moment might have killed a bad idea at the very outset and spared both him and the world a lot of future grief.

But, of course, Manning doesn't say no to the Chief of Staff's offer. Rather, he accepts immediately and the two of them begin to discuss how his job switch is to be accomplished.

As a matter of fact, the only thing Manning is reported to have said during this entire meeting is to be sure that he can have his man DeFries with him in his new post:

> There was talk of leaving me in Washington to handle the political details of Manning's office, but Manning decided against it, judging that his other secretary could do that, and announced that I must go along as his adjutant. The Chief of Staff demurred, but Manning was in a position to insist, and the Chief had to give in.

How sweet to be needed so desperately that you can even make the top general in the army jump through a hoop!

3

THE INVENTION OF K-O DUST

SO eager is Congressman Manning to get back into the familiar comfort of a pair of army boots that he doesn't linger in Washington long enough to make necessary phone calls and clear his desk. By the very next day, he and DeFries—now an instant new-made army officer—are off to Maryland to begin taking charge of the Federal nuclear research lab Manning's been given to command.

He doesn't pause at Walter Reed Army Hospital first for a routine physical checkup, either, just to be sure he's fit for duty. Nor, most strangely, does the Chief of Staff or anyone else in the army bother to insist that Manning undergo an exam before he begins his new assignment, even though you would think the state of his health would be everybody's first concern.

So why is everyone in such a hurry? What's so unique and pressing about this particular task that the army would find it necessary to look outside its own ranks and reach into Congress for a one-time officer with heart problems to place in charge here? And what military necessity could possibly be so urgent as to convince Manning to abandon his constituents and go rushing off to Maryland to assume this post?

We aren't told.

It's not because America is losing World War II and has its back to the wall. In the world of the story, it's as late as 1943, and the United States, while continuing to supply England with ships and planes to keep her fighting, still isn't an active combatant in the war.

In fact, rather than being immediate and pressing, the research the lab is doing into an Atom Bomb seems prospective and hypothetical. Things here at the lab are handled in a leisurely and informal way. Ordinary military discipline isn't observed. And there doesn't appear to be anyone from outside overseeing what they're doing.

The narrator says:

> We were searching, there in the laboratory in Maryland, for a way to use U235 in a controlled explosion. We had a vision of a one-ton bomb that would be a whole air raid in itself, a single explosion that would flatten out an entire industrial center …
>
> The problem was, strangely enough, to find an explosive which would be weak enough to blow up only one county at a time, and stable enough to blow up only on request. If we could devise a really practical rocket fuel at the same time, one capable of driving a war rocket at a thousand miles an hour, or more, then we would be in a position to make most anybody say "uncle" to Uncle Sam.

But despite this happy dream of a war rocket armed with the Bomb and America with its foot on the neck of the world, the development of a reliable and controlled A-Bomb eludes them. DeFries says: "We fiddled around with it all the rest of 1943 and well into 1944."

But if this is the case, what was the rush to get Manning on the job?

Eventually, however, the fiddling around has to come to an end. They're forced to conclude "that there existed not even a remote possibility at the time of utilizing U235 as an explosive" and to abandon their quest for a convenient one-county-size nuclear Bomb.

All is not lost, however. It isn't necessary to close down the atomic weapons program with its unlimited budget, and Manning doesn't have to admit defeat and go back to Congress. Instead, he's able to recognize the potential for an even more awful weapon in another project under his authority.

In taking command of the lab, Manning has inherited the ongoing research of a Dr. Estelle Karst into the medical application of radioactive isotopes. Dr. Karst has no use for Manning and the work he's doing and complains to him that her investigations have been hampered by lack of access to Dr. Obre, a spectroscopist whose services are being monopolized by the Bomb development project. She declares to Manning that Manning is "a warmonger" because he cares more about killing than curing.

She could be right about that, too. Manning was formerly one of the army's top experts in poison gas—the horror weapon of World War I, eventually banned—and when he familiarizes himself with her work and sees the radioactive dust her program produces glistening in the air and hears of fish kills in Chesapeake Bay from her waste water, he gets a gleam in his eye. Saying, "I think we may turn up a number of interesting things," he takes over Dr. Karst's research and pours men and resources into it.

Manning will demonstrate the gratitude he feels toward Dr. Karst for the preparatory work she's done by naming the radiological weapon he develops "Karst-Obre dust." And after it has been used to kill every living thing in Berlin and Dr. Karst commits suicide, he'll express his regret to DeFries.

"I wish," Manning added slowly, "that I could explain to her why we had to do it."

If Manning never lets Dr. Karst know why it's necessary to commandeer her medical dust and alter it into a weapon of mass extermination, neither does he report to his superiors about what he's up to. The Army Chief of Staff may have set him up here in the atomic research lab, given him all the money and resources he could ask for, and put him to work making a Bomb, but when Manning closes the Bomb project down and begins making Karst-Obre dust instead, he neglects to inform anyone that he's doing it.

Nobody keeping an eye on the program. No limit on funds. And a colonel with a secret weapon and no sense of obligation to follow the chain of command. What an unusual way to run an army!

It isn't that Manning entertains no doubts. At one point, he declares, "John, I wish that radioactivity had never been discovered."

And the narrator says, "Manning told me that he had once seriously considered, in the middle of the night, recommending that every single person, including himself, who knew the Karst-Obre technique be put to death in the interests of all civilization."

But DeFries can't understand these apprehensions. To him, the dust is just another weapon, only more potent, and we're the ones who have it.

He says to Manning, "I still don't see what you are fretting about, Colonel. If the stuff is as good as you say it is, you've done just exactly what you set out to do—develop a weapon that would give the United States protection against aggression."

Now, is *that* what DeFries thought they've been doing? If it is, then why didn't he just tell us so at the time Manning was given his assignment? More to the point, if Manning's goal all along has been to protect the United States from aggression, what on earth has he been doing trying to develop a one-ton A-Bomb capable of laying flat an entire industrial city?

It's no wonder that Manning tells DeFries he's stupid.

Manning spells out for his typist, gofer, and apologist that this weapon is a loaded gun held to the head of every man, woman, and child on the planet. And if any nation should use it, every nation will have to have it, and nobody will be safe.

Manning says:

> Once the secret is out—and it will be out if we ever use the stuff!—the whole world will be comparable to a room full of men, each armed with a loaded .45. They can't get out of the room and each one is dependent on the goodwill of every other one to stay alive. All offense and no defense. See what I mean?

So concerned is Manning that two weeks after this, he calls the Army Chief of Staff and tells him that he needs to speak to the President. And he won't tell his superior why.

If it should seem out of line for someone who's only a colonel to insist on bypassing the chain of command to talk directly to the President of the United States, we have to understand that Manning is a special case. He reminds the Chief of Staff: "I took this job under the condition that I was to have a free hand."

We've heard nothing of this previously. It seems to mean that from the outset Manning has not only had no explicit orders, no one to report to, and no ceiling on expenses, but even a guarantee that he can do as he pleases. No wonder he leaped to take the job. Under those circumstances, it might almost make sense for him to think he could see the President alone if he should want to.

If this reminder of the autonomy he's been given weren't enough, Manning plays again on his personal dominance over the Chief of Staff. He says: "Don't go brass hat on me. I knew you when you were a plebe."

This suggestion that the Chief of Staff should ignore the difference in their rank and do as Manning says is a reminder of the long-ago situation when Manning was an upperclassman at West Point and the Chief of Staff was a first-year man and Manning could make him snap to.

We aren't permitted to hear what the Chief of Staff has to say in response to this impertinence and insubordination. But it doesn't seem to be to inform Manning that he's forthwith relieved of his command and should hold himself ready for court martial.

Rather, he responds by doing exactly as Manning desires, running his request for a personal meeting with the President upstairs to his own superior, who just might be able to arrange it. And what he has to say to him is apparently so compelling that within the hour the Secretary of War himself is calling up Manning on the phone.

We never learn what the Secretary has to say, either. We're just allowed to overhear Manning telling him, "All I want is thirty minutes alone with the President. If nothing comes of it, no harm has been done. If I convince him, you will know all about it."

This is really remarkable stuff—an army colonel telling his ultimate superior, the Secretary of War, to get him an appointment with the President of the United States but refusing to tell him what for. If he can't convince the President of what he has in mind, the Secretary doesn't need to know any more about it. And if he does convince the President, what it's about will be revealed to the Secretary in good time.

Underlings don't usually talk to their superiors this way and get away with it, yet somehow, this wide-eyed insolence is enough to convince the Secretary of War to place himself at the service of his subordinate and use his influence to set up the appointment that Manning desires. Even more marvelously, the White House is so responsive to the urgency and persuasiveness of the Secretary when he calls that it agrees to give this obscure congressman/colonel exactly what he's seeking—a thirty-minute meeting alone with the President with no indication of what it might be for. And as soon as tomorrow!

This readiness to cooperate with Manning is all the more extraordinary since he will later tell DeFries that the President has a nose like a bloodhound: "In his forty years of practical politics he has seen more phonies than you or I will ever see, and each one was trying to sell him something. He can tell one in the dark."

DeFries waits patiently outside the Oval Office while Manning's half-hour one-on-one with the President stretches into two-and-a-half hours. In view of the qualms Manning has expressed to DeFries, we can imagine that he's been unburdening himself to the President, telling him about this horrible new weapon he's made which is so awful in its consequence and so irrevocable that he hasn't even dared to mention its existence to his superiors.

Instead, however, when DeFries is called within at last, it's to be told that in keeping with Manning's recommendation, the dust is going to be given to the British to use to end their war with Germany. And DeFries has been chosen to take it to them because he knows about it and understands nothing of how it was made.

It seems that far from working to convince the President that the dust must never be used, Manning has spent his time talking him into injecting this new super-weapon into the European conflict the United States still has no official part in. The price of our intervention will be that we get to dictate the terms of peace to the Germans and British.

In short, it seems that Manning's intent all along in insisting on speaking privately with the President hasn't been to spare the Army Chief of Staff and the Secretary of War unnecessary and intolerable knowledge. Rather, it's been to evade any intervening authority, including theirs, which might be inclined to stand in the way of his determination to see K-O dust—this weapon he's said he should be put to death for knowing how to make, this weapon he's said must never be used—employed as an instrument of war.

And he's right to anticipate that such opposition would have been forthcoming since later, the Secretary of Labor will declare: "The dust must never be used again. Had I known about it soon enough, it would never have been used on Berlin."

But Manning has an uncanny ability to operate the system without ever being held to account for it by acting as though its structure and rules are going to be observed by everyone but him, while somehow convincing people in positions of authority to order the things he wants done.

And whether it's through the warmth of his smile or his possession of the secret power to cloud men's minds, in the space of just two-and-a-half hours alone with a President of the United States who knows a phony with a dubious scheme when he sees one, he's been able to mesmerize him into not only ignoring established governmental and military procedure and trashing the Constitution, but also, more practically, into foregoing the counsel of all his usual associates and advisors in order to introduce a hideous and destabilizing new weapon into someone else's war and send Capt. John DeFries on a special mission to see that it's done.

PART TWO: USING THE DUST

THE DEATH OF BERLIN

IT might be possible to make a case that up 'til this point DeFries bears only limited responsibility for the events that have been taking place. To be sure, he was the leading member of the political committee that, snowed by Manning's charm, made the mistake of choosing him as a reform candidate for Congress. DeFries has served as a minder of detail for Manning both in Congress and in the army. And he did stage manage Manning's successful re-election campaign in 1944 from his army office, even though Manning has come to think of his congressional career as old hat, and it is against the law—the Hatch Act of 1939—for DeFries to have done it.

Perhaps the most damning thing he's done is to speak up at the right wrong moment about the fish kills in the Chesapeake Bay and set Manning to thinking of Dr. Karst's radioactive medical dust as a potential weapon of war.

Now, however, by agreeing to serve as the personal agent who carries the dust to England, DeFries compromises himself beyond all question. He joins the conspiracy. He becomes an active participant in an unconstitutional scheme.

It is a decision that will have fatal personal consequences. While "sitting on that cargo of dust" in the course of delivering Manning's weapon to the British, DeFries is exposed to "cumulative minimal radioactive poisoning," which in time is going to kill him.

It seems odd that something like that could be allowed to happen. For one thing, it means that the scientists and technicians who've been manufacturing and storing the dust haven't had sense enough to put it in shielded containers. And neither have they kept DeFries from harm by issuing him a protective suit and armor of the sort they habitually wear when dealing with radioactive materials. They haven't so much as pinned a strip of film to his lapel to fog up and reveal exposure to radiation.

Who was asleep on the job?

It's all the stranger since DeFries himself certainly ought to know better. He's told us over and over again just how toxic the stuff is and he's fully aware of the need to safeguard against it. We've seen him suiting up before entering Dr. Karst's lab and listened to him discussing protective gear as a possible defense against the dust with Manning.

So where was Manning in all this? Why wasn't he looking out for DeFries?

As it is, having been given responsibility for transporting the weapon to England, DeFries forgets everything he knows and doesn't trouble himself to ask anyone what precautions he ought to observe in handling the dust. Instead, he watches over it like a first-time babysitter. If we take him literally, he actually spends a week sitting on top of the canisters.

He must *really* be stupid—and he will pay for it.

On the other hand, just like the Army Chief of Staff pushing Manning's case with the Secretary of War, and then the Secretary of War working to convince the White House that it ought to give Manning a private meeting with the President as early as tomorrow, while DeFries is carrying out Manning's mission, he's temporarily granted something of Manning's magical ability to turn the head of higher authority.

After he's arrived safely in England with his cargo of dust, DeFries is commanded to appear at a royal audience. But he won't go. He won't leave the dust. Instead, he's called upon by a Member of Parliament and a "Mr. Windsor"—whom we are to take as the Prime Minister and King.

They ask him questions and DeFries answers them as best he can considering that ignorance is one of his major credentials for being here. Again, we aren't told what either the questions or the answers are. Nevertheless, this army captain must have managed to be persuasive because the next thing we know the British are ready to use the diabolical new weapon, even though to do so means agreeing to American terms of settlement of the war.

Surrender to the US, that is.

The Prime Minister's government will fall over this. And the King will violate constitutional precedent. Nonetheless, it seems that both men must have agreed to the plan. We just aren't allowed to hear them doing it or why they do it.

After British warnings of direness to come and German failure to capitulate, thirteen British bombers—a strange and ill-omened number—leave England bound for Berlin armed with the dust. At Manning's request, DeFries is aboard one of them as an official observer, as though it were somehow possible for him to become neutral and objective once again after all he's done to make the bombing happen.

The planes approach Berlin from different angles and slice the city like a pizza, dropping canister after canister of Karst-Obre dust as they go. The canisters are armed with explosive devices to disperse the dust as widely as possible.

These prototype dirty bombs leave the streets and structures of the city standing intact. But so lethal are they that every living thing in Berlin is killed: Men, women, and children—guilty and innocent alike. Dogs and cats. Parakeets and pigeons. Rats and mice. Earthworms, ants, and butterflies. All of them dead.

The narrator doesn't tell us how many casualties this amounts to—but at the time that Heinlein wrote "Solution Unsatisfactory" in 1940, the human population of Berlin was nearly four-and-a-half million people. And every last one of them imagined as dying from the dust.

As an index of the magnitude of the death toll resulting from this fictional bombing raid, when the United States dropped two Atomic Bombs on Japan in August 1945, the targets would be substantially smaller cities and the human deaths far fewer. A sober latter-day estimate suggests that 66,000 people were killed in Hiroshima and another 39,000 in Nagasaki. In both cases, three-quarters of the population would survive, at least for the time being. With more than forty times as many deaths as from both Atom Bombs put together, the radioactive sterilization of Berlin in this story has to rank as the greatest atrocity in human history.

DeFries may have transported the devil dust to England, helped persuade British leaders to use it, and borne witness to the dropping of the canisters over Berlin. But he doesn't immediately appreciate the overwhelming, disproportionate, and irrevocable nature of the human catastrophe he's been party to.

In contrast, Dr. Estelle Karst understands as soon as the dust has been used that Col. Manning has abused her trust and perverted her research in the medical use of radioactive isotopes. Her choice of the dust to commit suicide is not an accident or a convenience. It's an act of moral protest.

The awfulness of what has happened only becomes apparent to DeFries after he has seen films showing the death of Berlin. He says, "You have not seen them; they never were made public, but they were of great use in convincing the other nations of the world that peace was a good idea."

There's a gaping hole in the narrative at this point, all the more significant for being completely unacknowledged. What was American public reaction to the overnight death of four-and-a-half million people in Germany?

What did the newspapers and the radio pundits have to say about the British acting in such an overwhelming and barbaric fashion against the civilian population of an enemy city? Did they criticize them for having done it?

When did the American public learn that the weapon was actually a US invention, and England had only been given one-time use of it in order to test it on Berlin? Did the President speak up then and take personal responsibility for having sent them the dust and talking them into using it?

How did the Secretary of War and the Army Chief of Staff react when they found out that they'd allowed themselves to be deceived, used and outflanked by Col. Manning?

And was there protest when the public discovered that it wasn't going to be allowed to see what this new American secret weapon had done to Berlin, but films were being shown to people in other countries as a warning not to get out of line?

We're never told.

What we do learn from DeFries is that he himself is a changed man for having witnessed those reconnaissance films. They make an impression on him that watching canisters of K-O dust being dropped one by one from a bomber at night had not.

In the language of Christian belief, which Heinlein absorbed as a child but ordinarily didn't use in his science fiction stories, he has DeFries say, "So far as I am concerned, I left what soul I had in the projection room, and I have not had one since."

Heed what the man is telling us: For all his superficial appearance of artless speaking, he has no soul.

If he had told us so at the outset rather than at this late moment, it most certainly would have had an effect on what we've made of all he has to say. As it is, his lack of a soul—or lack of a conscience—might go a ways toward explaining all the gaps, contradictions, and unlikelihoods we've taken note of in this narrative.

5

SECRETARY OF DUST

AFTER the dusting of Berlin, Germany is ready to capitulate.

Britain is slower to surrender.

The immediate assumption of the British people is that the weapon which has ended the war is their weapon, and they're eager to make Germany pay for the years of bombing they've had to endure. Consequently, when the Prime Minister reveals the private bargain he's struck with the United States for its loan of the dust, his government falls.

However, British reaction turns around after the King, rather than uttering words that have been handed to him to read from the throne, as is customary, speaks out on his own authority.

Once more we aren't allowed to hear what someone actually has to say at a crucial turn, only to accept what takes place as a result, even though what happens may be unlikely. In this case, the King advocates surrender. And so persuasive is he that his voice "sold the idea to England and a national coalition government was formed" for the purpose of yielding British sovereignty.

Lucky thing for them, too. Until the British unite in a national consensus to throw up their hands, Manning is prepared to convince them to do it by taking out London, with the prospective death of another eight-and-a-half million people, including his sometime allies, the Prime Minister and King.

Or, in the more delicate way in which DeFries puts it, "I don't know whether we would have dusted London to enforce our terms or not; Manning thinks we would have done so."

What Manning thinks has now become significant. After Berlin, his power is greatly increased. Instead of being thanked for his services, given a retirement promotion to general, and sent back to Congress out of harm's way, a place is made for him at the President's side as a chief advisor and spokesman.

Once again, his righthand man is brought along with him. Or, as DeFries tells us: "By this time, Manning was an unofficial member of the Cabinet; 'Secretary of Dust,' the President called him in one of his rare jovial moods. As for me, I attended Cabinet meetings, too."

Speaking in his new capacity, Manning completely dominates his first Cabinet meeting. As "Secretary of Dust," it's his estimate that only a small window of time exists—ninety days or less—during which the United States has the advantage of sole possession of the new weapon. He proposes that all aircraft around the world not in the service of the United States Army be grounded, including American commercial and civilian planes.

He says, "After that, we can deal with complete world disarmament and permanent methods of control."

When it is objected that this would be unconstitutional, he answers, "The issue is sharp, gentlemen, and we might as well drag it out in the open. We can be dead men, with everything in due order, constitutional, and technically correct, or we can do what has to be done, stay alive, and try to straighten out the legal aspects later."

The Secretary of Labor—the newest and least powerful Cabinet member, but the most vocal among them now in resisting Manning's appeals to fear and urgency—concedes that control of the dust is going to be necessary. However, he says:

> But where I differ from the Colonel is in the method. What he proposes is a military dictatorship imposed by force on the whole world. Admit it, Colonel. Isn't that what you are proposing?
>
> Manning did not dodge it. "That is what I am proposing."

Let's not dodge this one, either. Instead of hurrying on just as though nothing remarkable has been said, the way the story does, let's consider what is happening for a second.

This is yet another unlikely event we're being asked to accept, another whopper like believing that an army colonel could win a private appointment with the President of the United States for tomorrow while declining to tell anyone what it's about.

Now we're being asked to imagine that everyone at a Cabinet meeting has been told to shove over, and an extra chair has been pulled up to the table so that this same army colonel can sit in. And not merely as a guest, either. The President introduces him to the various Cabinet members by telling them to consider Manning a *de facto* Secretary on a par with themselves.

What's more, this new unofficial Secretary is given the floor. The President of the United States, apparently in complete agreement with everything he has to say, is content to sit back passively through the rest of the meeting and "let Manning bear the brunt of the argument."

Speaking on behalf of the President, this colonel-who-is-more-than-a-colonel informs the Cabinet Secretaries that since the United States has sole possession of the dust for the moment, US policy, effective immediately, is going to be to violate the Constitution at home and to impose a military dictatorship on the world.

Even if we grant Manning all the unique privilege we're told in the story he now has, the course he is indicating is such a radical break with the usual assumptions of American politics that we have to wonder at the temperate way in which his words are received.

As a reality check, imagine the reaction of the Cabinet in 1945 if Gen. Leslie Groves, the army officer in charge of the actual development of the Atomic Bomb and a man not known for his modesty, had presumed to speak to the assembled Secretaries in such an arrogant, presumptuous and authoritarian a manner as this. At the very least, I think he'd have instantly lost all credibility, and that the good sense, if not the sanity, of the President would have been called into question for sponsoring this kind of power trip.

Even within the much more accommodating confines of "Solution Unsatisfactory," we have to wonder why the Secretary of War—whose equivalent today would be the Secretary of Defense—doesn't speak up.

I mean, there he is, seated across the conference table from Manning at the left hand of the President. The military is his area of responsibility. This officer ought to be under his authority. And not only has Col. Manning already broken the oath he's sworn to support and defend the Constitution and is proposing to do it some more, he's betrayed him personally.

Manning has developed a radiological weapon of unprecedented deadliness at the army lab he commands without informing his superiors of what he is doing. By some arcane means, he has managed to persuade the Army Chief of Staff and the Secretary of War to arrange an urgent private meeting for him with the President while refusing to tell them why such a meeting is either necessary or appropriate. Then, over their heads, he has convinced the President to introduce this horrendous new weapon into the ongoing war between Britain and Germany, with the slaughter of millions of civilians.

As his reward for this usurpation of power, Col. Manning has been granted informal Cabinet status and now speaks on behalf of the President. It's his assertion that America's enemies—and maybe its friends, as well—are on the verge of launching an attack on the United States with radioactive dust of their own. The only way to be secure in this brave new world of Manning's making is for the US to use its advantage while it has it and impose military dictatorship on the world. Right now.

Under circumstances like these, you'd think that the Secretary of War would have a question or two for him. As one possibility, he might ask Manning just who he has in mind for the job of world dictator?

But in telling about this crucial Cabinet meeting, the narrator doesn't even so much as mention the Secretary of War. Maybe he couldn't make the meeting, and they had to go on without him, or perhaps he just had nothing to say that day.

What DeFries does recall happening in the wake of Manning's confirmation that he is advocating the imposition of a global military dictatorship is a counterproposal from the Secretary of Labor. He suggests that the present moment of opportunity be used to establish a worldwide democratic commonwealth, and then control of the dust be turned over to the new world government.

But Manning replies that this isn't feasible. While he personally would lay down his life in order to accomplish global democracy, most of the world has no experience of democracy nor any love for it.

He says:

"It's preposterous to talk about a world democracy for many years to come. If you turn the secret of the dust over to such a body, you will be arming the world to commit suicide."

Manning then sets forth a scenario of an inevitable series of back-and-forth dustings that will kill three-quarters of the world's population and reduce human culture to the level of peasants living in villages.

If previously it has been the territory of the Secretary of War that Manning has usurped, it's now the area of responsibility of the Secretary of State he's attempting to muscle in on. Up to this point, however, the Secretary of State has been silent, too.

DeFries tells us, somewhat patronizingly, that he was "really a fine old gentleman, and not stupid, but he was slow to assimilate new ideas."

Now this sweet old fudd speaks up on behalf of a policy of isolation, as though he were an old-time backwoods politician addressing a bunch of yahoos from a stump rather than the man in charge of American foreign policy now faced with the diplomatic challenge of a lifetime. He suggests that we just "keep the dust as our own secret, go our own way, and let the rest of the world look out for itself. That is the only program that fits our traditions."

But Manning dismisses this course of action, too. The research that other countries are doing—or might do—into the new weapon won't permit the luxury of going our own way. What if it had been Germany who'd made and used the dust first instead of the US? They might have done something awful with it.

He declares that "it is the best opinion of all the experts that we can't maintain control of this secret except by rigid policing"—just as though there were no problems with the words "best opinion," "all the experts," "maintain control," "secret," and "rigid policing."

In the event, neither the Secretary of Labor's internationalism nor the Secretary of State's isolationism has a chance. The President's mind is already made up in favor of Manning's fear of Karst-Obre dust in the hands of others who might be as ready to use it as the two of them have been.

With two more unconstitutional moves, the President declares martial law in the United States and, in what is called a "Peace Proposal," informs the leaders of every other nation that they must disarm themselves. As a start, all airplanes capable of crossing the Atlantic must be delivered into US hands and destroyed. Failure to comply with this will be considered an act of war.

Or, as DeFries translates this diplomatic ultimatum, the American answer to the touchy problem of a roomful of men all armed with .45s is, *"Throw down your guns, boys; we've got the drop on you."*

6

THE FOUR-DAYS WAR

THERE are three gunslingers in particular that the narrator singles out as posing potential threat to the United States—England, Japan, and the Eurasian Union.

However, America's friend and ally, England is no longer a problem. It's already in the act of throwing down its guns, thanks to the King's radio address.

(Unless, of course, like me, you're inclined to believe the persistent rumor that a canister of K-O dust went missing during the bombing raid on Berlin—I mean, all those planes, all those canisters, all that confusion—and only got found again afterward. And the British, not wanting to cause a fuss over nothing, were too polite to mention they had it.)

As for the Japanese, they may dismiss the lethal power of the dust as just a story, and they may be convinced that they cannot be defeated, but it's possible to bully them into submission by pressing the right psychological buttons.

DeFries tells us:

> The negotiations were conducted very quietly indeed, but our fleet was halfway from Pearl Harbor to Kobe, loaded with enough dust to sterilize their six biggest cities, before they were concluded. Do you know what did it? This never hit the newspapers, but it was the wording of the pamphlets we proposed to scatter before dusting.

Now, what do you suppose could have been said in those pamphlets—and, more importantly, with what spin—that wouldn't just anger the

Japanese, but which having been shown to them would be sufficient to make them instantly acknowledge their inferiority and bow low in submission? It must have been something devastating.

This leaves those unknown men who've been running the Eurasian Union since the death (on this alternate timeline) of Joseph Stalin in 1941. They've put Lenin and Stalin behind them. And they've held their country out of the war between England and Germany. Now they're quick to agree to American terms. They declare themselves willing to cooperate in every way with the President's ultimatum.

But they're only trying to trick the United States. Instead of delivering their long-range aircraft to a field in Kansas to be parked alongside the planes already surrendered by Germany and England, as they've been directed to do, they launch a series of bombing raids over the Arctic against New York, Washington and other cities with dust of their own.

Exactly how successful these attacks were, we are never told. DeFries says there's no point in repeating what's been in the newspapers. But we're assured that the Four-Days War was a near thing that America should have lost—"and we would have, had it not been for an unlikely combination of luck, foresight and good management."

How close did the United States come to losing the Four-Days War? At least some of the planes that failed to land in Kansas made it through to New York with radioactive dust. DeFries tells us, "We lost over eight hundred thousand people in Manhattan alone." Enemy planes must also have been successful in dropping dust on Washington since he says in passing that "Congress reconvened at the temporary capital in St. Louis."

But the Eurasian Union is promptly paid back for what it's done. The US sterilizes the cities of Moscow, Vladivostok, and Irkutsk, with a combined population of another four-and-a-half million people. And, just that fast, the war is over.

The part played by luck in America's victory is that one of the planes sent to bomb Moscow went off course and arbitrarily picked the city of Ryazan as the place to drop its dust instead. Completely by chance, this industrial center turned out to be the location of "the laboratory and plant which produced the only supply of military radioactives in the Eurasian Union," so the Eurasians are unable to make any more dust.

Very good fortune, that. Like firing a gun randomly into the air and having the bullet fall to earth and kill a cat. And not just any cat, either—the King of the Cats. Right between the eyes.

As for foresight and good management, that's Manning covertly at work. It seems that one more time, in his role as Secretary of Dust, his authority has grown.

DeFries says: "Manning never got credit for it, but it is evident to me that he anticipated the possibility of something like the Four-Days War and prepared for it in a dozen different devious ways."

Manning or somebody ought to have been anticipating an attack on the US since once again, as on other occasions in America's history, some of them alluded to in "Solution Unsatisfactory," an incident has been deliberately provoked in order to provide justification for the United States to go to war.

The Eurasians were goaded into fighting.

Just consider: One of the reasons America had for dropping the Bomb on Japan to end World War II was to make an impression on the Soviet Union. And enough of an impression was made to set off the Cold War.

Imagine, if you will, that in 1945, the United States had gone on to order the Russians either to disarm or suffer the consequences and called this a "peace proposal," as in this story. An ultimatum like that would have immediately triggered a Hot War exactly as it does here.

Not only are the Eurasians deliberately pushed beyond their tolerance by the demand that they surrender all their long-range aircraft to the US and then disarm themselves, but the door for their attack has been left invitingly open. Eurasia's bombers aren't collected and destroyed on Eurasian soil. Instead, they're pointed in the direction of Kansas and not inspected before they go.

No wonder the attack that follows has been anticipated. Air traffic in the United States is at a halt, and military planes are standing by, ready to intercept the Eurasian bombers and shoot most of them down before they can reach their targets.

America is also poised to make a counterattack. Vladivostok is a long way from anywhere; Irkutsk is off at the foot of Lake Baikal in Siberia, and it's possible to get lost while trying to fly to Moscow and wind up in Ryazan. In order to successfully launch immediate coordinated strikes on targets like these, distant from the continental United States and widely separated from each other, advance planning and logistical work must have been done.

If we call preparation to meet the Eurasian attack and then strike back decisively "foresight," the "good management" part is the holding of American casualties to an acceptable minimum.

New York City is largely empty when it is hit. A completely unfounded rumor of bubonic plague has been circulated and everybody able to do it has deserted the city. DeFries has no idea how so effective a whispering campaign was organized and carried out, but he gives Manning credit for having arranged it. And with such perfect timing that most people escape the Eurasian dust.

As for Washington, thanks to Manning's doing, Congress has gone into recess. The President has granted a ten-day leave of absence to the civil service (an authority I wasn't aware he had) and then left town himself to make a sudden political jaunt through the South. The only people who are still at home to receive the attack are the permanent population of the city.

DeFries suggests that it must have been Manning who put the thought of going off on a political swing in the President's head. He couldn't have split the scene to save his own skin: "It is inconceivable that the President would have left Washington to escape personal danger."

That puts a nice face on it, but it's bushwah.

Since the dusting of Berlin, international tensions have been running high. The President has declared martial law in the US and told all other governments that they must surrender immediately or fight the United States. As a precautionary measure, he's closed down official Washington and sent it to visit the folks back home. The American military is on alert, anticipating imminent war with Eurasia.

This is no time for kissing babies, and Manning hasn't suddenly turned into the President's chief political advisor. He's the Secretary of Dust. And when it's the Secretary of Dust who whispers in the President's ear that now might be a good time to pay a visit to Florida, the President doesn't need to hear it twice. He's on the next train south.

Anything else you may have been told is just a cover story.

It only takes four days for the war to be over—one day for the Eurasian attack, a day for assessment of the damage, American counterattack on the third day, and Eurasian surrender on the fourth. Very shortly, the President can join the other survivors at the new temporary capital in St. Louis.

So, how great has the cost been to America from this invited catastrophe?

With no newspapers to consult to find out what DeFries doesn't tell us because it's been in the papers, it's impossible to say with any certainty. But the largest city in the United States, hub of its commerce and center of its publishing and broadcasting industries, is now uninhabitable, and the nation's capital and all its buildings and records have been made inaccessible for years to come. The focal points of American life have been attacked, normal existence has been shattered and refugees are everywhere.

If eight hundred thousand people are dead in Manhattan alone, then at least several million Americans must have been killed in all the cities struck—666 times as many as the three thousand people who died in the attacks on the World Trade Center and the Pentagon on September 11, 2001.

Without luck, foresight, and good management, it would have been far worse.

PART THREE: MANNING AND DEFRIES

7 MR. COMMISSIONER MANNING

WORLD order has now been reestablished, at least for the moment.

However, a horrific new weapon has been unleashed, the world is no longer the same, and the problem originally set forth by Manning to DeFries still remains to be answered: How is Karst-Obre dust—which any nation can make, and which cannot be defended against—to be kept under control?

The Secretary of State's suggestion that the US should hold the dust a secret and go its own way has been overleaped by events. K-O dust has now been used and used again. It's no secret anymore.

The immediate answer America arrives at to the problem of controlling other people's use of the dust—*"Throw down your guns, boys; we've got the drop on you!"*—is only a temporary expedient at best. It can't be relied on to work for very long, as the Eurasian attack demonstrates.

So, who or what is to be in charge of overseeing the monstrous and deadly Karst-Obre dust and protecting the population of the world from it?

The Secretary of Labor's vision of a worldwide democratic commonwealth of nations controlling the weapon has been rejected. Most of the world simply isn't ready to handle that much self-responsibility.

Neither are the people of the United States. The President rules out unilateral US possession of the weapon because he doesn't think America is up to the strain.

As DeFries puts it:

> We were about to hand over to future governments of the United States the power to turn the entire globe into an empire, our empire. And it was the sober opinion of the President that our characteristic and beloved democratic culture would not stand up under the temptation. Imperialism degrades both oppressor and oppressed.

The solution that is arrived at is to establish a special body above and beyond all national governments—a "Commission of World Safety"—whose purpose is to control the dust benevolently. The Commissioners receive lifetime appointments to their post and take an oath to *"preserve the peace of the world."*

The Commissioners are to be backed up by a "Peace Patrol." The idea for this body—and perhaps for the Commission, as well, since one depends upon the other—is Manning's:

"Manning envisioned a corps of world policemen, an aristocracy which, through selection and indoctrination, could be trusted with unlimited power over the life of every man, every woman, every child on the face of the globe."

These patrolmen are to serve in any place except the country of their origin: "They were to be a deliberately expatriated band of Janizaries, with an obligation only to the Commission and the race, and welded together with a carefully nurtured esprit de corps."

Working together, the President and Manning personally select the Commissioners and the initial members of the Peace Patrol. The very first Commissioner to be chosen, the chief amongst them, is (did you guess?) Clyde Manning. In yet another effortless promotion, "Colonel Manning became Mr. Commissioner Manning"—yes, *that* Mr. Commissioner Manning.

As chutzpah goes, this might be compared to Dick Cheney being assigned the task of choosing the best candidate to run for Vice President of the United States, looking the country over and picking Richard B. Cheney for the job.

Were it not for his self-selection, Manning would be an unlikely choice for Commissioner.

It was, after all, Manning who conceived and developed Karst-Obre dust, and men who invent a weapon for the military aren't ordinarily allowed a determining say in what happens to it after it leaves their hands. They're tech people not decision makers.

But Manning has gotten past this limit by inducing his superiors to aid him in circumventing themselves and then by putting the whammy on the President of the United States. Though he says that if the dust is ever used, the world will be destabilized, he's insisted that dust be dropped on Berlin anyway and is given his wish. The result is millions dead in Germany, millions more dead in the US, and still more millions dead in the Eurasian Union—as many as eleven million people in all.

Manning was prepared for the death toll to be much higher.

The casualties in New York would have been worse if that black death rumor hadn't worked so well to empty Manhattan and if the fleeing people hadn't shown such admirable restraint while waiting in line to use the bridges and tunnels. And had it not been for that lucky dusting of Ryazan, millions more Americans would have died, and the US would have lost the war.

Another eight-and-a-half million people could have been killed if England hadn't decided to surrender, and London had been taken out as an object lesson. And if the Pacific Fleet had sailed on to Japan to dust its six largest cities, a further fifteen million people might have died.

Apparently, Manning understood that the initial death toll from use of his weapon might be as many as forty million people or even more and accepted the possibility. What's more, he's foretold the death by dust of three-quarters of the population of the earth if his plan for a military dictatorship imposed by force isn't adopted.

Not only is everybody in the world already suffering nightmares thanks to Manning, it seems that Manning is capable of killing every one of us in order to save us all from the genie he's let out of the bottle.

True, in his new role as First Commissioner, he will be restrained by the oath he swears to preserve the peace of the world. But such an oath is subject to interpretation. He's also a man who has been known to take an oath and then break it.

In view of Manning's responsibility for the existence of Karst-Obre dust, his willingness to use it and indifference to how many casualties it causes, and his personal history of insubordination, we have to ask whether someone like him, who looks on the dust as a loaded gun held to the head of every man, woman, and child on the planet and is prepared to use it that way, is the best possible choice to be the person in charge of worldwide oversight of this weapon?

Would the US Senate be likely to confirm the nomination of this man to be Head Fox in Charge of All Chickens? He's stirred up some bad feelings.

Manning has double-crossed powerful people in the course of his rise to power. By ignoring standard operating procedure and the chain of command, he's offended and angered others. Because of him, millions of people are now dead, and millions more like DeFries have been condemned to die a lingering death from cumulative minimal radiation poisoning if not from cancer. Life as usual has been radically disrupted, untold numbers of people have been displaced from their homes, and billions of dollars have been lost.

Manning has to have made enemies along the way.

By this time, he must be a highly controversial figure, this army officer detached from his command. Or is he really a congressman? This unofficial Cabinet officer. This mysterious man who lurks in the President's attic and creeps forth to whisper dire things in his ear.

Whether the colonel who invented the dust and then pressed for its first use has any business acting as Secretary of Dust, let alone being made World Czar of Dust, ought to be under question. Manning may not have gotten the credit he deserves for the dozen devious things he did to prepare for the Four-Days War, but he's in a perfect position now to be given the blame for anything and everything that's gone wrong at home and abroad since the war between England and Germany suddenly got so out of hand.

Can he escape all responsibility for the actions he's taken?

Under circumstances like these, it seems unlikely that Clyde "Devil Dust" Manning's confirmation as the most powerful person on Earth could have been nearly as uneventful a matter as the narrator would have us believe.

This is one more crucial transition that DeFries slides past.

When Manning moves on to his new post as Commissioner, DeFries goes with him yet again.

From his beginnings as just another high school teacher with an interest in politics, DeFries has now traveled to Congress with Manning to be his secretary, followed him into the army to serve as his adjutant, and sat at his elbow in Cabinet meetings. Each new place that Manning has gone, DeFries has been right there beside him.

It's not clear what special skills he possesses that make him so useful, but his continuing presence appears to somehow be essential to Manning.

Nothing is ever said in the story about the home lives of these two men. Is either of them married? With all the job changes they make, did their kids complain about being forced to switch schools again?

Or perhaps they're bachelors, which would explain why both of them are able to pack up and move at a moment's notice. We might even imagine their living arrangement as resembling that of lifetime FBI Director J. Edgar Hoover and his Assistant Director, Clyde Tolson, who shared a house together and were buried in adjoining graves when they died.

8

WHO'S ON TOP?

EVEN after the establishment of the new oversight agencies, it still remains an open question who actually controls the dust.

Is it the Commission of World Safety and that new aristocracy, the Peace Patrol? Or are they just a front for the United States of America?

From the point of view of the rest of the world, it would be difficult not to think so. For all their nominally international and disinterested nature, the Commission and the planetary police both wear a Made in America label:

They're the result of an initiative put forth by the United States at a moment when the US has exclusive possession of the weapon and has demonstrated its readiness to use it.

The first Commissioner to be chosen is the US Army officer who invented the dust. He and the President of the United States pick the rest of the Commission.

The majority of the Commissioners are American. And it's the US Senate and not an independent international body which confirms their selection.

Even the arms, ammunition, and aircraft of the Peace Patrol must be given to it by the United States.

Ultimate authority appears to remain with the US President.

That's an illusion, however.

In fact, Manning is in charge, just as he has always been. DeFries may keep suggesting that the President is a strong and savvy master of politics. He may characterize him as "a good President." But what he actually shows us is somebody who is putty in Manning's hands and does everything he wants him to.

The President falls under Manning's spell from the moment the colonel is shown into the Oval Office for their first one-on-one meeting. If Manning says dust should be dropped, the President drops dust. If Manning suggests the President leave town, the President heads south. And if Manning tells the President that he thinks it might be a good idea if he were to be placed in charge of overseeing the dust, the President names him First Commissioner.

It's Manning who calls the tune, and it's the President who dances.

Years pass with the President doing whatever he can to lend Manning assistance in the transfer of control over the dust from the United States to the new agencies that Manning directs.

The radioactivity in Washington was short term, and has abated, and the capital has been reoccupied. However, the emergency controls that were established in the US prior to the Four-Days War have never been lifted. Even after six years, commercial aviation still hasn't been allowed to resume operation.

Given America's privileged position, the economic and political restraint observed by the US has been remarkable. DeFries says:

> The President was determined that our sudden power should be used for the absolute minimum of maintaining peace in the world—the simple purpose of outlawing war and nothing else. It must not be used to protect American investment abroad, to coerce trade agreements, for any purpose but the simple abolition of mass killing.

To every appearance, America continues to run the world. In actuality, however, it's been engaged in a gradual process of ceding all of its special advantage to the Commission of World Safety. How this has been managed without active opposition within the US isn't explained.

But then, before the shift of power can be made complete, the comfortable working relationship between Manning and the President comes to an abrupt conclusion. On February 17, 1951—a day that conceivably might be the sixth anniversary of the dusting of Berlin—the President is killed in a plane crash.

The narrator tells us no more than this. He never says a single word to suggest that foul play was involved. However, I think questions have to arise any time a plane with an important political figure aboard falls out of the sky.

In this case (and let me say again that DeFries never suggests it), my first guess is that the person behind the fatal crash was the Vice President of the United States.

We're told that the Vice President was a compromise candidate placed on the ticket to preserve party unity when the President was re-elected in 1948. He was an opponent of the legislation which originally brought the Commission of World Safety into being. DeFries calls him a confirmed isolationist.

But that's not true.

At least, what I take the Vice President for isn't someone who wants the United States to keep the dust a secret and go its own way in the manner that the old Secretary of State did, but rather somebody who sees America as having a power advantage over the rest of the world, and who can't bear to stand by and watch the President give it all away.

The first thing the new President does after he's sworn into office is to send for Manning.

DeFries expects to accompany him to this meeting just as he always does. But Manning tells him he has another job for him to do. He opens his safe and removes a sealed envelope containing orders that were apparently prepared some time ago in anticipation of a moment like this and gives them to his assistant to execute.

For once DeFries won't claim our attention because he was present at some pivotal historical moment only to skip over what was actually said and done when it comes to telling us about it. This time—even though he wasn't there himself—he's able to tell us more than he usually does.

When Manning arrives at the White House, it's to find the President waiting for him with an entourage of bodyguards and supporters. If I read the new President as a proponent of American private interest and not an isolationist, it's because one of the allies he has at his elbow is a House committee chairman who wants to re-establish commercial air travel and another is a Senator who would like to use the Peace Patrol to safeguard American-owned assets in Africa and South America. The new President attempts to assert his authority over Manning. He reminds him that he's still a member of the US military by addressing him as "Colonel Manning." And he informs him that he's relieved from duty—something which perhaps might more usefully have been said to him back in the old days when he first got out of line.

It's too late now. Manning tells the President that he's to be addressed as "Mr. Commissioner Manning" and says that his appointment is for life. It can't be rescinded.

When the President tries to place him under arrest, Manning points to six bombers in the skies over the Capitol. They're piloted by members of the Peace Patrol, none of them American. Unless Manning is given his way, everyone present is a dead man.

It appears that DeFries has carried out the orders he was handed.

Thanks to the former President, the United States has turned over all means of resistance. And the new man lacks the nerve and sense of social responsibility necessary to call Manning's bluff by having him shot down in his tracks as the threat to the world he's demonstrated himself to be.

Instead, just that easily, the new President gives in—although, as usual, we don't see him do it.

We may find we have to reconsider. Judging by who ultimately benefits from these changes in power and by the fact that DeFries doesn't tell us the truth about who and what the Vice President really is, perhaps it wasn't he who caused the old President's plane to crash after all.

9
THE CHEESE STANDS ALONE

THE American President's capitulation represents the surrender of everybody. Now that Manning's disguise has at last been cast aside, he stands revealed as Big Cheese of the World.

This last self-promotion to military dictator of the planet has to be the least likely of the many unlikely promotions that Manning receives in the course of this story. It's a big leap from pointing at half a dozen bombers overhead to establishing your authority as supreme ruler of the world and making it stick. But as far as DeFries is concerned, we can just consider it done.

How Manning manages to dispense with the other Commissioners and take sole control of the Commission of World Safety is not revealed to us. But maybe there's no need. In the six years the Commission has existed, we haven't heard so much as a peep out of any other Commissioner.

Beyond the Commission, however, Manning's power base isn't obvious. It's not clear which people, organizations, or nations would have reason to support him or why anyone would choose to obey his orders. And the lack of challenge to his assumption of authority isn't explained. He's in charge now, that's all.

Henceforth, Manning is to be military dictator of the world, and the Peace Patrol will serve as his handpicked enforcers.

DeFries says:

> There were incidents thereafter, such as the unfortunate affair at
> Fort Benning three days later and the outbreak in the wing of the

Patrol based in Lisbon and its resultant wholesale dismissals, but, for practical purposes, that was all there was to the *coup d'état*.

Manning was the undisputed military dictator of the world.

But now that Manning has made such an effort to make himself ruler of the world with the power to tell everybody what to do, how does he use this authority? What is his ideology? What are his programs? What edicts does he make?

That we aren't told. Manning's accession to undisputed power is, as far as the story goes, as though this was the point it had really been aiming for all along.

All that remains in DeFries' account are a few paragraphs of summation and a final bid for sympathy for Manning.

He says:

> Whether or not any man as universally hated as Manning can perfect the Patrol he envisioned, make it self-perpetuating and trustworthy, I don't know, and—because of that week in a buried English hangar—I won't be here to find out. Manning's heart disease makes the outcome even more uncertain—he may last another twenty years; he may keel over dead tomorrow—and there is no one to take his place. I've set this down partly to occupy the short time I have left and partly to show there is another side to any story, even world dominion.
>
> Not that I would like the outcome either way. If there is anything to this survival-after-death business, I am going to look up the man who invented the bow and arrow and take him apart with my bare hands. For myself, I can't be happy in a world where any man, or group of men, has the power of death over you and me, our neighbors, every human, every animal, every living thing. I don't like anyone to have that kind of power.
>
> And neither does Manning.

Poor Manning. Forced to run the world all by himself because the prospect of K-O dust in the hands of others who just might be tempted to use it isn't acceptable to him. And never mind that he himself is the person responsible for the dust and its use in the first place, or that he's quite ready to use the dust again to back up his authority now if anyone tries to challenge it.

The poor man is dying, too. He might drop dead as soon as tomorrow.

We haven't heard a word about Manning's heart since Congressman Manning set off at too brisk a pace for the War Department to listen to a no-strings-attached job offer the Army Chief of Staff wanted to make him. And his heart disease hasn't visibly slowed him down for a moment at any time since. It's only now, when a little sympathy is desired that the precarious state of Manning's health is being brought up again. But we won't quibble about that.

The unfortunate part is that there's nobody to succeed Manning as dictator of the world. Certainly not DeFries, who not only is dying himself, though taking a good long time about it, but who's never shown a sign of being anything more than a convenient tool.

If Manning truly is concerned for the good of all, it's not clear why he's taken no thought for who is to be in charge after he's gone, especially since if he were to start on a search tomorrow, he might live long enough to find a responsible successor. Things being what they are, however, his lack of provision for the future is just one more unfortunate circumstance the world is going to have to cope with when he's dead.

The nearest Manning has to a plan of action is to perfect the Peace Patrol and make it self-perpetuating and trustworthy. If he could manage to do that—and it's by no means certain that he can—then the Patrol might be able to keep a lid on things. But Manning needs twenty years to bring this off and there's no guarantee that he has that much time.

He's also hampered by the fact that everybody in the world except John DeFries hates him.

DeFries would like us to know that Manning's been misunderstood. The true purpose of his account has been to show a world that doesn't properly appreciate Manning how things appear from his side.

The person really at fault is the man who invented the bow and arrow and set off the arms race in the first place. (If DeFries could only get his hands on the bloody bastard, why, he'd murderize him, he'd tear him limb from limb, that's what he'd do.)

Manning, in his wisdom and benevolence, has just been doing what's necessary to keep the problem under control. If he had his druthers, he'd really prefer that nobody had the power of death over you and me, our neighbors, every human being, and every living thing.

But if someone has to do it, well, he's tough-minded enough for the job. He'll do it even though he'd really rather not.

That's DeFries' story, at least.

But if he's right in saying that every story has another side, then we have yet to hear the other side of this one. DeFries may be aware of what everybody else in the world thinks of Manning and why, but we can only guess. His version is the only one we've heard.

We may never be able to say exactly what has happened. However, by taking things slowly and not allowing ourselves to be hustled, it has been possible for us to assess the likelihood of the account that DeFries has given us.

He may imply that we're lucky to be able to get the inside story from him at a moment when he feels a need to tell it. He may be folksy and confiding. He may be certain and plausible. But he's a partisan with all the verbal moves of a con man.

Over and over, when exactly what happened matters, his story has gotten vague. Again and again, he's set us up for one thing but delivered something else and then moved right along as though nothing had happened. And he's told lies—lots of lies.

By his own admission, he has no soul.

So what are we to believe?

10

MANNING'S NATURE

IF the events of this story have been nothing but a series of accidents, imperatives and improvisations, as DeFries would like us to accept, then what a strange and unlikely trip it's been to watch the metamorphosis of Clyde Manning, retired early from the army with a heart condition and reduced to addressing women's clubs, into Mr. Commissioner Manning, master of dust and ruler of all.

However, if that was his goal all along, then he finally got where he was aiming to be.

But which of the two is it?

Why Manning behaves the way he does is a mystery. Aside from DeFries' crucial murkiness and uncertain reliability, again and again in the course of the story, there's a difference between what Manning says and his real intention:

When he addresses those women's clubs after he's first retired from the army, he's suave and urbane and makes an excellent impression. He's just dazzling them with charm.

When Manning answers the inquiries of a political search committee looking for a candidate to replace a two-bit chiseler in Congress, he allows them to think he's a liberal. He's only feeding them what they want to hear.

He flatters Dr. Karst by telling her that he sees interesting possibilities in the medical research she's been pursuing. He really means he perceives the basis for an unprecedented weapon of mass annihilation.

Manning tells DeFries that if the weapon he's made should ever be used, the world will be destabilized. Shortly thereafter, we learn that he's talked the President into using it anyway.

And he assures the Cabinet that he would willingly lay down his life in order to achieve global democracy. But this is just him striking a pose for effect. All that we are shown is Manning making unilateral decisions for everybody in the world.

DeFries presents Manning as a genius of common sense responding to changing circumstances by doing what needs to be done—as though he had no responsibility for the new conditions that he's reacting to. However, if we judge Manning not by what he professes but by what he actually does and its result, he looks very much like someone who's been aiming to make himself dictator of the world all along, following a path as straight as a dog's hind leg to get there.

The most mundane explanation I can offer for him (and it's clearly insufficient) is that—like Robert Heinlein at the Naval Academy—Manning was assigned to engineering at West Point and not placed on the command track. He always had dreams of being in charge but was never allowed to be. He's resentful about that, and this is his way of showing everyone better.

Dr. Karst accuses him of being a warmonger—someone who learned to love the stench of rotting corpses on the battlefield or maybe somebody who'd been too late for the Great War and now is trying to catch up. And Manning does proceed to kill a lot of people just to demonstrate he can.

But there's more to the man than someone who merely wants to run up the body count as efficiently as possible. He's got a vicious streak, as well. Something in Manning takes active pleasure in the pain he causes.

He links Dr. Karst's name to the horrific weapon he makes from the medical dust he co-opts from her, knowing that nothing could be more excruciating to her than to be "honored" in this fashion. DeFries says he doesn't know whether Manning ever told her what he intended to do with the dust he's permanently attached her name to. I believe he did, which is why she committed suicide after Berlin.

DeFries declares that there are some people who see Manning, the dictator, as a traitor and a mad dog. This has to be a specifically American reaction. It takes people from the United States to perceive him as a traitor.

It's certainly true that Manning breaks the military oath he's sworn, violating the US Constitution rather than defending it. He casually sets off a war that results in the death of millions of American civilians, a war that would have been lost had it not been for luck. And ultimately, he even stages a *coup d'état*, which overturns the American government.

Yet, he's not the usual kind of traitor to the United States who betrays his country for money, for sex, or because of allegiance to a foreign power. Manning isn't greedy for money, he's got all the sex he'll ever need at home, and his only loyalty is to himself.

Should we take him for a mad dog, then—solitary, antisocial, rabid, and ready to sink his teeth into any available target? There's no question that Manning is ruthless enough to kill eleven million people in the space of a few weeks and not care if the number is higher or that he's prepared to set a series of events in motion that will either make him world dictator or knock humanity back to the Stone Age.

Within the context of the story, his readiness to be this excessive—doubtful and dangerous though it might seem to us—appears to be the only reason for the extraordinary support he's given. Manning wants to develop a horrifying weapon, see it used, and make it his excuse for taking over the world. And because he does, one person after another bends himself out of shape to see that he can.

He might be a trickster figure like Loki, the Norse god of discord and mischief who hangs out with the gods of Asgard and plays games with their heads but who owes them no allegiance and is destined to stand against them in the final battle.

It's certainly true that everyone in this story who trusts in Manning eventually gets betrayed by him. He's got the power to mess minds, even over the phone and at secondhand. People in authority unaccountably do whatever he wishes. He has a particularly tight hold on the psyche of the American President, who prides himself on his ability to spot a phony but is never able to spot one in Manning.

There's even a whiff of sulfur hanging about Manning.

He defiles DeFries, corrupting both his body and his soul. He takes a simple-minded schnook of a high school teacher who only wanted to see a dirty congressman voted out of office, and before he's done with him, makes him a crucial figure in the development and the pivotal agent in the first use of an archetypical weapon of mass annihilation that Manning himself calls "devilish stuff."

If that were not enough, Manning hands DeFries the order to initiate the coup which makes Manning dictator of the world. And DeFries carries out this little chore for him.

Of course, he doesn't tell us this directly. DeFries never comes right out and admits to us that even though he's been passing himself off to us as "an ordinary sort of man who, by a concatenation of improbabilities, found himself shoved into the councils of the rulers," in fact he's the person responsible for putting Manning in power. If not for him executing Manning's orders, the coup could never have happened.

Poor deluded DeFries! Robbed of what little soul he ever had by Manning. With the blood of millions on his hands, thanks to Manning. A traitor to the United States because of his greater loyalty to Manning. Now slowly rotting all over from radiation poisoning, courtesy of Manning. And in a world united in hatred of Clyde Manning, the only person with anything good to say for him.

But then, even the Devil needs a defender. It's a job.

What a diabolical story this is! If Manning really was the Devil all along and not just some prematurely retired military man daydreaming about what he might have been and what he might have done if only he'd been given the opportunity, it would explain a great deal.

PART FOUR: INTERPRETATIONS

11

 POINTING IN FOUR DIFFERENT DIRECTIONS

"**SOLUTION** Unsatisfactory" is like nothing else Robert Heinlein would ever write for *Astounding*, either under his own name or as Anson MacDonald.

A chart in the same May 1941 issue of *Astounding* in which "Solution Unsatisfactory" appeared demonstrated that all the stories that had been published there under the Heinlein name were part of a common fictional future. The one partial exception to this, a novelette entitled "Universe" also published in that May 1941 issue of the magazine, would later be confirmed to be part of the Future History, too.

The pseudonym Anson MacDonald was reserved for stories which didn't fit within this framework. That would include some of Heinlein's most provocative work, like *Beyond This Horizon*, a novel which set forth an alternative line of future historical development, the time travel tangle "By His Bootstraps," and "Waldo," in which reality shapes itself according to how we conceive it.

But "Solution Unsatisfactory," the second of the seven stories under the Anson MacDonald byline, wouldn't be like the rest of MacDonald's or Heinlein's work. As a memoir of American military and governmental operations a few years in the future, it might well be the most apparently "realistic" story ever published in the pages of *Astounding*.

Underneath its plausible surface, however, it was a pack of lies.

That "Solution Unsatisfactory" should seem so sure of itself at the same time that it contained so many untruths was completely by intent. Heinlein was bent on fooling the readers of *Astounding* by appealing to their taste for certitude and then covertly working to subvert it.

He would take in Crown Publisher's editor Edmund Fuller, too, four years later. So successful was Heinlein at the appearance of just knowing the facts and reciting them, and so immediately striking would be the resonances between "Solution Unsatisfactory" and the actual end of World War II, that Fuller would insist that the story ought to be put at the front of *The Best of Science Fiction* as a demonstration of science fiction's ahead-of-the-headlines relevance.

So devious and tricky was "Solution Unsatisfactory," however, that what he actually wound up publishing wasn't the example of confident prophetics he'd intended to present but rather a four-way quarrel over what the story meant.

12

FOREIGN POLICY—WHAT FOREIGN POLICY?

THE first person that Robert Heinlein set out to mislead was John W. Campbell. When the editor of *Astounding* initially announced "Solution Unsatisfactory" in the April 1941 issue of the magazine, he informed his readers that the author's title for it had been "Foreign Policy."

Even though he may have altered the title, however, Campbell was sufficiently taken by it to repeat in his preface to *The Best of Science Fiction*: "The author's original title for this story was 'Foreign Policy'—in reference to the fact that the United States never has had a consistent, predictable, or understandable foreign policy."

The opening lines of the story reinforced Heinlein's faux title by declaring emphatically that its subject was American foreign policy and how the dust forced it to change. It begins:

> In 1903, the Wright brothers flew at Kitty Hawk.
> In December 1938, in Berlin, Dr. Hahn split the uranium atom.
> In April 1943, Dr. Estelle Karst, working under the Federal Emergency Defense Authority, perfected the Karst-Obre technique for producing artificial radioactives.
> So American foreign policy had to change.
> Had to. *Had to*. It is very difficult to tuck a bugle call back into a bugle. Pandora's Box is a one-way proposition. You can turn pig into sausage, but not sausage into pig. Broken eggs stay broken. "All the King's horses and all the King's men can't put Humpty together again."
> I ought to know—I was one of the King's men.

The narrator is saying that taken in sum the invention of the airplane, the splitting of the atom by a German scientist, and the atomic research of Dr. Estelle Karst forced American foreign policy to alter, and that everything else followed inevitably. Once it had the dust and the means to deliver it, what else could the US do?

But what he is actually doing is feeding us the story's first lies.

Because the false information given to us by DeFries comes before we're able to know that he's lying, it's only natural to take everything he has to say at face value. Rather than orienting us within the story, however, the effect of those initial dry statements of fact, some of which aren't facts, followed by a barrage of cleverness for emphasis and distraction, is to lead us astray from the outset.

Estelle Karst wasn't working under the direction of the Federal Emergency Defense Authority, a body we never hear of again. She was doing medical research for the US Army under the command of Col. Manning.

American foreign policy did not have to change because Dr. Karst perfected the Karst-Obre technique in April 1943. She didn't perfect it in April 1943.

She never perfected it at any time.

K-O dust was in no way her doing. It wasn't produced until late in 1944 after Manning had separated Dr. Karst from the fruits of her work and eased her out of the picture.

So, as definite, exact and authoritative as the things we're told about her may sound, none of them is true beyond the fact that Dr. Karst worked with artificial isotopes. Instead, the effect of what the narrator says is to point a finger at her and assign responsibility to her that she doesn't deserve.

DeFries is also lying about his own role. As one of the King's men—or, more properly, as Manning's man—his job was always to assist in kicking American foreign policy to pieces. It was never to attempt to put it back together again afterward.

The phrase "foreign policy" is used on three occasions in the course of the story. And each time it has a different significance.

The first time it's used, it means that as an inevitable consequence of Dr. Karst's medical research (or rather Manning's development of K-O dust), the US has to use the dust as a weapon in the war between England and Germany. Has to, *has to*.

The second time it's used, it means that the dust having been dropped, the US must take charge of the world and rule it benevolently for the next hundred years.

The third time it's used, it means that because American politicians can't be trusted with that much power, control of the dust is to be turned over to Manning. Whatever this sequence may be, it doesn't amount to a consistent, predictable and understandable new American foreign policy. And after this point in the story, with Manning now established in place as First Commissioner, we hear no more about it.

"Foreign Policy" was an intentionally deceptive title for a deliberately misleading story. It set forth a promise the story was never intended to keep. It focused attention where it didn't belong and led it in the wrong direction. Then, it flowed into the desert sand and disappeared.

No wonder John Campbell felt the title needed to be changed.

13

WATCHING THE WATCHERS

THE title Campbell substituted, "Solution Unsatisfactory," was more in keeping with the nature of the science fiction he aimed to publish in *Astounding*.

The proper business of science fiction, as the editor presented it, wasn't to predict the future as much as it was to anticipate problems the future might bring and then deal with them imaginatively before they happened.

By retitling this story and thereby reemphasizing it, Campbell turned attention from American foreign policy to control of the dust by what he described as "a dictatorship and a super-police force of the most ruthless and autocratic kind imaginable."

We're told by DeFries that this super-police force, the Peace Patrol, is the only thing standing between humanity and self-destruction. In the name of keeping the weapon under control, these global policemen are prepared to use the dust to kill the President of the United States and even their own Commissioner Manning. They're prepared to go anywhere and do whatever is necessary to see that nobody in the world has the dust or the means to use it but them.

In order to offset any inclination toward national favoritism, the Peace Patrol consists of men without a country, expatriates severed from their cultural roots, never allowed even to pay a visit to the places they were born. Instead, they're turned into a new aristocracy loyal to each other and to the Patrol, above and apart from the ordinary mankind they serve.

Manning's plan for this group of law-enforcers to become a new elite separated from their origins and bonded to each other had better work. As DeFries says, "There would be no one to guard these selfsame guardians. Their own characters and the watch they kept on each other would be all that stood between the race and disaster."

If this solution seemed less than satisfactory to John Campbell, the reason may have been that in two stories published in *Astounding* during 1940, "The Roads Must Roll" in June and "Blowups Happen" in September, Heinlein had already set forth the problem of a fallible mankind attempting to control overwhelming future technology. And in neither case had the problem been convincingly resolved.

In both these stories, once people put a new technology in place—in one case, highways that move, in the other a nuclear power plant—they then become hostage to it and to the good sense and stability of the men responsible for operating it. In both cases, too, the situation becomes all the more precarious when the new technology is taken to the brink of disaster and the superior men in charge find themselves threatened by torturing storms of emotion suddenly bursting free of the inner compartments where they're usually kept in lock-down.

The answer that Heinlein attempted to offer in the course of these stories—greater and greater watchfulness with added layers of ever more able men keeping guard—had become untenable by the end of "Blowups Happen."

But now, once more in yet a third story, another advanced technology, Karst-Obre dust, has to be used. It's capable of killing most of humanity and knocking civilization back to the Stone Age. And all that prevents it is the superior personal character, constant vigilance, and emotional stability of the chosen men of the Peace Patrol.

This third time around, however, John Campbell was no longer willing to accept that character, ability, indoctrination, training, and oversight were going to be enough to deal with the problem.

The Peace Patrol is a disaster waiting to happen. It can't possibly work as it's supposed to.

It's a thin force, predominantly American in origin. It isn't fully operational. Its schools aren't even in place, and who can say what someone who hasn't been properly trained and indoctrinated at the Academy might do?

Nonetheless, even though there are as yet relatively few Patrolmen and they're inadequately prepared, they're already expected to be everywhere at once all over the world right now, peeking in windows, poking through trash cans, sniffing out secret underground laboratories, preventing the dust from being made.

Realistically, they're never going to be able to do it, no matter how bright and dedicated they are or how hard they try.

As in Heinlein's two earlier stories, once again, this is another untenable situation in which overconscientious men of superior ability and exceptional responsibilities must attempt to do the impossible by bearing down harder and harder, holding on tighter and tighter, and becoming more and more frantic until at last they reach the limit of their ability to cope and come to pieces.

Given this group of stressed-out men who've been taught to regard themselves as a breed apart, the only people worthy of possessing the dust, it seems just a matter of time before John Campbell's fears come true and the Patrol starts using the threat of the dust to coerce and control lesser folk. In fact, they've already begun to do it with their bombers in the skies over Washington.

Not their least problem is that the last line of defense against the dust is the Peace Patrol.

At the same time, the Peace Patrolmen are also the only ones who *have* the dust.

It seems their work is cut out for them. These elite, tightly bonded, alienated men are just going to have to keep a closer and closer watch on each other at all times to be sure they're sure the dust is safe.

With more hope than sense, DeFries may insist, "It stood a chance of working. Had Manning been allowed twenty years without interruption, the original plan might have worked."

But Manning doesn't have twenty uninterrupted years to devote to getting the Patrol squared away.

In fact, the Peace Patrol may already have been fatally compromised thanks to Manning and his coup. It's a subordinate arm of the World Safety Commission. As soon as Manning seizes sole power, the World Safety Commission loses its former authority, and the Patrolmen no longer have a job.

Whom are they to serve now? Do these men of the utmost ability and character simply fall into line and become Manning's personal military force? Or is their individual bonding, their esprit de corps, and their hubris great enough for them to attempt to seize power for themselves? Or do they just throw up their hands and go back where they came from?

That outbreak in the wing of the Peace Patrol based in Lisbon with its resultant wholesale dismissals may be a sign that the Patrol has already begun to come apart under the strain.

If the future of the human race depends upon perfecting the Peace Patrol and even DeFries is not sure that the Patrol can be made both self-perpetuating and trustworthy, then it seems that the fate of the world is in unstable hands.

So when John Campbell retitled this story, he was correct—the solution it offered to the problem of control of the dust wasn't satisfactory.

However, recognizing this and even making a point of it would not prevent the editor from buying and publishing the story anyway.

14

DIRTY BOMBS DON'T WORK

AND that is where things might have remained, with "Solution Unsatisfactory" a half-forgotten curiosity buried in the graveyard of old magazine issues—a story which might have been about American foreign policy but really wasn't or else a story that offered an inadequate solution to the problem of control of an atomic weapon too awful to tolerate. But then World War II was ended by the dropping of two American atom bombs on Japan, and overnight, "Solution Unsatisfactory" came back to life with a new emphasis.

In the immediate postwar moment, with *The Best of Science Fiction* in the making, this story became a bone of contention between the editor of the book, Groff Conklin, and Edmund Fuller, overseeing the project for Crown.

I think the argument between them developed this way:

In the early fall of 1945, while they were still in the process of selecting work for the anthology, Conklin handed Fuller a copy of the May 1941 *Astounding* for him to read the cover story, "Universe" by Robert Heinlein.

In this novelette, a society living aboard a giant spaceship traveling from Earth to the stars has forgotten its original purpose. When one man sees the stars again and then tries to remind his fellows of what they no longer correctly understand, not only isn't he believed, he finds himself sentenced to death for heresy.

This commentary on human shortsightedness and resistance to truth was written immediately before "Solution Unsatisfactory." Both stories would then see publication, along with the Future History chart, all three together in the same May 1941 issue of *Astounding*.

In the six-and-a-half years of the Golden Age of *Astounding*, from the middle of 1939 to the end of 1945, this issue would be pivotal. It both consolidated the changes Campbell had been making in the magazine and set forth the nature and scope of the new modern science fiction that he was working to put in place.

These two stories—one of them by Robert Heinlein with an interstellar setting hundreds of years from now, the other by Anson MacDonald taking place in the United States the day after tomorrow—set forth the size of the territory encompassed by Campbellian science fiction, while the Future History chart indicated its depth and connectedness. The readers of *Astounding* would rank "Universe" as the top story in the issue, with "Solution Unsatisfactory" a solid second.

After he read "Universe," Edmund Fuller approved it for use in *The Best of Science Fiction*.

But then, as he paged on further through the magazine, "Solution Unsatisfactory" would catch his attention. Reading it only a few weeks after the bombing of Hiroshima and Nagasaki and the conclusion of World War II, he was amazed to see just how on target the story had been, with an American atomic weapon bringing the war to an end in 1945.

How right that was! It seemed perfect to go in the book.

But when he brought the story up with Groff Conklin, Conklin surprised him. He wanted no part of it. He'd never liked "Solution Unsatisfactory." And he didn't like it any better because it had made a lucky guess or two.

Just how prophetic was it, anyway? The resemblance to current events that had captured Fuller's attention all happened by the time the story was half done. In getting caught up by the similarity to the end of World War II, he was managing to ignore the rest of what took place in "Solution Unsatisfactory"—the runaway Cabinet meeting, the Four-Days War with its millions and millions of casualties, the fatal plane crash, Manning making himself dictator. Did that foretell the future, too?

Conklin didn't think that declaring successful prophecy and shouting hurrah for science fiction was reason enough to use the MacDonald story in his anthology, let alone for putting it in a place of special prominence.

But he wasn't able to dissuade Edmund Fuller. Fuller recognized a good sales hook when he saw it and he didn't want to let go of this one. He kept coming back at Conklin about using "Solution Unsatisfactory" in *The Best of Science Fiction*.

And after the editor saw a newspaper account in the *Washington Post* in which a Nobel Prize-winning scientist said the existence of atomic weapons meant the United States might have to be ruled by a dictator, Conklin finally capitulated. With the argument he'd been making about the story's accuracy of prediction gone, he felt he had to concede to Fuller and give him his way.

But then just as soon as he did it, he regretted having done it. He still couldn't abide the story.

So he didn't let go of the matter, either. Instead, in the course of the introduction he wrote for *The Best of Science Fiction* placing this unfamiliar sort of story in context, Conklin would express his discontent and hang a warning sign around the neck of "Solution Unsatisfactory."

He wrote genially, or almost genially. He said his say in bits and pieces, a little here and a little there. But he got it all out:

He said that science fiction was a branch of fantasy. It was an exercise of the imagination offered to readers as entertainment. Its value was that it took them to places they had never been before. But it wasn't prophecy except by accident or by appearance.

He wrote:

> That professional S-F writers (as they are familiarly known in the pulp-magazine trade) were able to write with some knowledgeability of the nature of atomic fission as far back as 1940 does not prove they had second sight. It only proves that they read the right science journals.

He said that Edmund Fuller was still his friend. But that he'd learned to like science fiction so well in the course of working on the book it sometimes seemed he was about to take over the project and run away with it. In the name of Crown Publishers, Fuller had forced "Solution Unsatisfactory" on him against his better judgment.

Conklin said he thought "Solution Unsatisfactory" was dangerous. He didn't want to endorse its power politics or to help the story come true. Reader take heed.

Edmund Fuller didn't—or else couldn't—keep Conklin from casting doubt on the opening story in his very own book. But neither was he willing to remove "Solution Unsatisfactory" from the anthology.

The answer he found was to invite John Campbell, the original editor of this story, to write a preface to put in front of Conklin's introduction to help offset the damage. And Campbell obliged him.

In his preface he too would discuss the nature of science fiction and talk specifically about "Solution Unsatisfactory."

Campbell said that some SF stories were simple adventure. Some like "Universe" were philosophical in nature. But some were prophecy, and "Solution Unsatisfactory" was a Grade A example. He said he knew it had been read and discussed by physicists and engineers working on the Manhattan Project to build the Bomb.

The prophetic success of this story was no accident. A good science fiction writer armed himself with the facts. The author of this one had experience both as an engineer and as a politician and consequently knew what he was talking about. He recalled a conversation he'd had in 1942 with a friend who was fond of fantasy but didn't like science fiction. He specifically disliked "Solution Unsatisfactory."

John Campbell—who was founding editor of the fantasy magazine *Unknown* as well as editor of *Astounding*—said: "… this man felt an overwhelming pressure on the part of the author to convince him that the story was possible, and could happen, a driving sincerity that oppressed and repelled him."

His friend wanted his fantasy to stay fantasy. He didn't want his fantasy coming true, and "Solution Unsatisfactory" was more plausible than he was quite comfortable with.

Campbell concluded his preface by adding that "secrecy" was no answer to the existence of atomic weapons. Congressional Representatives—and, by implication, the reader, too—ought to study the Smyth Report on Atomic Energy.

This was a reference to "Atomic Energy for Military Purposes," an official report by Henry De Wolf Smyth released on the heels of the Bomb in August 1945 to inform the American public about atomic weapons in a properly authoritative way.

Campbell would show it to Edmund Fuller. And to further counter Groff Conklin's introductory comments, Fuller would see that "Solution Unsatisfactory" was preceded by three consecutive numbered paragraphs excerpted from the Smyth Report.

These prefatory paragraphs had not been published with the story when it originally appeared in 1941, of course. Neither would they be printed with the novelette when it was republished in the 1965 Heinlein collection, *The Worlds of Robert A. Heinlein*, or in the much larger 1980 version of this book, *Expanded Universe: The New Worlds of Robert A. Heinlein*. They were included in *The Best of Science Fiction* for the express purpose of contradicting Conklin and verifying the authority of "Solution Unsatisfactory."

The paragraphs said it was possible to extract deadly radioactive fission products and use them "like a particularly vicious form of poison gas."

And also, that while the United States had not pursued such a weapon itself, serious consideration had been given "to the possibility that the Germans might make surprise use of radioactive poisons, and accordingly, defensive measures were planned."

With this testimony that the US had thought of the possibility of something like the dust—although not exactly—and feared its use during the war, and even planned to defend against it—though Smyth didn't say how—there was reason to take the story that followed not merely as fantasy written for entertainment but to see it by the light of America's new atomic weapon and read it as serious prediction.

There would be two problems with this, however.

In the fall of 1945, it may have seemed obvious and overwhelming to read "Solution Unsatisfactory" as being about anticipation of the Bomb. But this take on the story was simply the perspective of a particular instant. Its power wouldn't last.

The postwar moment passed as all moments will. New headlines came along to replace the old ones, and the apparent predictive success of "Solution Unsatisfactory" would not be repeated by other science fiction stories. Gradually, the one-time impact of this story's fictional anticipation of the end of World War II wore off until the-same-but-not-the-same mirroring of a portion of the story by the end of the war came to seem more like a coincidence or a similarity or even a bit of trivia than the vindication of science fiction it had briefly appeared to be.

The second problem is that time would reveal that dirty bombs do not work. As tests by the US government have demonstrated, and *The Bulletin of the Atomic Scientists* has made a point of repeating, when radiological dust is spread by conventional explosives, more damage is done by the explosives than by the dust. Far from sterilizing a whole city, killing the entire population, at best it would only have a chance of triggering cancer in a few people. Most likely, it would blow away in the wind.

The main effect of a dirty bomb would be to cause fear.

15

DR. NO NO NO

THIS leaves one last interpretation of "Solution Unsatisfactory," on the face of it the most simple, obvious and complete. That's the way Groff Conklin, the leading anthologist of science fiction through the 1950s, saw the story.

According to this reading, "Solution Unsatisfactory" is about the rise to world domination of a ruthless man using K-O dust as his means.

That this could be what the story is about is something the narrator attempts to deny and obfuscate at every turn, from the opening where responsibility for the weapon is assigned to poor Estelle Karst and her medical dust, to the end where the villain of the piece is suggested to be the man who first made the bow and arrow and touched off a human arms race which hasn't ended yet. In either case, DeFries suggests it wasn't Manning who done it. He was just a victim of circumstance.

But, in fact, Manning's quest for absolute personal power is confirmed by every event in the story. It's Manning who brings the weapon into being. It's Manning who insists that it be used. It's Manning who asserts the necessity of a military dictatorship. It's Manning who draws up plans for seizure of power. And it's Manning who points to the Peace Patrol bombers in the sky over Washington and takes over the world.

It is this assumption of power by one man that is the politics that Conklin so abhorred. And he certainly wasn't wrong to believe that adopting Manning as a model of behavior could prove dangerous.

If a youngster of ten or twelve read "Solution Unsatisfactory" in its original appearance in *Astounding* in 1941 or in its favored position in *The*

Best of Science Fiction—someone like a young Donald Rumsfeld, say, or a Dick Cheney—and found it impressive, it's possible that he might grow up believing that special exemptions from ordinary honesty and decency are permitted to a wise and benevolent genius of hard sense who happens to know better than everyone else.

If such a reader of "Solution Unsatisfactory" were to rise to a position of power, the result could indeed be dangerous. From reading this story, he might have learned the mouthing of euphemisms and false pieties to divert attention from true intent, evasion of accountability for the consequences of one's actions, the breaking of solemn oaths, deliberate violation of the Constitution of the United States, the invitation of attack as an excuse to go to war, the institution of a permanent state of martial law in America, the use and threatened further use of horrific weapons in order to convince other countries not to make those weapons themselves, and the extralegal seizure of power.

However, when Groff Conklin suggested that behavior like this might be the politics of the author of "Solution Unsatisfactory," I don't believe he was right.

Robert Heinlein had a need to fly the flag and also an urge to revolt—both of these in the name of freedom. In the thirties, he'd been an active participant in Upton Sinclair's End Poverty in California campaign for governor, regarded by many as radical and socialist. In his later years, he was perceived as a libertarian and an extreme conservative.

It's not simple to pinpoint what his politics were in conventional terms. However, I cannot believe the revolutionary patriot present in Heinlein at all stages of his life, and not least at the time he wrote this story, would ever have permitted him to support a man like Clyde Manning.

"Solution Unsatisfactory" actually has no readily identifiable political content at all, just like Heinlein's postwar political operating manual *Take Back Your Government*, eventually published in 1992. Instead, in keeping with the conventions of pulp storytelling, which weren't prepared to alienate any part of an audience prepared to buy a copy of this month's magazine, there's an avoidance of specific political identification in any conventional sense in the story.

At every point that the subject of recognizable policies and affiliations might be brought up, DeFries finesses the issue:

What party does Manning represent in Congress? We aren't told. We aren't so much as given the compliant President's name, let alone his political orientation or which party he belongs to. And Manning offers the world no political program or direction beyond his own personal control of the dust.

Rather than resembling Hitler, Mussolini, or Stalin, or any other known dictator, Manning doesn't really seem a creature of politics at all. He's more a story figure. His nearest relatives are James Bond style super-villains ready to hold the world at ransom with threats of mass destruction if they aren't given all they demand by a chosen hour.

Though it might be frightening to imagine a man like Clyde Manning making himself dictator of the world—and even though this interpretation manages to account for more of the content of "Solution Unsatisfactory" than any of the other candidates proposed—there's something fundamentally implausible about it.

It takes a lot of special arrangement of circumstance, deliberate looking away, unlikely assistance, and handwaving to promote Major Clyde Manning from prematurely retired army officer to Big Cheese of the World, ruler of all.

And even if we should accept all the unlikeliness for the sake of the story and agree that someone like Clyde Manning really might succeed in putting himself in charge of everybody in the manner he's said to have done, we have to wonder by what means he would be able to hold on to power and for how long?

He's a solitary figure. Unless some remnant of the Peace Patrol chooses to support him, Manning has no military muscle to enforce his will. He has no secure base of operations. He has no economic foundation or political allies. Everyone in the world hates him. He has no successor, and his future lifespan is limited.

Not an unstressful set of circumstances for a man with a bad heart, and a situation that is destined to come to an end in pretty short order.

In fact, if Manning doesn't drop dead from the strain of it all, in all likelihood there are enraged common men brandishing slide rules and monkey wrenches at the gates of his castle even as we speak.

It seems that one way or another, shortly after this story ends, the breach of normal reality that is Manning is destined to go *poof* and disappear.

PART FIVE: SOLVING THE RIDDLE

16  NOTHING CAN BE BELIEVED

WE'RE left with an enigma. If on examination, each and every one of the various attempts to take "Solution Unsatisfactory" at face value proves to have been partial at best—deliberately misleading, an unsatisfactory solution, the perception of one particular moment, or just a bogeyman—what makes this story so hard to pin down? What did the author intend by it?

Let's begin by recognizing that "Solution Unsatisfactory" is not on the level. It may have a believable surface, filled with the promise of testimony from someone who ought to know. And it may be told in a confident manner, with authoritative-sounding detail buttressed by historical references and some true scoop. But that's all window dressing.

As we've seen, the teller of this tale is a liar. Beneath his presentation of himself as an ordinary man who just happens to have been a conveniently-placed witness to important historical events, DeFries is in fact nothing less than Manning's chief henchman.

And the story he has to tell is about a man who can't be trusted. Manning betrays everyone he deals with. If he isn't actually the Father of Lies, he's a master of deceit. He's able to lie six different ways in a single breath. We've seen him do it.

But it's not only the narrative voice and the central character of "Solution Unsatisfactory" that are deceptive. False speaking is built into the very bones of this story as a principle of its construction. It opens with that flurry of lies about Dr. Karst. It closes with an assurance of Manning's personal regret we have no reason to believe and every reason to doubt. In between, it's filled with one untruth after another.

One tipoff to the consciously fraudulent nature of "Solution Unsatisfactory" is the series of job promotions that enable Manning to do his dirty work. Each is unlikely, and every one of them is accomplished by a wave of the hand.

Reluctantly, Congressman Manning has command of the atomic weapons program thrust upon him: "But it *was* possible, and Manning agreed to it after the Chief of Staff presented his case."

Col. Manning morphs into Secretary of Dust: "By this time Manning was an unofficial member of the Cabinet …"

The completely unauthorized yet unaccountably powerful Manning is made the initial member of the World Safety Commission: "… Colonel Manning became Mr. Commissioner Manning."

And Commissioner Manning becomes undisputed military dictator of the world: "… for practical purposes, that's all there was to the *coup d'état*."

All it takes is a wink and a nod, and he's on to the next higher station of power.

In a similar fashion, the key facts and crucial persuasive statements in "Solution Unsatisfactory" are hidden away behind gloss-over phrases that assume the existence of some improbable result without bothering to tell us how such a thing could ever happen.

The King of England speaks to the British people and advises them to surrender: "In this greatest crisis in his reign, his voice was clear and unlabored; it sold the idea to England and a national coalition government was formed."

New York is duped into evacuating itself:

> And then, there was the plague scare. I don't know how or when Manning could have started that—it certainly did not go through my notebook—but I simply do not believe that it was accidental that a completely unfounded rumor of bubonic plague caused New York City to be semi-deserted at the time the E.U. bombers struck.

And the Cabinet Officers give in to Manning's desire to run the world: "They came around."

"Solution Unsatisfactory" is a series of straight-faced whoppers covered over by a plausible line of misdirective patter. It's made out of contradictions, unlikelihoods and impossibilities, exaggerations for effect, sleights of hand, and bait-and-switch, with new lies standing on the shoulders of the lies that came before.

Could it really be possible for a freshman congressman to be instantly transformed into a colonel, be placed in charge of an urgent weapon development program, and then be left to his own devices with no limit on funds and no supervision?

If we're supposed to believe that nuclear weapons are so esoteric that Manning can be billed as the only person in the United States capable of developing them, how is it that the Eurasian Union manages to have huge quantities of the dust at the same time the Americans do, and that everyone else is going to have it within three months? If it was all that obvious and inevitable, why wasn't poor Manning just left at peace in Congress?

How about an army colonel walking into the Oval Office on an urgent appointment made at a day's notice for a half hour alone with the President, and then emerging two-and-a-half hours later with a glassy-eyed President ready to atomically sterilize Berlin to end a war the US isn't fighting?

Is it likely that a King of England would ever pay a petitionary visit to a US Army captain seated atop a throne of canisters in a secret underground airplane hangar and strike a bargain with him there to surrender British sovereignty to the United States in exchange for sufficient Devil Dust to take out the city of Berlin?

And just imagine an army officer with no official standing except his concurrent status as a Congressional Representative assuming control of a Cabinet meeting after the President has introduced this unknown person with a flash of his trademark grin and the announcement, "This is Clyde Manning, everybody. Clyde is my new Secretary of Dust. I want you to give a listen to him. He can be very persuasive," with the colonel then proceeding to insist that the Constitution be trashed, and a military dictatorship imposed on the world.

Would the Cabinet really fall in line behind Manning and this new policy? Isn't that a whopper? I hope it is.

And could it really be possible for the wording of a pamphlet to be so compelling that a country like Japan would surrender without a fight rather than permit its citizens to read it?

How ever so much better the dropping of that kind of pamphlet on Germany would have been than dropping the dust. We have to wonder why pamphlets like that aren't written all the time as a substitute for war and as a sufficient answer to the existence of the likes of Clyde Manning.

There is a name for stories that have a superficial appearance of plausibility but an underlying content that begs to be doubted. I think "Solution Unsatisfactory" was a hoax, a deliberate attempt to trick the reader and trick the reader again.

This is a story that doesn't mean what it seems to say. It isn't sincere about its lies, either.

The truth it has to tell is hidden.

17

THE TRUTH THAT COULD NOT BE SPOKEN

WAS Robert Heinlein really capable of playing mind games of this kind?

At the time, it wouldn't have seemed likely. Except for one short story in *Astounding*, "And He Built a Crooked House," a bit of foolery in which a California hillside house folds into a fourth-dimensional shape after an earthquake, and another story in *Unknown* entitled "They," in which ordinary reality is a falsity constructed to keep the protagonist distracted, the pre-war Robert Heinlein had an air of being a very solid and reliable writer. He was the author of interconnected Future History stories for *Astounding*—fiction that was sincere and straightforward.

The actuality was a bit different, however.

Robert Heinlein, writer of dependable stories, was not only responsible for the work of Anson MacDonald as well, but of even stranger writers for Campbell.

He was capable of many things that could not be contained within the bounds of the Future History. Over the course of his career, he would write some very unstraightforward stories:

There was Heinlein's final story for John Campbell before joining the war effort, the 1942 John Riverside fantasy short novel, "The Unpleasant Profession of Jonathan Hoag," in which our world is suggested to be a promising but flawed piece of art destined for dismantling—but we will never find out for certain because the story ends first.

In 1958, there would be the Möbius strip short story, "All You Zombies," in which a person is both mother and father to her/himself and the existence of the rest of us is a matter of doubt.

And in Heinlein's longest work of fiction, *The Number of the Beast* (1980), the book is full of anagrams and puzzles, the realms of the imagination are countless, and the author is ultimately revealed as a persistent intruder in his own story, a mysterious figure who keeps causing turmoil for the four central characters.

For someone with a head full of ideas like these, it was perfectly possible to craft a pseudo-realistic story that concealed a hoax which served to divert attention from the unspoken ending of the story, all in order to obscure a truth he wasn't willing to speak directly.

The inevitable ending of the story from which DeFries' lies distract us is that all of Manning's actions have been dedicated to bringing ultimate catastrophe into being and making it happen. When his work on earth is through at last and he finally dies—which could happen just as soon as DeFries finishes speaking and we're done feeling sympathy for poor Manning—all hell is going to break loose.

If Manning's long-term goals are fulfilled, three-quarters of humanity will perish with him and for those who survive, life will be much more simple.

Alteration in American foreign policy can't avert this. A monopoly on the weapon counts for nothing. Elite international peace patrolmen aren't sufficient to prevent it. Nor will one tough-minded man keeping watch over mankind guard us from harm. It will happen.

Manning's culminating evil act, after first conjuring up the means for disaster to occur and demonstrating its awfulness, and then seizing dominion over the world, will take place at the proper dramatic moment. Then his hands will uncup and, like the opening of a new Pandora's box, unleash the irrevocable power of death upon you and me, our neighbors, every human, every animal, and every living thing.

That's what's going to happen because that is what has been set up to happen.

Like every other crucial turn in this story, however, we won't read about it when it does. The Devil Dust will begin to drop only after the music for Manning has stopped playing and the curtain has fallen.

That's a bitter conclusion to hide. But it's the way this story really goes—the story, being what it is, will probably be played out in terms of a free-for-all among nations paying off old scores and scrabbling for power using the dust they've been cooking up all this time in the secret labs the Peace Patrol was never able to find while there still was a Peace Patrol.

But why tell this implicit story under cover of a narrative that doesn't mean what it says and isn't willing to say what it does mean?

An epigraph from George Bernard Shaw in Heinlein's next-to-last novel, *The Cat Who Walks Through Walls*, declares: "The truth is the one thing nobody will believe."

As though in illustration of this, "Universe," written just prior to "Solution Unsatisfactory" and published under Heinlein's square writing name in the May 1941 *Astounding*, was about a man who attempts to tell the truth to his society and is sentenced to death for doing it.

Robert Heinlein had been keeping clipping files of news stories on technological change and social behavior since 1930. After doing this for ten years, I think he believed himself to be in possession of a truth that John Campbell and the readers of *Astounding* wouldn't want to hear. It was so contrary to the mythos of the magazine that if by chance they did take in what he really had to say, he thought he would be made to pay for having spoken.

The unacceptable truth he saw was that the ability of society to produce new and ever more powerful technology had already reached a point that tested the capacity of fallible human beings to deal with. And sooner or later devices of our own making that were too much for us were going to escape our control and come back to haunt us.

During the course of 1940, he'd pointed to this fatal human weakness in "The Roads Must Roll" and "Blowups Happen"—stories which had pull-the-punch endings in which human frailty is overset, and control is reestablished, but unconvincingly.

In "The Roads Must Roll," a striking workforce deliberately brings a moving highway to an abrupt stop, causing horrendous casualties. When the man in charge of the road tries to cope with the emergency, he comes very near to cracking:

"He had carried too long the superhuman burden of kingship—which no sane mind can carry light-heartedly—and was at this moment perilously close to the frame of mind which sends captains down with their ships."

The answer ultimately found to the clash between advanced technology and human vulnerability pointed to by the story is pure whistling-in-the-dark: "Supervision and inspection, check and recheck was the answer."

Supervision and inspection, check and recheck would be the starting condition in "Blowups Happen." Psychiatrists keep ordinary workers in the world's only atomic plant under close observation at all times, watching for any signs of unusual thought or behavior.

This time, instead of moving roadways adapted from the stories of H.G. Wells, the future technology involved would be something to which Heinlein gave serious credence and that genuinely unsettled him.

In "Blowups Happen," it's suggested that the Moon is the sterile ball we see today because of an atomic disaster long ago. If the atomic plant in this story should explode, the same thing could happen to Earth.

And in this story, someone in authority—one of the psychiatric observers—does flip out under the strain of the situation and deliberately tries to induce the disaster himself. But the catastrophe is averted by physically overpowering him at the last moment. An answer of a kind is then found in shutting down the plant and moving its operation into Earth orbit.

But this was no solution, either. Check and recheck might not be a sufficient answer to the underlying problem of human-monkey cleverness producing technology which even superior people aren't able to deal with without going down with their ship or blowing up—but out of sight, out of mind was no improvement. Human frailty remains.

It was in the wake of the publication of "Blowups Happen" in the September 1940 issue of *Astounding* that Heinlein wrote "Universe," a story about the difficulty of trying to convey truth to an audience that wasn't disposed to receive it.

Then he took a deep breath and wrote "Solution Unsatisfactory," in which he finally did let out the truth he saw, or something closer to it. But he did it under the protective cover of every straight faced lie he could tell.

The problem Heinlein perceived is given in the first lines of "Solution Un-satisfactory" before the lies begin: The invention of the airplane in 1903, followed by the splitting of the atom in 1938.

Heinlein thought of himself as someone who could look out of a moving train, see another train coming towards them on the same track and predict a collision. And it was his conclusion that the combination of airplane and atom must inevitably lead to the delivery of atomic weapons from afar. In the worst-case scenario so cheerfully set forth in passing by DeFries, county-flattening A-Bombs would be sent by rocket—American, by preference.

If "Solution Unsatisfactory" can be said to be truly prescient about anything, it is nuclear proliferation. Heinlein imagined a coming world like a saloon full of drunken cowboys packing six shooters. "All offense and no defense," as Manning says to DeFries.

That was the situation Heinlein foresaw in 1940. And eighty years later, this scenario has yet to be played out to its conclusion.

The character of Manning was just Heinlein's device for dramatically fore-shortening the coming state and then getting out of the story clean with plausible deniability before the moment when everything goes to hell.

And even so, in order to indicate his dark truth at all, Heinlein had to bury the bone deep:

He placed a false title on the piece. He disguised it as a memoir told years later. He phrased it as a bunch of lies. He threw in misdirection at the beginning and the end. He set up the collapse of civilization to happen and then closed things down fast before it did.

And then, he published the story under a pseudonym.

18

JOHN CAMPBELL'S RESPONSE

WE can say it again—no wonder the editor of *Astounding* chose to call Heinlein's novelette "Solution Unsatisfactory."

John W. Campbell, Jr. was a man with insight into the nature and meaning of the stories that he published in his magazines. He didn't say everything he thought; a good many of the things that he did say were for effect, and, as the preface to *The Best of Science Fiction* demonstrates, he was perfectly capable of putting forth more than one idea about "Solution Unsatisfactory" at a time.

I think he understood more of the story's true nature than he was ready to admit.

So why, then, did he buy and publish a story like this that came to him with a deliberately misleading title, that didn't satisfactorily resolve the situation it presented, and that was full of lies to boot?

The most obvious reason was that he had to.

In order to fill the pages of his magazines every month, the editor needed at least one professional writer he paid at a better rate in order to guarantee himself a regular supply of copy. L. Ron Hubbard, who would eventually found Scientology but who was then an all-purpose pulp story writer, was the first to serve this role. And Hubbard did an adequate job of it for three years until he joined the Naval Reserve and then was called to active duty in 1941.

During the summer of 1940, Campbell came to a similar professional understanding with Robert Heinlein. Heinlein was the most able and reliable of the new writers he'd drawn to *Astounding* and *Unknown*, far better at playing the editor's game than the man he would replace.

But while Heinlein may have been the logical candidate for the job, the arrangement would be an insecure one from the outset.

With the check for "Blowups Happen," Heinlein had paid off his mortgage, the reason he gave for having taken up story writing in the first place. So when Campbell offered to buy all the work he could supply at his best rate, he agreed—but with a proviso. He would turn out copy only as long as the editor accepted everything that he sent him. If Campbell should ever reject one of his stories, Heinlein was through.

Consequently, Campbell didn't have much choice when Heinlein sent him "Foreign Policy." He had to buy it whether he liked it or not if he wanted Heinlein to continue to write for him.

And there were a number of things about the story the editor didn't like. The title didn't work. And he wasn't satisfied with the abrupt ending. In the ordinary way of things, he'd have returned a story like that to the writer and asked him to finish it properly—except he wasn't able to do it.

And he also couldn't help but notice that it was full of deliberate lies.

"Foreign Policy" must have seemed like a test of their relative power by Heinlein, a deliberate attempt to use his new-found leverage on the editor and see how much he could get away with.

However, during the Golden Age, John Campbell was highly creative. And he didn't choose to contend with Heinlein. That would come later.

Instead, like the dervish who picked up a coconut a monkey threw at him, drank the milk, ate the meat, and shaped what remained into a bowl, he found things to do with this story.

Heinlein may have been intentionally acting as a devil's advocate in writing "Foreign Policy" and forcing it on him. But the editor didn't have to take it negatively. In order for modern science fiction to address future problems, future problems had to be identified.

So Campbell changed the title of Heinlein's story from "Foreign Policy" to "Solution Unsatisfactory," and by doing it redefined the novelette as a problem in need of an answer. He altered the fact that it wasn't satisfactorily resolved from an intolerable omission into the focus of the story.

Then in the "In Times to Come" spot, the last item he completed for the April issue of *Astounding*, Campbell spelled out explicitly for his readers that "Solution Unsatisfactory," the Anson MacDonald story that would be appearing the following month, was incomplete and invited them to do what the author hadn't been able to do. He wrote:

> Read the yarn, and let's have your suggestions as to how to get a satisfactory solution that does not involve either, (a), a dictatorship and a super-police force of the most ruthless and autocratic

kind imaginable to preserve any remnant of civilization as we know it, or, (b), a chaos ending only when the simplest industrial facilities—even the one-man shop—have been wiped out.

The editor would print two responses to his challenge, one in the July 1941 issue, the other in November, both from the same reader, L.M. Jensen of Cowley, Wyoming.

In his first letter, Jensen said, "Every person must believe *beyond any possibility of doubt* they are being 'watched' and curbed continually by a superbeing."

In other words, "God help us all!"

In his second letter, Jensen said, "It will be a race to determine whether society can advance to the point where it can take care of itself before such a weapon is invented."

There was one more thing that Campbell would do.

Two days before Christmas 1940, he had a writing conference with his young story writing apprentice, Isaac Asimov. At that point, Asimov had only managed to sell to him three times, most recently "Reason," a story about an uppity robot he was running in the April issue.

The editor had been giving thought to this story, and he wasn't comfortable with the idea of a rebellious robot. That was a prime example of human technology out of control.

Now Asimov, having sold him one robot story, had the idea for another. How about a robot that was telepathic?

Campbell answered by setting forth the fruit of his thinking—three laws of robotics he wanted Asimov to consider: First, a robot must not cause harm to humans or allow them to be harmed. Second, it must follow human orders. After that, but only after that, a robot must preserve its own existence.

If fallible human beings weren't up to the job of guarding themselves against their own technology, then build the technology to do the job for them.

The editor asked Asimov to imagine what a telepathic robot bound by these rules might find it necessary to tell lies about, and asked what would happen if it did lie, and sent Asimov home to write a story.

So when Campbell came to assemble the May issue of *Astounding* it would be no accident but more in the nature of a covert editorial comment when in between Heinlein's two novelettes—one about the perils of knowing the truth and revealing it and the other which told the truth in a way the author pretended he didn't mean—he placed a story called "Liar!"

Though Asimov had no way of knowing it, his story would serve as a response to "Solution Unsatisfactory" twice over—once calling it for the lies it told and again addressing the problem of uncontrolled technology it didn't resolve.

But Campbell wasn't done. Fourteen months after the publication of Heinlein's novelette, he published a second fictional reaction to it by A.E. van Vogt, the most visionary of his new contributors and Heinlein's successor as his contract writer, as the lead story in the July 1942 issue of *Astounding*.

The editor would call no attention to what he was doing except for the title of van Vogt's story, which echoed the title Campbell had placed on Heinlein's novelette.

Just like "Solution Unsatisfactory," "Secret Unattainable" took place during the current war and had a "realistic" form. But instead of being a memoir, it was presented as a file of documents captured from the Germans after the war was over.

These documents detail the promising beginning and the catastrophic outcome of a super-scientific project designed by a scientist named Kenrube—the building of a machine to bridge hyperspace and produce limitless quantities of raw materials to fuel the German war effort.

But when the full-scale version of the machine is demonstrated, it behaves contrary to expectation, and there's a disaster. Many people are killed, and the Fuehrer himself barely escapes with his life.

Professor Kenrube anticipated that something like this would happen and counted on it to happen. He explains:

> My invention does not fit into our civilization. It's *the next*, the coming age of man. Just as modern science could not develop in ancient Egypt because the whole mental, emotional, and physical attitude was wrong, so my machine cannot be used until the thought structure of man changes.

Kenrube appears mysteriously at the scene of the catastrophe as it is unfolding even while being held a prisoner elsewhere. Here he reveals that his machine will only do unanticipatable, incomprehensible, and undesirable things for the Germans: "It is not that the machine has will. It reacts to laws, which you must learn, and in the learning, it will reshape your minds, your outlook on life. It will change the world."

The answer offered by van Vogt to the problem of coping with the dangers of technological advance set forth by Heinlein in "The Roads Must Roll," "Blowups Happen," and "Solution Unsatisfactory" was that the time has come for us to move on to the next age of man, and the catalyst for this will be nothing other than our own advanced technology and the problems it poses.

In a new era, when people have learned to think, feel, and act differently, Devil Dust and rolling roads will become as irrelevant and outmoded as chariots, mummies, and pyramids and be left behind.

But if Kenrube's actual purpose is to stimulate this kind of change, we're offered reason to think again about Clyde Manning.

It's true that Manning in "Solution Unsatisfactory" deliberately presents people with science-beyond-science that causes catastrophe—but that's also what Kenrube does in "Secret Unattainable." Kenrube doesn't even claim that what he's doing *has to* be done to end the war. He's certain that the Nazis are going to lose in any event because of the way they think and act.

And if it's true that Manning is a traitor, so also is Kenrube. Any distinction between them is only a matter of partisanship and point of view. Professor Kenrube has our sympathy because he betrays the Nazis, the bad guys of World War II, while we're more ready to point a finger at Colonel Manning because it's the United States of America that he turns on.

But both of these men are traitors to their national governments, and both men cause disasters with super science. The difference is that Manning is deadly serious about what he's doing and is willing to kill three-quarters of humanity to see it done, while Kenrube is out to make a point and sow a seed for tomorrow.

However, if Kenrube is ultimately to be applauded for what he does because his underlying motive is to change the way people think and stimulate a transition to a new age of man, then Manning may be entitled to the same benefit of the doubt.

If what Manning is doing isn't merely sparking a change from one era to the next but providing the necessary provocation for an even more radical transformation in the human condition to take place, then perhaps he might not merely be a mad dog, or the Devil in disguise, or the living representative of the dangerous consequences of modern technology after all, but might actually be the misunderstood genius that DeFries claims him to be.

It all depends on what he is aiming for.

We might consider this: In the last story that he contributed to *Astounding* in June 1937 before becoming editor of the magazine, John Campbell himself pointed to the sort of human development that might be sufficient to justify a Manning and earn him forgiveness for what he does.

In "Forgetfulness," an expedition of aliens not too different from ourselves lands on a far future Earth after an interstellar voyage that has taken them six years. Here they discover abandoned crystalline cities with machines they can't understand, but which they recognize as the work of the godlike beings who long ago brought them fire.

Nearby, they find the descendants of these city builders living simple lives in domed houses set amongst the trees. They no longer recall how the cities and machines were made. Atomic power means nothing to them.

The invaders determine to move these fallen creatures out of the way, take possession of the cities, and recover the lost secrets of the machines.

But in fact, our descendants are not degenerate; they've moved on. Humanity abandoned the cities and machines because it no longer had need of them.

Anything they have to do now, they're able to do with mind. And by mental power alone, they're able to instantly send the invaders back where they came from.

One invader explains to the others:

> Seun is not a decadent son of the city builders. His people never forgot the dream that built the city. But it was a dream of childhood, and his people were children then. Like a child with his broomstick horse, the mind alone was not enough for thought; the city builders, just as ourselves, needed something of a solid metal and crystal to make their dreams tangible.

John Campbell's ultimate answer to the threat posed to our existence by our own artifacts was that mankind needs to grow up and leave its crude childhood toys behind. Growing up is the only satisfactory solution to Heinlein's nightmare of self-induced human disaster there can be.

Whether we will be able to do it has yet to be seen.

AFTERWARD

19  AFTER THE BOMB

ROBERT Heinlein wouldn't go back to writing for *Astounding* after World War II. Instead, he sought to break free of the confines of the pulps and working for John Campbell to find less specialized and better-paying markets for what he wrote. Sometimes he would be successful, sometimes not.

One thing he did in the immediate aftermath of the war was to produce one article after another—by his own count as many as nine—warning of the dangers of a nuclear world and how they might be survived. But he wasn't able to sell any of them.

In two of these articles eventually included in *Expanded Universe*, Heinlein recommended that people leave the large population centers and head for the hills. Heeding his own advice, he moved from California to the mountain town of Colorado Springs, Colorado.

However, in due time, he would be followed to Colorado Springs by the North American Air Defense Command, which located itself inside Cheyenne Mountain immediately next door. The place he had selected as a refuge from the Bomb became the number one nuclear target in the United States.

Heinlein would respond by building and stocking a fallout shelter. He recommended that others do the same.

FALLING DOWN
A RABBIT HOLE

1

PICTURE YOURSELF IN A BOAT ON A RIVER

ON Friday afternoon, July 4, 1862, a rowing party left Oxford to go on an outing up the Thames River. At the forward set of oars, dressed in white flannels and a straw boater, was Charles Dodgson, a thirty-year-old lecturer in mathematics. Rowing as well was his friend, Robinson Duckworth, another Oxford fellow. Their passengers, seated at the bow and stern of the gig, were the three young Liddell girls, daughters of the Dean of Christ Church, the college where Dodgson taught.

The eldest, Lorina, who was thirteen, demanded that Dodgson tell them a story as he'd often done before. The middle sister, ten-year-old Alice, Dodgson's special favorite, seconded the request more nicely. And she asked that the story have nonsense in it.

In most situations, Charles Dodgson was an intensely inhibited man. He hid out from life in his teaching position which required him to take nominal religious vows and remain unmarried. He was meticulous and proper and feared ridicule. When he had to talk to adults, he stammered, and the opinions he expressed were always conservative and conventional. Some of his students thought he was the most boring teacher they'd ever had.

But there was another side to this man that could be brought out by a young girl encouraging him to talk nonsense. He didn't stammer then. Instead, he became capable of saying anything at all that popped into his head.

This is a rare gift. Most people aren't able to place everything they're sure they know on hold and then just make stuff up, saying whatever outrageous, unlikely, or impossible thing happens to fly off the tongue next. But this shy young man, who ordinarily found speaking so difficult that his very fear of being made fun of turned him into a figure of fun, was practiced at doing this for the right sort of audience.

Charles Lutwidge Dodgson had grown up in relative social isolation as the third child and eldest son of a country parson. He was a precocious boy who took his greatest pleasure in entertaining his seven sisters and three younger brothers. He set up a railroad line in the garden with stations and tickets. He dressed up as a sorcerer in a brown wig and white robes and did magic for them. And he built a marionette theater where he performed puppet plays that he wrote himself.

Over a period of time, from 1845 to this very year of 1862, he even produced a series of magazines by hand for his family featuring his own drawings and writings. The last of these, a scrapbook entitled *Mischmasch*, included a so-called "Stanza of Anglo-Saxon Poetry" written when he was twenty-three. It went:

> *Twas bryllyg, and the slythy toves*
>   *Did gyre and gymble in the wabe:*
> *All mimsy were the borogoves;*
>   *And the mome raths outgrabe*

His explanation of this, after learned definitions of all the strange words, was: "Hence the literal English of the passage is: 'it was evening, and the smooth active badgers were scratching and boring holes in the hill-side; all unhappy were the parrots; and the grave turtles squeaked out.'"

To this, he added:

> There were probably sundials on the top of the hill, and the "borogoves" were afraid that their nests would be undermined. The hill was probably full of the nests of "raths," which ran out, squeaking with fear, on hearing the "toves" scratching outside. This is an obscure yet deeply affecting relic of ancient poetry.

Nonsense like this was a nineteenth century amusement in which a recognizable form of some kind—such as a stanza of poetry—was filled in with an absurd content. Here, for example, is a mock letter that was sent to a friend in this same year of 1862 by one of the acknowledged masters of nonsense, the gentleman artist Edward Lear:

Thrippsy pillivinx,

Inky tinky pobblebockle abblesquabs?—Flosky! Beebul trimble flosky!—Okul scratchabibblebongibo, viddle squibble tog-a-tog, ferrymoyassity amsky flamsky ramsky damsky crocklefether squiggs,

Flinkywisty pomm,
Slushypipp

It is obvious that this stuff is being invented even as it is being written. The shape, the sound, and the rhythms are all familiar—but whatever does it mean? Is it just tomfoolery? Is it funny? Or is it deeply critical of all meaningless formalities and ritualistic phrases and that aspect of society that, above all, wanted the proper appearances to be observed?

The Victorians didn't press these questions. It was sufficient that the nineteenth century was a period in which a certain limited exercise of the imagination had become socially acceptable. Adults might play parlor games, novels were read aloud to the family, and the professional houseguest like Lear or the Oxford don like Dodgson who was able to do it was given leave to utter extravagant and untrue things for the amusement of children.

Nonsense was outside ordinary rules. By its very name, it was acknowledged to be harmless inconsequential fun. Not sense. Nonsense.

Dodgson came by this form of verbal play honestly. His own father was someone who had a taste for nonsense. When Charles was eight, for instance, Rev. Dodgson had traveled to Leeds, and his son made a special request that a file, a screwdriver, and a ring be bought for him there. In the course of the journey, his father wrote to young Charles detailing the hubbub and uproar that would follow if the city should fail to comply with this commission:

> Then what a bawling & a tearing of hair there will be! Pigs & babies, camels & butterflies, rolling in the gutter together—old women rushing up the chimneys & cows after them—ducks hiding themselves in coffee cups, & fat geese trying to squeeze themselves into pencil cases—at last the Mayor of Leeds will be found in a soup plate covered up with custard & stuck full of almonds to make him look like a sponge cake that he may escape the dreadful destruction of the Town.

In order to write nonsense like this, a certain confidence in nonsense is required. There must be trust that the spontaneous flow of oddly juxtaposed objects and whimsical events or of made-up words that sound as though they should refer to familiar objects but don't is going to take care of itself and come out right.

It might very well come out wrong. Nonsense is fragile and ambiguous. There is always a risk when talking nonsense of having the wind taken out of your sails by someone who just doesn't want to play this game, or of being understood a little too well and causing offense, or simply of sounding like some babbling idiot and leaving your audience shaking its head.

The imaginative young Charles Dodgson faced his own measure of incomprehension. In his teen years, he was sent off to boarding school in the manner typical of his class. Scholastically, he did well there, but the creative side of his nature got stuffed at Rugby.

In this place where the future masters of the growing British Empire came to learn how to dominate each other and excel at sports, he had much of the nonsense knocked out of him. During his time at school, Dodgson became fixed in the shy, over serious, stammering public persona that he would display throughout his adult years.

And yet he didn't lose all touch with his former playfulness. When he first left Rugby, it wasn't immediately possible for him to take up residence at Oxford, so he spent a year studying at home. During that time, he produced *The Rectory Umbrella*, his most ambitious and creative homemade magazine yet, for the eyes of his family.

While he was at Oxford, he continued to write as he could. Eventually he began to accumulate the scrapbook of his best new work which would become *Mischmasch*.

In 1854, his last year as an undergraduate, Dodgson contributed two poems to a short-lived Oxford advertising sheet. And during his long vacation that year, he published a poem and a story in a local newspaper. But, as he would note in the diary he had begun to keep, he didn't count these as "real publication."

He had hopes for better. He began submitting material to *Punch*, the premier humor magazine of the day, but with no success.

Then, in the summer of 1855, Frank Smedley, a novelist who was the cousin of a cousin of his father, proposed to him that he should contribute to a new humorous weekly, the *Comic Times*, which was about to commence publication. Dodgson, who had now become a tutor at Oxford, sent Smedley a travesty of some lines in Thomas Moore's Romantic poem *Lalla Rookh* that *Punch* had previously turned down.

His humorous verse was published in the second issue of *Comic Times*. During the four months the publication lasted, Dodgson contributed to it four times. And when it folded and was succeeded by a monthly called *The Train*, he wrote for that, too, even though its hopes of ability to actually pay contributors never came to anything.

At first, he tried to hide behind the false initials "B.B." His editor, Edmund Yates, suggested that he adopt a pen name instead. Dodgson proposed "Dares." That was short for Daresbury, the town in Cheshire where he was born. It may also have been an indication that he intended to follow an unconventional line of development.

The editor replied that this name had too much of the appearance of a typical newspaper signature and asked him to try again. So Dodgson offered Yates four possibilities. Two of them were anagrams of Charles Lutwidge, and two were Latinized versions of his first two names. The editor passed over the likes of "Edgar Cuthwellis" and settled upon his final suggestion, "Lewis Carroll." Henceforth, that would be the name he would use for all the stories, poems, and puzzles he would publish.

However, professional acceptance of his writing wasn't enough to satisfy Dodgson. He also felt a continuing urge to be visually creative.

He tried sending *Comic Times* humorous drawings he'd done for *Mischmasch*. But contrary to his expectation, the paper didn't use his pictures. Instead, it rejected them, saying they were "not up to the mark." At this point, Dodgson, who could be extraordinarily sensitive to any hint of rebuff, determined he wouldn't send any more drawings to the publication.

That didn't mean he was ready to accept this assessment of his artwork as final, however. In October 1857, he noticed John Ruskin, an Oxford don who was the best-known art critic of the day and whose opinions he respected, having breakfast in the Christ Church Common Room. Dodgson took advantage of this unusual opportunity. He overcame his shyness enough to show his drawings and ask for an opinion. Ruskin looked them over and, as nicely as he could, told him that he lacked sufficient talent to make sketching worth his time.

This was a blow. However, Dodgson was someone who had a stubborn nature and an active need to express himself in visual terms. He continued to produce his amateurish but amusing drawings anyway. And though he might drop all thought of professional publication of his artwork for the moment, such was the quiet persistence of this man that the day would eventually come when he would arrive at a way for his drawings to be seen by a wider audience.

However, the immediate remedy that Dodgson found for the deficiencies of his draftsmanship was to develop an alternative. In the aftermath of his rejection by *Comic Times*, he took up another form of picture making, the recently created art of photography.

Like so many people of the mid-nineteenth century, Dodgson was deeply impressed by the technical advances of the era. In 1851, he attended the first international exhibit of modern technology in the Crystal Palace, an amazing new structure that enclosed and covered twenty acres of Hyde Park in London in iron and glass. He was awestruck by what he saw there. He wrote to his family: "I think the first impression produced on you when you get inside is one of bewilderment. It looks like a sort of fairyland."

For Dodgson, the innovations of the day were marvelous new toys. He would own and use an early typewriter. He would ride a velociman, an adult tricycle powered by hand, and give thought to how it might be improved. And he himself would invent a nyctograph, a device for taking notes in the dark.

Of all the man-made wonders of the age, however, it was photography that Dodgson loved first and loved best. Somehow it was the very essence of the new magic of technology that it had now become possible to project a view of the world through a lens onto a polished glass plate and capture it there in negative form with the aid of chemicals, and then by a further application of chemicals translate this image-in-reverse into a positive picture on paper.

Dodgson had first seen photographs on display in the fairyland of the Crystal Palace. But it wasn't until early in 1855 that it finally became feasible for an amateur enthusiast with the necessary time and money and patience to take pictures. And through the course of that year, he was persistently intrigued by this new possibility.

At last, in January 1856, Dodgson went to an exhibition of photographs that was being held in London. He came back the next day to see it again. The following week he wrote to a knowledgeable uncle asking for help in obtaining a photographic apparatus of his own.

It took some arranging, but that spring he managed to buy all the equipment that was necessary: A camera and a tripod for it to stand on, along with a chest of chemicals, and a portable dark tent for preparing and sensitizing photographic plates and then fixing and varnishing them after they had been exposed. Over the next twenty-five years, one of Dodgson's primary modes of dealing with the world would be crouched behind a camera, covered by a cloth drape, and peering through a lens.

He quickly became a skilled photographer—one of the best of his time—with a gift for taking pictures of people, especially youngsters willing to put on costumes and assume attitudes for him. Theater was a particular passion of his, and he applied ideas about composition and grouping he'd taken from observation of the stage to his photography.

Dodgson went through a period in which he was ready to presume upon the novelty of photography and his ability to take a good portrait in order to make the acquaintance of various eminent people of the day. And he would also use photography as a convenient reason to meet and make friends with children.

Having child friends—and there would be troops of them over the years—was absolutely necessary to him. All that seemed most worthwhile about human life, Dodgson identified with childhood. The first work that he published under the name Lewis Carroll was a poem he'd written when he was only twenty-one entitled "Solitude," which ended:

> *I'd give all wealth that years have piled,*
>   *The slow result of Life's decay,*
> *To be once more a little child*
>   *For one bright summer-day.*

In our time, a photographer with a fixation on little children might be suspected of harboring dubious sexual intentions. But that wasn't the nature of this man. Dodgson had both a keen awareness of social propriety and an exacting conscience. He went to lengths to be sure that all his interactions with the young were first approved by their parents. More important is that he was confident in his own mind that his relations with children were "innocent and right in the sight of God," as he put it in a letter to one of his sisters.

What he wanted from children was simple. He was looking for people to play with. He sought someone to think his nonsense was amusing, somebody who would do her best to answer a difficult question for him, or pose for a picture, or listen to him tell a story and respond to it.

One half of Dodgson's two-sided nature sustained the other. In his teen years, he had constructed his outward adult persona of stodgy, proper Do-do-dodgson, shy, sometimes exact to a fault, but earnest and reliable, in order to make a safe space within which his inner self—the part of him which loved nonsense, stories, and games and didn't want to ever give them up—might continue to function even though childhood was over. And the activities of this creative self—call it "Charles Lutwidge" or "Lewis Carroll"—went to make life tolerable for the otherwise constricted adult Dodgson.

But Charles Lutwidge was always and ever a boy. He needed to get out and play. That's why it would be Dodgson's practice whenever he set off on a train journey or went on vacation at the seaside to carry a black bag filled with puzzles and toys and other items of interest to the young and look for children to entertain.

Charles Lutwidge primarily sought his playmates where he'd found them in the days before the adult Dodgson was bound to the social wheel—among young girls. Although he did make friends in early days with a few boys, such as the eldest Liddell child, Harry, he would be much less fond of them. But then, when the time arrived that his young female friends reached the age of puberty and were no longer as eager to dress for the camera or figure out a brainteaser, he got out of their way and allowed them to move on with their lives while he discovered new friends who were the right age and temperament to like the things that he liked best.

When she was seventy, Enid Stevens, to whom Dodgson's final work of fiction is dedicated and who regarded herself as having been his last special child friend, said of him: "The truth of the matter is that he had the heart of a child himself, so when he spoke to a child she understood—even about the deeper things of life—because he spoke her own language."

Enid thought of him as a much-loved grandfather in the same way that earlier child friends had looked on him as a favorite uncle. Several times a week, Dodgson would "borrow" her to go on walks with him. He made up stories and songs to amuse her and played hide-and-seek with her among the chimney-pots on the roof above his rooms. He took her to the theater for the first time. And when she was cut off from all society for six weeks with scarlet fever, he wrote to her every day with a cipher, a puzzle, or a game.

Enid Stevens Shawyer would be speaking for more than one of his child friends when she said:

> I never realized—as I do now—what jewels were being poured out for my entertainment. I know now that my friendship with him was probably the most valuable experience in a long life and that it influenced my outlook more than anything that has happened since—and wholly for good.

Dodgson actively avoided all talk about his child's play and what it meant to him. The outer man—the mathematician, the don, the deacon—kept vulnerable, creative Charles Lutwidge shielded behind a wall of silence to protect him from the world at large.

In his autobiography, the American magazine editor Edward Bok tells of being introduced to Dodgson at Oxford and spending two delightful hours in his company. Bok was shown some of the college buildings, and they had lunch together. But first and last, Dodgson informed him, "You are not speaking to 'Lewis Carroll.'"

Even a long-time theatrical friend, the playwright Augustus Dubourg, in writing a brief appreciation of Dodgson following his death at the beginning of 1898, would conclude regretfully: "I may truthfully say that throughout much friendly intercourse with Charles Dodgson, the remembrance of which I value greatly, I never met that exquisite humorist, Lewis Carroll."

When he was with adults, Dodgson didn't even like to admit that he knew Lewis Carroll. He would refuse any mail for Carroll that was addressed directly to him at Oxford and not sent to him by way of his publisher. Since he laid no claim to that man's work, it was presumptuous for anyone to assume that it had anything to do with him.

Even in the diary that Dodgson kept for his own eyes, his play with children would hardly be mentioned. There is just one entry—for June 26, 1857, a day spent with the Liddell children at the Christ Church Deanery—in which it almost becomes possible to catch the outward Dodgson admitting his identity with that eternal boy, Charles Lutwidge:

> I had Alice and Edith with me till 12, then Harry and Ina till the early dinner at 2, which I joined, and all four children for the afternoon. The photographing was accordingly plentifully interspersed with swinging, backgammon, etc.
>
> I mark this day most specially with a white stone.

We should take note of both the rarity and the reticence of these remarks. Not only does that apparently casual "etc." contain the essence of everything that went to make this day a particularly special one for Dodgson, but it also must serve as the nearest thing we have to an expression by him of all the playtime activities he actually lived for but wasn't permitted to speak about.

We don't know what age he was when he first began to mark the days he found notable with a white stone. But it does seem like the sort of thing a boy in school might find to do. The days Dodgson singled out with a metaphorical white stone in his diary most often were spent with some young person.

There is only one single recorded occasion when Dodgson let down his barriers and allowed himself to talk frankly to someone about his association with children and what it meant to him. A student who had stopped by his rooms on business asked him—"incautiously"—if children never bored him, and Dodgson replied that he couldn't understand how anyone could be bored by small children.

He said that whenever he was weary of the world and too much thinking, play with children was like a tonic to his system. He told the student outright, "They are three-fourths of my life."

The Liddells were among the earliest child friends that he made outside his own extended family. He first met them in 1856, in the same spring season in which he took up the camera. Lorina was turning seven then, Alice was just short of four, and Edith was a toddler.

At the time of this afternoon excursion in July 1862, the Liddells were the children he saw most frequently. When the three girls went on this boat trip—which wasn't the first ride on the river this same party had taken that summer—it could seem to them that they had known Dodgson for as long as they could remember. So it was nothing at all new for Ina to ask him for a story, as she did that day. One of Dodgson's most successful modes of relating to the young was through storytelling. During his years of friendship with the Liddells, he'd told the children many a story.

It was a fairytale that Lorina specifically wanted to hear. That was the collective name Victorians gave to marvelous tales of magic and giants and talking animals.

In an earlier day, stories like this had been told to a general audience. But the men of the Age of Reason in the Western world, striving to be rational and shun all superstition, had no use for old wives' tales. When it became evident in the eighteenth century that children were not yet capable of reason, and the childhood state began to be set apart as a separate and distinct phase of human development, this sort of story had been abandoned to the young—not without considerable misgiving and objection—as something specially their own.

For the Victorians, the models of the fairytale were French stories like "Cinderella," "Puss in Boots," and "Sleeping Beauty" which had been written down by Charles Perrault at the end of the seventeenth century, the *Märchen* collected by the brothers Grimm in Germany, and the fantastic oriental stories of rocs and genies gathered in *The Arabian Nights*. Dodgson knew all of these, of course. Storybooks formed an important corner of his library.

When he told a fairytale, it could be something familiar like Hans Christian Andersen's "The Ugly Duckling." Or it might be a story about a strange talking beast that he'd invented himself. But Dodgson always had some wonderful narrative to enchant a child.

Many years later, as an old lady, Alice would remember:

He seemed to have an endless store of these fantastical tales, which he made up as he told them, drawing on a large sheet of paper all the time. They were not always entirely new. Sometimes they were new versions of old stories: Sometimes they started on the old basis but grew into new tales owing to the frequent interruptions which opened up fresh and undreamed of possibilities.

This picture of the man improvising a story, sketching to embellish the tale as he talked, and changing course in response to the promptings of his listeners is confirmed by Gertrude Chataway, who was an important child friend of Dodgson's a dozen years after this boat ride. After his death, she would recall:

> I had the usual child's love for fairy tales and marvels and his power of telling stories naturally fascinated me. We used to sit for hours on the wooden steps which led from our garden on to the beach, while he told me the most lovely tales that could possibly be imagined, often illustrating the exciting situations with a pencil as he went along.
>
> One thing that made his stories particularly charming to a child was that he often took his cue from her remarks—a question would set him off on quite a new trail of ideas, so that one felt one had somehow helped to make the story and it seemed a personal possession.

Charles Dodgson, Self Portrait, circa 1960s

2
LIFE IS BUT A DREAM

BUT that July day on the Isis, as they called the Thames at Oxford, Ina's command that Dodgson tell them a story and that he start it right then came to him as an intrusion.

Dodgson had fallen into a strange mood that afternoon. It may have been something about the quality of the summer light, with the sun playing with the trees and the river as they rowed along, that gave this particular moment a heightened clarity. It's possible, too, that "Row Row Row Your Boat," with its suggestion that life is only a dream, had come into his head. In any case, his state of mind that day on the water was such that next to the vividness of the present instant, life as he ordinarily knew it didn't seem altogether real to him.

At those times that he put on C.L. Dodgson's clerical hat and strove earnestly to live up to established expectation, conventional social life could be all too much of a reality. But not today. Compared to the immediacy of this floating moment on the Isis, the modern world was a distant dream ... Victorian England, a dream ... Oxford and Christ Church, just a dream.

So strong was the grip of this feeling, and so firmly associated with the day would it be for him, that nine years later, in recalling this moment in the acrostic poem spelling out Alice's full name, which ends *Through the Looking Glass*, he would conclude with the lines:

> *Ever drifting down the stream—*
> *Lingering in the golden gleam—*
> *Life, what is it but a dream?*

But if familiar life as he usually knew it seemed a dream to Dodgson just then, what was he able to take as real?

In every time and place, there have been people with a conviction that ordinary human social life isn't as substantial as it appears to most of those who live within it and that somewhere just beyond our grasp, there exists a realer reality that is more perfect and complete and closer to the essence of things. But mid-nineteenth century Europe, dedicatedly materialistic and fact-minded and intoxicated by the visible progress and power of modern Western civilization, was a particularly challenging cultural context within which to be otherworldly.

Dodgson had felt most in contact with another more wonder-filled order of existence when he was a boy living in an isolated country parsonage in Daresbury and his younger sisters and brothers were still very small or had yet to be born. Playing by himself, it seemed that anything that he could conceive might be true. That special feeling of being alive in a magical realm of infinite possibility was connected in his mind with the light of summer so that when he remembered his childhood, it could seem a "fairy dream" to him—"bright, beyond all imagining"—and he could long to be a child again on a beautiful summer day.

But as Dodgson had grown older and become enmeshed in the demands of the adult social world of time and obligation, the door to heightened experience that had been open to him as a little boy had begun to swing shut. If he sought out the company of children, it was because he valued their innocent truthfulness, their ability to love without reservation, and their immediate receptivity to novelty and wonder. He envied that openness, and he strove to keep the door to wonder ajar for himself through association with the freshness and honesty of the young.

It was more difficult for Dodgson to perceive a reality beyond the one he saw immediately around him when he was a grown-up living in Oxford within the shadow of the great city of London. However, he did manage to find two avenues that led from things as they presently were toward things as they potentially might be. These were the theater and photography.

As a newly independent Oxford don in 1855, during the same long vacation in which he began to write for *Comic Times* and also looked on while his Uncle Skeffington experimented with his recently acquired photographic equipment, Charles went to see a play. His father might expressly disapprove of the professional stage, but this was Shakespeare, and so Dodgson had the excuse that it was uplifting.

He found himself enchanted by what he saw. After that first experience, he declared that he'd never enjoyed anything so much in his life. He wrote in his diary: "I almost held my breath to watch; the illusion is perfect, and I felt as if in a dream all that time it lasted."

The theater offered him an opportunity to see beyond the visible surface of existence. It showed him things he couldn't ordinarily witness, and expressed thoughts and sentiments that his own uncertain tongue could never utter. He returned to the theater again and again, and he would continue to go as long as he lived. It was the public C.L. Dodgson's greatest rebellion against the authority of his father.

This form of adult imaginative play quickly became a necessity for him. Dodgson would find his way backstage and satisfy some of his curiosity about stage mechanics and effects. He would faithfully read and collect *The Theatre* from its first issue, and even contribute to the magazine himself. And he would form an important continuing friendship with Ellen Terry, a well-known young actress he had admired since she appeared as a child in two of the earliest plays he attended. Eventually, he'd even send several aspiring, talented young girls to live with her as dramatic apprentices.

The stage was so essential to Dodgson that if he had been asked to make a choice between his position at Christ Church and the theater—as for years he thought might happen—he was never certain which he would finally choose.

In a similar way, Dodgson was attracted to photography by the ability of a picture to reveal things that are not usually apparent. From an early moment, he recognized that it was possible for a well-composed photograph, taken with care and then effectively framed, to show a deeper level of human existence than the eye can normally perceive. He wanted to be able to do that himself.

Making a photograph at all in that era was a difficult and complex process, with each step subject to chance and mishap. Many of the pictures that Dodgson took failed. When he did manage to obtain a good likeness, true to the appearance and spirit of the sitter, he could count that a considerable success.

Every now and then, however, with the intervention of some mysterious element that he might hope for but could never control, the picture that Dodgson so painstakingly produced turned out to be something more than just an accurate representation of a particular person. His camera was able to penetrate beyond the specific details of the time and place and subject to capture an image that was eternal and enduring and not merely of the moment.

This rare result happened most often in photographs of children playing for the camera. He had taken at least three pictures of Alice Liddell that had this timeless quality—once dressed as a beggar child leaning against a wall, once sitting sideways pensively on a wooden chair outdoors, and once perched on a draped table with a potted fern to her right and an expression on her face that was innocent and trusting yet unfathomable.

But life also seemed to present Dodgson with barriers at every point, which baffled him and kept him at a distance from the wonder he sensed. He might try to hang onto the experiences and perceptions of his childhood, but he wasn't an innocent child any longer.

While he could remember what it was like to see things by a certain light, most of the time, he wasn't able to see things that way himself.

In his adult years, the theater or a photograph might still sometimes serve as a window into another order of reality for him. But between the audience and the wonders they witnessed on stage there was always an invisible gulf. And a photograph, even at its best, was an indirect image—like a view of freedom that a prisoner can glimpse in a carefully placed mirror, but never directly, and only when the light is right.

Dodgson often had difficulty sleeping at night, kept awake by questions and doubts. In those troubled hours, it was possible for him to feel that there was nothing of substance to any of the things he loved and that everything he cared about most deeply was only something he'd dreamed. The magic he'd experienced as a child and was able to perceive at times on the stage or in a photograph was completely intangible. It existed in memory or in the eye of the beholder. There was no way for Dodgson to prove it to anyone.

As time passed, his convictions on this score would only grow stronger. Eventually, he would declare: "My view of life is, that it is next to impossible to convince *anybody* of *anything*."

Dodgson's way of getting through his sleepless hours was to embrace the things he loved all the more strongly, simply because he loved them. Love—not mere sentiment or romantic love, but the genuine love of anything worthy—was a fact that held a central importance for him.

In his eyes, love had its own validity. It was an inner recognition that was true simply because it existed. He aimed to live by "the spirit of a maxim I once came across in an old book, 'Whatsoever thy hand findeth to do, *do it with thy might*.'"

That was a lesson to be learned from children. They had the natural gift of loving whatever they found to love uncritically and wholeheartedly. To those able to emulate the young, he would suggest that "the best work a man can do is when he works for love's sake only, with no thought of name, or gain, or earthly reward."

The object of this love might be anything that lifted the spirit. Dodgson loved the look of the light at that moment in the boat on the river. Something in him stirred to see it. Its bright golden gleam was like a knock on the door of Charles Lutwidge and a call for him to come out and play. A sample of that light could never be trapped in a bottle for analysis. And yet, to him it was magical.

The repeated invocations of love made by Dodgson could be intensely discomfiting to anyone for whom immediate social reality is all that exists, and only quantifiable fact can be true. Nobody would ever go so far as to call his abiding love for a certain kind of golden summer light directly into question. And if again and again, he associated light of this sort with his most visionary moments, that would be allowed to pass without comment. But a time would eventually come when there would be an attempt to discredit Dodgson's description of the light on this one particular afternoon on objective scientific grounds.

Almost ninety years after this day, *The Observer* of London made a request that the weather records for July 4, 1862, be checked. The answer it received said that it had been cool at Oxford and that during the twelve hours after two o'clock in the afternoon, there was an accumulation of

.17 of an inch of rain. And more than one scholar or annotator of the mid-twentieth century would bow before the power of this information, invoking it as the real truth, which unfortunately must trump Lewis Carroll's fond but demonstrably inaccurate memory.

But one thing that a weather bureau does not do is record the tonal quality of the light on a given day. For that, our best witness must be Charles Dodgson.

Not only was he there, but he also had a photographer's eye for the character of the light. This was a man who, even at his most playful, would insist that anything he told you three times was true. And on at least three occasions over a span of more than twenty years, he would consistently describe the afternoon as golden.

Alice Liddell Hargreaves would also remember the day as a beautiful one. And this testimony from two people who were actually present in the boat that afternoon isn't to be set aside simply on the basis of someone's eventual interpretation of old weather records.

It almost seems possible that both versions could be true. Golden light sounds like slanting sunshine bursting through the clouds. On an in-and-out English summer day, Oxford could have been persistently shadowed and comparatively cool. There might even have been a shower. At the same time, a few miles away on the river, it is possible to imagine the sun finding a hole in the clouds and the weather being altogether brighter and warmer.

That was just the opposite of what had happened during the last river outing the same group had made several weeks earlier. That time, they'd gotten drenched by a sudden rain, and Dodgson had led them to a house where a friend had lodgings to dry themselves out.

However, what gives this controversy about the state of the weather that afternoon a special note of mystery is that Dodgson wouldn't remember there being any clouds at all. He would say specifically:

"I can call it up almost as clearly as if it were yesterday—the cloudless blue above, the watery mirror below, the boat drifting idly on its way, the tinkle of the drops that fell from its oars, as they waved sleepily to and fro."

Ultimately, there is only one thing we can take as indisputable. A state of mind that was usually only a memory to Dodgson could be triggered by a certain kind of bright summer light. And even though he might no longer be a dreaming boy lying all alone on a silent hill, on this particular day, there was something about the quality of the light he was experiencing that he recognized and responded to.

In this light, anything seemed possible. Something more wonderful than life ordinarily allows might be waiting just around the next bend in the river. Extraordinary things could happen.

In an entry in his diary, Dodgson had once written, "May we not then sometimes define insanity as an inability to distinguish which is the waking and which the sleeping life? We often dream without the least suspicion of unreality: 'Sleep hath its own world,' and it is often as lifelike as the other."

This was an allusion to Byron's poem "The Dream," which begins:

> *Our life is two-fold: Sleep hath its own world,*
> *A boundary between the two things misnamed*
> *Death and existence: Sleep hath its own world,*
> *And a wide realm of wild reality*

Could he be in that other world now? Was it possible that he was asleep and this vivid moment on the river was only a dream?

He certainly felt as though he were somewhere other than usual. And yet, at the same time, what he was experiencing was completely convincing to him. Just now, and in this magical light, it was ordinary daily life that seemed like a faraway dream.

So which of them was the dream and which was real—the mundane Victorian world or this golden moment?

Or was it necessary to make a choice between the two? If life did have more than one aspect, might it not be possible for both states to be equally real but for each to appear as a dream to the other? Both of them true at once, separate and distinct—yet also somehow intimately connected.

After all, the waters on which the gig was riding now could simultaneously be the workaday Thames River and the mythic River Isis. And it was possible for him to be both stodgy C.L. Dodgson and playful Charles Lutwidge.

Alternative modes of anything were fascinating to Dodgson, and all the more so when a variant displayed some wild quality that the familiar version lacked. He loved the ability of mathematics and logic to produce changes from one state to another. And he was attracted by any device or method of transformation which allowed him to turn everyday expectation on its head.

He would obtain a distorting mirror and place it in his rooms. He practiced until he could write from right to left in reversed letters. And he liked to tinker with the works of the vast array of music boxes he owned in order to make them play songs backward.

The children who visited him found queer things like this amusing. But to most adults, they would be travesties of reality that deserved to be ignored.

Dodgson knew better. For him, a strange reflection, wrong-way writing, and a back-to-front song would be every bit as real, evident, and meaningful as the more familiar versions. Not only did they exist—and by the very fact of their existence demand to be taken account of—but they would be a more compelling demonstration of the possibility of other modes of being than any argument he could ever make.

It was even possible for him to imagine a mirror world in which things like this were completely at home. A song in reverse could sound normal there. To the inhabitants of such a place, it would be everything that we are accustomed to and take for granted, like writing from left to right, that would appear odd.

So which was *really* the proper direction to write, and which was all wrong? Dodgson didn't know how to tell.

Perhaps it was we who had things backward.

And then, as the gig hung suspended between the cloudless depths above and the watery mirror below, Dodgson slipped into a state of even greater uncertainty in which he was no longer sure what was real and what was not. It seemed to him that any number of different modes of being could all exist, with each of them just as real or just as unlikely as the next.

There was nothing specially privileged about our usual waking attitudes and assumptions. In his present state of mind, it was clear to Dodgson that if you looked at familiar daily life from outside with the eyes of a stranger, it wouldn't appear necessary and inevitable, but arbitrary and even humorous.

Many other modes of being were possible. The mirror world, the realm of sleep, and the present floating moment were not the same as the ordinary waking state but were just as meaningful. And by existing at all, each of them laid claim to its own rightful place in human experience.

Even when they seemed to conflict with each other, one state wasn't to be favored as more real than another. A dream at night had just as much or as little significance as the activities people pursue so single-mindedly each day.

Every aspect of life was equally real—or else all of them were equally a dream. Then—as Dodgson was seeing things in this way, with every different mode of human awareness and existence granted its own right to be—a conviction of a sort that he implicitly trusted flashed across his mind: Life *was* a dream.

Every bit of existence was a dream. And all of our experiences were part of that dream.

That was how it was possible for there to be so many different states of perception and being. The dream just kept shifting from one set of circumstances to another the way that dreams do. And the dreams that we have at night were only one more phase within this larger dream.

Having arrived at the fundamental insight that life is a dream, Dodgson would hold fast to it for the rest of his days. He would never distress himself or anyone else by insisting on this point, but on more than one occasion he would offer it as a question for others to consider.

In the final words of the acrostic poem recalling this special afternoon that he placed at the end of *Through the Looking Glass* in 1871, Dodgson would ask specifically, "Life, what is it but a dream?"

And eighteen years later, he would deliberately echo the last three lines of this poem in the first three lines of the dedicatory verse he included at the beginning of his long fantasy story, *Sylvie and Bruno*:

Is all our Life, then, but a dream
Seen faintly in the golden gleam
Athwart Time's dark resistless stream?

3

FREE FALLING

WHEN Ina interrupted his train of thought with her order to tell them a story immediately, Dodgson's mind was elsewhere and the insistent sound of her voice was enough to put him off his stroke.

He was in no mood to tell a fairytale just then. He was lost in a vision of all existence as a dream that included many different states of being, each one of them as meaningful as the next. At that moment, to tell still another story about some magic beast that sits up and talks appeared as unrewarding a prospect as to engage in an earnest discussion of adult affairs with Duckworth.

But then Alice and Edith came chiming in as well. Both younger girls wanted to hear a fairytale, too.

Dodgson may have had good reasons for hesitation. And yet, if he resisted Lorina's request because telling a story seemed limiting, because his mind was already occupied, and because Ina's manner was too overbearing by half, what Alice added next was enough to cut through his reluctance. She hoped the story would have nonsense in it.

That spoke to Dodgson. He'd never combined nonsense with a fairytale, and he wasn't sure that it could be done. Magic and nonsense seemed to point in opposite directions.

In a story, real magic was possible—at least once upon a time in fairyland. This was a basic premise whenever he told a tale of wonder and enchantment to the girls. And for the duration of the story, they'd accept that it was true, listening wide-eyed and hanging on every word.

But when he talked nonsense, he expected them to understand that he was only joking and the things he was suggesting weren't really possible. So he might play one of his music boxes backward and then declare that since it was now the day before yesterday he'd better stop before they turned into babies or even disappeared altogether. And the girls would giggle because it almost seemed like something that could really happen and yet it was so absurd.

However, when he described an encounter with a marvelous scaly dragon lurking in the deep, dark wood, he didn't want them to burst into laughter. He wanted them to believe and to inch closer. If he were to declare that dragons and all they do were nonsense, the spell of the story would be broken.

And if it was a joke for him to suggest that time changes direction when a music box plays in reverse, he couldn't turn around and say in the next breath that it might actually happen through magic. It would no longer be nonsense then, but something else.

As Dodgson had always perceived things, you could either have nonsense or you could have magic. But you couldn't have both at once.

However, Alice didn't appear to recognize that she might be asking for anything that wasn't possible. Her request for a fairytale with nonsense in it was stated so simply and sincerely that it seemed a truth uttered in innocence.

The words she spoke struck Dodgson like an oracle—wise and yet also baffling. But the puzzle they presented him was so uncannily well-suited to his present state of mind that he immediately resolved to do what she was asking.

He wasn't daunted by the impossibility of combining nonsense and magic. As much as anything else, it was the very incompatibility of these two things he loved that attracted him.

Life for him at that moment was an inclusive dream where everything the mind can conceive had its own right to be. Since magic and nonsense each had a place in this dream, to single one of them out as true at the expense of the other had to be a mistake.

Dodgson's problem was how to tell a tale in which they existed simultaneously. He had to find a way for them both to be in the story at the same time.

And then a radical solution to this dilemma occurred to him which reversed his previous conceptions of nonsense and magic completely. It took these two things he'd always thought of as distinct and different and made them into one, like a three-dimensional image leaping into sight when separate pictures are brought together in a stereoscope.

What if magic and nonsense didn't merely exist at once in the story? What if they should be the very same unknown observed from two different partial points of view?

An inexplicable event that was utter nonsense to one character might be magic for another. What this mystery was thought to be would depend upon the assumptions and perceptions of the observer.

Wonderful occurrences were a normal fact of life for the inhabitants of fairyland. Magical transformations were always taking place there.

However, to anyone who took contemporary English customs for reality, the very same marvelous happenings would appear doubtful and absurd. If somebody like that were to pay a visit to fairyland, everything they experienced might seem like so much nonsense to them.

Things fell into place for Dodgson then, and he saw how to tell a story.

It could be the fairytale that Ina was demanding, with talking animals in it, and giants, and magic as well.

It could also be full of the nonsense that Alice wanted. Above all, however, it would have to be a dream.

As they rounded the next bend in the river, Charles Lutwidge Dodgson began to talk. He started his story with two girls, much like Ina and Alice, on a hot summer day that was much like today.

What he said went something like this:

> Alice was beginning to get very tired of sitting by her sister on the bank and of having nothing to do: once or twice, she had peeped into the book her sister was reading, but it had no pictures or conversations in it, and where is the use of a book, thought Alice, without pictures or conversations? So she was considering in her own mind (as well as she could, for the hot day made her feel very sleepy and stupid) whether the pleasure of making a daisy chain was worth the trouble of getting up and picking the daisies when a white rabbit with pink eyes ran close by her.
>
> There was nothing very remarkable in that, nor did Alice think it so *very* much out of the way to hear the rabbit say to itself, 'Dear,

dear! I shall be too late!' (when she thought it over afterwards, it occurred to her that she ought to have wondered at this, but at the time it all seemed quite natural), but when the rabbit actually *took a watch out of its waist-coat pocket*, looked at it, and then hurried on, Alice started to her feet, for it flashed across her mind that she had never before seen a rabbit with either a waist-coat pocket or a watch to take out of it, and, full of curiosity, she hurried across the field after it, and was just in time to see it pop down a large rabbit-hole under the hedge. In a moment, down went Alice after it, never once considering how in the world she was to get out again.

The Alice of the story, who is described as bored and drowsy, has slipped into sleep almost imperceptibly right in the middle of wondering whether she should get up and pick some daisies. And immediately, things begin to depart from the ordinary waking state.

As Dodgson would say directly in a letter to playwright Tom Taylor in 1864, at a time when his tale had grown into a book-length manuscript of still-uncertain title: "The whole thing is a dream, but that I don't want revealed until the end."

Dodgson was familiar with more than one story that claimed to have some kind of connection to dream.

The play by Shakespeare that he loved best was *A Midsummer Night's Dream*, in which the affairs of men and fairies magically intersect one night in a wood near ancient Athens. The humans all interpret their experience as something they've dreamed—and in a mischievous concluding speech, the fairy Puck invites anyone in the audience who has found the play disturbing to do the same.

But dream in story didn't usually present a challenge to the sufficiency of the ordinary waking state. More commonly, these "dreams" were just a literary convention or a conceit—either a nominal means of travel to reach some more perfect society or else a convenient excuse for an author to turn away from what he'd just imagined and deny its reality.

During Dodgson's own lifetime, however, a number of writers had published stories that were more adventurous in their use of dreams, evoking or imitating dream states as a way of being fantastic. Charles Dickens' *A Christmas Carol* had appeared when he was a boy, with the miser Ebenezer Scrooge brought to a change of heart by a series of ghostly confrontations on Christmas Eve which Scrooge experiences as actual encounters but an adult reader is intended to interpret as a night of dreams. Dodgson had read the nightmare-like tales of Edgar Allan Poe, such as "The Fall of the House of Usher" and "The Masque of the Red Death."

And he was the owner of a copy of his friend George MacDonald's "faerie romance" for adults, *Phantastes,* in which a man rises one morning to find his bedroom turning into fairyland and undergoes a number of irrational but meaningful experiences there before waking again in the familiar world on a hilltop near his home after three weeks have passed.

However, what Dodgson aimed to do was more ambitious than any of these. In his story, dream wouldn't just be a secondary matter—an implied rationale, the model for extreme effects, or a road by which to reach fairyland. Instead, it would be all of these at once and more.

Dream would be what the story was about. From beginning to end, it would have an elusive shifting dreamlike quality.

The transformations start with the rabbit that comes running by. Whatever this dream-creature may seem to be at any given moment, at the next its nature is different. Our idea of what it is changes from one word to another until all that makes a single thing out of it is the continuing impression it gives of rabbitness.

At first glance, we might be inclined to take it for a common rabbit of the sort that hops around the field and lives in a hole in the ground.

But while it does have the appearance of an ordinary animal, there's also something about it that's out of place here. It isn't wild. This is a domestic rabbit with white fur and pink eyes. Whatever is it doing running about loose by the river?

Before we can make anything of this, however, the creature alters and becomes something different. Now it's no longer a normal rabbit of any sort. Like an animal in a fairytale, it has the power to speak.

But the way it uses this ability is very odd. It doesn't address Alice and her sister directly. Instead, it halts nearby and talks out loud to itself, as apparently oblivious of their presence as an actor is of an audience. As though the possibility were just occurring to it, it begins to fret about being late.

Where could this marvelous white rabbit be going, and what might have delayed it? And why should it stop here to dither this way?

But even though Dodgson would again and again describe the Alice of this story as curious, none of this is enough to cause her to wonder. In the state she's in, it seems a perfectly normal thing for a talking white rabbit that behaves as if she isn't there to come running close by her and pause within easy earshot to speak its thoughts aloud.

Then this rabbit changes again in a way that Alice can't overlook. Now it's not only standing on its hind legs just as though it had been doing so all along, it's hauling a watch out of its vest pocket and checking the time like some Victorian man of business with an urgent appointment to keep.

This nonsense is finally enough to arouse Alice's curiosity. A talking animal might not seem anything out of the ordinary to her, but a rabbit that wears a waistcoat and consults a pocket watch is clearly beyond the bounds of reason.

Now that its message that time is pressing has been delivered and then acted out again with the aid of an unlikely but appropriate prop and Alice's attention has been captured at last, the mysterious rabbit hurries off—on two legs or on four, however you prefer to imagine it—with Alice up and chasing after it through the wildflowers like an American Indian boy pursuing an animal ally in a power dream. She catches sight of it entering a large rabbit hole under the hedgerow bordering the field, and she follows after.

How could that be? People aren't usually able to fit into rabbit holes, even large ones.

But his story was a dream, even if Dodgson wasn't yet ready to say as much directly. So when he described the hole as large, he didn't just mean that it was large as rabbit holes are commonly reckoned. Instead, "large" became an indeterminate dream word that meant as large as large needed to be in order to be large enough. Not only does Alice fit easily within a hole that's as large as that, she's even able to continue chasing after the white rabbit.

Perhaps because this rabbit of many parts popped into it first, the hole has been firmly identified for us as a rabbit hole. But if it really is a rabbit hole, it's every bit as peculiar as the rabbit.

At the outset, it goes straight ahead like a tunnel, which isn't at all the sort of thing that rabbit holes usually do. And then suddenly, there's nothing beneath Alice's feet, and she finds herself falling down what seems to be a well.

Ordinarily when we fall, experience says that very shortly we're going to bang into something, and the fall will come to an end. But on this occasion, things aren't like that. This fall goes on and on. Alice has so much time on her hands while she's falling that she's able to look all around her.

Now maybe—Dodgson suggested to his listeners—she was falling slowly. (Which might well be the case, they would have to agree, if she were very composed as she fell and managed to descend with gravity.)

Or it might be that this well was deep, where "deep" was another dream word that didn't just mean deep as wells go, but really deep. As deep as deep can be imagined to be.

Or perhaps both these possibilities were true at once: Her fall is slow. And the well is also deep.

But now that Dodgson had thrown Alice into this state of complete uncertainty—falling and falling down a rabbit hole that was no common rabbit hole, which had somehow contrived to alter into a well that wasn't any usual kind of well—he had no idea what would take place next.

His total lack of foreknowledge of what was going to happen in this story would still seem remarkable to him after the passage of a quarter of a century. As he would recall things then:

> That was many a year ago, but I distinctly remember now as I write, how, in a desperate attempt to strike out some new line of fairy-lore, I had sent my heroine straight down a rabbit-hole, to begin with, without the least idea of what was to happen afterwards.

Since at the outset Dodgson had nothing more specific in mind than setting Alice to falling, at first when she glances about her nothing is all that she's able to see. The white rabbit she has followed ought to be falling, too, just ahead of her in the well. However, when she attempts to look beneath her, it's so dark down there that she can't make out a thing.

But then as Alice continues to fall, what previously was lost to her in darkness becomes visible. She is able to see the sides of the well as she goes falling past them.

What does she notice there?

She sees walls that are filled with bookshelves and cupboards, and every now and again pictures and maps hanging from pegs, as though the well—without ever ceasing to be a well—had also become the rooms of an Oxford don, not unlike Dodgson, especially gifted with an ability to live at right angles to everyone else.

This image of somebody dwelling under conditions that ordinarily would be impossible in three different ways could have been intended to be fairytale magic.

Or it may have been meant as nonsense, a humorous juxtaposition of things that don't ordinarily belong together, like Rev. Dodgson's comic vision of panic-stricken old women outracing the cows in their hurry to seek refuge up chimneys and fat geese doing their best to squeeze themselves into pencil cases.

Or perhaps Dodgson was overwhelmed for just a moment by a recognition of the uncertainty he'd embraced in launching himself into the arms of the unknown this way, setting himself and the heroine of his story to falling and falling in a space whose nature wasn't fixed ... and then grew accustomed to the strangeness of this place by acknowledging how appropriate a residence it could make for somebody like himself who was capable of living with his books in the middle of the air without ever noticing how unfounded he was.

Given a story like this, where everything has its measure of mystery and meanings are never simple or final, it's impossible to be certain about the nature of this peculiar manifestation. The only thing we can be sure of is that as Dodgson rowed along making up a new kind of fairytale that was also full of nonsense, but above all was a dream—with Alice gazing all around her while she is falling but unable to see anything definite—the first specific image to come into his mind was rooms resembling his own at Christ Church, but arranged vertically. And as fast as he thought of this, he made it a part of the story—so that when Alice looks at the sides of the well, not only is she able to make things out there now, but it is cupboards and bookshelves, maps and pictures she sees.

For those listening to Dodgson tell this story that July afternoon on the river—the three Liddell sisters riding in the front and back of the boat and his friend Duckworth rowing stroke in the middle—the things he was saying seemed amusing, baffling, and intriguing all at once. What do you suppose might be kept in a cupboard in mid-air inside a dream rabbit hole that has contrived to alter into a well?

The youngest of the sister, Edith, was the most curious, always eager to have an explanation of everything she didn't understand. Again and again her need to be told how or what or why things were would cause her to come breaking in on the story with another urgent question.

But Dodgson welcomed the girls' desire to know more, especially on this particular day. Attempting to find answers for the questions they asked helped him bring the story into being.

So when he said that Alice saw cupboards and shelves there in the well, and the girls just had to know what sort of thing they held, he was able to use their curiosity to provoke Alice's.

In his story, then, another shelf conveniently happens along. (How vertically the unseen occupant of these strange quarters does manage to live! And how responsive this dream is!)

Immediately it becomes possible for the girls' question to be answered. As she goes falling by, Alice reaches out, takes something from the shelf, and examines it.

Since this is a dream, however, the object proves to be one more mystery. It's a jar with the label "Orange Marmalade"—except it's empty.

Why should a jar that has a label on the outside but nothing on the inside be kept here on this shelf? And why does the description of what the jar doesn't contain read "Orange Marmalade?" Might it just as readily have said "Mango Chutney" or "Library Paste?"

But even though Alice may have been curious enough to pick up the jar in the first place, no questions like these occur to her. Instead, she's disappointed that there's nothing within so she can't eat marmalade while she's falling.

And now she has an empty jar on her hands that she doesn't wish to drop for fear that it will hit somebody standing below and kill them. As though anyone who was foolish enough to lounge around at the foot of this particular well wasn't just begging to be struck on the head by the constant shower of empty marmalade jars and other litter that comes raining down from the residence above.

Obligingly enough, however, another cupboard happens along just then, so that Alice is able to rid herself of the jar, setting it down inside as she goes falling past.

Perhaps because she's too young to have studied physical science yet, Alice is not aware that she is already traveling as fast as any object she might drop ... unless, of course, in this dream, she isn't. Nor does it occur to her that she might land on anybody herself, to their harm or hers.

She's just proud of how brave she's being and thinks how much more ready she'll now be to take a tumble at home after experiencing such a great fall as this: "Why I wouldn't say anything about it, even if I fell off the top of the house."

(Which—the storyteller was quick to add—most likely would be so.)

This was a humorous way of confirming our usual presumption that a fall from a Victorian rooftop would likely be fatal. At the same time, however, it suggests yet again that what is presently happening to Alice isn't ordinary.

And either because she truly is brave or because something within her is aware that this is all a dream, Alice isn't frightened but remains completely calm as she falls down and down and down.

4

A DREAM WITHIN A DREAM

ALICE is curious about how many miles she has fallen now and speculates about whether she has reached the center of the earth yet. She wonders, too, just what longitude and latitude that would be.

This was a joke, of course. It doesn't occur to her that at least two circumstances exist in which the concepts of latitude and longitude can have no meaning. One is in a dream. The other is at the center of the earth.

Charles Dodgson wasn't the only storyteller of the moment to play with the thought of leaving everything conventional and familiar behind and finding a way down to the heart of the world where things are no longer the same. Two years after this tale was told for the first time, but a year before it finally appeared in book form under the title *Alice's Adventures in Wonderland*, the French writer Jules Verne would publish the third of his pioneering scientific romances, *A Journey to the Center of the Earth*.

In Verne's story, a party of contemporary explorers is led down an extinct volcano in Iceland by a rational-minded geology professor. After they've descended eighty-eight miles, well into a region that the science of a later day would regard as hot enough to melt rock, they come upon a mysterious underground realm perpetually lit by some unknown means which they conclude must be electrical in nature.

Here, in a place where neither wind nor water should exist, they set sail on a storm-tossed subterranean ocean. From the safety of their raft, they witness a battle to the death between two monstrous sea reptiles out of the Age of Dinosaurs. And later, they look on as a herd of living mastodons grazes violently upon a ghostly forest where the plants have no color, and there are trees from every time and climate, the oak growing next to the palm and the eucalyptus beside the fir.

However, the significance of what they are seeing is something the men don't allow themselves to think much about. Again and again, they find themselves confronted with things that by normal daylight standards of truth cannot possibly be. And the only way they can manage to live with this weirdness is by taking refuge in familiar habits and attitudes.

The professor plays the privileged scientific observer confirming what he already knows must be so because he's seen it in a book. He constantly delivers self-confident impromptu lectures which are long on numbers and technical names but in the event always prove to be a less-than-adequate assessment of what the party is encountering.

His Romantic nephew, the narrator of the story, would like to be just as knowledgeable and sure of himself, but on any occasion that what he's experiencing is more than his state of understanding can accommodate, he's apt to faint. He never manages to be completely certain that this adventure is as real as his uncle takes it to be. At one moment, he can feel as though he were standing on a distant planet, at another that what is happening is a dream come to life.

The third member of the expedition is an Icelander who has been brought along to do any job too practical or dirty for a gentleman. His response to the bizarre other realm they are passing through is to bury himself in his work, concentrating all his attention on whatever task he's been assigned as though nothing out of the ordinary was taking place.

The postures they adopt of rational self-congratulation, emotional hyperventilation, and nearsighted devotion to duty are all intended to minimize the impact of what they are experiencing and keep the strangeness at arm's length. But, just as with Alice and the watch and waistcoat of the white rabbit, eventually a moment does arrive when the cumulative queerness of the world beneath the world becomes more than Verne's characters can continue to ignore.

As the professor and his nephew are observing the mastodons foraging in the colorless forest, stripping away great masses of leaves with their trunks and stuffing them down their cavernous maws, it suddenly becomes apparent to them that these intimidating creatures aren't wild. They have a keeper—a human figure standing over twelve feet tall with an unkempt head the size of a buffalo's.

A forest of a kind that has never existed growing far under the ground! A herd of extinct American elephants living upon it! And now an antediluvian giant brandishing a tree limb for a shepherd's crook watching over these brutes and protecting them from harm!

A leading tenet of the new materialistic faith of the day was that if only the facts of any matter could be gathered and codified, they would prove to be intelligible and coherent and add to the ever-increasing power of Western scientific man. And here we are given one close observation and exact fact after another—from the names of all the plants in the forest to the height of the shaggy herdsman.

Only the result is not greater knowledge and control. Rather, it is mystery heaped upon mystery.

This irrationality is more than either of the two onlookers, both of them good children of the nineteenth century, can manage to accept. Uncle and nephew turn tail together and flee from the nightmarish sight.

But when they run away, it is only to find themselves confronted by yet another hard fact. A great rock appears in their path, which prevents them from proceeding any further toward the center of the earth.

The response of the men is to assault the object with technology. They attempt to blow the rock to pieces with gun cotton, an explosive four times as powerful as gunpowder.

But this is no way to behave in the strangely responsive region they have penetrated. These modern explorers of the underworld have shown how oblivious they can be to all the unlikely things that have been taking place before their eyes. They've displayed an inability to accept anything which fundamentally contradicts their present state of understanding. And now they intend to show how willful and violent they are capable of being.

It's not enough for them to have worn out their welcome here. They seem actively bent upon making their continued presence intolerable.

When they set off the gun cotton they've brought with them all this distance, the result is not the removal of the obstacle that they are anticipating. Instead, the three men find themselves launched upon an involuntary return journey back to the surface of the earth.

Up and up they are lifted on their raft by a succession of fortuitous events that are fully as fantastic a means of getting from here to there as the rabbit-hole-turned-well down which Alice is falling—only going in the opposite direction. They are taken a certain distance by a rising column of water and the rest of the way by lava until they reach the familiar daylight world again, ultimately being spit forth unharmed by an erupting volcano near Sicily.

Is it possible for something similar to happen to Alice? If she were to persist in thinking and doing all the wrong things, could a strange wind suddenly rise in the well, change her direction from down to up, and blow her back to the field of daisies and her sister's side? Perhaps it might. In this other realm of existence, it seems that almost anything could happen if it had a mind to.

But then Alice isn't about to set off any powerful explosions down here in the realm of mystery in order to have things her own way. She is even careful about how she disposes of an empty marmalade jar. Nor is she attached to schoolroom knowledge about latitude and longitude, which she doesn't really comprehend and which has no relevance here. She just likes the grand sound these words make when she says them aloud.

However, her thoughts of reaching the center of the earth do serve to indicate her uncertainty about how deep this well may actually be. In the next moment, it even occurs to her that she might fall all the way through the world and emerge on the other side—just as Baron Munchausen had claimed to have done. She wonders how funny everybody there will look walking around upside down and whether she would be making a fool of herself if she were to ask someone if she'd arrived in New Zealand or perhaps Australia.

In order for that to happen, of course, she would have to fall against the force of gravity from the center of the earth to the far side of the world. But this doesn't appear to be a problem to her. Just now, falling is the only thing of which Alice is sure, and it seems that she could keep right on falling until there was no farther to fall.

Down and down she falls, keeping occupied by chatting to herself as she goes. She thinks how nice it would be if she had her cat Dinah with her for company. But then, what would a cat find to eat in the middle of the air where there aren't any mice? Bats, perhaps?

Alice is feeling drowsy and dreamy, and her thoughts have begun to drift. From wondering "do cats eat bats?" she finds herself asking the opposite question—"do bats eat cats?" It doesn't seem to make much difference which way 'round she puts it since she doesn't know the answer in either case.

What a strange state to be in! Alice has fallen asleep but is dreaming that she is still awake and falling down a large rabbit hole that somehow or other has turned into a well. And the well is so deep that even while she's falling down it, she could slip off to sleep and begin to dream a dream inside her dream.

A dream within a dream! The party in the gig with Dodgson had all listened to him tell stories before, but never anything like this. The mystery and uncertainty of the tale held the girls enthralled. How could any well be as deep as that?

Even Robinson Duckworth was fascinated. The story he was privileged to overhear was like nothing he was familiar with. Long afterward, he'd remember that he'd checked his impression of its originality by turning his head as they were rowing and asking over his shoulder, "Dodgson, is this an extempore romance of yours?"

And that the answer which came back to him was: "Yes, I'm inventing as we go along."

It was somehow the nature of this particular moment that Dodgson could be able to continue to help row the boat and also hold conversations on the side with his friend at the same time that he was dropping down an eternal well with Alice, improvising this fantastic tale as they went. But if Alice in his story was able to be in more than one place at once—so that while she was fast asleep on the river bank, she was also falling down a rabbit hole, and as she fell, she could grow sleepy and drift off into a dream within the dream which she was dreaming—such a thing was possible only because the consciousness of the teller of her tale was already in more than one location that day, and this story was a way of expressing and maintaining his own special state of mind.

In the course of an afternoon boat ride on the waters of the Isis, with the oars of the gig swaying back and forth in a rhythm he found hypnogogic and in precious golden light which reminded him of former times when the things he imagined were more real to him than the things he'd been assured were so, Charles Lutwidge Dodgson had slipped into a waking dream-state in which he continued to be completely aware of his immediate surroundings, but his mind was able to wander freely from one vantage to another.

The accepted truths of the present day were all reduced to just another perspective among the many that were possible. In the condition of lucid dissociation he was in, one point of view appeared as valid to him—and also as partial—as the next.

Men and women of a certain bent in societies all over the world have been subject to episodes of this kind of dislocalized vision ever since the most remote human times. But indoctrination in the values and beliefs of modern Western civilization was ordinarily enough to ensure that no well-bred, well-educated Victorian gentleman would ever fall under the spell of anything that might be taken for a shamanistic trance.

Even so, however, by the evidence of his own testimony, it seems that on the first Friday in July 1862, during the course of a boating picnic up the Thames River from Oxford, the Rev. C.L. Dodgson did pass into a psychic state in which, while he was still conscious, every single aspect of life took on a dreamlike appearance for him.

It was as though his thoughts had come drifting free of all the assumptions that customarily bounded and defined the life he was given to lead as a lecturer in mathematics at Christ Church and a member of the class of privilege in a nineteenth century Britain of technological might and worldwide colonial empire.

The place where he found himself then was the grand, all-encompassing dream where everything the human mind can imagine has existence. And it appeared to him that there was nowhere he couldn't travel within this immense realm of possibility, and there was no perspective from which he couldn't look at things—and all without ever leaving the boat on the river.

He was brought up short, however, when Lorina Liddell came bursting in on his thoughts seeking a fairytale. Dodgson was jarred by the intrusion. In looking back on this moment at a later time, he'd even describe the manner in which Ina asked as "imperious."

He only felt more unsettled when Alice and Edith added the strength of their voices to their sister's. The last thing he wanted to do at the moment was to tell a fairytale. But Dodgson also found it difficult to deny the girls anything that the three of them were all yearning for.

It was Alice, seated at the tiller of the gig doing the steering, who rescued him from his dilemma with her innocent wish for his story to contain both nonsense and magic. The obvious impossibility of this spoke directly to his ambivalent feelings.

Then, quick as a flash, he saw not only how he could satisfy both requests, but also how to hold onto his condition of disconnectedness from any one thing and connection to everything. A way occurred to him to tell a story which would share his unfixed state of mind with the girls.

All life had the appearance of a single great dream to him just then, and Dodgson wanted his sense of that to continue. So while he was in a waking dreamstate, and was aware that he was, he determined to tell the girls a dream story about someone who was asleep and having a dream but didn't know it.

One dream nested inside another …

In a story that was made from level upon level of dream, whatever he said might be nonsense, or might be magic, or might even be both at once. That was a way to hold onto his present certainty that different states could be mutually exclusive and nevertheless still have existence at the same time.

Anything at all might take place in a dream inside a dream. And even he would never be able to tell what the tenor of an event really was.

Nor could he ever know what was going to happen next:

It was nonsense that Alice was asking for, and nonsense is spontaneous and unpredictable. The three girls all wanted to hear a fairytale, so the story had to have magical transformations in it. And then, because the narrative was a dream, it must change and change again.

There was nothing that Dodgson could be sure of in telling this tale. He could only hurl himself headlong into the story with no thought for how he was going to get out of it. He had to start speaking and count upon words and images that could be taken in more than one way to come to him as he had need for them. He had to surprise himself as well as his listeners.

And yet, if he placed his trust in the tale and was ready to go wherever it led him, it seemed possible for him to satisfy everyone. Ina could have her fairytale. Alice could have her nonsense. And he could have his dream.

But a story has requirements of its own that he also needed to observe.

Until that moment, it had been enough for Dodgson to see things from a particular point of view and then from some other that contradicted it completely and understand that there could be truth in both of them. But looking at things from various conflicting standpoints and smiling upon each of them wasn't enough to make a tale.

A story has meaning and consequence. And though he might intend this one to be fantastic, and also absurd, and to shift and alter as well, it still needed to follow a narrative thread and to come to a conclusion.

What sort of person would it take to find a path through a tale as uncertain as this one? Who was the dreamer in his dream story to be?

That was when Dodgson began to speak, and as he did, he entered a further, more focused phase in the shamanistic state he was in. He changed in form and nature and became someone very different from his usual self:

He was thirty years old. In his story, he turned into a child again.

He might have an element of maiden aunt in his makeup, which only grew more visible as he got older, but Dodgson was a man. In the tale, he'd speak with the voice of somebody of the opposite sex.

He was a college teacher who had his own extensive personal library. He set all his learning aside. In his narrative, the person that he was-and-was-not wouldn't know very much at all, and half of that was wrong.

Then, having assumed the viewpoint of this ignorant child, he allowed her to fall asleep on a riverbank and begin to dream.

It wasn't just happenstance that Dodgson should select an innocent little girl like that to serve as the eyes and ears of his story. Her very lack of attachments, fixed habits, and formal knowledge would be a distinct advantage to her in the state of complete uncertainty into which she is thrown. She'd be burdened with none of the adult baggage of social role, fashion and ambition which so hampers and distracts Verne's people in their quest to reach the world at the heart of the world.

Instead of that, she'd have characteristics in common with each of the three Liddell children:

The girl's name would be Alice, just like Alice Liddell. And these two would be alike in their readiness to accept what was ordinarily completely impossible as only natural. When a white rabbit with pink eyes suddenly comes running close by her, only to pause and begin speaking aloud to itself about its lateness, as though it regarded the errand it was bound upon as so urgent and absorbing that it had no attention to spare for her and her sister, this Alice wouldn't be taken aback. She'd accept the fact of its presence without giving the matter a second thought.

Her age in the story would be seven—the same as Edith—and both of them would have a distaste for being ignored and want to find out immediately whatever it was they wished to know. So when she witnesses the rabbit reaching into its pocket and looking at its watch before hurrying on, Alice rises at once to follow this animal herald across the field, and chase after it down a large hole under the hedge.

Not least, she would share Lorina Liddell's sense of regal self-possession—her unspoken certitude that since she knew very well who she was, she could never be out of place because, after all, she was she and this just happened to be where she was right now. So when the rabbit hole unexpectedly turns into a well beneath Alice's feet and she begins to fall and fall, she never loses her aplomb but is able to descend into the unknown with poise.

With her goes no worldly power, position, or privilege. Her only resource is the nature of her character.

In time, Dodgson would state explicitly what he took Alice to be like in an essay by Lewis Carroll which saw publication at the time the story was brought to the stage.

He would say that she is as loving as a dog, as gentle as a fawn, and as courteous to everyone she meets as the daughter of a king. She is wildly curious and completely trustful—"ready to accept the wildest impossibilities with all that utter trust that only dreamers know." And she takes pleasure in expanding her knowledge of life.

Though children may be open to experience, it's not every seven-year-old who is able to be as receptive and accepting as this. However, for Dodgson to find his way from one end of the story to the other, it was necessary for him to be just this unpresuming and full of goodwill. In consequence, as his own contribution to Alice's nature, he made her the gift of a gentle and loving spirit.

Down the well, then, this Alice goes falling, and Dodgson along with her. At times as they fall, their point of view is just the same. He knows what she knows, and he sees what she sees. At other times, he would separate himself from her enough to find humor in her limitations of awareness, knowledge and understanding.

The people who were listening to his story would be there, too, swept up by the ongoing flow of his account and carried away with him on this trip into the unknown. Without the assistance of Dodgson, they wouldn't have been able to perceive a thing, but by following his narrative as it unfolded, each of them would be able to envision everything that was taking place.

A mysterious reversal was at work here:

For those in the boat that day, Alice was not in sight except as her image was evoked in their minds by Dodgson's words. Yet within the scope of the story that he was telling them, it was they who would be neither audible nor visible—like eavesdropping spirits—while Alice could not only be seen and touched but acted on behalf of them all in addition to herself.

So what is this seemingly endless well down which she and they go falling? What is this place?

It's known by many different names. It may be called the World Tree, or the Gate of Clashing Clouds, the Isthmus of Similitudes, or the *axis mundi*. When perceived as a well, it's known as the Well of the Worlds.

This is the route that travelers take when they journey to reach the Other World. And in this in-between space, the sincerity and good intentions of all who would proceed are tested:

There is darkness at first. Those who come this way are deprived of their usual sense of direction. Then they are shown fantastic forms that resemble things they know, but which are plainly impossible. Their reaction to this exact reflection of their limits of understanding determines whether or not they will be permitted to go any farther.

In this intermediate place, both Alice and the men in *A Journey to the Center of the Earth* would be given recognizable things to see under conditions that make no sense at all. The wonders revealed to Alice are of a simpler kind than those the adults witness because she knows so much less than they do. But because she is more at ease in her state of disequilibrium, as well as more accepting of things that ordinarily could never be but are anyway, what is shown to her can be less threatening yet far stranger.

This means that Verne's underworld explorers watch great sea monsters attacking each other—ancient fossils reclothed in flesh and brought to life again—and recognize them as an ichthyosaur and a plesiosaur, while Alice only sees a rabbit. Except this one is wearing a vest and carrying a pocket watch to remind it of the hour. And they look on as a herd of fierce mastodons feasts upon a subterranean forest. Alice merely traverses the familiar living quarters of an Oxford don—only somehow these rooms have made a place for themselves in mid-air down the shaft of a well that's deeper than deep.

Eventually Verne's men of fact and reason find the scientific anomalies they're witnessing more unsettling than they can stand and flee from them in terror. But Alice never attempts to avoid the much queerer order of things that she encounters. She always wants to have a better look.

As she passes a shelf in the vertical living quarters, she even picks up an object just to see what it might be. It's that jar labeled "Orange Marmalade" which has no marmalade inside.

The meaning of this puzzle eludes Alice—though it might be a way of hinting that the container is not the content. Despite her inability to comprehend, however, she still treats the enigmatic object with care, and when she is done with it, puts it back down in the next convenient cupboard.

Because the initial response of Verne's characters to that which exceeds their understanding is to attempt to ignore it, then to retreat in panic before its strangeness, and finally to try to obliterate it when it seems to block their path, they are found unacceptable and sent home again. Alice, on the other hand, is open and innocent enough to engage what is beyond her comprehension without fear or force, and she is permitted to pass.

On down the well, then, she goes falling and falling. So long and so far does the fall continue that eventually she can even grow drowsy, nod off to sleep, and begin to dream …

This dream within a dream would be an intimation of just how impossibly deep this well is. It would also be a way for Dodgson to share the true nature of his story with his audience. Most of all, however, it would serve as an indication that Alice has now entered a new state of consciousness and is ready at last to reach her destination.

Down she comes then with a couple of bumps—somewhere else other than usual.

The landing isn't nearly as great a shock as falling off the roof of a house. Instead, it seems about as hard as if she'd taken a leap from the top of a wall that wasn't too high for a little girl to climb up on. She isn't hurt a bit.

In fact, now that her fall has finally come to an end, it's no longer possible to say whether it really did go on for a very long time, or whether it just seemed that way while it was happening.

And it's no great heap of trash dropped from the rooms above that she has landed upon. Instead, her fall has been broken by a pile of sticks and shavings—as though someone upstairs had been doing some whittling. But when she looks back overhead where she's just been, it's now dark up there once more, and she can't make out a thing.

There is only one detail in the story to this point that Dodgson would alter when he expanded this tale for book publication. For the shavings at the bottom of the well, he would substitute dry leaves.

This change may have been intended to remind us that what we've grown used to thinking of as an endless well which also doubles as somebody's home was a rabbit hole to begin with.

Alice hasn't laid eyes on the white rabbit since it first popped down the hole and she ran after it and began falling. But there it is again—as though now that she's finally gotten here it is time for it to pop back into being.

She spies the creature hurrying down a passageway in front of her, as apparently unaware of her presence as it was before. This spirit guide speaks to the air one more time about how late it is getting to be. Then it turns a corner and is gone.

Alice rushes after it. But when she turns the corner, too, the white rabbit is nowhere to be seen. Instead, she finds herself alone in a long, low hall with doors all around it.

What waits behind each of those doors?

We can only imagine.

MAN BEYOND MAN

1 AN ORGANIC UNIVERSE

THE most radical and visionary of the writers of the Golden Age of *Astounding*, Alfred Elton van Vogt, was born on his grandparents' farm in Manitoba, Canada on April 26, 1912. At this time, van Vogt's father and three of his uncles were partners in a general store in the village of Neville, Saskatchewan and his father was studying by correspondence to earn a law degree.

Like another significant Golden Age writer, Isaac Asimov, who developed a case of double pneumonia at the end of his second year from which it was feared he wouldn't recover, van Vogt had an early brush with death. When he was two, he fell from a second-floor window onto a wooden sidewalk, knocked himself unconscious, and remained in a coma for three days.

Van Vogt was like Asimov in another regard—the original language of this writer-to-be was not English. Until his mother put her foot down on the matter when Alfred was four, it was a dialect of Dutch that was spoken in the van Vogt household.

Young Alfred had something of a divided nature. He was an insatiable reader who, for many years, devoured two books a day and knew early that he wanted to be a writer when he grew up. But there were also moments when he was "an extrovert of extraordinary energy"—as he put it in a 1981 memoir entitled "My Life Was My Best Science Fiction Story."

Van Vogt was a horseback rider as a youth. In summers during his teens, he worked as a separator man on a threshing outfit and drove a truck for a combine. He was a good rifle shot, and even came close to going off on a trapping expedition to northern Canada.

In later years, van Vogt would look back upon his younger self and try to determine just when it was that the more outgoing part of himself had gotten suppressed. Did it stem from that traumatic fight with another boy that occurred when he was eight? Was it the teacher who had caused him to doubt himself for reading fairytales at twelve? Or was the crucial event when he was seventeen-and-a-half and killed a snake and then suffered a revulsion against doing harm to any wild creature?

Though van Vogt might make guess after guess, he would never be able to pinpoint the exact moment when it happened. And, in fact, even well into his twenties, when he was an advertising space salesman and writer of interviews for a string of trade papers, van Vogt could still call on some lingering residue of brashness in his character to gain the attention of businessmen and store owners—as long as no one challenged him.

The truth of the matter seems to be that van Vogt's withdrawal into himself took place over a considerable period of time. The beginning of it may lie in the fact that young Alfred was a highly idealistic small-town boy with a number of wide-eyed notions about right and truth and justice in his head. When the world failed to conform to his expectations, he found that a substantial shock.

Beyond this, it was also true that Alfred was a boy who had something a little strange and left-footed about him. He didn't think or talk exactly like everyone else, and reaction to this may have had its effect on his developing personality.

As the twenties boomed, van Vogt's lawyer father moved his family once and then again, first to the larger town of Morden, Manitoba, and then to the city of Winnipeg, where he became the western Canadian agent of the Holland-American Shipping Lines.

These moves were very difficult for van Vogt. He would recall: "Childhood was a terrible period for me. I was like a ship without anchor being swept along through darkness in a storm. Again and again, I sought shelter, only to be forced out of it by something new."

Morden was twice as large as Neville. It was a conservative community with a predominantly English population, and here, van Vogt was made aware that Canada was British but that he was not.

Winnipeg was even more trying. It was a city of 250,000—two hundred times the size of Morden—and Alfred felt lost there. He quickly fell behind in school "in the five subjects that you just can't catch up on easily: Algebra, geometry, Latin grammar, Latin literature, and one other that I can't recall." In consequence, he was asked to repeat the tenth grade.

The broader horizons offered by science fiction—still not yet called this—were one answer he found to his difficulties. He came across SF first in Morden at the age of eleven in a British boys' magazine called *Chum*, the yearly collected volume of which he contrived to borrow for a dime from another boy who soon became his best friend.

Then, in Winnipeg, in his dark days of failure in school, he discovered the November 1926 issue of *Amazing Stories* on a newsstand and recognized it as what he was seeking. During the next three years—until Hugo Gernsback lost control of the magazine and it came under the more conservative editorial direction of ancient T. O'Conor Sloane—van Vogt would read *Amazing* assiduously, seeking signs of another and higher order of being than that which was to be found in Winnipeg, Manitoba in the late 1920s. As van Vogt would eventually come to express it:

> Reading science fiction lifted me out of the do-be-and-have world and gave me glimpses backward and forward into the time and space distances of the Universe. I may live only three seconds (so to speak), but I have had the pleasure and excitement of contemplating the beginning and end of existence. Short of being immortal physically, I have vicariously experienced just about everything that man can conceive will happen by reading science fiction.

If *Amazing* had defects and limitations, this wasn't apparent to young Alfred. What he saw in the pioneer magazine of science fiction was the wonders of man's progress-to-come, and his imagination was fired by one grand new concept after another:

> ESP, trans-light speeds, exploration of space, the infinitely small turning out to be another universe, new super-energy sources, instant education, the long journey, shape changing, vision at a distance, time travel, gravity minimization, taking over another body, etc.

A considerable impression would be made on van Vogt by E.E. Smith's *The Skylark of Space*, of course. But the writer in *Amazing* who had the most to say to him was A. Merritt, the author of *The Moon Pool*.

When Gernsback left the magazine, the youngster couldn't help but notice the change. *Amazing* lost the magic it had held for him and became dull. Consequently, in 1930, in one of the utterly abrupt transitions that were to become typical of his conduct of life, van Vogt put science fiction aside.

He wouldn't look at SF again for more than eight years until, just as abruptly, he was ready to begin to write it. In the meantime, however, he had a great deal of self-preparation to do.

Lack of spare cash was one reason for his ceasing to buy science fiction magazines. The stock market crash of 1929 took place at the beginning of van Vogt's last year in high school. Before that school year was over, van Vogt's father had lost his shipping lines job, and it was apparent there wouldn't be sufficient money available for Alfred to go to college. Although in later life, van Vogt would sit in on college courses in many subjects, from economics to acting, this was to be the end of his formal education.

For the next six months, he hid out in his bedroom and wondered what to do with himself. Mostly he continued to read. He read hot pulp fiction—historical romances, mysteries and Westerns. He read serious turn-of-the-century British fiction and nineteenth century French novels. He read history and psychology. And he also read books of science.

The science that interested van Vogt the most was not familiar Newtonian science. It seems possible that the unrecallable essential subject he flunked in tenth grade, along with Latin and math, just might have been chemistry or physics. Unlike his contemporaries, John Campbell and Robert Heinlein, van Vogt hadn't spent his youth building radios or carrying out a search for a better way to blow up the basement. There was never much likelihood that he would grow up to become an aeronautical engineer like L. Sprague de Camp or a biochemist like Isaac Asimov.

The science that van Vogt did care about was the new wider science of atoms and galaxies. But even here, what interested him was not the details, but rather concepts and overviews—the philosophy and meaning of science. And so it was only natural that he would find his way to the writings of Arthur Eddington, James Jeans and J.B.S. Haldane.

However, the book that had the greatest influence on the formation of his thinking may have been Alfred North Whitehead's *Science and the Modern World* (1925). At one time or another, this pioneering work of post-materialistic philosophy passed through the hands of most of the youngsters who would grow up to become the science fiction writers of Campbell's Golden Age. But it was van Vogt alone amongst them who would be able to take insights derived from this difficult little book and make them the basis for his SF writing.

Until the year preceding the publication of *Science and the Modern World*, Alfred North Whitehead's career had been spent as a mathematician, first for twenty-five years at Trinity College, Cambridge, and then, from 1911, at the University of London. Whitehead had been Bertrand Russell's teacher and then his collaborator on the *Principia Mathematica* (1910–1913), a heroic three-volume attempt to reduce all mathematics to logic.

In his brilliant 1931 metamathematical paper, "On Formally Undecidable Propositions," the German Kurt Gödel had demonstrated that it was impossible for either the *Principia Mathematica* or any like system to be self-consistent and complete. Certain statements must necessarily be admitted as true that the system itself was incapable of either proving or disproving.

Even before the publication of Gödel's paper, however, Alfred North Whitehead himself had already come to perceive the inadequacy of his and Russell's monumental effort. In fact, Whitehead had been led by his understanding of mathematics, of the new quantum physics, and of physiology and psychology to doubt the sufficiency of the entire modern scientific philosophy.

He would object: "We are content with superficial orderings from diverse arbitrary starting points." And, with disarming gentleness, he would further inquire: "Is it not possible that the standardized concepts of science are only valid within narrow limitations, perhaps too narrow for science itself?"

So it was that in 1924, at the advanced age of 63, Whitehead traveled across the Atlantic to join the faculty of Harvard University as a professor of philosophy. And the first fruit of this new career was *Science and the Modern World*, based in the main on eight Lowell Lectures that he delivered in 1925.

Two complementary lines of argument were to be found intertwined in this remarkable book. In one, Whitehead reviewed the entire history of Western objection and exception to scientific materialism: The philosophical arguments that had been raised against it at the outset of the modern Western scientific adventure during the Age of Reason. The experiential objections—often phrased in poetic terms—of the Romantic Era. And finally, the problems that had been recently raised for scientific materialism by the strange new science of the later Age of Technology.

And meanwhile, in his other concurrent line of argument, Whitehead sketched out a basis for an alternative post-materialistic philosophy—"a system of thought basing nature upon the concept of organism and not upon the concept of matter." As Whitehead would draw the distinction:

> The materialistic starting point is from independently existing substances, matter, and mind. The matter suffers modifications of its external relations of locomotion, and the mind suffers modifications of its contemplated objects. There are, in this

materialistic theory, two sorts of independent substances, each qualified by their appropriate passions.

The organic starting point is from the analysis of process as the realization of events disposed in an interlocked community. The event is the unit of things real.

Following the arguments that Whitehead was setting forth in *Science and the Modern World* was not at all easy. His presentation was intricate, wide-ranging, dense, and elusive, as though Whitehead himself wasn't always completely sure just what it was he was attempting to say.

In the course of his discussion, Whitehead would draw a contrast between thinkers who are clear yet limited and thinkers who are muddled but fruitful. Beyond question, he himself was a thinker of the second sort. In consequence, following out the nuances and implications of Alfred North Whitehead's arguments and attempting to determine exactly what they meant would remain something of a challenge even for professional students of philosophy.

It was little wonder, then, that van Vogt's contemporaries—the other boys who would grow up to write the science fiction of the Golden Age—should largely find *Science and the Modern World* unintelligible. Or that in the places where these earnest young scientists of the basement could comprehend Whitehead—as in his repudiation of scientific materialism—they would not be prepared to accept and follow him.

However, it would be quite otherwise with van Vogt, in large part precisely because he was not a professional student of philosophy, and neither did he have any special allegiance to the given assumptions of Western science. He was just an out-of-step kid from farther Canada who above all things desired to broaden his mental horizons and was ready to take his ideas wherever he could find them.

For van Vogt, reading *Science and the Modern World* provided him with exactly what he was seeking. From out of the general murk of Whitehead's argumentation, certain key remarks leaped forth to speak directly to him.

As one example, there was this:

> My theory involves the entire abandonment of the notion that simple location is the primary way in which things are involved in space-time. In a certain sense, everything is everywhere at all times. For every location involves an aspect of itself in every other location. Thus, every spatio-temporal standpoint mirrors the world.

What a mind-boggling suggestion this was—that everything is everywhere at all times so that each and every standpoint, to some extent, mirrors all that exists! Now that was food for thought.

So was this:

> If organisms are to survive, they must work together. Any physical object which by its influence deteriorates its environment, commits suicide.

And this:

> Successful organisms modify their environment. Those organisms are successful which modify their environments so as to assist each other.

It mattered little to van Vogt that he might not be picking up every last detail of Whitehead's reasoning. What did matter was that he grasped the whole: In place of a Universe of constantly competing particles effectively going nowhere, Whitehead was offering the alternative vision of an organic and interconnected Universe evolving through creativeness and cooperation.

Thinking such as this—neither spiritual nor materialistic, but holistic, organic, environmental and evolutionary—was a genuine rarity in the twenties. But the young Alfred van Vogt found it highly appealing and took to it eagerly.

The extraordinary ideas that he stumbled upon in *Science and the Modern World* would linger in the back of his mind. Eventually, after they had incubated long enough and become his own, they would emerge again as the philosophical basis for the science fiction van Vogt would write for John Campbell's *Astounding*. And the fundamental difference distinguishing his stories from the Golden Age SF produced by all the writers who still remained card-carrying scientific materialists would be van Vogt's Whitehead-inspired post-materialistic sense of a Universe of interconnected organisms evolving together.

As the months that followed high school wore on, it became clear that there was a limit to the length of time that young Alfred could go on burying himself in his books and insisting to everyone that he was a writer even though he had never written anything. Early in 1931, van Vogt took a Civil Service examination, was offered a temporary government job, and accepted it. He traveled east to Ottawa, the capital city of Canada, where he would spend ten highly formative months as a clerk tabulating the Canadian census.

Van Vogt's imagination was captured by the holistic quality of the census, with its populations of information to be examined first from this angle and then from that. One result of this fascination would be that in years to come, when a Doc Smith was still describing the thinking machine of tomorrow as no more than a gigantic card sorter, and a Robert Heinlein had gotten no further than to conceive of a ponderous and unreliable "ballistic calculator" used for the single specialized purpose of working out spaceship rocket burn requirements, A.E. van Vogt would be envisioning the computer of the future as an information machine capable of containing a quadrillion facts all cross-referenced by names, dates, and keywords, and available to an inquirer at the touch of a button.

Another thing that would stick in van Vogt's imagination from his sojourn in Ottawa—and eventually find expression in his SF stories—would be a powerful secret that he was let in on by his boardinghouse roommate, a young man who had recently been brought over to Canada from Scotland. He informed Alfred that his flag-waving neighbors back in Morden, Manitoba, had had it all wrong: The English didn't rule the British Empire at all; they only thought they did. The actual covert masters of the empire were the Scottish, taking their revenge for the defeat of Bonnie Prince Charlie at Culloden. And just as soon as the roommate had earned his college degree, he expected to assume the place that was being held for him behind the scenes in the Canadian government.

Since van Vogt enjoyed no comparable secret support from well-placed Dutch-Canadian cabalists, he had no alternative but to catch a freight train back to Winnipeg when the work of compiling the 1931 census was over. But during his time in Ottawa, he'd made a serious start toward learning how to become the writer he was already claiming to be. From the Palmer Institute of Authorship, he took a correspondence course in "English and Self-Expression." The long-term consequence of this course would be to set him thinking about the possible subliminal effects of particular sounds and unorthodox word selections.

Then, back home in Winnipeg, he took out of the library Thomas Uzzell's *Narrative Technique* and two highly useful books by John Gallishaw, *The Only Two Ways to Write a Story* and *Twenty Problems of the Short-Story Writer*—precisely the manuals of instruction that a young Jack Williamson, newly dropped out of college to become a full-time writer, was choosing to study at about this same time. From Gallishaw, van Vogt learned the necessity of writing sentences that conveyed either emotion, imagery, or suspense and how to break a story down into a series of short scenes, each with its own distinct purpose. From Uzzell, he took the idea that a story should make a unified impact upon the reader.

At last, after all this study, the twenty-year-old van Vogt felt ready to try writing a story of his own. But what kind of story should it be?

He didn't read confession magazines himself, but van Vogt had noticed that *True Story*, the top such magazine, had a prize contest in every issue. So he decided to be audacious and take a shot at that. He went off to the library, and with Uzzell and Gallishaw backing him at either elbow, he managed to write the first scene of a story.

What he was attempting seemed chancy to van Vogt. All the time he was working, he kept waking in the night and going round and round about what was to come next. After turning out one scene each day for nine days, he managed to finish a story which he called "I Live in the Streets." This was about a girl who had run into hard times in the Depression and been thrown out of her rooming house. It didn't win any prizes, but *True Story* did buy and publish it.

During the next three years, from 1932 to 1935, van Vogt had regular success selling simple, emotional, anonymous little stories to the confession magazines and even won a thousand dollar prize with one. But then—as though his inner being had come to the sudden conclusion that if practice was what he had been after in writing these stories, he had had practice enough—in the middle of another true confession, he felt disgusted with himself, threw down his pen, and wrote no more of them.

But if it was not sufficient to write whatever was easiest to sell, then what was his writing for? Van Vogt wasn't altogether sure. In the middle thirties, he would write trade newspaper interviews, short radio plays, and an occasional short story for a newspaper supplement or a pulp magazine. He learned from this work, but none of it was completely satisfying. At the same time, he had been told that he had the ability to write for the slick magazines, but he felt a strong aversion to attempting this, which he couldn't altogether explain.

Because he was a reader, a writer, and a thinker, van Vogt regarded himself as an intellectual. But if he was an intellectual, it was not of the usual sort. He wasn't silver-tongued or swift-witted. He had very little ability to remember a precise fact or an exact niggle, and no talent at all for linear thought and logical analysis. He was not a conventional man of reason.

Rather, van Vogt's usual method was to fix on some question or subject in a highly single-minded way—to surround it and dwell upon it and absorb it. He might get nowhere with a problem for the longest time, but then at last the penny would drop and some insight would pop into his mind.

When van Vogt had enough insights accumulated on a topic, they would assemble themselves into what he would come to think of as a system—a methodology or mode of approach that had its own consistency, if only in the manner in which it was applied by him. In later days, van Vogt would even take pride in describing himself as "Mr. System."

The insight that he might write science fiction and that he *should* write science fiction dawned on him in the summer of 1938. It came with typical suddenness and indirection. After eight years in which he had not read any science fiction, one day, when he was in McKnight's Drug Store in Winnipeg, van Vogt casually picked up the latest issue of *Astounding*, a magazine he had never paid any attention to before. He flipped on through to the middle pages and began to read a story.

But not just any story: Amazingly ... coincidentally ... significantly ... perhaps even inevitably ... the story that he singled out in this apparently completely random fashion was "Who Goes There?" by Don A. Stuart—the prototypical example of modern science fiction.

Van Vogt was immediately hooked by the mood and the flavor of what he was reading. And so he bought the magazine and hurried on home to finish the story he'd started—to savor it, to linger over it, and to think about it.

What struck van Vogt most forcibly about "Who Goes There?" wasn't exactly the same thing that would catch the attention of those readers who were still staunch scientific materialists. All that they would see was the morally neutral message that even a shape-shifting otherworldly monster might be subject to the universal power of human scientific knowledge. Isaac Asimov, for instance, responding to this very same story, would write his first attempt at modern science fiction—"Stowaway," or "The Callistan Menace"—about another threatening alien creature that human beings come to understand scientifically.

But what van Vogt took from his reading of "Who Goes There?" was something quite a bit different from this. What intrigued him about this story was its intimation of a cooperative ethic—a new ordering of value appropriate to the post-materialistic Universe he had been turning over and over in his mind since he first read Whitehead.

That is, van Vogt noticed that those human beings in the Antarctic party of "Who Goes There?" who retained their sanity were able to work together to overcome a creature who, on an individual basis, was far more powerful than any of them. And conversely, he saw that the horrific alien, even though it might be both telepathic and originally one being, was not able to join its various parts together to take concerted action. Indeed, its selfishness and egoism were so complete as to affect even samples of its blood so that at the threat of a hot wire, these would scream and strive to escape and thereby betray their nonhuman nature.

And this all had a rightness for van Vogt. It seemed to him that in an organic, interconnected Universe, cooperation would be a fundamental value, a reflection of the purposes of the whole. And selfishness would be a fatal ethical defect no matter how outwardly powerful the entity might appear to be.

"Who Goes There?" altered van Vogt's life. Just as surely as if someone had seized him by the shoulders and physically realigned him, reading this story turned van Vogt around and pointed him in a new direction.

In the science fiction stories that he would come to write during the next half-dozen years, van Vogt would work out the answers to a cluster of questions that were first aroused by his reading of "Who Goes There?"

In an organic universe, wherein does true superiority lay? Does might in and of itself make right?

What connection exists between evolution and altruism?

And—his most persistent line of inquiry—how would a genuinely superior creature behave? What would it do? How would it act? And how would it be perceived by lesser beings?

For us to say all this, however, is not only to anticipate the direction in which

A.E. van Vogt would travel, but to state with some clarity what was not necessarily at all clear to him in the summer of 1938 when he put aside the August *Astounding* to reach for a sheet of letter paper and an envelope. It is perfectly possible, perhaps even probable, that he had no explicit memory of *Science and the Modern World*, or thoughts of post-materialism, or formed convictions about the moral nature of transcendent being in his mind at all. In the immediate moment, all that he may have known for certain was that he had an urgent idea for an SF story.

2
COSMIC HOSTILITY

IN complete unawareness that Don A. Stuart, the nominal author of "Who Goes There?" and the editor of the magazine he'd been reading were one and the same, van Vogt drafted a letter of inquiry. As an indication of his serious intent, he summarized his past experience as a writer. Then, in a paragraph, he outlined his idea. Would *Astounding* be interested in taking a look at a story like this?

He mailed the letter off to New York and then waited for some sort of answer to come. One moment, he was rarin' to go—ready to take over the whole Universe and transform it with his imagination. He knew how to tell a story, after all. And from his teenage reading of *Amazing*, he knew his way around science fiction. So why shouldn't he write SF and do it well? In the next instant, however, he would start to feel all unsure of himself, like a shy five-year-old new to the neighborhood who has to have an invitation before he can bring himself to come outside and play.

But if encouragement was what he had to have in order to begin writing SF, John Campbell did not let him down. Van Vogt would say later:

> I feel pretty sure that if he hadn't answered, that would have been the end of my science fiction career. I didn't know it at the time, but he answered all such letters.
>
> When he replied, he said, "In writing this story, be sure to concentrate on the mood and atmosphere. Don't just make it an action story."

This was precisely the right thing to say to van Vogt. It had been the splendidly atmospheric opening sentence—"The place stank"—which had first hooked him into reading "Who Goes There?" And the creation of story mood was the very thing van Vogt felt he knew how to do best.

So, feeling under some real obligation to follow through now that he had received this go-ahead from Campbell, he set to work on his story. He called upon the familiar methods he'd derived from the Palmer Institute, John Gallishaw, and Thomas Uzzell: Particular words and sounds used strangely for effect, sentences of constant suspense, imagery and emotion, one purposeful scene after another, all aiming toward a final unified impact.

The eventual title of the story would be "Vault of the Beast." It began:

> The creature crept. It whimpered from fear and pain. Shapeless, formless thing yet changing shape and form with each jerky movement, it crept along the corridor of the space freighter, fighting the terrible urge of its elements to take the shape of its surroundings. A gray blob of disintegrating stuff, it crept and cascaded, it rolled, flowed and dissolved, every movement an agony of struggle against the abnormal need to become a stable shape. Any shape!

This creature bears an immediately apparent resemblance to the menace of "Who Goes There?" It, too, is a telepathic shapeshifter capable of assuming the form of any human it encounters. But it also has its differences from Campbell's monster. It isn't able to proliferate and take over other beings, and it isn't autonomous.

In fact, this half-hysterical, half-terrified, yet casually murderous thing—which van Vogt called both a "robot" and an "android" and described both as organic and as a machine—is a construct that has been made by "great and evil minds" from another and slower dimension than ours. It has been dispatched to Earth to find a mathematician capable of freeing one of their kind who, millions of years ago, fell into our space and, while helpless, was imprisoned in a vault by the Martians of that day, who sensed its underlying ill intent.

If this mighty prisoner should become free, it can show its fellows the way to transfer from one dimension to another. And that is what they yearn for. As they admit, at the moment they think their designs have finally been achieved: "Our purpose is to control all spaces, all worlds—particularly those which are inhabited. We intend to be absolute rulers of the entire Universe."

The malevolent aliens use their shape-changing robot creature to manipulate, delude and sweet-talk an Earthman into divining how the vault might be opened. But when this has been accomplished, they give their true nature away. They propose to use the android as the key to the lock and take evident pleasure in the pain it suffers as they wrench it out of the human form it has assumed and twist it into the requisite shape.

Brender, the Earthman, cannot avoid the recognition that he has been tricked. At exactly the same moment, however, he also comes to the sudden realization that the act of opening the ancient, sand-buried Martian prison is going to cause the destruction of its occupant and ruin the aliens' schemes for conquest.

The poor screaming robot can still read Brender's mind. It knows what he knows. Even yet, it might warn its makers and possibly save its own life—but it elects not to. It permits itself to be sacrificed. The vault is opened, and the evil alien within perishes—and with it, its knowledge of how to travel from one dimension to another.

As the now-dying robot struggles in vain to return to human form, it explains to Brender:

"I didn't tell them ... I caught your thought ... and kept it ... from them ... because they were hurting me. They were going to destroy me. Because ... I liked ... being human. I was ... somebody!" The aliens, it seems, have been undone by their own remoteness, deviousness, and casual cruelty. And while Brender looks on in pity, the android dissolves into a puddle of gray, which then crumbles away into dust.

When he had finished this story, van Vogt mailed it off to *Astounding*. And just as van Vogt had managed to recognize "Who Goes There?" when he needed to, so John Campbell was able to reciprocate and to perceive from the outset that in this new Canadian storyteller he had discovered someone most unusual.

The very first thing that he noticed in reading "Vault of the Beast" was just how immediate and raw-nerved and intense it was. It didn't sit still for one minute but moved ahead with the inexorable pace of a fevered dream. Writing as relentless as this had never been seen in the SF pulp magazines.

The story was also boldly, even extravagantly science-fictional. Only five years earlier, the venerable H.G. Wells had suggested that to include more than a single wonder in any SF story was to step over the line into irresponsible silliness. He had declared, somewhat testily, "Nothing remains interesting where anything can happen."

But here was a rank beginner who seemed to have no compunctions at all against throwing a profusion of marvels into one brief novelette:

A protean monster/robot/android, space travel, telepathy, malevolent higher aliens, a multiplicity of dimensions operating at different time rates, inter-dimensional transference, a long-vanished Martian civilization, antigravity, the "ultimate prime number," no less than two different kinds of "ultimate metal," and an irresistible universal force. What's more, van Vogt came very close to making this superabundance of wonders add up to a real and meaningful story.

But the most original and impressive aspect of "Vault of the Beast" was that a considerable portion of the story was told from the point of view of a whimpering, blobby, shape-altering *thing*. Not only this, but van Vogt even asked the reader to empathize with the creature and to regret its passing. This was completely unheard of. Nobody had ever dared before to write from inside the psyche of so different and monstrous a being.

As powerful, imaginative, and unusual as van Vogt's story recognizably was, however, Campbell couldn't help feeling that it wasn't yet as sound and effective as it might be.

To begin with, it wasn't altogether plausible. If the headlong pace of the narrative should be interrupted for even an instant and exact questions be asked, there was much in this story that would not hold up under examination.

This would, in fact, always be van Vogt's weakest point. Like his mentor, Alfred North Whitehead, he would be muddled and fruitful, rather than limited but clear. In later times, van Vogt would say of the writers of the Golden Age: "In a sense, we were all One Great Big Author." And there would be considerable aptness to this observation. However, to the extent that the body of Campbellian modern science fiction did amount to a whole—the synergetic product of many separate and partial individual contributions—it would be writers other than A.E. van Vogt who would supply it with its detailed, plausible arguments. Without the comparatively restrained and careful work of de Camp, Heinlein, Asimov, and the others, van Vogt's flights of dreamlike imagination might very easily have seemed completely unfounded—just as without his work, many of their stories might have seemed lacking in mystery.

There was a further difficulty with "Vault of the Beast" beyond its imperfect plausibility. Despite the sound advice of Thomas Uzzell, it wasn't unified in its effect.

The central questions raised by the story appeared to be how the android creature was to contrive to win the freedom of the long-imprisoned alien, and what this evil being and its kind might do if it were allowed to escape from the Martian vault. At the climax of the story, however, all this possibility and danger prove to be nothing more than illusion. At any time that the vault should be opened, it appears the alien inside must inevitably perish.

So the main story problem was not a problem at all—and never had been. At this point, the emotional weight of "Vault of the Beast" shifted over to the death of the shape-changing robot and the flattering taste this wretched creature had acquired for the assumption of human form.

This alteration of emphasis did not work perfectly. At the very least, it appeared to Campbell that if the reader was to be hooked into identifying with this monster and looking upon it with pity, then more emphasis would have to be placed upon the emotions of the creature early in the story.

So Campbell returned the manuscript to van Vogt. He praised it highly but suggested that it still needed some fine-tuning. The Earthman, Jim Brender, could use additional motivation. And the monster should be made more pitiable from the outset. Would van Vogt have a try at that?

Instead, however, his new would-be contributor overleaped Campbell's expectations entirely. By the time he heard from the editor, van Vogt was already at work on a second SF story that incorporated all he had learned in writing the first one. And it was going so well that he didn't want to set it aside.

It would be a good while before van Vogt got back to "Vault of the Beast" to rewrite it. In this form, arguably stronger, yet still not wholly satisfactory because of the central nonproblem of the imprisoned alien, it would appear in the August 1940 issue of *Astounding* as his fifth published SF story. And this one, extended delay for revision would be as close as he would ever come to having a story rejected by John Campbell until after the end of World War II.

It was the novelette "Black Destroyer," his second science fiction story, which convinced Campbell that this "Alfred Vogt"—as he would address him at the outset—wasn't just another highly promising beginner who required tutoring and guidance. On the basis of this singular story, it became evident to the editor that this 26-year-old from Winnipeg—just two years younger than Campbell himself—had already arrived as a wild, imaginative talent unmatched in science fiction.

Van Vogt demonstrated in "Black Destroyer" that the apparent virtues of his first effort had been neither an illusion nor a fluke. His new story had the very same strengths: Once again, he started his story with a dynamic and gripping first line—"On and on Coeurl prowled!"—and then hurtled along from there. Once again, he asked the reader to identify with the drives and purposes of a powerful alien creature. And once again, he offhandedly mixed together a multiplicity of SF concepts, any one of which another writer might have thought more than sufficient to serve as the basis for a story.

But this time his plot was more integrated. Better than that—unlike "Vault of the Beast" and its model, "Who Goes There?," which still retained overtones of the conventional Techno Age alien invasion story—"Black Destroyer" had a situation that was completely new and different.

And still better yet was that this novelette was a brilliant anticipation of science fiction as John Campbell thought it ought to be and wished it to become.

The direction in which the great editor desired to move science fiction was toward human dominion over the future and outer space. And in "Black Destroyer," van Vogt imagined an exploration vessel from a future human civilization that spans the galaxy, landing on a planet of a red sun that is separated from its nearest neighbor by nine hundred light years.

What a premise this was! An interstellar survey team from an Earth-derived human civilization that is as broad as the galaxy! Some fifteen years later, in the mid-fifties, a story background of this kind would be commonplace in *Astounding*. But in 1939, nothing quite like it had ever been imagined before.

It was John Campbell's conviction that if it was going to be possible someday for men to travel to the planets and the stars and establish control over the wider Universe, the necessary job for science fiction had to be to identify every possible problem or hindrance to this, and then imagine how each one might be dealt with. The real flaw in "Vault of the Beast," from the editor's point of view, was that it didn't actually pose any problem of responsibility and control for men to resolve.

But "Black Destroyer" did.

In this story, the human scientists exploring the isolated world they have discovered set their spherical ship down near the remains of a long-destroyed city. And here, they encounter the bizarre and powerful Coeurl, a catlike creature with fangs and massive forepaws, tentacles that grow from his shoulders, and tendrilled ears, whom they will eventually identify as a degenerate survivor of this ruined civilization.

As the Techno Age would reckon matters, Coeurl is a clearly superior being, more than a match for any one man. Not only is he immensely long-lived, but he is quick, strong, and deadly. He is able to breathe chlorine or oxygen indifferently. Through his ear tendrils, he can hear sounds, pick up the vibrations given off by the precious life-substance *id*, and also detect, broadcast, and control electromagnetic phenomena. And with his prehensile tentacles, he can instantly operate sophisticated machinery he has never encountered before, including the great globular human spaceship itself.

Coeurl is a living example of cosmic hostility. He is a ruthless and practiced killer. He and his kind have leveled their civilization, fought amongst themselves, and devoured all other living things in this world in a desperate death struggle to obtain "the all-necessary id"—eventually identified by a human scientist as the element phosphorus.

Before the humans manage to recognize Coeurl's true nature and power, this utterly rapacious being has ripped one man to pieces to obtain his id and then murdered another twelve men as they sleep. When he is found out at last—his carnage discovered—Coeurl escapes to the spaceship engine room, barricades himself there, and then launches himself and the human party into interstellar space.

However, if Coeurl is a representative of unrelenting Techno Age cosmic hostility, it is as perceived through revisionist Atomic Age eyes. And the Atomic Age would not only doubt that there can be such a thing as total difference or absolute superiority but would boldly assert that men may scientifically investigate anything and everything that exists in search of the most convenient handle to grab it by.

We might compare this with the members of the Antarctic party in Campbell's "Who Goes There?" Though confronted by a shapeshifting alien monster, they are able to calmly say, "This isn't wildly beyond what we already know. It's just a modification we haven't seen before. It's as natural, as logical, as any other manifestation of life. It obeys exactly the same laws."

In highly similar fashion, even though the human scientists of "Black Destroyer" may find themselves up to their knees in corpses and gore as their spaceship screams toward the stars under the guidance of an id-crazed cat-creature endowed with powers like none they have ever encountered before, Commander Morton, the leader of the expedition, is able to overcome any impulses he might be feeling toward fear and panic and deal coolly with the situation. He declares: "We're going to find out right now if we're dealing with unlimited science or a creature limited like the rest of us. I'll bet on the second possibility."

And that's a pretty good bet. Capable and dangerous Coeurl may be, but he is by no means either all-powerful or invulnerable. He has a number of weaknesses and limitations—crippling defects of ability, knowledge, mentation, and perspective.

Foremost among these is Coeurl's animalism. Ever since H.G. Wells' invading Martians, alien beings had displayed a taste for human blood and proved their own superiority by looking upon men as cattle. For van Vogt, however, Coeurl's insatiable appetite for id identifies him, and not his human victims, as the animal.

Coeurl is driven by lusts and hungers and lacks self-control. It doesn't take a lot to unbalance his psyche.

He can be thrown by his greed for phosphorus: "The sense of id was so overwhelming that his brain drifted to the ultimate verge of chaos."

Unexpectedness—even so little as the closing of a door and the movement of an elevator—can unsettle him: "He whirled with a savage snarl, his reason whirling into chaos. With one leap, he pounced at the door. The metal bent under his plunge, and the desperate pain maddened him. Now, he was all trapped animal."

And mayhem can make him manic and cause him to forget his purposes: "It was the seventh taste of murder that brought a sudden return of lust, a pure, unbounded desire to kill, return of a millennium-old habit of destroying everything containing the precious id."

Over and over, Coeurl gives himself away by these descents into animality. They cause him to act prematurely, to betray his intentions, and to reveal his awesome but combatable powers.

Moreover, when Coeurl isn't acting like a heedless beast, he is a blind egotist. All that he can see in the human scientific expedition is new inferiors to serve as a fresh supply of essential id. And beyond that, an opportunity for himself and the others of his kind who still survive to leap to the stars and seize even more id:

> For just a moment he felt contempt, a glow of superiority, as he thought of the stupid creatures who dared to match their wit against a coeurl. And in that moment, he suddenly thought of other coeurls. A queer, exultant sense of race pounded through his being; the driving hate of centuries of ruthless competition yielded reluctantly before pride of kinship with the future rulers of all space.

At every turn Coeurl believes himself to be more powerful and able and in control than he actually is, and he automatically dismisses the human opposition he faces without ever pausing to think very deeply about its true nature.

But, in fact, there is a profound difference between the humans and him. Their galactic civilization has solved the problem of cyclical history, while Coeurl and his kind have not, so they know a great deal about him while he knows nothing about them.

The men can look at his historical context and his behavior and gauge Coeurl accurately as a degenerate and a criminal. As the archaeologist Korita observes: "In fact, his whole record is one of the low cunning of the primitive, egotistical mind which has little or no conception of the vast organization with which it is confronted."

It is wholly typical of Coeurl that he should take over the engine room of the spherical spaceship under the apparent assumption that being where the power is located will be sufficient to make him master of the situation—and also typical that he should be mistaken. In fact, it is the humans who occupy the ship's control room who actually direct the ship and its machines.

What's more, they possess science that Coeurl does not have and dares not face. He may be able to blank out remote pictures of himself, to take a shot in the head from a vibration gun without suffering harm, to disrupt electric locks, and to harden the door to the engine room by increasing "the electronic tensions of the door to their ultimate." But he cannot redirect, ward off, or absorb atomic power. Consequently, once the humans do manage to break into the engine room, they have an effective weapon with which to attack him.

Coeurl must escape from this threat. So able is he, within his limits, that he can throw together an individual spaceship right then and there in the machine shop of the great ship. And in this little ship, he attempts to flee back to his own planet to gather his kind.

But alone in space is just where the humans would like to see Coeurl. They have vast experience there, while he has none. As Korita says: "We have, then, a primitive, and that primitive is now far out in space, completely outside of his natural habitat."

And, indeed, Coeurl does find space disconcerting. Given his tendency to lose his head, it isn't surprising that he should be thrown into confusion when all his usual expectations begin to be overturned. First, the human ship suddenly disappears from view. Then it seems that he is going backward, away from his planet, rather than toward it, as he should. And finally, the human ship—which, by Coeurl's reckoning, should be far behind—suddenly proves to be waiting in front of him.

It is all too much for Coeurl, and he becomes overwhelmed by panic. Fearing the flames of men wielding atomic disintegrators, he wills his own death:

> They found him lying dead in a little pool of phosphorus.
> "Poor pussy," said Morton. "I wonder what he thought when he saw us appear ahead of him after his own sun disappeared. Knowing nothing of anti-accelerators, he couldn't know that we could stop short in space, whereas it would take him more than three hours to decelerate, and in the meantime, he'd be drawing

farther and farther away from where he wanted to go. He couldn't know that by stopping, we flashed past him at millions of miles a second. Of course, he didn't have a chance once he left our ship. The whole world must have seemed topsy-turvy."

And, in fact, with this brilliant novelette, van Vogt would turn all Techno Age perception upside-down. In previous science fiction, it had always been invading aliens who had the Universe on their side and men who had to overcome a limited Earth-bound perspective. But in "Black Destroyer," these values were reversed. Despite their power as individuals, it is Coeurl and his kind who are the limited offspring of a small and isolated planet, and it is human beings who have the knowledge and resources of the galaxy behind them.

What a promise! When he saw this, John Campbell's heart had to leap.

The editor wrote to van Vogt, saying, "You've done a perfectly beautiful job on this yarn about the Black Destroyer." And he would place this new writer's first published SF story on the cover of the July 1939 *Astounding*, the issue which is generally considered to have marked the beginning of the Golden Age.

In his letter accepting "Black Destroyer," Campbell described *Unknown*, a fantasy magazine he was starting, at some length, and asked van Vogt to consider it a wide-open market. Campbell thought that writing fantasy would come naturally to van Vogt, with his gift for evoking mood and horror. The editor declared, "If this 'Black Destroyer' had not been interplanetary, had not involved atomic power, mechanism, etc., it would have been grand for the new magazine."

And van Vogt did his best to oblige Campbell by giving him what he was asking for. More or less immediately, he wrote a story about a Polynesian shark-god—"The Sea Thing" (*Unknown*, January 1940)—that was his attempt to do something like "Black Destroyer" in fantasy dress. And in 1942–1943, he would contribute three more stories to the magazine, including a novel, *The Book of Ptah* (*Unknown Worlds*, October 1943), in the very last issue.

But even though van Vogt might not be a man for facts and exactitude, and had a certain talent for evoking moods, writing rational fantasy just wasn't his thing. Ultimately, stories like that hinged on providing material explanations for bits and pieces of remnant spiritualism, and playing that game wasn't what van Vogt had returned to SF to do. Consequently, he wrote stories he thought of as fantasy only with the utmost difficulty, and his work for *Unknown* was no match for his science fiction in either originality or effectiveness.

Van Vogt only caught fire when he was writing what he believed in, and his true beliefs were post-materialistic. His great aim in writing SF was to look deep into the time and space distances of an organic, interconnected, evolving Universe and imagine man transcending himself.

Between the sale of "Black Destroyer" and its publication, van Vogt married Edna Hull, a woman seven years older than he. She was a former executive secretary, a freelance writer of newspaper features and short-short stories for church magazines whom he had met at the Winnipeg Writers Club. After their marriage, Mrs. van Vogt would transcribe her husband's handwritten drafts on the typewriter, and in the process, become sufficiently intrigued by SF that she would eventually write a dozen stories of her own for *Astounding* and *Unknown* under the name E. Mayne Hull.

The first story van Vogt completed after his marriage was a direct sequel to "Black Destroyer" entitled "Discord in Scarlet" (*Astounding*, December 1939). Here the same human survey ship, this time traveling from our own galaxy to another, comes upon Xtl, a red six-limbed alien being even older, more powerful and more frightening than Coeurl, floating there in the void where a cosmic explosion had hurled him eons ago.

Once he has been permitted inside the barriers that protect the human ship, Xtl proves to be able to rearrange his atomic structure so as to pass through floors and walls at will. Then he begins playing an elaborate game of hide-and-go-seek in which he suddenly appears out of nowhere, seizes and paralyzes a man, preferably a nice fat one, and carries him away to deposit one of his eggs in.

The humans are awestruck by the creature's ability to survive in space and to walk through walls. And one of them declares, "A race which has solved the final secrets of biology must be millions, even billions of years in advance of man."

Psychologically, however, Xtl is much less advanced. Despite the opportunity he has been granted for heavy meditation all alone there in the timeless quiet of the extra-galactic darkness, his thinking remains cycle-bound. And Korita, the archaeologist, is able to recognize that Xtl displays the blinkered vision typical of a peasant.

As a peasant, his first aim is to safeguard his posterity. It is his overriding concern to find hosts for the eggs he carries within his breast that gives men the time they need to organize themselves and to devise plans against him.

Furthermore, having a peasant's personal attachment to his own little territory, Xtl is unable to conceive until too late that the men might actually halt their ship in the middle of intergalactic space and then abandon it in order to trap him alone inside while they temporarily turn their ship into "a devastating, irresistible torrent of energy" to rid themselves of him.

After Xtl has fled into the intergalactic dark, one crew member suggests that they had a natural advantage over the creature: "After all, he did belong to another universe, and there is a special rhythm to our present state of existence to which man is probably attuned." But another replies:

> You assume far too readily that man is a paragon of justice, forgetting apparently that he lives on meat, enslaves his neighbors, murders his opponents, and obtains the most unholy, sadistic joy from the agony of others. It is not impossible that we shall, in the course of our travels, meet other intelligent creatures far more worthy than man to rule the Universe.

In these first three science fiction stories by van Vogt—"Vault of the Beast," "Black Destroyer," and "Discord in Scarlet"—there were two common elements. The more readily apparent of these was monsters possessing more-than-human powers. Indeed, so obvious was this that it would begin to seem to some—van Vogt himself among them—that it was possible he was only a one-plot author.

A more complete and sympathetic assessment, however, would understand that van Vogt was yet another intuitional SF writer following his nose wherever it chose to lead him—and, moreover, one who had rather less conscious awareness of where he was bound and what he was really up to than was usual even amongst this gang of creative sleepwalkers.

Van Vogt would begin writing a story when he had nothing more to work with than some faint glimmering—an image or a mood—and then grope his way toward the end one scene at a time, working by feel and by inspiration. He would say frankly: "I have no endings for my stories when I start them—just a thought and something that excites me. I get some picture that is very interesting, and I write it. But I don't know where's it's going to go next."

He would throw in every single idea that he had during the time he was writing a story, holding back nothing. And when he got stuck, van Vogt found that the necessary new turn he needed would arrive in a dream that night or in a flash sometime the following morning:

> Generally, either in a dream or about ten o'clock the next morning—bang!—an idea comes, and it will be something in a sense non-sequitur yet a growth from the story. I've gotten my most original stories that way; these ideas made the story different

every ten pages. In other words, I wouldn't have been able to reason them out, I feel.

Earlier writers of SF, in imagining their stories, had again and again taken their cue from some dream or sudden insight. But A.E. van Vogt was the first writer of science fiction to attempt to turn this into a system and rely upon nonrational processes to light his way through one story after another.

However, the truth of the matter may be that he simply couldn't help but do this. Writing out of mental imagery, lack of conscious foreknowledge of what was to come next, and dreamstuff was the only effective way that van Vogt knew to produce science fiction at all. He says, "I have tried to plot stories consciously, from beginning to end, and I never sell them. I know better, now, than to even attempt to write them that way."

3

THE MUTATION-AFTER-MAN

THE less obvious, less superficial, common element in van Vogt's earliest stories—the message from his unconscious that he was forced to repeat until at last he understood it—was morality, or, as the more psychologically minded Atomic Age would prefer to call it, sanity. In each of his first three science fiction stories, super-powered monsters are undone by their drives and hungers, by their egotism, ruthlessness, and cruelty, and by their inability to surrender cherished attachments, while people constituted much like ourselves are able to prevail over them through decency, self-sacrifice, cooperation and breadth of vision.

After three of these science fiction monster stories—plus that paler imitation for *Unknown*—and just when he was beginning to think that this might be all he could write, van Vogt finally came to a conscious recognition of what his unconscious mind had been getting at all along. It was telling him that true superiority was not a matter of age or biology or personal power. Rather, it lay in being able to distinguish between mere self-interest and the good of the whole.

Having finally gotten this message, van Vogt would state it as explicitly as he could in his next science fiction story, the aptly titled "Repetition" (*Astounding*, April 1940).

In this story, an envoy has been sent from Earth to persuade the stubbornly defiant colonists of the Jovian moon Europa to allow their world to be ceded politically to Mars in order to bring Mars into union with Earth and Venus and forestall a Solar System-wide war. The envoy admits that short-term suffering for this colony is a real possibility but argues that it should lead to a greater long-range good:

> Remember this, it's not only Europa's recoverable metals that will be used up in a thousand years, but also the metal resources of the entire Solar System. That's why we must have an equitable distribution now, because we can't afford to spend the last hundred of those thousand years fighting over metal with Mars. You see, in that thousand years we must reach the stars. We must develop speeds immeasurably greater than light—and in that last, urgent hundred years we must have their cooperation, not their enmity. Therefore, they must not be dependent on us for anything, and we must not be under the continual mind-destroying temptation of being able to save ourselves for a few years longer if we sacrifice them.

The envoy's concluding exhortation, which convinces a young Europan to switch from being his enemy to being his earnest protector, is this:

> I have talked of repetition being a rule of life. But somewhere along the pathway of the Universe there must be a first time for everything, a first peaceful solution along sound sociological lines of the antagonisms of great sovereign powers.
> Some day man will reach the stars, and all the old, old problems will repeat themselves. When that day comes, we must have established sanity in the very souls of men, so firmly rooted that there will be an endless repetition of peaceful solutions.

The story had little of the intensity, heat, and drive that had made van Vogt's three previous science fiction stories different from all other SF. Next to them, "Repetition" was merely conventional—similar in appearance and scope to other short fiction in *Astounding* in 1940. More than that, it was a talky story, in essence no more than a dramatized lecture.

Even so, it did have one highly important statement to make. If men were ever to become the beings that van Vogt had described in "Black Destroyer"—if they were ever to reach the stars at all, let alone inherit the galaxy—they would first have to learn simple sanity: Breadth of vision, surrender of self-interest, and peaceful cooperation. And if they couldn't achieve this, they would be just so much chopped liver for creatures far simpler and less powerful than Coeurl.

That this indeed was the point implicit for van Vogt in "Black Destroyer" and "Discord in Scarlet" would be confirmed in 1950 when he put these stories together with two others and added new material to make what he would call a "fix-up novel"—*The Voyage of the Space Beagle*. The overall point made by this book would be the necessity for integrated vision. Sanity.

In the novel, van Vogt would introduce a new central character, Elliot Grosvenor, a Nexialist, or applied holist. He might be understood as the van Vogtian equivalent of Heinlein's ideal man—the "encyclopedic synthesist" or master of all knowledge. The difference between them was that in Heinlein's version the weight of emphasis was on photographic memory and perfect command of fact, while in van Vogt's case the emphasis was on holistic vision.

At the outset of the story, Grosvenor is something of an odd man out aboard the exploration vessel. He is all but invisible:

> He was becoming accustomed to being in the background. As the only Nexialist aboard the *Space Beagle*, he had been ignored for months by specialists who did not clearly understand what a Nexialist was, and who cared very little anyway. Grosvenor had plans to rectify that. So far, the opportunity to do so had not occurred.

Grosvenor intends to apply Nexialism to the splintered viewpoints of the various scientific specialists aboard the ship and to resolve the small-minded political infighting that divides the men of the *Space Beagle*. His opportunity to demonstrate the value of holistic thinking arrives in the encounters with Coeurl and Xtl—here given as Ixtl—and other bizarre life forms. With his broader view of things, Grosvenor becomes the person most responsible for the survival of the expedition.

By the end of the book, the need for Nexialist thought has become sufficiently well-established that Grosvenor is giving classes in holism to the men of the *Space Beagle*, which even his former chief antagonist has begun to attend. Grosvenor says:

> The problems which Nexialism confronts are whole problems. Man has divided life and matter into separate compartments of knowledge and being. And, even though he sometimes uses words which indicate his awareness of that wholeness of nature, he continues to behave as if the one, changing Universe has many separately functioning parts. The techniques we will discuss tonight ... will show how this disparity between reality and man's behavior can be overcome.

In late 1939, however, van Vogt's thinking had not yet explicitly progressed as far as this. Rather, we can say that with "Repetition," he had answered one question for himself but then raised another. He had satisfied himself that men who were well-integrated into the Universe could face any selfish Village-minded creature to be found in this galaxy or beyond it and prevail. But he had also begun to wonder what men must become if they were to be successful in making their own transition from the Village Solar System to the wider Universe.

It seemed to him that men would have to transcend themselves and become better attuned to the Universe as a whole. So to John Campbell, van Vogt suggested the possibility of a novel about Homo superior emerging out of man as we presently know him. This story, *Slan*, would be told from the point of view of the new, higher order man.

Campbell's immediate reaction to this proposal was that what van Vogt wanted to do simply couldn't be done. It wasn't possible.

Some twenty-five years later, in a letter to Doc Smith, Campbell would recall what he told van Vogt: "I pointed out to him that you can't tell a superman story from the superman's viewpoint—unless you're a superman. He pulled a beautiful trick in that yarn and proved me 100% wrong."

What Campbell threw at van Vogt was nothing less than orthodox wisdom, received truth. During the Age of Technology, it had been presumed that superior meant *superior*—clearly better in every significant regard. If a being were to be acknowledged as a superman, by definition that must mean that his thoughts and motives and values were completely beyond the ability of lesser men to understand.

The very unfathomability of the superman would be a central evidence of his superiority. Consequently, a superman story in the Techno Age, like Olaf Stapledon's *Odd John*, would invariably be told by some uncomprehending but tolerated human who is allowed close enough to the New Man to look upon his radiant splendor in something of the same way that a dumb but adoring cocker spaniel might gaze upon its lord and master.

The "beautiful trick" that van Vogt would pull off in *Slan* was to tell his story from the point of view of an isolated, ignorant, and immature superman—a young and vulnerable boy on the run, seeking to learn more about himself and his kind.

And this was something that John Campbell could accept. Not only would he be willing to concede that a superman who wasn't very old and didn't know all that much might be within the power of ordinary human beings to comprehend, but he would be thoroughly delighted with van Vogt for demonstrating the insufficiency of an accepted truth. There was nothing Campbell liked better than that.

So much did Campbell like it, in fact, that he would adopt the narrative argument of *Slan* as his own and attempt to pass the lesson he'd learned on to others. Here is how Campbell would phrase that lesson in a letter to Clifford Simak:

> The super-*man* can't be fully portrayed. But since ontogeny recapitulates phylogeny, a super-human must, during boyhood and adolescence, pass through the human level; there will be a stage of his development when he is less than adult-human, another stage when he is equal to adult-human—and the final stage when he has passed beyond our comprehension. The situation can be handled, then, by established faith, trust, understanding, and sympathy with the *individual as a character* by portraying him in his not-greater-than adult human stages—and allow the established trust and belief to carry over to the later and super-human stage.

This Campbell-eye view of *Slan* would be accurate and perceptive—but only as far as it went. For instance, it would be quite true that van Vogt would portray his superman, Jommy Cross, at different moments in his early life—in boyhood, in adolescence, and as a young man. But to van Vogt, these different points would not represent a series of discrete stages, climaxed by a leap to some single final stage of supermanhood in which Jommy passes beyond our power to understand. Rather, they would delineate a steeply rising curve of growth that might well continue on to even higher levels.

For van Vogt, being a superman was a relative condition, not an absolute one. Because he was more able and together than an ordinary human being, Jommy Cross would be *a* superman. But he wouldn't be *the* superman—the one and only kind of superman there could be—in the old Techno Age sense.

Again, Campbell would be perfectly correct in noting that trust and belief in Jommy's motives and behavior were established when it was easiest, while he was a helpless, hunted, innocent kid. There can be no doubt that van Vogt, the writer who had evoked empathy with blobby creeping androids and id-thirsty tentacled cat-monsters, spared no effort to hook the reader into making an emotional identification with his nine-year-old telepathic boy with golden tendrils in his hair, separated from his mother on a city street and forced to flee for his life.

What's more, he would make the boy an unflagging idealist as well, and completely convince the reader of Jommy's constant desire to find out the truth and to do right.

Where Campbell would be mistaken, however, would be in thinking that Jommy Cross' innocence and idealism were only a narrative ploy, a device to gain reader identification and sympathy. In fact, Jommy Cross' purity would have its own reason for being. It would be the very essence of what van Vogt was attempting to express in this novel.

The central plot-problem of *Slan* would be young Jommy's struggle against all the old Techno Age stereotypes which insisted that the superman must be a remote, unfeeling, hyper-intellectual—Big Brain's younger brother. Jommy would be told that this was the true nature of his own kind, the tendrilled slans. Again and again, he would be offered reason to perceive them as utterly cold and ruthless and cruel.

In the meantime, however, through his own maturation and gradual self-discovery, Jommy would demonstrate what it really might be like to be a superior human being. We'd see for ourselves that a superman didn't necessarily have to be brainy, heartless and amoral, because Jommy himself would not be at all like that.

Jommy Cross would be the first example of a new and radically different sort of Earth-born superman—good and noble and altruistic.

It was van Vogt's holistic sense of an organic, evolving, interconnected Universe that permitted him to reconceive the superman in these terms. More than permitted him—compelled him.

If the Universe was indeed a whole and not merely a jumble of unrelated parts, then it was obvious to van Vogt that true superiority must consist in being relatively more in tune with the purposes of the whole. To be superior was to be more integrated and less partial. To better approximate the wholeness of the whole.

However, it would be one thing for van Vogt to come to an apprehension of this *gestalt*—to have a sudden gut awareness that there was a novel demanding to be written about a superman whose superiority ultimately lies in his relatively greater integration with the purposes of the Universe—and another to actually write the story. Like most of van Vogt's work, *Slan* was completed only with considerable effort.

Because van Vogt was so often vague and implausible and had so little concern for exact factuality, there would be those among the readership of *Astounding* who would take him for a hasty and careless writer. That wouldn't exactly be the case, however.

The truth of the matter was that A.E van Vogt toiled endlessly over the stories he wrote. He wasn't facile—anything but. It was often difficult for him to find any words, let alone the right words set down in the right way to express the images and relationships that came to him in dreams or sudden flashes.

Like a Romantic of the previous century, he struggled to express the all-but-inexpressible: His sense of where transcendence was to be found. And with his eye fixed on the whole of things, he was always capable of tripping over the English language and taking a header.

It wasn't that van Vogt had no ear at all for the language. One of his real pleasures in writing lay in coining names like Coeurl and Xtl and Jommy Cross. And he loved what he liked to call "the great pulp music," and aimed to emulate it, most successfully in his ringing final lines.

But the truth must be admitted—his prose wasn't as consistently clear as Asimov's, as consciously clever as Heinlein's, or as exquisitely cadenced as Theodore Sturgeon's. Van Vogt was capable of bashing words together in the most dismaying manner without seeming to take any notice of the damage he was inflicting. One example of this is the phrase "fix-up novel"—but there have been and will be others that we may quote without lingering over.

At the same time, however, it is also true that a considerable portion of what looked to be clumsiness on van Vogt's part was, in fact, deliberate and hard-won technique: A word used more deliberately for its sound value than for its meaning in order to set up some subliminal resonance. Or a provocative vagueness introduced in order to prevent his readers from understanding too clearly and exactly what was happening and thereby losing their sense of mystery. As van Vogt would eventually say:

> Each paragraph—sometimes each sentence—of my brand of science fiction has a gap in it, an unreality condition. In order to make it real, the reader must add the missing parts. He cannot do this out of his past associations. There *are* no past associations. So he must fill in the gap from the creative part of his brain.

On several different occasions, van Vogt would offer this passage as an example of what he meant by this kind of writing: "The human-like being reached into what looked like a fold of skin and drew out a tiny silver-bright object. It pointed this shining thing at Hagin."

But so difficult and trying did van Vogt find it to write in this way—in dream-born, emotion-charged, headlong sentences, each with its own special element of oddness or not-thereness—that there were times when he would more than half-envy those SF writers like L. Ron Hubbard who could just sit down at the typewriter and bang out finished story copy as fast as they could type.

He would think of writers like that as intuitional—and himself as not. Indeed, van Vogt's own self-description would be: "The writer with the slowest natural intuition—meaning the least naturally talented, in terms of normal creativity availability—of any successful writer that I, personally, have ever met."

It was van Vogt's firm belief that it was only his systems for contacting his unconscious processes and for writing stories that allowed him to produce science fiction at all. He would say: "People do not seem to realize that form does not bind. It frees. If your form seems to constrain you, learn others."

We should also take note, however, that at another moment, he would say:

> I mean, I'm always trying to write by methods, see. I'm mad about methods and I sometimes feel that's the only thing that makes my stories worth it, but it's really not true. There is a place for method in writing, but I've overdone that many times and had to back away from it and start all over.

So here we have A.E. van Vogt, for whom words always came with a certain difficulty, systematically at work on his first novel, the revisionist superman story *Slan*. It would take considerable self-alignment and constant self-monitoring to produce this story. But, with the aid of his methods for contacting his creativity and engaging the intuition of his reader, and the further systems he used to guide him in the construction of his stories, science-fictional sentence by science-fictional sentence and scene by scene, van Vogt would inch his way along only occasionally having to back away and start over.

Making *Slan* go slower, however, was the fact that van Vogt was a part-time SF writer who had to steal his moments to work as best he could. Most of his attention was required elsewhere.

Until two months after the publication of "Black Destroyer," van Vogt still continued to write trade paper interviews for the likes of *Hardware and Metal, Sanitary Engineer*, and *Canadian Grocer*. But then, in September 1939, Hitler's armies invaded Poland and World War II began, and Canada was carried into the war along with the rest of the British Empire.

Poor eyesight rendered van Vogt unfit for active military service. But the Civil Service, rummaging through its files, recalled him as someone who had worked on the census eight years before. A telegram was sent to van Vogt, offering him a job as a Clerk II in the Department of National Defense.

In his heart, van Vogt didn't really want to take this job. Working as a low-level paper-pusher once again felt like taking a big step backward.

But he thought that everyone should try to be of some use in the war effort, so he accepted the offer.

He traveled to Ottawa by bus, leaving Edna in Winnipeg to pack, sell their furniture, and follow. It was November by then, and the newspapers told them there were only fourteen apartments to be had in the entire city. They felt highly fortunate to locate a nice place to live, even though the monthly rent was $75, and van Vogt's take-home pay was just $81.

The gap between his pay and their actual living expenses could be made up for a time out of the money for the furniture they had sold back home. But it was evident that if they wished to eat, to meet the time payments on their new furniture, and to have such amenities as a phone, a working stove, or lights, it was going to be necessary for van Vogt to push ahead and finish that novel of his and bring home some writing income.

But the new job didn't leave him very much time for it. Van Vogt had his Sundays free, and half a day on Saturday, but for the most part he did his writing in the evenings, when he wasn't too tired. He'd come home from the job, eat dinner, take a short nap, and then press on with *Slan* until eleven at night.

At the times when it was going well, he could complete a scene in longhand during a single writing session. And sometimes, especially toward the end when the narrative had gained a momentum of its own, it might be two scenes. Then, the next day while he was off at work, Edna would transcribe what he had written.

It took six months for van Vogt to write his story, all the time existing in such a state of tension that he was constantly waking and worrying over his novel in the middle of the night. Somehow, however, between Campbell's pronouncements, his own vision of things, his conscious methods for writing, his dreams, his urgent need for money, and the ever-dwindling amount of time he had in which to write, he finally managed to complete *Slan* in the late spring of 1940.

Van Vogt rushed his novel off to John Campbell, who not only received it with considerable pleasure but backed his enthusiasm with a swift check which included a highly welcome quarter-of-a-cent per word bonus.

Van Vogt says: "Checks from Campbell were always prompt. He evidently knew writers starved because you could send him a story and, apparently, he'd read it almost immediately and put the check through."

Slan would be serialized in *Astounding* from September to December 1940 and would be far and away the best-liked story published in the magazine that year—more popular than either Robert Heinlein's story of the overthrow of the Prophets, "If This Goes On—," or L. Ron Hubbard's endless war story, *Final Blackout*.

But what a completely unusual story *Slan* actually was! The more closely it was examined, the stranger and more elusive it had to seem. Like all of van Vogt's early stories, except for his most recent, "Repetition," it had that bizarre, intense, dreamlike quality—but this time at the extended length of a novel.

At the outset of *Slan*, nine-year-old Jommy Cross and his mother are on a city street, surrounded by an unseen but mentally sensed circle of hostile humans. People blame the slans for their use of the mutation machines of ancient scientist Samuel Lann, which have caused ordinary humanity to give birth not only to slan babies, but also to grotesque failures and botches. They aim to exterminate the tendrilled telepaths.

As the humans close relentlessly in on them, Jommy's mother sends her son running in a desperate but successful try for life that has him clinging with super-strength to the rear bumper of a speeding "sixty electro Studebaker." But before she is cut down, she gives Jommy a final mental admonition to kill the man behind the anti-slan campaign, the dictator of Earth, Kier Gray. She thinks, "Don't forget what I've told you. You live for one thing only: To make it possible for slans to live normal lives. I think you'll have to kill our great enemy, Kier Gray, even if it means going to the grand palace after him."

When he is fifteen, Jommy follows a hypnotic command from his long-dead scientist father. He enters the catacombs underneath the city to recover his father's great discovery, the secret of controlled atomic power, from the place where it has been hidden. However, he is caught in the act, and in order to escape he must use an atomic weapon to kill three guards. This is something that causes him continuing remorse, and which he becomes determined not to repeat.

In his own right as a teenage super-scientist, Jommy develops "ten-point steel," a metal that approaches the theoretical ultimate in hardness. And he invents "hypnotism crystals," which enable him to control the thinking of ordinary human beings.

Jommy also roams the world looking for other slans with golden tendrils in their hair—but he is never able to find any. Where can they be?

However, again and again, he stumbles across a widespread network of "tendrilless slans," who are also products of Samuel Lann's mutation machines but lack telepathic ability. They have mastered anti-gravity and built spaceships and established settlements on Mars that are completely unknown to ordinary Earthbound humanity.

But these half-slans look on Jommy as an enemy, too. It seems that when the tendrilled slans were in ascendancy, they persecuted the slans without tendrils, and the tendrilless slans have neither forgiven nor forgotten. They call Jommy "a damned snake" and strive even more diligently than the simple humans to kill him.

Jommy steals a spaceship from them and has the opportunity to kill a tendrilless slan, Joanna Hillory. But he forbears in spite of the enmity she shows him. Instead, he assures her of his goodwill. "Madam, in all modesty I can say that, of all the slans in the world today, there is none more important than the son of Peter Cross. Wherever I go, my words and my will shall rule. The day that I find the true slans, the war against your people shall end forever."

And he sets Joanna Hillory free.

Then, at last, when he is nineteen, Jommy finds another slan like himself, a girl, Kathleen Layton, seeking refuge in a long-abandoned slan hideout, an underground machine city. Kathleen has been kept for observation by Kier Gray ever since she was a child, but now, with her life in imminent danger from the slan-hating secret police chief, John Petty, she has fled the palace.

The meeting of Jommy and Kathleen is a wonderful moment of mutual recognition:

> *And she was a slan!*
> *And he was a slan!*
> *Simultaneous discovery!*

But almost in the moment in which they find each other and fall in love, John Petty invades the cave hideout and surprises Kathleen there alone. He shows her no mercy at all but straightaway puts a bullet into her brain.

Jommy arrives on the scene with Kathleen's dying telepathic goodbye to him still ringing in his mind. He might pay John Petty back in kind by blasting him into nothingness with his atomic weapon, but he stays his hand. He leaves the crucial button unpressed and withdraws under heavy fire in his car made of ten-point steel.

Then, when Jommy is twenty-six—still not fully mature by slan standards—the tendrilless slans launch an all-out attack upon his secret laboratory and his spaceship, hidden under a mountain twenty miles away. But Jommy signals his spaceship, and it tunnels its way to him, and he escapes.

He travels to Mars to spy upon the tendrilless slans. Posing as one of them, he confirms his speculation that they soon intend to make a general attack upon the Earth.

But no sooner is he certain of this than he is suspected of being himself. He is taken to the office of Joanna Hillory, now the tendrilless slan military commissioner who has the job of tracking him down. She has written no less than four books on the subject of Jommy Cross.

While he waits, he is allowed the opportunity to consult what we today would think of as a computer:

> Inside the fine, long, low building, a few men and women moved in and out among row on row of great, thick, shiny, metallic plates. This, Cross knew, was the Bureau of Statistics, and these plates were the electric filing cabinets that yielded their information at the touch of a button, the spelling out of a name, a number, a key word.

Jommy asks these electric filing cabinets to tell him about Samuel Lann—and in no time he is reading Samuel Lann's diary for 1971, and then further random entries from 1973 and 1990, and from them is discovering that there never was a mutation machine at all. From the very outset, the tendrilled slans were and always have been a purely natural mutation.

Then, when he is called into the office of Joanna Hillory, he finds that his idealism as a fifteen-year-old was so convincing to her that she has spent the years since maneuvering herself into a position to help him in just such a moment as this. She aids him to escape and to return to Earth with the knowledge of a secret entrance to the slan-built palace of Kier Gray.

Van Vogt has said, "From a fairly early time, towards the end of my stories ... I would launch my subconscious into free associations, and, within the frame of what I was writing—roughly—would just let it rattle on." This kind of creative process would seem to underlie what happens next in *Slan*.

In a very strange scene, Jommy hurls himself down a hole in the palace garden, and when he reaches the bottom, he is two miles beneath the surface. There he encounters signs which presume him to be a slan and tell him where he is and what his circumstances are. Then walls close together around him, and in a kind of prison-elevator, he is raised high up into the palace to the most private inner sanctum of Kier Gray.

And once again, as in the Greek plays that van Vogt had read, a scene of recognition takes place. Jommy looks on the ruthless and powerful but noble face of Kier Gray and knows him for what he really is:

Kier Gray, leader of men, was—

"*A true slan!*" exclaimed Cross.

At first, Gray's manner is cold and hard. He even threatens to amputate Jommy's tendrils. But then, Jommy demonstrates his own power by effortlessly freeing himself from his bonds, and the recognition becomes mutual. Kier Gray knows that this must be the son of Peter Cross, the master of atomic energy, and immediately, his manner completely alters:

"Man, man, *you've done it!* In spite of our being unable to give you the slightest help! Atomic energy—at last."

His voice rang out then, clear and triumphant: "John Thomas Cross, I welcome you and your father's great discovery. Come in here and sit down ... We can talk here in this very private den of mine."

And Gray then proceeds to tell Jommy all.

Slans, he says, really rule the world from behind the scenes—something like those Scotsmen running the British Empire: "What is more natural than that we should insinuate our way to control of the human government? Are we not the most intelligent beings on the face of the Earth?"

Slans are "the mutation-after-man." Despite the fact that ordinary humanity hates and fears them, the slans are watching out for poor feckless old-style man, who is now growing sterile and beginning to pass from the scene. And if the slans in the past gave the tendrilless slans something of a hard time, well, that was all for their own good, to keep them tough.

The fact of the matter is that all unknown to themselves, the tendrilless slans *are* the true slans. Their special characteristics—tendrils, double hearts, more efficient nervous systems, and so on—have been temporarily genetically suppressed to keep them safe from the wrath of humanity. But one by one, the slan characteristics have been re-emerging. And in another forty or fifty years, the tendrils and telepathic power will start coming back, too.

The problem for the slans-behind-the-scenes is to make the transition from man to slan a smooth one. They would like to keep the humans from launching one last desperate anti-slan witch-hunt. And they would also like to keep the tendrilless slans from exterminating ordinary man before he passes naturally from the scene.

Now, however, it appears that both problems can be solved. With the aid of Jommy's atomics, the tendrilless slan attack from Mars can be turned away. Those slans who are in the know will "make a big noise with a small force" that should send the invaders back to Mars until the tendrils of their children grow in. Then, with the hypnotism crystals that Jommy has developed, it will be possible to soothe the hysteria, jealousy, and fear of man-as-he-has-been and make his passing painless and happy.

With this solution worked out, *Slan* concludes with a dramatic entrance and a final recognition scene. A young woman comes into Gray's private study—and it is Kathleen. Kathleen resurrected! Kier Gray then introduces her to Jommy.

It was at that moment that Kier Gray's voice cut across the silence with the rich tone of one who had secretly relished this moment for years.

"Jommy Cross, I want you to meet Kathleen Layton—my daughter!"

And so the story ends, leaving us all aglow. But also with a thousand rational questions that we might ask if we were of a mind to:

If Kathleen Layton really is Kier Gray's daughter, why should he have endangered both her and him by keeping her near him as she grows up? And if Gray is such a sentimentalist that he must have her close by, why is it that when Kathleen first meets Jommy, she doesn't yet have the slightest suspicion that Kier Gray might really be a slan, let alone her own father?

It only takes Jommy a matter of moments to find out from the tendrilless slans' electric filing cabinets that there never was a mutation machine. Why is it that the tendrilless slans don't know this fundamental fact? And if the tendrilless slans suspect him of being their most feared adversary, Jommy Cross, why do they so casually allow him free access to their data banks without anyone even bothering to take a peek over his shoulder just to see what he might be up to?

And, in its own way, perhaps the greatest oddity of all: What in the world is a Studebaker car with a protruding rear bumper in the style of the 1930s doing on the streets six hundred and thirty, or eight hundred, or fifteen hundre years in the future? (The figures for how much time has passed between now and then keep shifting, like so much else in this story.)

4
HOLISTIC PERCEPTION

OF the thousand questions that might be asked about the novel, van Vogt himself would attempt to address perhaps fifty or a hundred in the revised second hardcover edition of *Slan*—but with mixed results. Some matters for doubt, like that anomalous Studebaker, could be tidied up easily enough with the help of an eraser. But the effect of some of the other changes that van Vogt made would just be to swap one question for another.

The truth is that the essence of *Slan* did not lie in logic and reason, and no amount of tidying could ever be enough to make this story add up neatly and consistently. It might even be argued that the unintended result of those 1951 revisions aiming to make *Slan* more reasonable was actually to diminish some of the irrational power of the original serial novel.

In either version, however, the fundamental nonrationality of this story can't be emphasized strongly enough. In fact, if there is any obvious defect in our brief account of *Slan*, it is that by the very act of compressing and summarizing the story line, we have necessarily made the novel appear a good deal more transparent and coherent than the unsuspecting reader is likely to find it.

In *Slan*, things operate according to the dictates of dream logic. Characters gifted with unaccountable knowledge and equally unaccountable ignorance suddenly loom into view, only to disappear again just as abruptly. Anything that seems fixed—like a date, or an attitude, or an identity—may alter without warning and become something other than it was before. In this story, coincidences, unlikelihoods, and radical transitions abound—but as within a dream, this just seems the way that things naturally ought to happen.

Far more even than we've managed to indicate, van Vogt's future world is filled with secret passageways, underground hideouts, caves, catacombs, and tunnels. Here it seems perfectly normal for a spaceship to be parked within a building or underneath a flowing river, or for someone to leap down a rabbit hole two miles deep, and then rise again. The world of tomorrow and the labyrinths of the mind become one and the same place in *Slan*.

The Golden Age *Astounding* had plenty of writers who were prepared to be rational, plausible and responsible in what they imagined. But it had only one A. E. van Vogt, a writer convinced that he could be most true to the real underlying actualities of existence if he gave control of what he wrote to his nonrational mind and allowed it to go wherever it wished to go and say whatever it pleased to say.

In placing his unconscious in charge of his storytelling this way, van Vogt took the risk that it might blurt out something outrageous or paranoid or sexual or stupid. And, indeed, his stories were capable of being any or all of these things. However, there was one great redeeming virtue to his method, and this was that again and again, van Vogt was able to evoke vistas of transcendent possibility and human becoming in his stories such as no other SF writer of his era could begin to equal.

To be sure, among the readers of the Campbell *Astounding* there would be some who were too rational-minded to swallow van Vogt. They couldn't bring themselves to cast aside all logic and common sense to read him in the uncritical fashion in which he had to be read in order to be effective. Not only would the cheering that greeted *Slan* be baffling and annoying to these logicians, but the exasperation they felt would only increase as time passed, and van Vogt just continued to persist in his perversely left-handed approach to science fiction writing.

When *Slan* was serialized in the fall of 1940, however, most of the readers of *Astounding* found themselves swept up by the hurtling power of van Vogt's narrative. And so exhilarating would they find the breathless motion of the story and the constant changes they were given to experience that they wouldn't be able to bring themselves to stop and worry about whether or not it all happened to be making strict logical sense.

After the roller coaster ride was over and the concluding emotional glow of Jommy and Kathleen rediscovering each other had faded, these wide-eyed readers might not be able to say where they had been or how it was that van Vogt had worked his special magic. But they would be certain that *Slan* had somehow managed to reach right into their minds and stir their imagination in ways they couldn't begin to utter or explain.

We might recall that John Campbell had told van Vogt at the outset that it would take a superman to write a story from the viewpoint of a superman. And, of course, A.E. van Vogt himself was no superman—at least, not in the old absolute Techno Age sense of the word. But then, it wasn't actually necessary that he should be a perfected being. It was enough that he had a grasp of emerging post-materialistic thinking at a time when others did not.

In something of the same way in which Jommy Cross was a relatively superior human being, able to do what the ordinary person could not do, so may we see van Vogt as a relatively superior SF writer, able to imagine what the ordinary science fiction writer of 1940 could not imagine.

SF writers throughout the modern scientific era, starting with Jules Verne, had always divided existence into two parts—an area of securely known things and another area of unknownness. But van Vogt no longer observed this distinction between *here* and *out there*, between the Village and the World Beyond the Hill. To his way of thinking, knowledge, and mystery were inextricably intertwined in all times and places.

As van Vogt saw it, so great was the imperfection of our perception and thought that even the here-and-now was all but a total mystery to us. At the same time, however, the farthest star and the most remote moment were part of the same ultimate Unity as we, and consequently, in some sense, might be knowable by us.

This new construction of things allowed van Vogt to operate freely and easily in mental and physical territory that was too far out for his more conventional colleagues. And it also allowed him to imagine utter strangeness close at hand where ordinary perception would never expect to find it.

To an audience that was still struggling to come to terms with materialism and the apparently accidental and meaningless nature of existence, van Vogt's new perspective seemed mysterious and elusive. It permitted him to come at his readers from impossible directions and to show them marvels completely beyond their ability to anticipate.

Even John Campbell was captivated, charmed, and awed by the sheer inexplicability of A. E. van Vogt. Shaking his head in wonder, Campbell would say, "That son of a gun is about one-half mystic, and like many another mystic, hits on ideas that are sound without having any rational method of arriving at them or defending them."

However, eighty years after the original serialization of *Slan*, with the advantages lent to us by hindsight, by the changes that have taken place in thinking patterns during the intervening time, and by van Vogt's own self-explanations, we don't need to be quite as baffled or as hypnotized by the story as readers were in 1940. We can see that what was present in *Slan* to be taken away by a reader—whether consciously or not—was precisely those elements that van Vogt had labored so long and so hard to put into his story in the first place: Names of significance. A sense of the mutability of things. Sudden emotional and intellectual recognitions. Patterns and relationships. Awareness of the whole.

In *Slan*, far more explicitly than in van Vogt's subsequent stories, the names chosen for key characters were emblematic of their roles. The slan-hating secret police chief was Petty. The ambiguously regarded dictator of Earth was Gray. And the name of the young protagonist—J.C./Cross—was a sign to the reader that this particular superman, at least, was no cold, ruthless amoralist but someone striving to be decent and noble and good.

As we've seen, a sense that things move and change was central to *Slan*. Perhaps as much as Robert Heinlein, another SF writer who had been brought in childhood from a small town to the big city, van Vogt was convinced that things must change and do change. But van Vogt's mode of expression of this crucial insight was completely different from Heinlein's, and, in its way, was far more subtle.

Heinlein, the engineer, student of math, and compulsive keeper of clipping files, envisioned change in terms of permutations and combinations of existing and potential factors. Through his keen powers of analysis, his encyclopedic knowledge, and his ability to combine and permute elements in an almost algebraic way, Heinlein was able to imagine modes of thinking and states of social possibility that were not the same as our own: Future societies variously organized around a charismatic religious dictator, or moving roadways, or even the laws of magic.

But A.E. van Vogt, the systematic intuitionist, had little or none of Heinlein's special gift for observing change, considering it intellectually, and then portraying it in objectified terms. Instead, he sensed change as a kind of kinetic force, and that would be the way in which he would represent it.

By making his stories up as he went along, by constructing them as a series of individual scenes, each of which had its own purpose, and by allowing dream flashes to constantly alter the direction of his narrative, van Vogt wove change into the very fabric of what he wrote. A story like *Slan* didn't discuss the dynamics of change. It didn't depict the effects of change. It just kept changing and changing.

The result of this variance in expression was that from Heinlein's 1940 stories like "If This Goes On—" and "The Roads Must Roll," a reader could anticipate the intellectual convictions that Heinlein would express directly in his 1941 guest-of-honor speech, "The Discovery of the Future." Heinlein's stories said quite clearly that the society of tomorrow would necessarily be different from the society of today and that, consequently, the man of knowledge and competence would be well-advised to make himself ready for change to come.

But the reader of van Vogt wouldn't be invited to think about change so much as to experience it. And he would put *Slan* down not just intellectually convinced that change was a potential of the future, but with a gut feeling that change was an immanent aspect of existence, something that might occur within the context of any given instant.

Likewise embedded in the structure of van Vogt's novel would be his conviction—based upon his own experience—that understanding comes as the result of sudden accesses of insight. Not only would there be recognition scene upon recognition scene in *Slan*, but also instance after instance where Jommy suddenly arrives at some answer or conclusion on the basis of what would seem to be insufficient evidence or no evidence at all but then proves to be correct.

There would be no discussion of this in the novel and no lingering upon it when it occurs. Rather, Jommy just *knows* something, the story moves on, and yes, indeed, what Jommy thinks he knows is actually the way things turn out to be.

We can, of course, recognize this as exactly the same ability that van Vogt himself had for hitting upon sound ideas without having any rational method of arriving at them or defending them. To Campbell, this talent in van Vogt would appear half-mystical—but that would not be the way the writer would see it. For him, as for many others in his generation, "mystic" was something of a dirty word, an epithet indicating spiritualistic woolly-mindedness. And, most definitely, van Vogt was not a spiritualist of any kind.

A more acceptable explanation would be that van Vogt was an organic holist, a pattern-perceiver, and so was his character, Jommy Cross. And it was their respective abilities to read patterns as wholes that would allow each of them to arrive at sound conclusions that could not be logically demonstrated or defended.

Here is van Vogt on his own thinking processes:

> For years I may mentally stare at something that has aroused my interest, and, in a manner of speaking shake my head the entire time. This means that, for me, the pieces do not seem to be falling into a coherent shape. Years later, I'm still looking, still patiently waiting for *the* insight that will bring it into focus. Suddenly—and I do mean suddenly—the pattern flashes into view.

Similarly, within *Slan*, the achievement of holistic perception would be Jommy's most important mental attainment during the seven years from age nineteen to age twenty-six. In this new state, he is able to be aware of his surroundings as a whole. Nothing significant escapes him. As van Vogt-the-narrator describes Jommy's new condition of mind: "Details penetrated, a hard, bright pattern formed where a few years before there would have been, even for himself, a blur."

One example of such a pattern falling into place in *Slan* might be Jommy's sudden realization that Kier Gray, leader of the humans of Earth and the archenemy of all tendrilled slans, is, in actuality himself a true slan. Here, to be sure, is an unusual relationship: What at first seem to be separate contending parties, which ultimately prove to have common leadership.

What is more, variations upon this situation would appear in one early van Vogt novel after another. What ever should we make of that?

Van Vogt's first serious critic—a young fan named Damon Knight, who in time would himself become an SF writer and editor of note—would single out this recurrent relationship as a major flaw in van Vogt's work. He would characterize the situation as "the leader of the Left is also the leader of the Right" and condemn it as a plot device of "utter and imbecilic pointlessness."

And, admittedly, so it might very well seem to a sober, rational, rule-abiding person of democratic convictions, certain that in any contention between parties the apparent issues must in fact be the real issues and one side more correct than the other.

As we cannot help being aware, however, twentieth century history wasn't altogether devoid of examples of political parties that were infiltrated and subverted by their rivals or of revolutionary leaders who turned out to be secret police agents as well. To a person of this cast of mind—authoritarian and conspiratorial, contemptuous of rules and hungry for the exercise of power—the situation presented by van Vogt might not appear quite so stupid or pointless as it did to young Damon Knight writing his criticism in 1945.

And certainly, there are some grounds for thinking that Kier Gray might be just this kind of man. He is a dictator over ordinary human beings. His arrival to power came via devious means, and to retain his grip, he shows himself perfectly ready to plot, conspire, misrepresent, threaten, and even kill. And there is no doubt that he does anticipate a coming day when ordinary men are gone from the face of the Earth, and true slans are all that exist. Given a person this ruthless and cunning, it seems possible that he might not care particularly about nominal distinctions like Left and Right or trouble himself overly about the illusory issues pursued by people who know less than he does. To someone like Kier Gray, it might very well be the separate contending parties that seem stupid and pointless and not his ultimate power over both.

Now, admittedly, a Kier Gray who was this kind of man would be a megalomaniac, fully as crazy, suspicious, and dangerous as the Adolf Hitler, with whom van Vogt's country was currently at war. Nonetheless, there would be sufficient basis for this kind of reading of van Vogt's stories that the writer himself would develop his own measure of concern with the question. He would wonder about the compulsion he felt to write again and again about the emergent superman, and say, "I had become aware of all the things I'd done that were somewhat on the paranoid, the schizophrenic side."

To make completely certain that he had a clear grasp of the difference between a genuinely superior man and the kind of unbalanced, self-justifying, and violent human male who becomes a Hitler or Stalin, van Vogt would undertake a systematic study of this aberrated type of person and eventually write a realistic contemporary novel, *The Violent Man* (1962), on the subject.

However, it isn't necessary for us to take Kier Gray as a player of pointless games. And neither do we have to interpret him as a power-seeker with a twisted psyche. A third and better reading of him and his dual leadership of man and slan is possible. And this is that Kier Gray is a genuine caretaker with a concern for things as a whole.

There is no doubt that Kier Gray can be coolly pragmatic and even sometimes outright ruthless. In the interest of making the transition from man to slan as untraumatic as possible, Gray shows himself ready to pamper and soothe failing mankind, to intimidate and bamboozle tendrilless slans, and to treat true slans coldly and roughly. He is even capable of raising his own daughter Kathleen as a kind of zoo exhibit in order to test contemporary reaction to the presence of a revealed tendrilled slan.

Nonetheless, Kier Gray—as van Vogt suggests in describing him—is a noble man. Despite the unique degree of power he wields, we never see him being greedy, lustful, vicious, vengeful, or self-aggrandizing. When Jommy suddenly appears in his private study bearing the gifts of controlled atomic energy, ten-point steel, and hypnotism crystals, Gray doesn't pause for an instant to consider how these might be used for his own personal advantage. Instead, he immediately begins to plan how they may be applied to the problems of the ongoing transition. If Kier Gray really does aim to be a dispassionate universal caretaker with a concern for the welfare of all, then it might not be altogether pointless or crazy for him to be the leader of more than one party, especially if the various sides aren't actually as separate and opposed as they believe themselves to be.

We might consider that what at first seem to be ordinary human beings prove instead to be communities of tendrilless slans living unnoticed amidst the general population. And further that what are initially identified as tendrilless slans eventually turn out to be all-unknowing true slans. And finally, that what are at first suggested to be the unnatural and inhuman product of a monster-making machine—the tendrilled slans—are ultimately revealed to be not only a completely natural mutation, but the next stage in the evolutionary development of man.

The truth is that behind the appearance of difference and the assumption of difference, man, tendrilless slan, and true slan are one.

This is the pattern that suddenly flashes into view in the climactic scene of *Slan* at the moment in which it is revealed that Kier Gray, the great human antagonist of the slans, is in actuality the most powerful and visionary of true slans and that the slans are the mutation-after-man. Even more than Jommy Cross' intelligible character and good intentions, it is the unifying nature of Kier Gray that demonstrates the continuity of man and slan to the reader.

Slan isn't really a story of politics or power relations at all. It's a story about a difficult species-wide transition of man to a new and higher state of body and mind.

The audience that received *Slan* had lately been reading stories about the passage from Neanderthal man to Cro-Magnon, like Lester del Rey's "The Day Is Done." And they had found themselves able not only to look back upon poor, vanished Neanderthal and pity him for his grossness and imperfection, but also to feel a genuine human kinship with him.

Van Vogt asked his readers to make a corresponding leap of imagination and empathy, but this time in the opposite direction, and to perceive the beauty and desirability of becoming man-beyond-man. He offered the opportunity and challenge of identifying with the tendrilled slans, and of seeing them not as intolerably Other but rather as the manifestation of the transcendent potential waiting within us.

If the underlying message of van Vogt's novel was that the possibility of transcendence exists even within our present moment and condition, this communicated itself to John Campbell. One year after *Slan* began serialization—in the same September 1941 issue of *Astounding* containing Isaac Asimov's "Nightfall"—Campbell would publish an article entitled "We're Not All Human."

Here he would suggest that superior human beings already exist among us without fully appreciating their own specialness. And he would name *Slan* as the initial stimulus for this line of speculation.

There would be readers of *Astounding* who not only got this message from *Slan*, but who were prepared to take it personally. Some fans, for instance, would give their boardinghouses or communal living places joking names like "Slan Shack" or "Tendril Towers."

Another, much more earnest about his identification with the idea of imminent human self-transcendence, would declare in the first issue of his amateur magazine, *Cosmic Digest*:

> Man is still evolving toward a higher form of life. A new figure is climbing upon the stage. Homo cosmen, the cosmic men, will appear. We believe that we are mutations of that species. We are convinced that there are a considerable number of people like ourselves on this planet, if only we could locate and get in touch with them. Someday we will find most of them, and then we will do great things together.

This youngster would announce a new organization called "the Cosmic Circle" and attempt to rally his fellow SF readers to its banner with the slogan "Fans are slans!" And even though his efforts would be greeted with more amused tolerance than visible success, nonetheless, it is clear that van Vogt had done his work in making slanhood seem a desirable condition to aspire to.

A.E. van Vogt became the first superstar of Campbell's Golden Age on the strength of two special stories—"Black Destroyer" and *Slan*. But then, with the serialization of *Slan* complete and van Vogt at a peak of popularity as an SF writer, he all but disappeared from the pages of *Astounding*.

During the fourteen months that followed *Slan*, through all of 1941 and into 1942, while Robert Heinlein was dominating the magazine with a great burst of stories, van Vogt would only manage to contribute two short stories to *Astounding*. And after the second of these, "The Seesaw" in July 1941, he would be completely absent for the next eight months.

The reason for this difference was that Heinlein was waiting for the war to catch up with the United States, and while he waited, he filled his time by writing science fiction stories. Van Vogt, however, was already caught up in World War II and scarcely had time in which to take a deep breath.

There had been months of inaction following the original declaration of war in September 1939. But just about the time that van Vogt was finishing *Slan* in the late spring of 1940, Hitler launched a lightning flank attack that swept across the Netherlands, Belgium, and France and pushed the remnant Allied armies into the sea at Dunkirk. Then, in the summer and fall of 1940, the Germans sent wave after wave of aircraft across the English Channel to bomb Britain, their last surviving opposition in Western Europe.

The worse that things went for the mother country, the more hours the Canadian Department of National Defence required of van Vogt. He was fortunate to find enough time in the space of the next year even to write two short stories.

Brief and rare as "The Seesaw" was, however, it would manage to be one of the most remarkable of all Golden Age science fiction stories. The line of thought that culminated in "The Seesaw" was set in motion when van Vogt read John Campbell's editorial note in the February 1941 *Astounding*, officially announcing that all of Heinlein's stories of the future fit together in one common historical framework. Seeing that note got van Vogt to thinking about the unity of his own fiction.

He says:

> Being a system thinker and a system writer, I realized at once that in the area of overall purpose, I had no system, except, yes, hey, wait a minute; yes, I had already started one but not called it anything.
>
> The underlying premise was: In every rock, in every grain of sand, in every cell, there is a "memory" of ancient origins, and of the history of that cell going back to the beginning of things. If we could but read the signals that these bits of matter are showing us, we would have the answers we seek.

Once his own continuing concern with identity and organic wholeness had become apparent to van Vogt, he set out to express this in the structure of his next story. "The Seesaw," more explicitly than any other van Vogt story, would be a representation in narrative form of his Whiteheadean sense of the holistic interconnection of all things. No writer who was working from a rational, linear, materialistic Village-centered point of view could possibly have conceived it.

"The Seesaw" begins with a newspaper story dated as recently as the middle of last week—that is, the week before the on-sale date of this very issue of *Astounding*. The clipping tells of the materialization of a strange building in the space on a city street normally occupied by a lunch counter and a tailor shop and the eventual disappearance of this anomalous store. The entire episode is presumed to have been the work of some unknown master illusionist.

It seems that across the front of the strange building, but directly readable from every angle, there was a large sign that said: "FINE WEAPONS. THE RIGHT TO BUY WEAPONS IS THE RIGHT TO BE FREE." And in the window of the store, along with a display of curiously shaped guns, another sign read: "THE FINEST ENERGY WEAPONS IN THE KNOWN UNIVERSE."

The newspaper clipping says that the door of the shop would not open when a police inspector made an attempt to gain admittance. But that it did open for a reporter, C.J. McAllister, who thereupon entered the building.

The story proper then proceeds to relate what happened to McAllister after he went into the gun shop—and saw the handle of the door swinging shut behind him writhe to avoid the grasp of the policeman trying to follow him inside.

Within the store, the reporter discovers that here it isn't June 1941 at all. Instead, the girl and her father who run this weapon shop inform him that it is "eighty-four of the four thousand seven hundredth year of the Imperial House of Isher."

This weapon shop and other similar shops, connected in a network by matter transmitters, serve as an independent force that counterbalances the power of this long-enduring empire. And the temporal displacement of McAllister is a sign to the gunmakers that something is seriously awry. Very quickly they determine that he has been jerked into this present moment as an accidental by-product of an invisible attack that has been launched against all of the weapon shops by the forces of the empress.

McAllister is informed that in his passage through time he has accumulated a charge of "trillions and trillions of time-energy units." If he should step outside the confines of the weapon shop or even be touched by another person, he would cause a monumental explosion. However, if he can be returned through time to 1941, this would have a significant effect on the great machine behind the Isher attack.

As one representative of the weapon shops explains to him:

> You are to be a "weight" at the long end of a kind of energy "crowbar," which lifts the greater "weight" at the short end. You will go back five thousand years in time; the machine in the great building to which your body is tuned and which has caused all this trouble will move ahead in time, about two weeks.

This maneuver will give the gunmaking guild the opportunity it must have to counter the threat of the Isher Empire and maintain its independent existence.

However, when McAllister is sent back through time, something completely unforeseen happens. He arrives where he started from in 1941—but he doesn't stay there long. Instead, he begins careening back and forth through time in a great series of pendulum swings that takes him ever further into the future and into the past.

If the great Isher machine is on the other end of this wild seesaw ride, then it seems certain that the attack by the empress on the weapon shops has been successfully disrupted. But even if someone were aware of what is happening to poor McAllister, there is nothing to be done for him.

The story concludes with a burst of van Vogtian music as a calm and contemplative McAllister comes to a recognition of what the eventual conclusion of his bizarre adventure must be:

> Quite suddenly, it came to him that he knew where the seesaw would stop. It would end in the very remote past, with the release of the stupen the great dous temporal energy he had been accumulating with each of those monstrous swings.
>
> He would not witness, but he would cause, the formation of the planets.

What an altogether unusual story! Taken in terms of characterization or social observation or simple plausibility, there was nothing at all to it. The central character, McAllister, has no specific personal nature whatever; he is more a function than an individual. The world of five thousand years hence is not a complete, complex, ongoing society. All that we ever see of it is the eternal naked polarity—weapon shops vs. Isher Empire—and not a single thing more. And the explanations and interpretations that are offered in the course of this story are, at best, simple images or metaphorical indications like "crowbars" and "seesaws" but nothing more consistently reasoned or fully imagined than this.

However, if we agree to leave aside the questions of plausible argument and fullness of detail and take this little story instead as a kind of pattern or general statement, there is a great deal more to be found in it. In fact, we can get the most from "The Seesaw" if we elect to look on it as an active meditation on the nature of the cosmos and our place within it.

Casting about for precedents and antecedents, we might say that it has a kinship with the "prehistoric daydream" in Verne's *Journey to the*

Centre of the Earth in which Axel, the narrator, travels back in his imagination through past evolutionary ages to the fiery creation of things. And it also has a relationship to all those tales of time travelers brooding over red and chilly suns and the fate of man, from Wells' *The Time Machine* to Don A. Stuart's "Twilight" and "Night."

But there was a crucial difference between "The Seesaw" and these older cosmological meditations. In the Age of Technology, a narrative overview of existence would be sure to present a story of birth in primal gas and fire, which in good time would necessarily be followed by entropic death in darkness, cold, and rubble.

However, that wasn't the story that van Vogt had to tell. Instead, he wrote of a Yin-and-Yang Universe of reciprocal maintenance. In the cosmos, as presented in "The Seesaw," there is no such thing as strict linear cause-and-effect. Rather, the whole Universe is seen as existing through the mutual collaboration and support of its subordinate aspects, and the aspects as existing through the overallness of the whole. At least four obvious examples of fundamental interdependence can be seen in van Vogt's short story:

First, there is the title and central metaphor—the seesaw. A teeter-totter in action is an instance familiar to everyone of a dynamic equilibrium that requires the active participation of two different parties.

Second, there is the interpenetration of 1941 A.D. and the year 4700 of the Isher Empire. Here we have a cross-connection of elements from very different eras, so that McAllister becomes a pivotal factor in the doings of time-to-come and the slogan that the right to buy weapons is the right to be free—a message that most assuredly had a point for a democratic yet still nominally neutral United States in early 1941—becomes impressed upon the here-and-now.

Third, there is the symbiotic nature of the weapon shops and the Isher Empire. Though one party can be seen as standing for the force of determinism, authority and control, and the other for the power of free will, free thought and free action, the two appear to be absolutely necessary to each other.

And fourth, there is the chicken-and-egg question of which comes first: The Universe that will produce McAllister, or the McAllister who will not witness but will cause the formation of the planets?

With all the intertwining, mutual dependence, and reversal of temporal sequence here, how are we to say what is really a cause and what is an effect?

It is because of the Isher Empire's attack on the weapon shops five thousand years from now that McAllister is snatched out of the year 1941 A.D. And it is for the purpose of defending themselves against the forces of the empress that the weapon shops send McAllister back through time again. And it is because of this joint effort by the Isher Empire and the weapon shops, and because of McAllister's movements back and forth through time that a primal explosion will result, which in due course will produce the conditions for McAllister, and subsequently, the weapon shops and the Isher Empire, to come into existence. Somehow, through their own mutual yearning to be, 1941 A.D. and 4700 I.E. work together to call themselves into being.

But even this can't be the whole story. It fails to take into account the counterweight on the other end of the seesaw. In order for McAllister to do his stuff, it seems essential for the great Isher machine to serve as a balancing force. And even though van Vogt may say nothing about the fate of the machine, imagination suggests to us that at the moment that McAllister is going bang at one end of existence, the great machine must necessarily be going ka-boom at the other.

By this reading, the various collaborations between the future and the present, the weapon shops and the Isher Empire, and McAllister and the Isher machine all add up to one crucial action-event that begins creation and also brings it to an end.

And were our perspective even broader, we might be able to see this as nothing exceptional. Perhaps as a result of collaborations just like these, the Universe is created and destroyed at every instant.

Just this would be the case in van Vogt's very next story, "Recruiting Station" (*Astounding*, March 1942). Here it is said, "Every unfolding instant the Earth and its life, the Universe and all its galaxies are recreated by the titanic energy that is time ... The rate of reproduction is approximately ten billion a second."

In any case, it is clear that van Vogt had accomplished something quite significant in "The Seesaw." In place of the old Village-centered orientation held for so long by the Western world, with its arrogant assumptions of self-importance alternating with tremulous fears of cosmic insignificance, van Vogt offered a Universe in which man and the present moment were completely essential—but were not sufficient.

5

MORAL RESPONSE

SHORTLY after van Vogt finished this potent little story, the conditions under which he was attempting to live and to write finally became too much for him. His wife Edna had needed operations in both 1939 and 1940. His monthly expenses continued to exceed his monthly income. The money the sale of *Slan* had brought in was all but gone. And the Canadian Department of National Defence wanted still more hours of work from him.

He says: "By April 1941, they had me working my full day plus four evenings a week plus all day Saturday and every other Sunday, all without a raise in salary. And so, since I could no longer support the job by part-time writing (no part-time being available), I resigned."

However, as much as van Vogt may have been pushed toward this decision by his lack of income, we shouldn't underestimate the part that was played by the inner need he felt to write more science fiction. Ultimately, that may have been his most compelling reason for resigning.

As he would say about this inner drive:

> I write on the basis of uneasiness. I should be working is my feeling, and so, when that reaches a certain level, I'm working. If it doesn't, I'm not. This has nothing to do with whether or not I am completely solvent right now. I feel as if I should be working all the time, and if I've been wasting time in some way too much, then this feeling intensifies. It's like a feedback system. It reaches a certain point and I'm at work, and that's all.

When this inner urgency was on him, van Vogt *had* to write stories, even if he didn't consciously know why:

> I was being swept along in an entirely compulsive situation—fundamentally a compulsive situation. I didn't know why I was doing it. I didn't know why I was interested in it. I was interested; I enjoyed it. I got fun out of it. I read my stories, when they were published, with interest: "Did I write that?"

As long as he was still permitted to have a few minutes every now and then in which to write, van Vogt could continue to go on working at the Canadian Department of National Defence. But when he saw his last precious moments of writing time about to be snatched away from him, he *had* to resign.

And once again, he was served by his uncanny sense of timing. If van Vogt had resolved to try to stick it out for even a few more months, he would have been frozen in place for the duration of the war. His request to resign would have been denied, no matter how impossible his personal living circumstances.

As it was, van Vogt was set free: Free from the demands of a grinding and unfulfilling job. Free from the burden of somehow managing to pay each month for his over-expensive apartment. Free from the close confines of the city of Ottawa. Free to pause for a long moment and catch his breath. Most of all, however, free once again to satisfy the compulsion he felt to write science fiction.

Just as soon as it was possible, the van Vogts sublet their apartment and moved up the Gatineau River into Quebec, where they rented a summer cottage five miles beyond the end of the nearest paved road. Van Vogt let Campbell know that he had quit his job and would now have more writing time available and set to work on a short novel.

Then, in September 1941, while van Vogt was still up on the Gatineau, he got a letter from Campbell saying that Robert Heinlein had it in mind to retire. And even though the editor had not totally given up hope of seeing further stories from Heinlein, it was evident that he would be needing a high-quality writer to take his place as a reliable regular supplier of material. If van Vogt was willing to have a try at it, Campbell declared himself ready to accept what amounted to 20,000 to 25,000 words of material a month from him for the two magazines, *Astounding* and *Unknown*.

What a splendid opportunity this was! Van Vogt had never previously had the chance to be a full-time science fiction writer. And after all the days he had spent trying to survive on $81 a month take-home pay, the prospect of an income of two or three hundred dollars every month was truly welcome.

But also, what a challenge it was! Over the past three full years, van Vogt had only managed to contribute one novel and seven pieces of short fiction to Campbell—a total of about 140,000 words. But now he was being asked to deliver quite a bit more than this every year—an average of a short story and a novelette, or a short novel, or an installment of a serial, each and every month.

Van Vogt was still a painfully slow writer, but nonetheless he decided to accept Campbell's offer. What others seemed to be able to do with speed and ease, he would attempt to accomplish by method and by diligent persistence.

As he would come to say: "In order to produce what I was producing, I worked from the time I got up until eleven o'clock at night, every day, seven days a week, for years."

No wonder van Vogt could speak of having been in the grip of a compulsion!

The first eight stories that van Vogt turned out after quitting his job would see publication in *Astounding* between March 1942 and January 1943. Not only would several of these rank among his all-time best, but in this initial burst of work as a full-time science fiction writer, he would confirm, consolidate, and extend the special lines of thought he had begun to set forth and explore in his earlier fiction.

Taken as a whole, these stories would declare that we live in a responsive Universe with different levels of being and consciousness. They would assert again and again the necessity for cooperation among sentient creatures. And they would suggest that the natural business of truly superior beings must be to serve as the guardians and protectors of lesser entities.

The moral responsiveness of the Universe can be seen most clearly stated in "Secret Unattainable" (*Astounding*, July 1942), a novelette that may in part have been van Vogt's self-justification for having given up on his war effort. The story is in the form of a file of documents brought to the United States after World War II which charts the beginning and end of a secret German scientific project.

It seems that in 1937 a scientist named Kenrube proposed the construction of a machine capable of bridging hyper-space and extracting limitless quantities of raw materials from distant planets to serve the purposes of the Fuehrer and the German Reich.

Professor Kenrube is another holist. He is reported as believing in "the singleness of organism that is a galactic system" and that "all the matter in the Universe conjoins according to a rigid mathematical pattern."

Kenrube's conclusions seem doubtful to more orthodox scientists. And he is by no means trusted by the regime, his brother having been executed in 1934 for opposing the National Socialists. But his machine is of such potential usefulness to Hitler's plans for world conquest that Kenrube's project is given official approval and funding.

The Nazis take every precaution they can think of to guard against any treachery that Kenrube may have in mind. And they are pleased and excited when the model machine that he builds works exactly as anticipated—except for an eventual unfortunate accident in the professor's absence that destroys the test model and kills an assistant who has been set to spy on Kenrube.

Indeed, so promising are the results of the project that the Nazis are encouraged to act upon their lust for power and launch World War II. And just as soon as a full-scale machine is completed and successfully tested in the spring of 1941, Professor Kenrube is placed under arrest and thrown into prison under constant guard.

However, at the formal demonstration of the hyper-space machine for the benefit of the assembled Nazi hierarchy, there is a great disaster. The machine is completely destroyed, many notables are killed, and the Fuehrer himself only narrowly escapes death.

More than this—it seems that Kenrube himself mysteriously escapes from confinement on this very same day, manages somehow to appear hours earlier at the scene of the disaster even as it was unfolding, and then disappears for good. From statements he made to his guards just before he vanished and from a further declaration made at the site of the demonstration, it becomes apparent that the entire project has been an elaborate plot of revenge by Kenrube for the death of his beloved brother.

Kenrube has successfully turned the greed and power-hunger of the Nazis against them. He has lured them into launching a war that they must inevitably come to lose by promising them a secret weapon that they are inherently incapable of putting to use.

As he says to his guards just before his disappearance from his cell:

> My invention does not fit into our civilization. It's *the next*, the coming age of man. Just as modern science could not develop in ancient Egypt because the whole mental, emotional, and physical attitude was wrong, so my machine cannot be used until the thought structure of man changes.

And to those assembled for the demonstration of the hyper-space machine, he says:

Here is your machine. It is all yours to use for any purpose—provided you first change your mode of thinking to conform to the reality of the relationship between matter and life.

I have no doubt you can build a thousand duplicates, but beware—every machine will be a Frankenstein monster. Some of them will distort time, as seems to have happened in the time of my arrival here. Others will feed you raw material that will vanish even as you reach forth to seize it. Still others will pour obscene things into our green earth, and others will blaze with terrible energies, but you will never know what is coming, you will never satisfy a single desire …

It is not that the machine has will. It reacts to laws, which you must learn, and in the learning it will reshape your minds, your outlook on life. It will change the world. Long before that, of course, the Nazis will be destroyed. They have taken irrevocable steps that will ensure their destruction.

Here, in "Secret Unattainable," is an assertion of the moral responsiveness of the Universe in the most immediate and relevant terms that van Vogt could imagine. The Nazis, his story declared, must inevitably lose World War II because of the deficiencies inherent in their fundamentally short-sighted, hostile, greedy, barbaric, and paranoid mode of thought.

When Professor Kenrube tells Hitler and his henchmen that their thinking fails to conform to the "reality of the relationship between matter and life," we might well be reminded that in *Science and the Modern World*, Alfred North Whitehead had suggested that any being which by its influence deteriorates its environment commits suicide. And that those organisms are successful which modify their environment so as to assist each other.

We should remember, too, that in his 1940 story "Repetition," van Vogt had specifically declared that if our species was ever to leave the Solar System and reach the stars, both individual men and human governments would have to learn to actively work together. Now, no less than three times over in his stories of 1942, van Vogt would assert the positive value of mutual assistance between mankind and alien beings. The first of these stories would even bear the explicit title "Co-operate—or Else!"

In this short novelette published in the April 1942 *Astounding*, humans have managed to attain the stars. There they have encountered a wide variety of sentient creatures. And through their conviction of the essential desirability of cooperation, men have managed to unite no fewer than 4,874 nonhuman races in one common alliance.

"Co-operate—or Else!," which concerns human relations with two lately encountered alien races, might be taken as a specific demonstration of how this was accomplished.

One race, the ezwals, are huge, three-eyed telepathic creatures native to Carson's Planet, which men have recently colonized. The ezwals, who live a life in nature, have no use for the artifice and constraints of human civilization. They are doing their best to drive men from their world by violent attacks—without giving away the fact that they are actually an intelligent species.

The other race, the wormlike Rull, is advanced and able enough to have spread among the stars. However, unlike humanity, they are so implacably vicious, intolerant, and bellicose that they will not allow any other thinking beings to survive within their sphere of control. Just as soon as they become aware of man's existence, they launch an interstellar war against him.

One human, Trevor Jamieson, has discovered that the ezwals are sentient, which nobody else suspects. He is in the process of taking one to Earth to demonstrate his case when a Rull attack on his spaceship causes him and the ezwal to crash-land on a primitive planet. In order for the two of them to survive both the blind, unthinking hostility of the jungle world and the threat of the Rull, Jamieson must and does convince the ezwal that cooperation is a necessity.

In a minor related short story, "The Second Solution" (*Astounding*, October 1942), a young ezwal gets loose in the wilds of northern Canada and is hunted as a dangerous animal. If it isn't to be executed, it must demonstrate the ability to overcome its immaturity, discipline its prejudices, and develop trust in a human being, an assistant of Trevor Jamieson who has also figured out the truth about ezwals.

At the same time, the man who has striven the hardest to kill the ezwal—doubting its intelligence and fearing the savage physical power that has led to the death of thirty million humans on Carson's Planet—must likewise learn to revise his own thinking and behavior. And, indeed, it is he who will ultimately prove to be the narrator of this story.

"Co-operate—or Else!" and "The Second Solution," together with a radically revised "Repetition," would eventually be included in a van Vogt "fix-up novel" on the subject of cooperation—*The War Against the Rull*, published in 1959.

Also forming part of the material of this book would be another novelette, "The Rull" (*Astounding*, May 1948). In this story, van Vogt would bring on stage one of the Rull—who in the two 1942 stories are no more than an incentive for man and ezwal to make common cause—and show that if they were only banged on the head hard enough to get their attention, they, too, might alter their behavior and be brought within the circle of cooperation.

The third van Vogt story in 1942 on the theme of mutual assistance between unlike beings would be "Not Only Dead Men," published in the November issue of *Astounding*. In this short story, however, instead of mankind being the style-setter, teaching other races the value of cooperation, it would be humans who would be moral pupils learning from more advanced beings.

In "Not Only Dead Men," a spaceship directed by reptilian aliens from a galaxy-wide civilization is attacked by a Blal, a fierce and mindless space-dwelling monster, while in the course of passing through our solar system. The creature is wounded, but the spaceship is severely damaged, and both fall to Earth on the Alaskan coast. There the scaly aliens manipulate an American whaling vessel into having no choice but to aid them in destroying the space creature.

It is a firm galactic rule that low-level beings such as us are not to be allowed to know of the existence of interstellar civilization. And we have been led to believe that when the usefulness of the whalers is past, they will be casually destroyed to keep the disturbing knowledge of galactic civilization from humanity in general.

Instead, however, the aliens consider it a moral necessity to pay their debts, while still protecting Earth from an order of knowledge it isn't yet prepared to handle. In consequence, as the story ends, the decision has been made to lift the crew of the whaling ship from our planet and transport them through space to the green and wonderful world from which Earth was originally colonized at some moment long past.

In this reward for services rendered, and also in the rules that protect vulnerable and immature beings from premature awareness of the existence of galactic civilization, it is possible for us to catch a glimpse of van Vogt's most profound and original new theme—the obligation of superior beings to look out for the welfare of those less advanced.

The first half-indication of this emergent insight came in Kier Gray's dual leadership of the tendrilled slans and ordinary mankind in *Slan*. And there would be a further hint of it in the first story van Vogt wrote after he resigned from his clerical job in the Department of National Defence, the highly provocative but overly complex short novel "Recruiting Station" (*Astounding*, March 1942).

In this story, the Glorious, an arrogant Earth-centered future race of man, is shanghaiing contemporary men and turning them into automatons to fight in a war between Earth and the planets that mankind has settled. But the very existence of the Universe has become imperiled by their careless manipulations of time. A race of the farther future, who will be the heirs and successors of the Planetarians—that is, if they manage to win the war—has become aware of the danger, but so tenuous has their past become that they are unable to travel back through time to correct the situation.

However, with their assistance, Norma Matheson, a young woman of the present day whom we have understood to be completely under the control of the ruthless Dr. Lell of the Glorious, develops superpowers far beyond his, and with her serving as a focal point, space and time can be manipulated to minimize damage to existence. At the conclusion of "Recruiting Station," Norma has been returned to the moment in 1941 when we first met her, where she will work to cancel all of Dr. Lell's efforts in our era.

The story ends with another of van Vogt's striking last lines: "Poor, unsuspecting superman!"

"Recruiting Station" would be notable for its presentation of a future containing not just change upon change, but level upon level of possible human becoming. And beyond any doubts superior humans do lend a hand to comparatively backward twentieth century people in a moment in which they are being victimized. The single point about which we might have question, however, is whether these highly developed human beings are acting out of a sense of altruism or out of a desire for self-preservation.

But there would be no doubt of this kind in three other van Vogt novelettes—"The Weapon Shop," "The Search," and "Asylum,"—that would easily be his best work of the year. In each case, the altruism of those more gifted or insightful or intelligent would not only be established beyond any doubt, but in fact would be a central point of the story.

"The Weapon Shop" (*Astounding*, December 1942) would be set against the same future background first glimpsed in "The Seesaw," with one (possibly careless) difference: The time, which in the earlier story was given as five thousand years in our future, is here said to be seven thousand years from now.

In this story, the central character, Fara Clark, is a very ordinary person, a motor repairman and totally loyal supporter of the empress—"the glorious, the divine, the serenely gracious, and lovely Innelda Isher, one thousand one hundred eightieth of her line." When a weapon shop appears in his village, he is the local citizen who is most adamantly opposed to it.

However, very shortly thereafter, an interplanetary bank and a giant corporation conspire to swindle him out of his life savings and force him out of business. And there is no one who will give Clark any help. Even his own family turns against him.

With his life in ruins, and driven to the depths of despair, Clark enters the weapon shop with the intention of purchasing a gun and killing himself. Instead, he finds himself transferred somewhere to a place called "Information Center." Here, inside an immense building that is also a machine, the weapon shops keep constantly amended census data for all the settled planets of the Solar System—and individual files on every living person.

Fara Clark is directed to a particular room, and there, in a most mysterious and summary fashion, his case is reviewed. He is informed that both the bank and the corporation that took advantage of him are among the many enterprises secretly owned by the empress. And somehow fines are instantly levied and collected against the offending businesses, with Clark getting back all he has lost and a good deal more.

He is also told a little about the history and nature of the weapon shops. It seems that some four thousand years past, "the brilliant genius Walter S. DeLany invented the vibration process that made the weapon shops possible, and laid down the first principles of weapon shop political philosophy ..."

This philosophy is moral and idealistic:

> It is important to understand that *we do not interfere in the main stream of human existence.* We right wrongs; we act as a barrier between the people and their more ruthless exploiters. As always, we shall remain an incorruptible core—and I mean that literally; we have a psychological machine that never lies about a man's character—I repeat, an incorruptible core of human idealism, devoted to relieving the ills that arise inevitably under any form of government.

The practical instrument of this philosophy of protection and justice for the common man is the man himself—armed with the guns that the weapon shops sell. A weapon shop gun is attuned to its owner, and whenever it is needed, it will leap instantly to his hand. Not only does the gun present a complete defensive shield against energy weapons of the kind carried by the soldiers of the empress, but there is no material object that its beam cannot penetrate or destroy. However, a weapon shop gun absolutely may not be used—and perhaps cannot be used—for either aggression or murder.

Here is a weapon whose nature is not so much scientific as moral. A gun of justice! With a sidearm like this, it would seem that any oppressed man could look tyranny in the eye and never need to blink.

And, indeed, back home in his village with a weapon shop gun on his hip and a new outlook on life, Fara Clark is able to stand up for his rights, reestablish his family, and regain his repair shop—and in the process discover that others besides himself are in actuality supporters of the weapon makers.

When van Vogt finished "The Weapon Shop" and sent it to John Campbell, the story proved to have a very strange effect on the editor. As he was reading this novelette, he recognized that he was enjoying it thoroughly. But when he attempted to analyze the story intellectually, he just couldn't see why it should be so effective.

Campbell's head assured him that nothing of any real consequence happened in "The Weapon Shop." A simple motor repairman loses his business, is given justice, and then gets his shop back again. Was that the stuff out of which a proper science fiction story should be made? The editor just couldn't think so.

And yet, at the same time, Campbell was aware that whatever his head might be telling him, in his heart he liked this novelette so much that he intended to pay van Vogt a bonus for it and use it for a cover story.

It was a highly intriguing puzzle—all the more so since it seemed to Campbell that it was the business of any proper editor to know exactly why a given story did or didn't work. He was even willing to share his perplexity with the author himself. Along with the check for the story, he sent van Vogt a letter in which he said quite frankly:

> "Weapon Shop" was, like much of your material, good without any detectable reason for being interesting. Technically it doesn't have plot, it starts nowhere in particular, wanders about, and comes out in another completely indeterminate place. But, like a park path, it's a nice little walk. I liked it, as you may have gathered from the 25% extra.

To understand the problem that Campbell had in coming to terms with his affection for the Canadian's unorthodox but curiously effective science fiction, it is necessary to look at van Vogt's stories with the eyes of an early forties pulp editor, a man expected to put a magazine on the newsstand each month that would grab a browser's attention and make him eager to buy and read.

The first rule in science fiction as Campbell knew it—and in pulp fiction in general—was that things must happen. There must be visible action.

In the stories that the young Campbell had made his initial reputation with, for instance, there had been clashes between cosmic antagonists contending for dominance, climaxed as like as not by a titanic space battle with rays of various colors shooting off and whole planets exploding like rotten tomatoes. Now there was visible action for you!

And even in the more thoughtful modern science fiction that the editor was pioneering in *Astounding*, there would typically be some well-defined public problem—a strike on the rolling roads, or a robot who can read human minds, or a disaster in an atomic plant—which would then be resolved through a timely application of the proper universal operating principle.

But van Vogt's fiction wasn't like that. Despite all the powerful forces, the overwhelming personalities, and the levels and levels of possible becoming that were represented in his stories, in most of them, very little overtly happened.

Van Vogt's stories were dreamlike—made up as he went along, deliberately written in such a way as to elude the reader's conscious grasp, altering with each new intuitional flash, changing direction completely every ten pages. And, like dreams, they didn't seem to observe ordinary daylight standards of cause and effect. Instead, the reader would find himself in the midst of some ongoingness, and then, after an abrupt transition, find himself dealing with some other given state—and then another, and then another. In a van Vogt story, things didn't seem to happen so much as they just were.

In van Vogt's work there was also very little in the way of public problem-solving, and almost no direct physical conflict. A typical van Vogt story would be far more likely to climax with a conversation than with a fight.

Even when we look for outright physical contention where we might most expect to see it, in van Vogt's earliest human vs. monster stories, we simply don't find it. Rather, those powerful, hostile creatures would ultimately fall victim to their own flawed natures, or panic and commit suicide, or turn tail and flee whimpering into the intergalactic darkness.

The true plane of action in van Vogt's fiction would not be physical, but mental and moral. The classic van Vogt story would start with the presentation of some limited attitude or level of understanding and, after all the changes were done, conclude with another that was more sane and inclusive—which might well be the complete opposite of the original point of view.

At the outset of *Slan*, for instance, Kier Gray is taken to be the principal persecutor of the tendrilled slans, the archenemy whom Jommy must someday seek out and kill. But at the climax of the story—which is not the scene of violent contention we have been led to expect, but rather a moment of recognition—Jommy sees Kier Gray in a new light, as a caretaker of humankind in all forms with whom he must henceforth ally himself.

In similar fashion, the powerful yet still less than self-sufficient ezwal in "Co-operate—or Else!" learns from the harsh reality of the jungle planet that it is necessary for him to alter his attitudes, surrender his prejudices, and learn to cooperate with whoever is there to be cooperated with. He must give up being a special partisan of his own kind and become a citizen of a galactic federation of unlike beings.

And in "The Weapon Shop," Fara Clark must cease to be a slavish idolizer of the empress—and a helpless victim of her exploitations—and become a self-responsible member of an alternate society of free and just people. At the conclusion of the story, Clark marvels that his sleepy native village can look so unchanged to his outward eye—the ordering of the Universe within his mind is now so utterly different.

It was just this kind of rearrangement that van Vogt aimed to bring about in the minds of his readers. If at the outset they presumed, in conventional mid-twentieth century fashion, that the nature of the Universe must be inherently amoral, accidental, competitive, and fragmented, van Vogt would cast doubt on these assumptions with his sudden unveilings of the new organic reality, and perhaps even succeed in transforming them completely with the impact of his brilliant revelatory flashes.

Again and again, the bold ringing lines that concluded so many of van Vogt's stories would zap home a startling new apprehension of the way things are. In a single lightning phrase like "Poor, unsuspecting superman!" or "He would not witness, but he would cause, the formation of the planets," the order of the Universe would be wholly remade.

ONENESS

WHEN John Campbell suggested that "The Weapon Shop" was a nice little park path walk, good without any detectable reason for being interesting, there was no rational answer that van Vogt could conceivably make to this left-handed compliment. He couldn't explain to the editor what he was actually up to; it was all that he could do to *do* it. The only effective response available to him was to write a story, "The Search," that was more of the same, send it to Campbell, and see what happened.

And, no doubt, John Campbell did find "The Search" another strangely fashioned piece of work. Like "The Weapon Shop," this new novelette was an access-of-knowledge story. But, if anything, it had even less action to offer—not even the implicit potential for purely defensive violence inherent in a weapon shop gun seated in a holster on the hip of a Fara Clark. In "The Search," everything was accomplished with a glance, a word, at most, a touch.

In true van Vogtian style, the story began with a state of ignorance and limitation. It shifted abruptly from one queer set of circumstances to another. It climaxed with a conversation. And it concluded with a striking final line in which the conventional ordering of the Universe was stood on its head. Along the way, it displayed haunting dream imagery and introduced a powerful new science fiction concept.

"The Search" was one of van Vogt's more effective stories, and John Campbell was the first to recognize it. Whatever the puzzlement and disquiet he might feel where van Vogt's fiction was concerned, he would buy this novelette with his usual promptness and publish it the month following "The Weapon Shop," in the January 1943 issue of *Astounding*.

As "The Search" begins, Ralph Drake, the protagonist, is lying in a hospital bed with a case of amnesia. This acute state of personal ignorance was a device that van Vogt would come to employ on a number of occasions in his fiction.

It seems that Drake was found in a ditch with papers identifying him as a salesman for a writing supply company. But the most recent events he can remember happened two weeks previously. He had just been rejected by his draft board for an odd but harmless reason—the location of his internal organs is reversed from the normal. And as his next move, he had decided to apply for this job as a traveling salesman.

There in the hospital, he is told that the territory he had been assigned to cover includes the area of farms and small towns around Piffer's Road—the little community where he was born and spent his boyhood. Drake determines that he will go back to the beginning of his route and retrace his steps in hopes of discovering the events he cannot remember.

Along the way, he falls in with another traveling salesman, who informs him that the two of them had been sitting together on his previous trip when a girl, Selanie Johns, boarded their train at a local stop with her basket of souvenirs. The girl's father is a buyer of old metal who makes a number of strange and wonderful gadgets—among them fountain pens that offer a choice of different colored inks and never need refilling and cups that provide a variety of refreshing liquids to drink. Young Selanie sells these, one to a customer, for only a dollar.

When the salesman had showed him the pen that he had bought from her, Drake had been astounded by it. His company simply couldn't match its quality or value, let alone its marvelous nature. But while Drake was examining the pen, a fine-looking old man seated across the aisle asked to see it, and when it was passed to him somehow it snapped in two.

Selanie was told of this accident as she passed through the train with her basket. Looking at the old man, she had gotten back such a powerful stare that she'd fled the train at the very next stop—Piffer's Road. Drake had followed after. And that was the last the salesman had seen of either of them until now.

Drake pursues the trail of his lost memory to Piffer's Road. He hopes to find the Johnses there, but the trailer they live in has been moved somewhere else. And when he makes inquiries at the house of a woman neighbor, he hears another strange story:

Two weeks earlier, the neighbor's son had seen Drake come from the train and enter the Johnses' trailer. And he'd spied on him as Drake found even more super-gadgets there—glasses that serve as anything from a microscope to a telescope, and cameras that deliver developed pictures instantly.

But when Selanie and her father came back to the trailer in a state of agitation, the boy had anticipated trouble and ran away. When he looked back, the trailer was gone—not driven away but suddenly vanished—with Drake still aboard.

Furthermore, it seems that very shortly after this, a fine-looking old gentleman had come around asking people about the gadgets they had bought from Mr. Johns. And two days later, every one of these items was missing, with a dollar left behind as payment.

Drake goes back to his hotel wondering what to make of all this, and there he sees a splendid-looking old man who has just broken another man's pen and is offering him a dollar in compensation. Drake confronts him on the sidewalk outside the hotel. But the old man suddenly seizes Drake's wrist with a grip impossible to resist and hustles him into a car, and there he loses consciousness.

When Drake opens his eyes again, he is lying on his back under a high domed ceiling in some immense building. A great marble corridor stretches farther than his eye can see in either direction.

He follows the main corridor, ignoring all the many doors and side corridors and branch corridors he passes, until it seems to him that the building must be fully ten miles long. At last, he comes to a great final door that opens onto clouds of fog. He descends a course of one hundred steps, and there he discovers that the building hangs unsupported in the mist.

Back inside the building, he enters an office. It contains journals, ledgers, and reports concerning the affairs of "Possessor Kingston Craig." This man is apparently capable of traveling nine hundred years into the future—or twenty-five thousand—in order to right wrongs, avert murders, or convince ruthless rulers to behave themselves, even though to do so means the creation of new "probability worlds." On one occasion, Craig spent months quietly working to establish "the time of demarcation between the ninety-eighth and ninety-ninth centuries." And whenever he has completed a job, this Possessor returns to "the Palace of Immortality."

It would seem that we are privileged to have a peek into the intimate file cabinets of an organization that has undertaken a truly vast responsibility—the care and direction of mankind through future time. We may recall that the weapon shops only dedicated themselves to the righting of individual wrongs; they didn't presume to interfere with the mainstream of human existence. But these Possessors from the Palace of Immortality apparently have no such reservations. They have both the ability and the moral confidence necessary to range ahead through time, altering, shaping, and guiding the future development of man.

When Drake is through examining the papers of Kingston Craig, he discovers a magnificently furnished apartment at the head of a flight of stairs off a side corridor. He eats there and then goes to sleep.

He wakes to find a handsome woman beside him in the bed, and she speaks to him as though they know each other well. And when he goes outside the apartment, he finds that the previously deserted building is now busy with people. A man approaches Drake, calling him by name. And shortly, they are joined by the handsome woman, who is introduced as Drake's wife—the former Selanie Johns.

It is explained that this place is the Palace of Immortality. It was built in the only known reverse time eddy, so that whoever lives here grows younger instead of older.

There are three thousand Possessors—people gifted with the innate ability to travel through time. All were born during a five hundred year period beginning in the twentieth century in the area around an infinitesimal rural American community called Piffer's Road. These Possessors share a common physical characteristic—the location of their internal organs is reversed from that of an ordinary person.

Selanie's father, it seems, is a Possessor who does not believe that the work the Possessors are doing is right. Through the influence of the gadgets he sells and the removal of metal from the area around Piffer's Road, he means to alter the conditions that originally caused the Possessors to be born.

If Mr. Johns succeeds, he will bring into being a probability world in which the Palace of Immortality stands silent and empty—just as Drake saw it yesterday. The only way in which he can be thwarted is for an untrained Possessor—specifically, Ralph Drake—to approach him and seize him by the shoulder with a special glove. Will Drake agree to do this?

As an influence on Drake's decision, Selanie then recounts her memory of what was said and done while Drake was hiding in the trailer that disappeared from Piffer's Road:

> Her father was mightily upset by the appearance of the pen-breaking old man on the train. As their trailer moved off through time to evade this Possessor, Mr. Johns exclaimed: "When I think of the almighty sacrilege of that outfit, acting like God, daring to use their powers to change the natural course of existence instead of, as I suggested, making it a means of historical research—"

And that was the moment in which Drake stepped forth from hiding, seized Mr. Johns by the shoulder with a gloved hand, and destroyed forever his power to pass through time.

Mr. Johns was completely downcast by this abrupt termination of all his efforts, but Selanie remembers her younger self being relieved and glad. At last she was free to admit her true feelings about the Possessors to her father and to herself.

She declared to him: "*They're* in the right; *you're* wrong. They're trying to do something about the terrible mistakes of Man and Nature. They've made a marvelous science of their great gifts, and they use it like beneficent gods."

When he has heard her account, Drake's mind is made up—whether it be by the mutually consistent stories he has been told about himself by one witness or another, or by the fascinating prospect of marriage to this magnificent woman, or by the attraction and challenge of becoming a trained Possessor capable of roaming at will through time-to-come, using power like a beneficent god and never growing old. He smiles at Selanie, and he says that he doesn't think he will muff what he has to do.

As the novelette comes to an end, Drake is walking down the great steps into the mist, toward Earth and the fulfillment of his destiny. The concluding lines of the story are:

"His memory search was over. He was about to live the events he thought he'd forgotten."

What a reversal of perspective! What a powerful and alluring dream of human possibility! What an Olympian park path walk!

"The Search" was the first science fiction story to imagine that a continuing organization of human beings might stand apart from the flow of history and then dip back in wherever it seemed appropriate to positively affect the direction of human affairs. Van Vogt's Possessors, ranging forth from their Palace of Immortality to play beneficent god with history and then returning to file reports on the subject, would stimulate the imaginations of many SF writers. During the forties and fifties, there would be stories aplenty about Eternals and Time Patrols and Paratime Police and Change Wars, all of which would reflect the influence of this novelette.

More immediately and specifically, however, "The Search" offered a heady promise of new possibility to the egalitarian children of the Atomic Age. This story said that anyone at all might prove to be super. The most apparently ordinary of contemporary guys—even, say, a farm boy from Nowheresville, USA, a draft reject turned traveling salesman—might discover a truer nature as a meta-man, a supra-man, a person capable of ignoring the normal constraints of society and time and matter, and of assuming a responsibility for the guidance and direction of humanity's future.

What's more, this was a story that had a basis in truth. "The Search" was nothing less than A.E. van Vogt's own life story cast in the form of science fiction:

Van Vogt was an essentially ordinary guy who was born and raised in rural Manitoba and Saskatchewan in places even more unheard-of than Piffer's Road. He had lived in boardinghouses, and hopped freight trains, and been turned down by his draft board for physical reasons. And he'd worked at totally commonplace jobs like driving a truck, clerking for the government, writing true confession stories, and selling advertising space in the pages of *Stationers Magazine* and *Canadian Paint and Varnish*.

But van Vogt had managed to step out of this background of ordinariness and obscurity and assume a new calling as a science fiction visionary. He had discovered that he had the ability to disengage his imagination from the ongoingness of the present moment and allow it to wander freely through the time and space distances of the Universe in search of wondrous glimpses of what humanity could aspire to become. And it was his belief that the visions he put down on paper would have their influence on the future direction that mankind would elect to take.

As van Vogt would say in regard to his intentions: "Science fiction, as I personally try to write it, glorifies man and his future."

In this aim, we can see the answer to the riddle of how it was that John Campbell could manage to love van Vogt and even pay bonuses for his work despite everything his professional judgment had to tell him about the formal inadequacy of van Vogt's stories. If Campbell had no other reason for putting aside all he thought he knew about the way that stories should be constructed in order to buy every single bit of fiction that A.E. van Vogt could produce, this purpose of van Vogt's would certainly have been reason enough.

It was, after all, Campbell's passionate wish for modern Western man to overcome his paralyzing fears of the vast material Universe, and of older, more powerful beings, and of the inevitable decline and fall guaranteed by cyclical history, and to reach out to grasp the stars. Toward the accomplishment of this end, he had armed the writers of *Astounding* with the power of universal operating principles and filled them with faith in the ability of man to learn whatever he needed to know, and then he'd sent them forth to clear away every obstacle standing between humanity and its higher destiny.

There is no doubt that Campbell's authors had labored diligently and often brilliantly at this task. Yet none of them, not even the omni-competent Robert Heinlein, had been brave enough to take the crucial imaginative leap and portray human beings who actually possessed the necessary confidence and moral authority to successfully establish control over the wider Universe.

None of them, that is, except the not quite plausible, not quite rational, not quite technically sound A.E. van Vogt, with his dream-visions of a glorious human future.

As early as his first published SF story, van Vogt had suggested that one day, the human race might be capable of ruling the entire galaxy. And, as we have seen, when considered as a whole, the overall body of fiction that he had published in *Astounding*, from "Black Destroyer" to "The Search," may be understood as a multi-faceted meditation on the subject of how man would have to alter and what he would have to become if human beings were ever to assume responsibility for themselves, for their fellows, for other beings, for time and for space, and for the entirety of existence.

There was no way that John Campbell could possibly turn away from that. It was too close to his own heart's dream. And yet, there would be fundamental aspects of van Vogt's thinking that would continue to baffle and elude the editor.

Campbell was a materialist, pragmatist, and holist—a person with an engineer's appreciation for things which work. What was important to him was establishing human control over the Universe, and anything that served to bring this about was good enough for him. We could fairly say of him that he still saw the nature of the Universe in twenties' terms, as a great machine—but modified by his advanced thirties' recognition of the synergetic power of whole systems. It was Campbell's belief that if human beings could only get hold of the handbook of rules by which the great cosmic machine-system was run, they could take command of its operation and direct existence as they wished.

If van Vogt was also a holist, it was of a more subtle kind. He was not just a materialist and a pragmatist. To him, the Universe wasn't merely an assemblage of dead parts, a motiveless hunk of machinery that men could take over and operate in any way they pleased. Rather, he saw existence as an integrated, living Whole that must be dealt with carefully and respectfully—according to its own terms and not ours.

It was a new moral order that van Vogt was offering in his stories, crucially different from the traditional moral order whose threatened collapse had been such a central issue in the great Technological Age contention between the embattled defenders of soul and spirit and the barbaric partisans of visible materiality. The difference was that the inherited cosmic and social order had been based upon degrees of descent from God and spirit, but van Vogt's new morality was based upon the relative ability of beings to incorporate and exemplify the essential qualities of higher Wholeness.

John Campbell was about as innocent of morality as a twentieth century scientific barbarian could be. But he was able to travel a certain distance in company with van Vogt by electing to treat his new moral order as though it were a variant form of Campbell's own doctrine of universal operating principles. That is, if the way in which the Universe actually *does* function is what you mean by the word "right," then right behavior and effective use of universal operating principles would be one and the same thing. Campbell could go along with that.

Of course, this highly selective interpretation of van Vogt would be something like the old woman of fable who had never encountered a hawk and, when she did, was unable to rest content until she had clipped its wings and beak and turned it into a proper bird. Similarly, Campbell's reasoning would deprive van Vogt of nothing that was of any real importance—merely his sense of the essential connection between matter and life and his imperative conviction of the cosmic necessity of moral behavior.

The truth was that if John Campbell was sometimes willing to do the right thing, it wasn't because he recognized it as the moral thing to do, but because it seemed the thing most likely to get the job done on a particular occasion. Other times, other expedients. But for van Vogt, doing the right thing was not just a means or an option. It was the only thing. It was mankind's road upward.

The result of this underlying disparity in perception and aim was that Campbell could willingly accept van Vogt's stories with their potent images of human beings ruling the stars, defeating monsters, traveling between galaxies, creating the planets, besting supermen, standing off the power of empire, and policing time-to-come. But the means by which van Vogt was able to arrive at these wonderful possibilities would always escape him.

With our advantages of perspective, however, we can see that, taken as a whole, the first eight stories that van Vogt produced after he left the Canadian Department of National Defence to become a full-time SF writer were an outline of a program for human conduct and human advancement within a moral, purposeful, interconnected, and organic Universe. These stories said that in such a cosmos, the way for mankind to move forward was through responsibility, cooperation, and altruistic behavior. They said that one level of becoming after another was possible, each of which was defined by its own relative degree of integration. And they said that a natural imperative attendant upon human progress from one level to the next must be for those who had managed to advance to reach back and lend assistance to those lagging behind and aid them in overcoming oppression and limitation, in widening their horizons, and in learning how to participate in higher patterns and systems of being.

Of these eight stories, the one that indicated the farthest range of potential human integration and action, and the one that van Vogt himself considered his best piece of early fiction, was an extended novelette entitled "Asylum." This story was published following "Recruiting Station" and "Co-operate—or Else!" in the May 1942 issue of *Astounding*.

In "Asylum," the human form is given as the standard for all intelligent life throughout the galaxy. But within the framework of this basic form, it seems that many different levels of organization are possible. We see six in this story, identified in terms of IQ scores.

At the bottom of the scale comes ordinary Earth humanity, represented by a young reporter named William Leigh. He is a normal guy with a slightly-above-average IQ of 112.

In his future world, psychology machines invented by Professor Garret Ungarn, a noble but reclusive scientist who lives with his daughter in a "meteorite" home near Jupiter, had been thought to have eliminated all war and crime. But Leigh is now covering a story about several bizarre and brutal murders—"the first murders on the North American continent in twenty-seven years"—which left the victims drained of blood and of static electricity and with burnt and bruised lips.

These killings are in fact the work of two space vampires called Dreeghs, a male named Jeel and a female named Merla. This unsettling couple has super-swift reflexes, overwhelming psychological presence, and IQs of 400. But if they are to sustain themselves, they must have constant supplies of blood and "life force" drained from other human beings.

As Merla eventually explains to William Leigh, a million years ago, the Dreeghs were a party of interstellar holidayers who were caught in the grip of a deadly sun:

> Its rays, immensely dangerous to human life, infected us all. It was discovered that only continuous blood transfusions, and the life force of other human beings, could save us. For a while we received donations, then the government decided to have us destroyed as hopeless incurables.
>
> We were all young, terribly young and in love with life; some hundreds of us had been expecting the sentence, and we still had friends in the beginning. We escaped, and we've been fighting ever since to stay alive.

Jeel and Merla have come stumbling upon Earth while suffering an agony of need for blood and life force. Beyond the borders of our solar system, their spaceship encountered an *"ultra"* information beacon which signaled to them that Earth is a Galactic colony just seven thousand years old: "It is now in the third degree of development, having attained a limited form of space travel little more than a hundred years ago." The beacon tells them that at such an early stage in its development, this culture isn't yet ready to cope with knowledge of the existence of the older, wider, ongoing Galactic world. Galactic ships are warned to stay clear.

Merla and Jeel are elated to hear this. To them, an ignorant, isolated third-degree planet like this represents a rich and easy source of blood and life energy for themselves and for the other members of the Dreegh tribe.

The one obstacle between them and what they crave is the resident Galactic Observer in this solar system. But Jeel and Merla do not anticipate any problem in identifying and then eliminating this man. The job of being Galactic Observer in a primitive backwater like this is the kind of menial work assigned to Kluggs, a human type with an average IQ of just 240 or so—and no match at all for the likes of a Dreegh.

The only thing the Dreeghs actually do fear is the possible intervention of a vastly superior sort of human being, a "Great Galactic" with an IQ of 1200. Thus far, however, in the course of a million years, these exalted beings have never taken personal action against them.

Jeel and Merla make an appearance in William Leigh's hotel bedroom—their spaceship somehow held coincident in space-time with what would otherwise be his bathroom—and turn the reporter into their helpless tool. Using his knowledge and resources, they identify Professor Garret Ungarn as the local Galactic Observer. Then they hypnotize Leigh into fancying himself in love with the professor's daughter Patricia and send him off to Jupiter to gain entry to the Ungarn meteorite and lower the defensive screens that protect it.

Leigh accomplishes exactly what they desire of him—but in the process, something most peculiar happens. While he is aboard the meteorite base, there is a sequence of events that plays itself through again and again:

In the first version, Leigh is being taken to an interview with a highly suspicious Patricia Ungarn when he knocks out his escort and escapes. He runs to an elevator. This carries him to a room of utter blackness. Here he encounters a *something* that flashes and sparkles and then seems to penetrate his head.

Abruptly, Leigh finds himself back at the moment of his escape. He is bidden to enter Patricia Ungarn's apartment, which he finds marvelous and magnificent.

In a state of some confusion, he tells her of the elevator and the blackness room, but she denies that either one exists. She even demonstrates to him that what he is certain is the elevator door is, in fact, the door to another corridor.

When Leigh declares his love for her, Patricia becomes convinced that he must have been hypnotized. She determines to put Leigh aboard a small spacecraft and send him off to take his chances with the Dreeghs outside.

Abruptly, however, Leigh once more finds himself returned to the moment of his initial escape. As he is bidden to enter Patricia Ungarn's apartment, it seems to him that Jeel must be dissatisfied with the way that things have gone and is somehow forcing them to repeat until they come out the way he wants them to.

Leigh now begins to sense the presence of another mind within his head—and then suddenly, he sees things with a strange new clarity. Patricia's apartment, which had seemed so fine to him before, now seems marked by flaws and disharmonies. And when he studies Patricia herself, she appears very different to him than in the moment of his declaration of love:

> On all Earth, no woman had ever been so piercingly examined. The structure of her body and her face, to Leigh so finely, proudly shaped, so gloriously patrician—found low grade now.
>
> An excellent example of low-grade development in isolation.
>
> That was the thought, not contemptuous, not derogatory, simply an impression by an appallingly direct mind that saw—overtones, realities behind realities, a thousand facts where one showed.

This time, Leigh is able to effortlessly dominate the situation. He overpowers Patricia and her father, and then he cuts the power supporting the screens that protect this Galactic outpost.

Leigh has done exactly what he was bidden to do by the Dreeghs. And when he is back in their hands once more, an exultant Jeel binds him and turns him over to a rapacious Merla. The female Dreegh has been lusting after Leigh with a passion and greed that seem as much sexual as hunger for his life force.

Merla begs Leigh to cooperate with her kiss of death. However, when their lips meet, it is not *from* him but *to* him that energy flows. There is a searing flash of blue, and Merla collapses.

As Jeel revives her with some of his own supply of life force, a terrified Merla confesses that she has been cheating. She has secretly killed dozens of men on Earth for their energy, and now Leigh has it all!

We might remember that at the climax of *Slan*, Jommy's bonds dropped away, thereby identifying him to Kier Gray as the son of Peter Cross. Now Leigh's bonds fall away from him. The being who was William Leigh stands revealed as a Great Galactic!

It seems that the Dreegh discovery of Earth was anticipated. This Great Galactic has deliberately suppressed nine-tenths of his energy and mental power in order to take on the persona of an ordinary Earthman. Now his normal level of energy has been restored, and he is prepared to collect the two hundred and twenty-seven Dreegh ships gathered here to fall upon Earth.

This supremely confident and able being dismisses the now-docile Jeel and Merla, telling them, "Return to your normal existence. I have still to co-ordinate my two personalities completely, and that does not require your presence."

To this point in "Asylum," we have seen five different levels of intelligence portrayed: William Leigh, Earth reporter, IQ 112; Professor Ungarn and his daughter Patricia, Kluggs, with IQs around 240; the Dreeghs, Merla and Jeel, with IQs of 400; the beginning-to-awaken Leigh, who is able to perceive the flaws and disharmonies evident in Patricia and her apartment, and the reenergized Galactic being who is able to dismiss the likes of Jeel and Merla with no more than a word. But another level now remains to be attained—the fully reintegrated Great Galactic with an IQ of 1200.

Whatever any such fabulous number as that might actually mean!

A.E. van Vogt, more than most, had reason to be aware that real intelligence was a far deeper and more complex matter than just the conscious, rational ability to juggle facts and figures. And so we shouldn't make the literal-minded error of interpreting the various IQ numbers given in "Asylum" as some exact index of relative skill at checking off the proper boxes in a cosmic pencil-and-paper test. Instead, we would do better to take these numbers as a rough indication of the variety of effective levels possible in the integration of all the different aspects of which "intelligence" is comprised.

If this wasn't specifically emphasized in "Asylum," it would be in a long-delayed but closely connected sequel, a short novel entitled "The Proxy Intelligence" (*If*, October 1968). Here, Professor Ungarn would comment that standard Earth IQ tests omit a number of relevant intelligence factors, including mechanical ability and perception of spatial relations. And Patricia Ungarn would look a Dreegh in the eye and say scathingly: "If altruism is an I.Q. factor, you Dreeghs probably come in below idiot."

What an awesome challenge it was for van Vogt to attempt to imagine the likes of a fully integrated Great Galactic! As a gauge of how difficult it could be in 1941 to conceive of an encounter with a radically transcendent being, we might compare Slayton Ford returning a broken man from his interview with the gods of the Jockaira in Heinlein's *Methuselah's Children* or the brief, unrecallable glimpse of a High One in Heinlein's "By His Bootstraps," which demoralizes Bob Wilson/ Diktor, turns his hair gray overnight, and leaves him feeling like a bewildered collie who can't fathom how it is that dog food manages to get into cans.

But it wasn't just a less traumatic meeting with radical superiority that van Vogt was proposing to imagine. What van Vogt aimed to show was nothing less than a normal Earthman—or something like one—being transmuted and melded and assumed into the highest state of awareness and responsibility that the writer was capable of conceiving.

Van Vogt says:

> The problem was to describe how a being with an I.Q. of 1200 would operate—what he would see, feel, and think. I couldn't have him on the stage too long, because he'd become unreal. I slept on it for several nights and I finally got it. I think it was completely satisfactory, nonetheless, even the writing was kind of an anguished hurt.

He also says, "That was the hardest scene I ever wrote."

Here are the concluding paragraphs of "Asylum" with the frightened and resistant subsystem that still imagines itself to be merely William Leigh, Earth reporter, IQ 112 and proud of it, facing its moment of integration into the Great Galactic:

> Amazingly, then, he was staring into a mirror. Where it had come from, he had no memory. It was there in front of him, where an instant before, had been a black porthole—and there was an image in the mirror, shapeless at first to his blurred vision.
>
> Deliberately—he felt the enormous deliberateness—the vision was cleared for him. He saw—and then he didn't.
>
> His brain wouldn't look. It twisted in a mad desperation, like a body buried alive, and briefly, horrendously conscious of its fate. Insanely, it fought away from the blazing thing in the mirror. So awful was the effort, so titanic the fear, that it began to gibber mentally, its consciousness to whirl dizzily, like a wheel spinning faster, faster—

The wheel shattered into ten thousand aching fragments. Darkness came, blacker than Galactic night. And there was—
Oneness!

The nature of all existence is One, van Vogt says. And the direction of evolution is toward the realization of Oneness.

Now there is a holistic ending for you, achieved not through rational thought, but by intuition, creative imagination and story.

www.ingramcontent.com/pod-product-compliance
Lightning Source LLC
Chambersburg PA
CBHW020331240426

43665CB00043B/215